MONSTER HUNTER
ALPHA

BAEN BOOKS by LARRY CORREIA

To purchase any of these titles in e-book form,
please go to www.baen.com.

MONSTER HUNTER ALPHA

LARRY CORREIA

M.H.I.

BAEN

A Baen Books Original

Baen Publishing Enterprises
P.O. Box 1403
Riverdale, NY 10471
www.baen.com

ISBN: 978-1-9821-9359-1

Cover art by Alan Pollack
Team Haven patch by Rabbit Boyett

First printing, August 2011
Second printing, May 2013
First leatherbound hardcover printing, July 2017
First trade paperback printing, July 2024

Distributed by Simon & Schuster
1230 Avenue of the Americas
New York, NY 10020

Library of Congress Control Number: 2024935147

Printed in the United States of America

10 9 8 7 6 5 4 3 2 1

This novel is dedicated to Hinkley

Acknowledgements

I would like to thank Reader Force Alpha for once again helping me make it look like I know what I'm doing. Thanks to the good posters on the Monster Hunter Nation blog for the translating and for being generally awesome. I want to thank Toni Weisskopf, Jim Minz, and all the wonderful folks at Baen for running a very cool publishing house. Most importantly, I want to thank my wife and kids for putting up with all the craziness related to being a writer. I love you guys.

"Evil looms. Cowboy up. Kill it. Get paid."
—Mission Statement from the
MHI Company Handbook

⚜ Prologue ⚜

The night that Deputy Joe Buckley got disemboweled by a werewolf had started normally enough.

The patrol car's radio chirped just after one in the morning. It was dispatch, reporting a 911 call. Buckley laughed when he heard the description. Something was scaring Nancy Randall's horses. It sounded like a complete waste of his time, but since Nancy held a seat on the county council, she became the priority call of the evening. Buckley, being the nearest available deputy, took the call.

The Randall farm was up 26, way out on Cliff Road. Since it was raining and the roads were slick, it took nearly twenty minutes for him to get there from Copper Lake. When he arrived, the farm was dark and quiet, shrouded in the miserable freezing drizzle. Buckley left the warm comfort of his Crown Vic and hurried for cover of the front porch.

Nancy answered the door with a shotgun. She stuck her head outside and glanced quickly in both directions. "About damn time you got here, Joe."

What did she expect? Copper County only had a handful of deputies and she lived on the tail end of nowhere. There was nothing out this way except for a few abandoned mines, scattered farms, and a whole lot of trees. "Easy, Nancy," Buckley chided. Though she had a reputation for being levelheaded, Nancy was pale and shaking right then. "Just put the gun away and calm down."

"You calm down! Did you hear anything on your way in?"

"Like what?"

"Growling," she answered, watching over his shoulder.

"Growling? What kind of growling?"

"The scary kind . . . And screaming. Lots of screaming." Buckley laughed nervously, but Nancy was dead serious. "At first there was some crashing and banging, then they started screaming. I thought somebody was hurt behind the barn, crying for help, but when I went to look I heard . . . something else . . . Hell, I don't know what it was. So I herded the kids to the back room and called 911."

"Probably nothing out of the ordinary." Buckley sighed. Some regular old animal probably got caught in something, got scared, maybe hurt, and made a racket. It could sound spooky enough. Calls like this weren't too unusual, though he expected better from a longtime local. "I'll check it out."

"Just be careful."

Buckley bid Nancy a good night and went to work, expecting to find evidence of either a raccoon or petty vandalism. Surprisingly, he discovered that the horses in the barn were freaked out about something, snorting and kicking at their gates. Their genuine fear was a surprise and made Buckley think that maybe Nancy wasn't completely wrong to be concerned.

He did a sweep of the property. It was too dark and wet to spot any tracks, and none of the equipment looked like it had been disturbed. After wandering fruitlessly around the barn in the dark with only his flashlight for illumination, poking around, tripping over things, and getting generally soaked and frozen in the rain, Buckley decided to call it a night. Whatever had been out there was gone now. He returned to his Crown Vic to call in, thankful that it had a good heater and a thermos of hot coffee.

There hadn't been any snow yet this year, but this was northern Michigan, which meant that when it came it was sure to be extra nasty. Moisture fogged the windows solid within seconds. Turning on the defroster and jamming his hands deep into his pockets, he decided to wait until his teeth quit chattering before calling dispatch.

The Crown Vic suddenly lurched on its shocks. He looked up, but with the windows fogged, he was blind to the outside world. Puzzled, his initial suspicion was that someone was screwing with him, but then there was a thud as something big struck the hood.

Screeeeeeech.

The sound sent an involuntary shiver running down his spine. Something had just scratched the hell out of his paint. He reached for the door handle. "Son of a—"

The windshield ruptured, pelting him with safety glass. Black limbs shot through the hole. Buckley yelped in surprise as black fur engulfed his face. Stunned, he tried to jerk the door open but was torn away and pulled against the steering wheel. His hands were swatted aside as long claws flailed, tearing him open. Blood struck the dash as nails sliced through his scalp. Paws clamped down on both sides of his head, and squeezed until his skull cracked.

He was dragged thrashing through the glass, down the hood, and hurled into the cold mud. The claws released, and Buckley shoved desperately against the mass of heat and hair, splashing and rolling in the muck. He ended up on his back. The thing towered above him in the headlights, and Buckley knew that he was going to die. Terrified, he struggled to get his gun from its retention holster as blood poured down his throat.

The animal seemed to smile six inches of razors as the Beretta came out in slow motion. The pistol disappeared into the night as a claw laid Buckley's arm open from elbow to palm. Then the animal was on him, and Buckley watched in shocked disbelief as it drove its long snout under the bottom edge of his Kevlar vest and bit deep into his abdomen. Fire lanced through him as the animal wrenched its head back and forth.

"That's enough."

The animal tore its bloody head free, something red dangling from its teeth. In shock, Buckley stretched out both pieces of his hand, as if to ask for that bit of himself back, but the creature was already retreating out of the headlights. He tried to speak, but all he could do was cough on the blood in his mouth. He felt as cold as the puddle he was squished into.

A figure walked into the light. He was saved! Somebody had chased off the animal. The man would call for help. He just needed to hang in there.

But this man didn't seem upset. He didn't call for help. He didn't tell Buckley to stay calm. Instead he just squatted next to him in the mud. His features were obscured by the shadow of a wide-brimmed hat, but somehow his eyes were visible, glowing like molten gold. The stranger studied the giant hole in Buckley's stomach and frowned. He made a *tsk-tsk* noise, and behind him the animal let out a mournful howl.

Buckley had lost too much blood to be afraid. He was just very cold. The man plucked the gold name tag from his shredded uniform shirt and studied it. "My apologies, Deputy Buckley," the stranger said. He tossed the nametag into the puddle with a little *plop*. "I doubt you're going to make it. The pack could've used you. Maybe I'll be wrong, but that doesn't happen too often. For now I leave you to the *vulkodlak*."

The stranger rose, adjusted his overcoat, and walked from Deputy Buckley's darkening vision.

PART 1

The Monster

⊰ **Chapter 1** ⊱

---

*I've been shot one hundred and fifty-three times. Stabbed, cut, or bit so
many times I've lost count. I've been blown up, electrocuted, frozen,
buried alive, set on fire, and was once hit by a train. I've fought in both
world wars and a few others. I've killed men on all but two continents.
I've killed monsters on them all. Other dimensions? Twice.*

I guess you can say I get around.

*Husband, father, grandfather, and now great-grandfather, I've seen
whole generations come and go. I've loved, protected, and watched over
my family, the Shacklefords, for decades. With a couple of notable
exceptions, most of them have turned out pretty good. Which is
important, because in the grand scheme of things, the Shacklefords are
a very special bunch. This particular journal is not about them.*

*I run Monster Hunter International, the best outfit in the business.
You work for MHI for very long, and you'll see some things. I've run
into some of the weirdest beings in God's creation and killed a whole
mess of them. You wouldn't believe the shit we've fought. There are a lot
of innocent folks alive right now only because one of my Hunters stepped
up and did what had to be done. The bravest men there have ever been
look at me to be their leader, and that's a humbling thing. But this
journal ain't about them, either.*

*I've already written those things down. Now I need to focus on the
hard part. This is the third journal I've attempted to write. If you are
reading these words, then I can only assume that you know the truth
about me. This book is about things I'd rather not share, things I'd*

rather have forgotten. But no one lives forever. I'm hoping that some of the things I've learned might help after I'm gone. A wise man once told me that we're no smarter than the Hunters that came before us. The only reason we've got a clue is because those guys bothered to write stuff down. So here goes.

I'm a werewolf.

You've got no idea how remarkably hard that was to write. I stare at those words and want to tear the page out and burn the evidence. We tend to be a secretive bunch.

See, I bear a curse. You learn to deal with it, or it deals with you. Crying about it won't change a thing. Embracing it will destroy you. I have stared into the face of evil, and I've been the face of evil. I've done some bad things in my life. Good thing I've lived a long time because I'm still trying to even that score. Some folks would call it penance. I call it my job.

I am a Hunter. I am a Monster. I was born Raymond Earl Shackleford Jr., son of the greatest Hunter who ever lived, in the year 1900. I've held many names since.

Today they call me Harbinger.

✢ ✢ ✢

"Well, ain't you Mr. Melodramatic?" Earl Harbinger muttered to himself after rereading the first page of the journal. Frankly, it was surprising that he'd managed to fill so many pages in it already, and reading through them had given him something to keep occupied while waiting for the meeting. The leather-bound book went back into an internal pocket of his battered bomber jacket and a pack of Marlboros came out. Shaking one loose, he put it to his lips while pondering on the book.

Writing his personal history had been Julie's idea. Originally he'd been resistant to the idea of chronicling his life, but the fight with the demon Rok'hasna'wrath had cost him dearly. Earl pulled out his Zippo and lit the cigarette. The lighter was a perfect example of the damage the minor Old One had inflicted on Earl's mind. The Zippo had been engraved with the MHI logo, and he knew it had been a birthday present, but for the life of him he couldn't remember when he'd gotten it or who it was that had given him the gift. It was one of hundreds of little things he had lost. Random memories had been ripped from his mind and swallowed whole or torn into indecipherable shreds and scattered. Rocky, devourer of souls and reaper of worlds, had been a real asshole that way.

There were gaps, blank spots, fuzzy bits where the original events were lost but he could recall telling the stories to others, like a weird secondhand report. He didn't even know the entirety of what was missing. The journals had been started as tools to find out just what had been taken away. He'd written one chronicling the Shackleford family history and another about Monster Hunter International. The realization of the sheer number of events he could not recall had been a slap in the face.

Thinking about it left Earl bitter. It was too bad that Z had driven Abomination's bayonet through Hood's black heart. Martin Hood had gotten off far too easily for Earl's tastes. Rocky had robbed him, but that creature had only been summoned to perform the job. It had been at Hood's bidding, whereas his old friend had wanted to make it personal.

Ironically, the thing that had brought him here was also about personal business. Once again, the past had come back to haunt him, but when you're over a hundred years old, you build up an awful lot of past.

The bar was kept purposefully dim. It hid the grime, and once the crowds came in the evening, would help mask the unattractive. There was an old-fashioned jukebox playing country music. He had picked a table in the back. It was still early in the day, so the only other inhabitants were the solitary types with nothing better to do than down a couple of beers before lunch. Earl took a slow drink of his. It was just the kind of out-of-the-way dive that somebody like Conover would pick for a clandestine meeting.

It had been decades since they'd last spoken, but Earl had not hesitated to drop everything when he'd gotten the message. Making up some excuses, he'd told the rest of his team that he was taking some vacation time—which had shocked everyone—promised he'd be back before the full moon, loaded some gear in his truck, and driven the six-hundred-some-odd miles to rural Illinois.

Earl didn't like lying to his people. Hunters lived or died based on trusting their team, but this wasn't MHI business. And if it was what he feared, then he definitely didn't want to involve them.

He studied the other patrons, normal working stiffs, just regular

Joes. A tired bartender was watching the TV on the wall and eating stale pretzels. There was one almost-but-not-quite-pretty waitress wiping tables. His heightened sense of smell confirmed that everyone here worked for a living. They stunk of chemical fertilizers, truck cabs, engine grease, and French fries. Earl could usually tell what someone did for a living long before they opened their mouths. If any of them were undercover Feds here to snoop on his business, they were extremely good at it. Considering the kind of work that he'd once performed for Conover, he'd fully expected the place to be bugged and surveiled by all sorts of government types. Instead, the most interesting scent was the fry cook, and that was only because Earl was hungry.

The captain's message had been short. He hadn't elaborated on what business they needed to discuss, but it sure as hell wasn't to reminisce about the old days. There could only be one reason. The Russian was back. Earl took a long drag from his cigarette as he stared off into space. The single baddest son of a bitch Earl had ever had the sad displeasure of squaring off against. Sure, he'd won last time, but a lot of people had died in the process. Good people. Sadly, Rocky had left most of *those* memories, the spiteful demon prick.

The Russian had dropped off the grid years ago. Earl had hoped that he'd had the decency to just die, but had known that was wishful thinking. There was only one reason he could think of that would bring Nikolai Petrov to America, and Earl had known the time would come eventually. Driving all night had given him time to think about what it meant, and it had made him glad that he was doing this on his own. His Hunters had faced some terrifying things, but Nikolai wasn't just another monster.

This time was going to be different. He wasn't going to play Nikolai's games. Things had changed since Vietnam. No contest, no bullshit, no hide-and-seek. This was going to be a straight-up, old-fashioned execution.

Thoughts of revenge were interrupted as a sudden rectangle of daylight appeared at the front of the room. A tall, stately gentleman with silver hair entered. He was wearing jeans and a flannel shirt, but somehow he even made that look a little too professional. Kirk Conover had arrived. The man stepped into the room, subtly breaking the bar into quadrants and scanning each one for threats like the trained operative that he was. Conover's head dipped briefly in acknowledgment as he glanced at Earl's table. Satisfied there were no obvious watchers, the former liaison officer of Special Task Force Unicorn started over.

Earl was distracted by a female voice. "You can't smoke in here."

He looked up to see the almost-pretty waitress standing over him, hands on her hips, disapproving. He let the cigarette dangle from the edge of his lip. It was only half done. "We're in a bar. . . ."

"No smoking," she said sternly.

"Seriously?" The frown said she was serious. He didn't think he could use the excuse that he had a medical condition, either. Saying that the nicotine helped keep him from massacring everyone in the room in a fit of bestial rage, though partially true, probably wouldn't help his case. "Please?"

She shook her head. "It's a state law. Sorry. We could get fined."

"That's a stupid law," Earl muttered. Everywhere he went now there were laws stacked on top of other laws until there was a mountain of laws ready to collapse in a giant avalanche of meddling. "Fine." He flicked his tongue, put the lit cigarette in his mouth, swallowed hard, and ate it. It burned going down. "Happy?"

"Gross," the waitress said as she quickly retreated.

"Hey, get me a drink too, honey. Whatever that cranky bastard is having," Conover called after the waitress. He stopped in front of Earl's table. Conover had aged, as was to be expected, since they hadn't spoken since Vietnam. The fighter-pilot-turned-spook had always been tall, several inches over Earl's average height, and in good shape. Now he was approaching old age and didn't seem quite so tall anymore, but still very fit for a senior citizen. Kirk had aged, but he'd aged well. "Well, you've still got a way with the ladies, I see."

"You were the lady's man, not me." Earl gestured with his bottle of Sam Adams. "Have a seat, Cap."

"I retired as a colonel," Conover replied as he pulled up a chair. "And that was a while ago. But damn, Earl . . . You look nearly the same. . . . Well, you did get a shave and a haircut."

"A couple since then, I suppose."

"Good thing, too. You looked like a filthy hippie."

Earl shrugged. "You kept us awful busy to worry about the state of our grooming."

"Things were crazy there at the end." Conover gave a little chuckle.

He hadn't meant it to be funny. Earl and the other *special* members of the task force had been one step above slave labor, and this particular Air Force officer had been their overseer. Earl studied his old boss. Conover watched him back, and the two sat in uncomfortable silence for some time. People always told Earl that he had an unnerving way of looking at people, but Conover had been one of the few that had always been tough enough to look him in the eye. At least that hadn't changed.

The waitress came back and left another bottle on the table. To be fair, Conover had been as decent a sort as could be expected, given the circumstances, and had actually looked out for the monsters, mutants, and misfits under his control. The Perpetual Unearthly Forces Fund was as blind as lady justice and far less merciful. If your kind were on the list, you were fair game. An individual had to *earn* the right to be PUFF exempt, so the government always had some *special* volunteers. After fulfilling the terms of the government's agreement, Conover had kept his word and made sure that Earl's name had been put back on the exemption list.

His former boss may have gotten old, but he hadn't gotten soft. Conover stared back at him, unblinking. There was no guilt there. This was a man given hard orders who'd done his duty, that was all, and that was something Earl could respect. They hadn't spoken since the last evacuation, and he was curious about the other survivors. "Have you seen Sharon Mangum?" Earl asked finally.

Conover smiled, still with that lopsided way that the Saigon bar girls had found so charming. "We got married not too long after your tour was over."

"I'm shocked," Earl said, perfectly deadpan. The two of them had a thing there going toward the end. The fraternization rules sort of went out the window in an oddball outfit like theirs. "I figured that might happen. Extremely late congratulations are in order."

"Best thing that ever happened to me. The agency bounced us all over the place afterward. She hated that part, as you can imagine. But we settled down finally when I got stationed in DC. Moved out here when I retired."

"Family?"

"We've got a son and three daughters."

"Human?" Earl asked.

"Mostly."

"Good to hear, Cap." With Sharon's condition, it could have gone either way. "She was a fine girl. Saved my bacon a few times."

Then Conover let out a long sigh. "She died last year," he said. "Car accident."

It had to have been a bad accident to kill a half-siren. "I'm sorry. I know how you feel." So much for trying to be cordial. "I'm guessing you didn't send me that mysterious letter just so we could shoot the bull over some beers?"

"It did get your attention, didn't it?" Kirk gave a sad little laugh before taking a long drink. "Old times . . . We were never really buddies, were we, Earl?"

Conover had been a decent man to work for, considering the circumstances, but Earl had still been there against his will. He didn't mind war. In fact, he was rather good at it and would have gone if he'd been asked rather than threatened. "I like to think of us as business associates with a relationship based on mutual respect. Well, and the fact that I'd have gotten executed if I disobeyed your orders."

"Smart-ass. You know, when you got assigned to me, your file said you had authority problems and I'd probably have to terminate you."

"Aw, they were still just sore because of that time I punched out Jimmy Carter." Sure, he'd only been governor then, and that little stunt had cost MHI some business, but he had deserved it.

"You always were the lone wolf, weren't you?" Kirk asked rhetorically. "Well, back to business. I've still got people who owe me. When certain things pop up, I hear."

Men like Conover tended to accumulate a lot of favors. "Nikolai's back, ain't he?"

"Afraid so. Last we'd heard he'd gone freelance. Mercenary werewolf for hire. Worked for various bad people eating other bad people, and then all of a sudden, nothing. He just disappears. Until this week. Any idea what would bring him out of the woodwork after all these years?"

Earl shrugged. "Nikolai's a badass Russian. Badass Russians only have three emotions: revenge, depression, and vodka. Where is he?"

"It isn't that easy, Earl. First I've got a question about what happens when you find him."

"You know exactly what'll happen when I find him."

Conover nodded. "Yeah, stupid. I contacted you, remember? You're about the most determined killer I've ever met. Once I set you on Nikolai's trail, that bastard's good as dead. I'd swear you're not part wolf. You're part bloodhound. Not the *what*, Earl. I want to know the *why*. I'm retired. This isn't going in a report. You can level with me."

Earl paused. How was he supposed to answer that? Nikolai was dangerous. He was everything bad about werewolves rolled up into one exceedingly ruthless and intelligent package. He was the big bad wolf. He was evil, but there were plenty of evil people in the world, and he didn't go around hunting them all down. "Revenge is as good a reason as any, I suppose."

"You can do better than that." Kirk leaned back in his chair and studied him. "That was war. We did what we had to do."

Since Kirk understood monsters better than most people ever could—hell, he'd married somebody that technically was one—Earl figured he might as well level with his old commander. "There's something else . . . There are certain rules, ways of doing things. It's been the same since the beginning. There's always one who's the strongest. He sets the rules."

"They form packs once in a while, that's about it. You trying to tell me that there's some werewolf society with rules? Werewolf law? I must've missed that briefing."

"Not in the way you're thinking of it," Earl answered. "Maybe rules ain't the right word, but it'll do. New werewolves break them because they don't know better. Most folks, when they turn, they go right to doing whatever urge strikes. For the ones that live, though, after a while, they'll sense what the rules are, and they either obey them, or somebody like me comes along and takes them out."

Kirk studied him for a moment. "Somebody like you, meaning a Hunter, or an Alpha werewolf?"

Earl nodded at the terminology. As usual, Kirk knew more than he revealed. "Same difference." Even though it wasn't. "Some old werewolves break the rules, but most know better than to piss off the strongest. When he finds out, then there's hell to pay."

"What're the current rules?"

"There's only a couple. But basically, leave humans alone. They live by the rules, and regular people never even know we exist."

From the look on his face, it was obvious that Kirk's suspicions had just been confirmed. "I thought so. You know, I've learned a few things about werewolves since we last worked together. Most of them don't care. They do whatever they want, regardless of what some old guy says."

"I didn't say it worked well, but you don't want the world's werewolves instinctively following the example of a real aggressive leader. The way it is now is better."

"What happens if there's a new boss?"

"They'll all sense it. The rules will change . . . and you don't want somebody like Nikolai setting the rules. He doesn't see us as people who are different. In his mind, we're superior and humans are prey. The curse will spread. Packs will grow. You do the math."

Kirk nodded thoughtfully. "I figured it was some sort of monster psychology like that."

"So why does the Russian have to die?" Earl leaned back in his chair and folded his arms. His minotaur-hide coat creaked. "Because *I'm* the king of werewolves, and I said so."

Apparently, that had been the answer Kirk was looking for. "Nikolai is in America."

"Figured that was the case. Where?"

"North of here. Middle of nowhere, Michigan. He was spotted arriving in the US last week. Intel says he was heading for a town called Copper Lake. Heard of it?"

"Can't say I have. How do you know all this?"

"I'm retired. Not dead. I've still got friends in the business who like to keep me informed." The nebulous answer indicated that he was not ready to give up all his secrets.

"Are the MCB planning to take him out?"

"The Monster Control Bureau doesn't even know he exists. When the task force was shut down, we passed most of our files on, but not everything. Back then the MCB were just glorified cops and damage control. Our op was national security on a need-to-know basis. They didn't need to know."

"Good. They'd just complicate matters." The last thing Earl needed was Myers's goons getting in the way. "So, I answered your question, Kirk. Now you answer mine. Why'd you bring me in on this?"

Conover's beer was half empty. He swirled the remainder around and stared at it. "You and me, we're the last surviving members of the task force."

"Turns out the Destroyer is still alive," Earl pointed out.

"Really? Pitt the crazy Green Beret? Huh . . . Didn't know that. He must have gone on to something so classified that even my department didn't get a whiff of it. Well, Nikolai was our problem, and I don't like leaving problems unsolved. I'm too damn old now. I can't take him. Hell, I couldn't back in my prime. You, on the other hand, can. Sure, I could call the MCB. They'd go crazy if they knew Stalin's pet werewolf was roaming around their turf, but I'd like this to stay in the family."

Earl could tell there was more. "And?"

Conover studied the tabletop, mulling over his answer. "Sharon used to have bad nightmares, all the time, our entire marriage. And it was always the same thing. Golden eyes and white fangs . . . The Russian would come for her, and he'd take our kids, too, just out of spite. She never had closure. He killed most of the task force. She always felt that he'd come back to finish the job."

Nightmares. Earl didn't have nightmares. He gave them.

"That son of a bitch stole years of Sharon's life, and I couldn't protect her. Now that I know he's alive, I need you to destroy him, Earl, absolutely *destroy* him. I want him to feel how she felt. I've seen what you can do. Do it for the task force. Do it for her. And when you're finished . . . Then I can go to Sharon's grave and tell her it's finally over."

Earl raised his bottle. "For the ones that didn't make it."

They clinked their beers together. "To lost friends and a shitload of dead communists."

Earl Harbinger could drink to that.

⇥ **Chapter 2** ⇤

The morning after the first night I changed I woke up naked in a pool of blood. None of it was mine. I was in a farm house, a little pueblo on the river. The flimsy door had been ripped off the hinges and was lying in the yard surrounded by pecking chickens. The farmer's family was spread from one end of the place to the other, splattered on the walls, dripping from the ceiling, and turning the dirt floor into mud. I could still taste them in my mouth. Bits of them were stuck in my teeth.

It's a hard thing to explain. The memories while I'm changed are different. They're difficult to put into people words. It was like waking up from a dream, one that I could only partly remember, but I knew exactly what I had done to them. MHI hadn't known much about werewolves back then. It was all a mess of myth and old wives' tales, but now I understood how the curse was transferred. A simple bite one month before. That was all it took to end my life.

I found the farmer's old Navy Colt tossed halfway to the well. Though I could still feel where a slug had punched through my ribs under the caked-on blood, there was no wound now. The hazy memories told me that the bullet had just driven me into a frenzy. The Colt hadn't done the farmer a lick of good, but under that bright morning sun, I prayed to God that it would work for me now. I destroyed monsters. I would not become one. I put the muzzle under my jaw and angled it to take the back of my head off.

The others would surely find this place soon enough. They'd probably already seen the gathering vultures. Hunters would learn from what happened to me and not make the same mistakes. That was the last thought I had before I dropped the hammer.

I came to later with a splitting headache. Like I said, back in those days we hadn't known much about werewolves.

⸪ ⸪ ⸪

Heather Kerkonen didn't have to work the night shift. She had enough seniority to claim days, but had always been a night person by nature. Working nights ruined any chance she had for having a social life, but excepting the occasional accident, bar fight, or somebody doing something stupid, nights were usually quieter, almost peaceful.

Last night had been an exception. It had been one call after another. The state police had found some drifter wandering around a campground, screaming about the end of the world, and had put him in the closest lockup, which happened to be Copper Lake, where the nut had promptly bit a chunk out of the jailer's hand when they'd tried to restrain him. Heather had just come on duty and took care of the problem with a liberal dose of pepper spray and an ASP baton. After that she'd gotten a call about two hikers who hadn't made it back to their camp yet, but that turned out to be Baraga County search and rescue's problem. Then she'd had to check out a missing-person call because Mr. Loira had never gotten home from work—probably passed out drunk again somewhere—but all that had been interrupted when she'd heard that Joe Buckley had been mauled by a bear.

Sure, they had bears in northern Michigan—wolves, too—but nobody could remember the last time one had actually attacked someone. Heather had been incredulous when she'd heard the panicked call over the radio. It had to be a mistake. She'd driven like a madwoman to get out to Cliff Road, but by the time she'd arrived they'd already loaded Buckley into the ambulance. The early prognosis was grim, and when she saw the deep red of the puddle they'd lifted him out of, she knew that her friend was surely going to die.

Nancy Randall had found him. The poor lady was in shock. She'd been telling the other deputies about how she'd heard howling, but that was absurd. No wolf could do something like that. There were claw marks that actually pierced the metal of the patrol car's hood.

She and the other deputies had been joined within half an hour by two representatives from the Department of Natural Resources and some volunteers with a few good hunting dogs, but they'd found no sign of the bear. The dogs wouldn't cooperate. They'd sniffed around Buckley's damaged car only to retreat with their tails between their legs. No amount of coaxing could get them to go back.

Heather had grown up hunting in those woods, less for fun than because they'd been poorer than dirt and the only meat that ended up on the family table had come from things that she had shot herself. However, she had no idea how to track an animal. Sitting in a tree stand and waiting for a deer to walk by doesn't exactly make you Davy Crockett. She'd taken the Winchester shotgun from her cruiser, loaded it with heavy-duty slugs, and set out anyway. The wet ground had been so churned by clumsy footsteps at that point that she couldn't spot a thing with her flashlight. Sunrise hadn't helped either, and though more volunteers had arrived, the damn bear had gotten away.

The place was covered in fish cops, and the sheriff himself had taken command of the scene by the time Heather returned. Kai Hintze had been sheriff since Heather had come back to Copper Lake from Minneapolis. He was fifty years old, fifty pounds overweight, and a hardcore sci-fi nerd, so Heather hadn't expected much from her new boss, but Sheriff Hintze had turned out to be a good leader who watched out for his men and his county. He kept getting reelected because he honestly cared about the people, and compared to his incompetent predecessor, the county loved him.

The sheriff was talking to one of the DNR men. The game wardens weren't very popular amongst the independently minded types that lived in places like Copper Lake. She'd had a few run-ins with game wardens back in her teens, when she hunted game regardless of season—the squishy environmentalist types were the worst. But this particular one conducted himself like an old pro and seemed to know what he was talking about. Heather approached from behind and didn't want to be rude and interrupt.

"I'm telling you, Sheriff. There is something seriously wrong here. Colleague of mine out of Washington State, Terril Erion, he had a case like this a while back. Animal attack that didn't seem to fit, just like this. . . . A particular government agency got involved. Do you *know* the agency I'm talking about?"

Sheriff Hintze was nodding his head. "Every sheriff in the country gets a vague briefing and a number to call in case of something weird. You really think there really are . . . Naw. That's ridiculous." He realized Heather was standing there and abruptly stopped. The DNR man looked away, sheepish, like they'd been caught talking about something naughty. The sheriff coughed. "Deputy Kerkonen. Any luck?"

"Nothing, sir. Any word on Buckley?"

"Not yet." He took in her soaked and muddy appearance. "How long have you been out here?"

"Since we got the call."

"You look beat, and your shift was over hours ago. There's really nothing else you can do here."

"Sir, I—"

"I understand. Joe is my friend, too, Heather. Why don't you go see him?" *Before it is too late.*

She waited until she was a mile down the road before she screamed in frustration, swore her head off, and punched the steering wheel until her hand hurt. Her department had lost people before, but to things that made sense, like a meth head or a car wreck. . . . Who got killed in the line of duty by a damned *bear*? This wasn't Alaska. This was *Michigan*.

It didn't make sense. Winter was coming. She was no zoologist, but shouldn't the stupid thing have been hibernating? The attack had occurred during a freezing rain: why was it even out and about, and why would it attack a car? Heather had no idea, and now her hand was sore, and she chided herself for the tantrum. She had always struggled with her temper.

Why couldn't she have been the one to take the call? Maybe if it had been her instead of Buckley, he wouldn't be dying right now. Maybe she could have done something different. . . . She knew it was stupid to blame herself, but Heather had always been protective of anyone she deemed to be *her people.* That attitude had always made her popular amongst her coworkers, but had gotten her into trouble a few times with her superiors in her last department. Copper County was different. This was her town, her people, and this department was *family*. Only now one of them was dying, there wasn't a damn thing she could do about it, and it was really pissing her off.

It had been several hours after the Buckley call that she had finally made it back into Copper Lake. Half the staff of their tiny department and several family members had gathered in the hospital waiting room. Buckley was a popular and beloved man. By some miracle he was alive, which had absolutely amazed the doctors, but they said that it was too early to tell what would happen and too risky to airlift him someplace better. Heather didn't like hanging out, nervous and emotional, in hospitals. She had done far too much of that in her life already, and though her shift was over she had volunteered to head into the office to see if she couldn't help out for a bit. She was still too fired up to go to sleep anyway, and it wasn't like there was anyone waiting for her at home except for her dog.

Back at the station, hungry and cranky, Heather had not been surprised to find that nobody had bothered to put on more coffee. She bought a Diet Coke and a package of expired chocolate doughnuts from the office vending machine instead. She didn't think that doughnuts were supposed to be crunchy, but they had sugar, and that was the important thing. She knew that despite religiously hitting the treadmill every day, if she kept up her junk-food addiction she ran the risk of turning into another Upper Peninsula "snow cow," but that was a risk she was willing to take.

"Did you see Joe, Kerkonen?" asked Chase Temple, one of the new road deputies from days. Heather didn't know him that well yet, just that he had recently gotten out of the Navy and was taking correspondence courses from Northern Michigan University toward a political science degree. His youthful enthusiasm made her feel ancient. She had just turned thirty-six. "I'd heard he was bad off."

She had to pause to not talk with a mouth full of doughnut. She didn't really know what to say anyway; it wasn't like she knew any more than anyone else. "I didn't see him myself, but yeah, the doctors said it was bad. Broken skull, massive lacerations to the abdomen, a lot of blood loss, missing a few feet of intestines . . ." Even if Buckley lived, he would be crippled and miserable the rest of his short life, and that left her feeling even more depressed. She changed the subject and pointed in the direction of the holding cells. "How's our favorite guest?"

The Copper Lake station was a small building, so Temple knew whom she was talking about right away. "Bill was ticked after that nut bit him," he said, referring to the deputy that had been manning the station last night. "He needed five stitches. But I heard you really walloped the guy for it. Pow! Right in the face! That how you guys did it in the big city?" Heather didn't respond to his idiotic grin, so he quit smiling and tried to be professional. "Didn't mean anything by it. I've just heard you've got a reputation is all . . . Keeping it together when the shit gets real."

Heather shrugged noncommittally. "I just did what I was trained to do."

"Whatever. I heard about—"

"Kid needed protecting. I was the only one around to do it. No big deal." One crazy case involving a sex-slavery ring could get you quite a rep. One sloppy gunfight later, she'd been publically cited for bravery, privately reprimanded for stupidity, and been on the fast track to a promotion to detective until her family's health issues had brought her back to her hometown. It didn't matter now. Copper Lake was a much quieter place than Minneapolis. She made sure to change the subject so obviously that Temple would know better than to bring it up again. "We got an ID on our biter yet?"

"Every time we ask for a name, he just stares off into space and mumbles about something humming. Still no idea who he is yet, but we're still checking."

One of her friends had just been eviscerated. She wasn't in the mood for dealing with random stinky lunatics, but the U.P. was virtually the edge of the world. Lots of crazy people ended up here for some reason. It's like they wandered out of Chicago or Minneapolis and walked through the woods until they hit Lake Superior, where they became *her* problem. "Anything else going on?"

"Those hikers down in Baraga are still lost."

"Probably eaten by the same bear," she muttered. Lost hikers weren't any sort of surprise. Except for a few clusters of small townships and farms, northern Michigan was thickly forested hills. It was easy to get turned around if you got off the trails. The locals loved the tourists' dollars, but finding lost suburbanites got old quick.

"Other than that, well, some federal agent called from Washington, wanting to know about the bear attack."

"Who?" Heather asked. That was fast. The Department of Natural Resources guy must have passed it up the chain to whoever it was he'd been talking to the sheriff about.

"I don't know. The guy was named something Jefferson, real snooty type, but I kicked it over to the sheriff. They were asking if there had been any other animal attacks or any unexplained disappearances, that kind of thing. They said they wanted to send some people to interview Buckley if"—he corrected himself—"*when* he wakes up. I told him he better hurry if the weather reports are accurate. Huge storm coming in tonight. He was real adamant that we call if anything else unusual happens."

Unusual? The little black bears that were native to the area normally stuck to knocking over trash cans, not smashing their way through car windows to eat healthy, armed men. *Unusual* was an understatement.

Agent Doug Stark of the Monster Control Bureau of the US Department of Homeland Security answered the ringing phone on his desk. He had already had a busy day, seizing a camera and video files from some teenagers who'd blundered into a Type 2 Unnatural devouring a homeless guy at the bottom of a drainage culvert. Stark didn't necessarily enjoy the part of his job where he intimidated witnesses and survivors into keeping their stupid mouths shut, but he was extremely good at it. "Agent Stark," he answered sharply.

"Hello, Doug," said the voice at the other end, and he recognized it immediately. Washington was calling. *Damn it.* Washington only called when something was wrong, and he had been hoping to get off early so he could catch his daughter's trumpet recital. "This is Grant Jefferson."

Stark didn't like the new guy—he was too smooth—but Director Myers thought Jefferson walked on water, had taken him under-wing, and had delegated all sorts of responsibilities to the former MHI man. Grooming him for leadership, probably because Myers had come up from the private sector, too. . . . Just like those contractor bozos to get all the money, glory, and then come into his bureau to take all the promotions. "Mornin', Grant. What can I do for you today?" he asked with zero sincerity.

"There's been a potential attack in your region. The profile fits a lycanthrope, but that's currently unknown. One survivor."

So much for getting off early. Regulations said they had to check it out as soon as possible. "Bitten?" Stark reached for a pad of paper and took a pen from the pink clay mug labeled "#1 Dad."

"Probable, but unknown. You should assume the worst. Take a test kit. You may need to eliminate."

Stark grunted in acknowledgment. Who was this upstart punk to tell him something so obvious? As a rookie MCB agent recruited straight out of the SEALs, Stark had learned how to take care of witnesses from the holy terror himself, Agent Franks. Stark was old-school MCB. Back when he'd run the Phoenix office, he'd once had a family of four get torn apart by reptoids, and he had managed to blame the entire incident on coyotes. Stark was still bitter he'd been given the Chicago SAC job instead of the interim director position that Dwayne Myers had scored. Myers had been Dallas SAC before the promotion, so they'd been equals, the jerk. "Location?"

"Copper Lake, Michigan," Jefferson said.

"Where the hell is Copper Lake?" He leaned back and studied the laminated US map on the wall. The office chair creaked under his weight. Though no longer in his prime, Stark still loved pumping iron and had biceps as big around as most men's legs. He took pride in the fact that he could still keep up with agents half his age.

"Up by Lake Superior . . . I think," Jefferson said. "Hang on, I'm pulling up Google Earth." It figured. Not only was he going to have to work today, he was going to have to drive to the damn U.P. and probably freeze his ass off in Yooper country. "Wait a second, Agent Archer is here with me." There was a pause. "He says that he grew up right down the road in Calumet. . . . He says to pack a coat." Grant laughed.

Just like those headquarters assholes to have a laugh at his expense, Stark thought. He'd been doing this for nearly twenty-five years. He knew more about this business than Director Myers did. Who were they to laugh at him? Stark idly wrote down the details as Grant kept on talking, but Stark's mind was somewhere else. He glanced at the PUFF table tacked to the wall beside the map. Government employees didn't get to collect PUFF, but those contractors got paid damn good money per lycanthrope . . . and by the time he said his good-byes, he knew exactly what he was going to do.

Like most things that depended on secrecy, the MCB was a relatively small agency. Even the ICE and FBI staff they shared the building with had no clue what the ultra-secretive MCB did for a living. As Special Agent in Charge, he had six agents working under him in the north-central region, and more that he could pull out of Minneapolis, but he'd keep this one close to the vest. He called for Agent Mosher, gave him the lowdown, and told him to get an SUV ready. Requisitioning a chopper was out of the question. The weather was turning nasty, and besides, the key to keeping a monster attack low profile was keeping a low profile. Land a black helicopter at some rural airfield and the locals got to talking, and since the locals were already calling it a bear, why go and mess that up with a Black Hawk?

"Should I put together a team?" Mosher asked. "If it turns out to be a werewolf, that could be dangerous." Gaige Mosher was the newest agent in his office. He was a tough kid recruited out of Force Recon, but even tough guys didn't screw around when it came to shapeshifters.

"Naw," Stark said. "I need to get out of the office. Just the two of us to talk to the witness. My intuition is telling me that it was probably just an animal," he lied. "And if it does turn out to be the real deal, we've got a few days before the full moon. Myers can send out his strike team, and they can use up their budget." In truth, he just wanted to do the minimum amount of work needed and then get a little kickback on the side. Extra agents could make that a hassle, and Mosher was so eager to prove himself to the experienced Stark that he could be trusted to keep his mouth shut.

Once Mosher was gone, Stark excused himself from the office, supposedly to pick up some snacks for the road trip. He stopped at a pay phone on the way. He didn't like Briarwood much, certainly didn't trust them, but a man had to provide for his retirement somehow. His pride wouldn't let him deal with their competitors. He couldn't stand those MHI punks, ever since he'd lost a drunken fistfight to that asshole Sam Haven all those years ago at a BUD/S reunion, but MHI wasn't the only game in town. These new guys were local, hungry, morally flexible, and not above passing him a little cut of the PUFF action under the table.

"Briarwood." That's all the receptionist said whenever she picked up. They liked that cool mysterious vibe, like if you didn't know what they did, then you shouldn't be calling them.

No names. "It's me. I've got a scoop for you." Stark glanced around the busy street. This was the kind of thing that could get him fired or worse if somebody like Agent Franks got wind of it. Traditional forms of reprimands kind of went out the window when that guy got involved.

"Your information is always greatly *appreciated*," she purred. The Briarwood receptionist had a sultry European accent. Stark had never met her, but he liked to imagine her as a sexy blonde who liked to dress in tight black leather. Stark had always had a thing for European chicks since way back when the Navy had stationed him in Italy.

"My standard finder's fee applies."

"But of course," she said. It was only money, and these private hunters were rolling in the dough. He imagined the hot receptionist working out of some secret posh office on top of some downtown high-rise, all black glass and marble. Twenty percent of the PUFF bounty was nothing to those people, but to a GS-13, it was a few extra mortgage payments. "What and where?"

"Possible lycanthrope. Copper Lake, Michigan. I'll know tonight for sure. Your boys don't do shit until I give the word, got it?" Stark hung up before she could respond. It was always good to let those contractor goons know exactly who was calling the shots. Agent Stark then used his cell phone to warn his wife that he would be pulling an overnighter, and he apologized in advance for missing his daughter's recital.

The offices of Briarwood Eradication Services were on the second floor of a crumbling brick building in a not-quite-terrible-but-getting-there section of Chicago. The first floor was a pool hall, the third was rented by a company that stuffed coupon mailers, and the fourth was untenanted except for the pigeons.

Ryan Horst stopped cleaning his carbine long enough to listen to Jo Ann take the call. She was still doing that Euro-trash voice, which told him that it was probably a potential job. Jo Ann Schneider was from Wisconsin originally and had the accent to prove it but had been working for a phone-sex line when he'd met her. The woman could sound like just about anyone over the phone, which did manage to add a little mystique to their tiny company. Horst knew that success was all about the marketing.

"Ryan! It was that asshole, Stark," Jo Ann shouted across the large open space. She yanked off her headset and tossed it on the desk. "We've got us a big one!"

"About damn time," he muttered as he finished tugging the

boresnake through the barrel of his FAL. He'd assembled a tough crew, but the boys were getting restless. He'd promised that there was lucrative money in this business, far better than what they were used to making for their particular set of skills. Men that good at hurting people weren't the kind that he wanted to string along. "What've we got?" he asked as he pointed the barrel at the overhead lights and squinted at the rifling. The chrome was perfectly clean and shiny as expected. Horst took meticulous care of his weapons.

"A lycanthrope up in Michigan. I think that means werewolf! You know what one of those is worth?" She was practically squealing.

"Of course I do, babe. I am the expert, remember?" he said. Jo Ann stood off to the side, bouncing up and down eagerly, the aesthetics of which he especially appreciated when she wore a tank top. Horst could almost see the dollar signs flashing in her eyes. Even a brand new werewolf was worth at least forty large. The older they were or the more people they'd killed, the more you could make. The sky was the limit on a lycanthrope. Horst had memorized the PUFF tables before those squeamish pansies in Alabama had booted him out of their training camp.

Sociopath. That's what that broad, Paxton, had called him right before they'd fired his ass. Well, he didn't need them. Horst had always been an entrepreneur, and he'd always done best on his own. Sure, most of those business dealings had been of questionable legality, but he'd never gotten busted or served time for any of his many ventures. He was far too smart for that.

Horst had filed the paperwork, borrowed some money from his uncle Mickey, got his own PUFF charter, got the Title 13 FFL for the weapons, and recruited his own team of badass killers. Now that he had his own license to print money, all he needed to do was start collecting some fat monster bounties. Even with Stark taking his normal cut, this trip could pay a few bills. So far Briarwood Eradication Services had only taken down a few small, local monsters. Killing a werewolf, hell, any shapeshifter, would launch him into the big time. Horst took his time putting his gun back together. He worked the charging handle a few times. Smooth as silk.

"Good work, babe. Now do me a favor and call in the boys. We're gonna bag us a werewolf."

⤐ **Chapter 3** ⤏

One of the old wives' tales about werewolves said that if you could destroy the werewolf that bit you, the curse would be broken. Turns out that's wishful thinking. We know now that it's an agent present only in the werewolf's saliva, that must be introduced in quantity directly into the victim's bloodstream to cause the mutation to human DNA. But in the 20s, it was all just considered black magic and curses. But after I'd been infected, I was willing to try anything.

It took a magic spell, but I found the werewolf that had bit me. I tracked her for nearly a year. Ten moon cycles, at least three nights each time, and occasionally more if I lost control. I had something of a clue by the time I caught up. I knew that I could keep some semblance of control when I was changed, except for during the full moon, so I figured out how to restrain myself during those nights. I'd learned about the weakness to silver by then, but had developed the hope that I wouldn't need to use it on myself if I could just catch the evil thing that had inflicted this on me.

She went south, deeper into Mexico. Unlike me, she loved the killing. Whenever the trail grew cold, I'd just stay for a spell and wait for the next tale of mutilated bodies to reach me. It made her easier to follow. I just missed her in Honduras, where I broke the chain I'd used to tie myself to a tree and ended up murdering a goat herder. She doubled back and headed north. I lost her for a while when she went into the Gulf, but I caught her eventually. The thing about werewolves is that once we've got a scent, unless the prey knows a few tricks, we're almost impossible to shake.

Across the sea, I finally caught her in Havana. Killing her was intensely satisfying, but as soon as it was over I knew it had been for nothing. I could still hear the Hum. When the moon was full, it would be back to the same old thing.

I was dead to my wife, dead to my kin. I was dead to my fellow Hunters. Raymond Earl Shackleford Jr. had ceased to exist after that first night. No one knew where I was or what had become of me, all in the hope that I'd be able to cure myself by destroying a single werewolf. I was such a sucker. Now she was dead, but so, still, was I.

Every day was a struggle to stay a man. All I wanted to do was change. Hunt. Kill.

And so at dawn I found myself on the walls of an old Spanish fort in Cuba, with a bottle of fine whiskey in one hand and a Smith & Wesson 1917 loaded with a single silver bullet in the other.

✤ ✤ ✤

Heather knew that if she went home now she'd have time to get a decent amount of sleep before she had to come back in for work, and she still wanted to stop by the hospital again just as a show of support, but for whatever reason she decided to take one last look at the prisoner.

There were only a couple of cells at the Copper Lake station, nothing fancy. If they needed anything bigger, there was the larger jail in Houghton one county over. They still had no idea who this man was. He wasn't talking sense, had no ID, and there was no match on his fingerprints. Odds were that he'd be taken in for a psych evaluation by the state and that would be the last that the Copper County Sheriff's Department would ever see of him.

The prisoner was sitting on the thin mattress, staring off into space. Heather stopped in front of the bars and watched him for a second. He was probably thirty, bulky and a little too well fed to be homeless, pale with dark hair and a scruffy beard. For some reason an uneasy feeling settled in her stomach, and it didn't feel like the expired doughnuts. "Hey!" Heather shouted, but the prisoner didn't look up. He just kept rocking slightly.

Something wasn't right about this one, and it wasn't just the fact that he was batshit crazy and violent. When she'd heard Bill screaming earlier, she'd come in, yanked the prisoner off, sprayed him good, and then, when he hadn't sat his happy ass down like she'd asked, she'd pelted him with her baton. On the paperwork, she'd called it a pain-compliance technique, and the first few hits to the arms and legs probably had been, but the last one that she'd put alongside his head had been because he'd pissed her off.

Heather was the only female officer in a testosterone-soaked small town filled with unemployed miners. She wasn't a bully and actually really disliked hurting anyone, but she'd made a career out of not messing around. She wasn't nearly as tough as everyone thought she was, but as long as the local troublemakers thought she was tough, it made life a lot easier. Heather tried to avoid confrontation but she never hesitated to get physical if the job required it. That ASP hit to the face had finally taken the fight out of the guy. Since he'd been wrestling one of her friends, she felt that the nasty welt she'd given him last night had been earned.

The prisoner finally seemed to realize that she was there and turned his head slightly to watch her through squinty eyes, still rocking. Something was odd. It took her tired mind a second to realize what was wrong. There was no bruise on his face. In fact, there was no sign that he'd been struck at all, and she'd really nailed him. Heather walked a few more feet along the bars, just to make sure that she wasn't remembering wrong and maybe she'd got him on the other side. Still nothing.

Weird. She should have been thankful there was no bruise, because with her luck the prisoner's brother was probably a civil rights attorney or something, but instead she found herself creeped out. She remembered exactly how hard she'd struck him, and there definitely should have been some evidence of it.

"What's your name?" she demanded. "It's hard to help you if we don't know who you are."

The rocking stopped. The man paused, as if listening to something in the distance. He smiled, and Heather was astonished to see how perfectly white and straight his teeth were. For some reason she'd been expecting him to have bad teeth. The man looked right through her, and the blankness of the gaze was simply unnerving. "You're pretty."

In normal, polite company, she might have said *thank you*. This company was neither normal nor polite. Here, it was simply uncomfortable. Agreeing with crazy people only reinforced the delusions, and disagreeing only got them riled up. It was better just to stick to business. "What's your name?" she asked again.

The man slowly rose from the bed. The springs creaked. There was something unnatural about the movement, as if he was far too graceful for someone of his size. "You're lucky to be so pretty. Does he like redheads? I don't know. We don't have any redheads. He'll probably want to keep you for himself. He's selfish like that."

She should have walked away and just gone home, maybe stopped by the florist first to pick up a bouquet for Buckley, but she knew that she definitely shouldn't be talking to this man. There was just a sense of wrongness about him, but the question came out before she could stop herself. "Who is?"

The prisoner cocked his head to the side. "The Alpha, of course. He picked this place special, you know. They'll all be dead soon. It begins here. The snow is coming, then everything changes. Then it'll be like an avalanche. You can't stop an avalanche. You'll probably be one of the lucky ones that he'll keep. Everyone else gets harvested." His nostrils flared as he breathed deeply, tilting his head back, like he was drinking in the air. "But you . . . you smell *nice.*" His eyes grew wide with realization, and the blank look was suddenly replaced with one of desperation. "Your scent! You've got the same blood as the one he's looking for!" Heather stepped back instinctively as the prisoner flung himself hard against the bars. "Where is it? He has to have it!" Spittle flew from his lips as he reached for her. "Koschei's treasure! Where did the thief hide it? *Where?*"

Having finally had enough nonsense for one day, Heather turned and left the cells. The lunatic continued shouting at her, but she just kept on walking, mentally damning bears and crazy people, both.

Agents Stark and Mosher arrived in Copper Lake before sunset. The hospital had been easy enough to spot as it was one of the larger buildings in town. They'd used some of their many fabricated government IDs to lie their way in, take their sample, and get back out.

"What a hole," Stark muttered as they walked outside. It was miserably wet. The weather report said it was going to turn to snow. Sitting in the Suburban for the long ride had made his old knee injury, received while chasing a stupid Bigfoot, act up. He unclipped the CDC ID from his coat and stuck it back in his pocket.

"I don't know," Mosher said. "This place used to be a lot bigger. They had a thriving mine business up here. The town used to have a lot more people, but then there was a big accident. The mining company went out of business. Lots of people lost their jobs. Everything kind of dried up after that. The place never really recovered."

"How do you know this crap?"

"I checked the Internet after you said where we were going. And the people here do seem really friendly. The town has just had some hard times."

Just like a jarhead to stick up for a bunch of hillbillies. "It's a shithole," Stark pronounced with finality. This was the kind of place that he hated working in. When he had to cover up activity in a city, it was easy. People disappeared or died violently there all the time. Out here, it got tougher. Everybody knew each other, and they all liked to talk. Good thing there were wild animals to blame things on.

Agent Mosher was young and not quite educated on when to shut up. "Well—"

"Shithole!" Stark snapped. He was in an especially foul mood because Grant Jefferson had neglected to mention that the victim was a cop. Offing a regular infected was one thing, but offing a cop was something entirely different. For one thing, it caused more paperwork. "This part of the country is only good for growing trees and gambling at the Indian casinos."

"Yes, sir," Mosher replied as he got into the driver's seat of their government Suburban.

The primary responsibility of the MCB was keeping the existence of monsters secret. Most survivors could be intimidated into staying quiet. The stupid were taken care of in various ways, either through making them look like crackpots, or, if that didn't work, then through more extreme measures. MCB agents were granted a lot of flexibility in dealing with that kind of problem. Stark liked to call it his *license to kill.*

So if this Deputy Buckley was infected by a werewolf, then Stark had every legal right in the world to put a silver bullet in him. But then the three other cops that had been sitting in the waiting room would probably end up shooting him. Which meant that if the test came back positive, he'd have to go talk to the sheriff and fill him in about the complete mission of the MCB, which would require paperwork, and *then* go kill the deputy, which would require even more paperwork. Stark hated paperwork.

He studied the glass vial in his hand. It was a werecreature field-test kit. The solution was a pinkish red from the drop of Buckley's blood dissolving in it. It took up to a few hours for the chemical reaction to work. If it stayed red, then the deputy was clear, and if it was a false alarm he would only have to do a little bit of paperwork. If it turned blue, he'd have to do a lot of paperwork.

Stark had been doing this a long time, though. He'd looked at the extent of the unconscious man's injuries and had spoken briefly with some of the cops who'd been to the scene. His gut told him that it was a werewolf. Which meant that there was one in the area, and since there were clear bite marks on the victim, on the next full moon there would be two.

Maybe he was thinking about this the wrong way. . . .

If Briarwood were to kill *two* werewolves, then Stark stood to make a lot more money, and if he didn't have to pull the trigger on the deputy himself, that would save him from doing all that bothersome paperwork. He bounced the vial in his hand a few times. *These tests aren't always reliable.* Nobody at headquarters would bat an eye if the test came up negative but the deputy turned anyway. That kind of thing had happened before.

"So, where to now?" Mosher asked, tapping his hand on the steering wheel.

If it turned blue, he'd just call Briarwood and then tell Mosher that it had come up negative. The werewolf would still get popped, society still got protected, only Agent Stark would actually get paid what he was worth for once. "Let's see what there is to eat in this dump," Stark ordered. He was feeling better already.

Earl Harbinger had driven another hundred miles after leaving Conover before parking at a truck stop, pulling the brim of his ball cap over his eyes, and grabbing a few hours of sleep. He'd need his wits about him when he arrived.

Werewolves dream, just like anyone else. Yet he'd found that the closer it was to the full moon, the more his dreams turned to the fevered images of his animal state. Maybe it was early this time because of the nature of his current mission, but Earl awoke to the memory of running through the trees, hunting, killing, perfectly in his element. He took that as a good omen.

Back on the road, hours passed, fields turned into city, then back into fields, and then the view turned to trees. He had never been to upper Michigan before, but found it pretty. Hills and forest, just like home. But Alabamans were smart enough not to live someplace that got this damn cold. It seemed like whenever there was a break in the trees, there would be another abandoned mine hoist building, splintering wood and rusting steel constructions. Some of them were surprisingly tall. The industry of the area had fallen on hard times.

The clouds were thick and rolling in hard. Lights from the ground reflected against the snow in the air and gave the whole area a pinkish tint. It was just itching to snow hard. The hour was late by the time the GPS told him he'd reached his destination. The sign said that it had a population just over two thousand. There was a main street with one stoplight. The downtown area was made up of two- and three-story buildings, mostly brick, constructed back in the boom days. Many of them were empty now. There was a vast, pointy Lutheran church across from the surprisingly big, ugly Sixties-era high school. The cars parked along the street were humble. The people who lived here worked hard for a living. It was typical small-town America.

It positively stunk of werewolves.

⚜ **Chapter 4** ⚜

I didn't want to die.

I had never been a quitter. That's one of the things that made me such an effective Hunter: sheer absolute stubbornness.

Sure, I'd tried to do myself in that first morning when I'd woken up with a stomach full of human flesh. What sane man wouldn't? But I'd managed to live with the curse for nearly a year, driven by a desperate mission of revenge, and the truth was, I didn't want to die.

But it was my duty. I'd sworn an oath to my daddy that I would fight monsters to the end. The possibility of becoming one hadn't really entered my mind, but then again Bubba Shackleford's Professional Monster Killers had never come up against any werewolves before the one that got me. Undead were different. If you turned into an undead, that didn't count; you weren't a person anymore. Undead are just shells, with no souls, just going through the motions of living. But here I was, changed, the foulest of murderers, but I still considered myself human. I still felt like a person, but I knew the truth. I was a monster. And monsters had to be destroyed. By the time that bottle of whisky was half empty, the decision had been made. And this time I had a silver bullet to do it right.

The crumbling fort was isolated, but I heard the footsteps on the stone steps long before I saw whom they belonged to. I was polite enough to not want to share the sight of my fresh brains with some random passerby, so I put the Smith back under my shirt.

But the stranger wasn't just passing through. The man was tall and very thin, with a beak nose, not too old but nearly bald, and wearing a black suit with a padre's collar. He looked suspiciously vulture-like, but then again I was rather drunk. The priest said that he'd been sent to find me and that he was in dire need of my assistance.

"No offense, Father, but I'm a little busy right now," I told him.

He bobbed his wispy head in agreement. "Of course. You were trying to have a contemplative moment before shooting yourself. I understand, but if I could have but a moment of your time first?" He looked like a local, but his English was excellent, hell, better than mine for sure.

"Is it that obvious?"

"Yes, but I have been watching you for quite some time. I know exactly what you are."

I was certain that I'd never seen or smelled him before. I'd come here trailing a werewolf. I had been the predator. I had been the one running the night through the streets of the old city. If anyone had been following me, I would have seen them for sure. "Really? And what would that be?"

"Someone who bears a curse." The priest dusted off a spot on the stone next to me and took a seat. "Someone who bears the mark of Cain." He stopped, as if waiting for me to argue. "I'm sure you are aware that what you are contemplating is a terrible sin."

"Yeah, yeah. Add it to the list. I'm going to hell. You got a point?"

"My impression is that you are a decent man who has had an unfortunate turn of events. I do believe that if I were to throw my life away, I would do it in a manner more useful to my fellow man. There is great nobility in sacrifice."

I was drunk, but not that drunk. "I'm not really fit to become a man of the cloth. I've killed a whole mess of people. . . . Ate a few of them."

"Oh no, oh my, no." The priest laughed until he started to choke. I'd never seen a vulture laugh before. "That is not what I had in mind." It took him a moment to catch his breath. Apparently the idea of me finding that much religion was downright hilarious. He watched the sunrise with me for a while before making his pitch. "I know of a village in need of help."

"What kind of help?"

"The kind that will almost certainly get you killed in the process."

⁜ ⁜ ⁜

Heather was just getting ready to go to work when she was startled by a knock at the front door. She had just finished securing the Velcro straps of her much-hated bulletproof vest. *Hated* may have been a strong word for something designed to save her life, but the vest was uncomfortable, annoying, and made her look dumpy. It was also mandatory. At least it was a *princess*-cut vest, which was a nice way of saying that it didn't squish her breasts like the one she'd been issued in Minneapolis. Heather threw on her green uniform shirt and started buttoning.

Even though the old Kerkonen family home was right in the middle of town, she didn't get very many visitors, and on the rare occasions that she did, Otto usually warned her a long time before they got up the driveway. Normally her old, three-legged, retired police German shepherd would be bouncing around the living room, shedding everywhere, eager at the prospect of company, but he was nowhere to be seen. "Some guard dog you are," Heather muttered.

There was a fearful answering whine from under the kitchen table. She spotted her dog backed into the farthest corner, his head down, ears flat, obviously afraid. His black eyes were fixed on the front door.

"What's wrong with you?" Otto hadn't been a particularly well-trained K9 even before he'd been retired. Copper County never had much of a budget, so when the chief decided they needed a dog, they'd bought Full Otto the Über Hund from a second-rate trainer. He'd been relatively useless to the department, except the kids loved him at the DARE events. She'd kept him ever since he'd chased a tennis ball in front of a snowplow and ended up as Otto the Amazing Tripod Dog.

There was another knock, and Otto whined a little louder, almost as if he was begging her not to answer it. He was a little goofy, utterly loyal, too friendly for his own good, but Heather had *never* seen him scared before. He may have had only three legs, but he was still eighty pounds of righteous Teutonic muscle. It was so unlike him that she found it a bit unnerving. "Chill out, dog, jeez," she admonished as she looked out the peephole.

The bulbs on the porch didn't cast much light, but enough that she knew she'd never seen the man before. Otto let out a low, out-of-character growl. The security chain was still in place, but she'd worked enough break-ins to know how useless those things were. Heather put one hand on her issue Beretta as she opened the door a crack, just enough that the visitor could see her uniform. The "No Soliciting" sign was more effective against annoying people when there was somebody with a badge in the doorway.

"Good evening," the stranger said politely.

"Can I help you?" Heather had a lot of practice scanning people and recording the pertinent facts. Caucasian male, a pretty good-looking guy, remarkably handsome, actually, probably around her age, dark hair cut short, neatly trimmed goatee, six foot, hundred and seventy, athletic, dressed nicely, with a white button shirt and a wool overcoat, hands in his pockets. The car parked on the street was a newer model BMW M3, silver. The Beamer stood out on the street full of pickup trucks and older cars. Her initial thought was that he was probably either going to try to sell her something or he had the wrong place.

His smile was rather disarming, or would have been to most women. Heather was too jaded to be swayed that easily. "Why, I hope so. My name is Nicholas Peterson. I'm sorry to bother you so late, officer."

He looked nice enough, but Heather had inherited her family's Finnish heritage of being sullenly suspicious of anything new. "And?"

"I was given directions at the library. I'm looking for someone." He had just a little bit of an accent. Heather couldn't place it, but he certainly wasn't from around here. New Yorker? "And I can see from your name tag that I've found the right place. Do you know an Aksel Kerkonen?"

Great. Somebody else Grandpa owed money. She had thought that she was past dealing with this kind of thing. The first year had brought a long line of creditors out of the woodwork, but it had tapered off eventually. "That was my grandfather, but he's passed away."

"I'm terribly sorry to hear that," he said. "My condolences."

"It's been a few years. What do you want?" She got ready for the invoice to come out, because if there was one skill that Grandpa had been good at, besides drinking, fighting, gambling, and mining, it had been absolutely driving the Kerkonens into poverty.

"Perhaps you may still be able to help me. You see, I'm a historian by trade. I'm doing some research for a book that I am writing. Your grandfather immigrated here from Finland in 1947, correct?"

"Something like that," she replied suspiciously. There really wasn't anything about her grandfather that a historian would be interested in, unless it was the history of random drunken knife fights of the Great Lakes region. "Lots of Finns around here, though. You're probably looking for someone else." Heather was Irish on her mother's side and didn't really know much family history either way.

"Did he fight in the Winter War?"

Grandpa had. He'd been some sort of sniper, in fact, but he hadn't spoken of it much. Up until the year he died, he'd been a crack shot with his old Nagant rifle and could still move like a ghost on cross-country skis. It was only when he got to drinking that he'd started referring to Russians as "game animals with no bag limit."

When she nodded, Peterson pulled a piece of paper from his pocket. Instead of the expected bill, it was a photocopied drawing. "Did he have a medal like this?" He held the picture up. "About an inch across, relatively flat. It may have been on a simple chain. As you can see, the workmanship is very rough. It would be silver in color."

Her first instinct was to wonder if it was supposed to be valuable, as there were a few scams that started that way, but most hustlers were smart enough to prey on widows and the stupid, not suspicious cops. She gave the picture a brief look. It was shaped like an animal track, only comically distorted with three long claws. A facsimile of a human hand was carved into the center. "Sorry. I've never seen that before. I can't help you. Look, Mr. Peterson, I need to get to work."

"I'd be willing to pay a large sum of money for it." The stranger was insistent. "Perhaps he would have left it to your father?"

Heather really wasn't in the mood. "He's dead, too. So is everyone else, and if my grandpa ever had anything that might have been worth something, it would have ended up at a pawnshop a long time ago. Good night." She started to shut the door, but he quickly jammed his foot in the way before she could close it.

Heather looked incredulously at the leather dress shoe blocking her doorframe. *The nerve.* "Are you kidding me? Listen—" But when she looked back up, the stranger's manner had subtly shifted. His head was tilted a bit too far to one side, and he was studying her intently through the crack. There was something not quite right about the way his eyes reflected the porch light, and suddenly Heather realized that Otto was right behind her legs, growling and shaking. A shiver ran up Heather's spine as her hand automatically tightened around the butt of her gun.

The man studied her for a moment. Even his voice was different, deeper. "She is telling the truth. . . ."

There was a noise from the street. A group of teenagers was walking down the sidewalk, laughing and screwing around. Peterson's eyes flicked away for just a split second toward them, and Heather could have sworn that she actually saw the pulse in his neck. He turned back to her, just the slightest smile visible at the corner of his mouth.

Heather shouldn't have been frightened. She was armed. She'd stood her ground physically against men far scarier than the historian—back in Minneapolis, she'd had a gun stuck in her face by a lunatic sex offender and had stayed cool until the situation was under control—but for some awful reason that slight bit of smile scared the hell out of her. She tried to keep the tremor out of her voice. "Get your foot out of my door, or—"

And just as quickly as his manner had changed to threatening, it returned to normal, almost meek. His posture changed, the strange gold reflection gone from his eyes so quickly that Heather wondered if she'd imagined the whole thing. The foot retreated. "I apologize," he said, dipping his head. "This is just very important to me. If you happen to remember anything about the amulet, I will be staying at the Boddington Inn for a few days. I'm sorry to have troubled you, officer."

Without another word the stranger turned and walked down the steps. He crossed the sidewalk, got into his car, and drove away without looking back. Heather watched until the taillights of the Beamer disappeared around the corner. She closed the door and realized that she'd unconsciously opened the retention hood on her duty holster. Her hands were shaking.

What the hell? She'd been in life-or-death fights, and those hadn't affected her like the dude who had just stood on her porch. Heather took a seat on the couch. He'd stuck his foot in the door and smiled; he'd been rude. That was it. No one would have ever accused her of being a wimp, and she wasn't the type to freak out. Maybe it was the stress from Buckley's attack. Maybe it was the insomnia. She was just on edge. She was seeing things that weren't there.

But even as she thought it over, she knew that there was something *wrong* about the mysterious Mr. Peterson. When he'd tilted his head, there had been a feeling, something primal, something terrifying. He had unnerved her.

Otto whimpered. There was a fresh puddle on the carpet. Apparently her dog was in agreement.

We should have killed her.

"Shut up," Nikolai said. He turned the blinker on and turned right onto Copper Lake's Main Street. Nikolai was always careful to obey all the traffic laws of whatever country he was operating in.

Took her. Hurt her. Murdered her. Ate her. I like redheads.

"She did not have the amulet. I will not jeopardize the mission for your good time." There was only one stoplight in the whole town, and unfortunately Nikolai had caught it. The BMW pulled to a stop behind a truck. "Violence will only attract attention, especially against one of the authorities."

Too late for that.

Indeed it was. He had heard about the attack on the other deputy. There would be others as well that these people did not yet know about. The *vulkodlak* were being gathered. It was already starting. A single fat snowflake landed on the windshield. He watched it for a moment as it sat there, not even bothering to melt, taunting him. More flakes joined their brother. Within seconds his view was peppered white. Time was running out.

It would have served her right, spawn of that treacherous, thieving Finn.

Nikolai shook his head. It had become far more demanding lately. It made it difficult for Nikolai to think clearly. "Focus." There was still much work to do, people who had known Aksel to interview, places to investigate. These were problems that could not be solved with tooth and claw, nor with the rifle in the trunk, for that matter. "We must be discreet."

Do you smell that?

He did. "Wolfsbane . . ." The scent coming through the heater vent was distinct, barely detectable, and only recognized because Nikolai was used to its effects. Its presence served as a general warning, though the herb would cloud his normally acute senses and mask the precise location of the most important thing of all, other werewolves, specifically the one that was wearing it.

Harbinger.

The light turned green. Nikolai activated the wipers and knocked away the collecting snow.

The Quinn Mine had been closed for years. Operations had already been winding down from the glory days when it had been the region's largest employer, so that by the time the tragedy had occurred the Quinn Mining Company had been but a shadow of its formerly great self. Only two of the company's dozen shafts had still been in operation, pulling copper from the bowels of the Earth on the day when a rock burst had trapped twenty miners at the base of Shaft Number Six. Over the next seven days, the rescue attempt proved fruitless and was finally called off when two rescuers were killed on the surface by a malfunctioning piece of equipment. It had been the final nail in the coffin of the financially struggling Quinn Mine.

Surrounded by forest and isolated by hills, most of the buildings still stood. Equipment that had been caught up in the ensuing lawsuits had been abandoned to rust. Volunteers from the Copper County Historical Society conducted a tour a few times a year, and some of the faculty from MTU would do the occasional field trip, but otherwise the warren of offices, rock house, hoist building, and warehouses remained empty and decaying.

Ethan Pedde had been a miner there when the Quinn had finally shut down and had been working as the night watchman ever since. Usually the most interesting thing he got to do was chase off teenagers looking for somewhere to screw around or to scare themselves silly in a place that everyone in town said was haunted by the ghosts of trapped miners. Last year he had even let in a group from a cable TV show that had come in hunting for ghosts with a bunch of cameras and recorders. They hadn't found anything, but Ethan still knew that the place was haunted.

For example, the building he was currently strolling through, that stood on top of Shaft Six, always gave him an eerie feeling. It was several narrow stories of splintering wood and hanging tin, home to rats and pigeons. The wind always made the whole place creak and cry. There was a hole under his feet that went down five thousand feet, farther than God ever intended man to go, an inclined nine thousand feet of tunnels, all coated in red iron dust, and somewhere in a pile of rocks under all that wet red hell were the skeletons of twenty of his best friends who'd asphyxiated in the pitch black. Oh, yeah, if anyplace was truly haunted, it was the old Number Six.

He'd taken a few days off for Thanksgiving, then took a sick day because of a nasty cold. The broken chain lying in the snow at the gate had told him that somebody had snuck into Number Six while he was away. Damn kids. They were probably long gone by now, but if they weren't, braining one of them with his nightstick was mighty tempting.

Ethan saw the gleam of a flashlight bouncing ahead of him before it disappeared down the stairs, and it ticked him off. Because it was the source of the legends, Number Six was where the morons liked to break in to impress their girlfriends, so Ethan always made sure he walked through it at least twice a night, even when it was piercing cold, like tonight. Though he wasn't a religious man, Ethan thought of Number Six as a tomb, and therefore sacred, and not to be broken into by idiot teenagers.

Kids looking for a scare . . . They didn't know what scared was. Scared was going back down that hole, even while the rock was screaming around you, ready to break again, and trying to cut your way to men who any sane person knew were probably already dead while choking on clouds of dust. Ethan had gone down twice, working twenty straight desperate hours. The really brave one had been that madman Aksel Kerkonen, the supervisor of Number Six, who'd gone down by himself one last time, even once they'd called the rescue off. That stubborn old bastard hadn't known when to quit.

The footprints were visible in the dust. These kids were braver than most. They were going right down to the shaft entrance, following the crumbling railroad ties. The steel tracks had been pulled up and sold for scrap years ago. Ethan lost the prints on the metal catwalk.

Ahead and below were the twin giant spools of cable that raised and lowered the cars. It would take a particularly stupid teenager to go down there. It was pitch black, and there were lots of sharp bits of rusty metal to bang into. The holes had been covered with heavy grates for safety. Although the shafts themselves had crumbled during the cave-in, leaving them choked with broken ledges that you could barely crawl between, even the shortest drop was still a couple hundred feet.

Ethan had stopped to pull the cobwebs from his hair when he heard the crunching. At first he thought it was boots on the gravel around the top of the shaft, but this was different. It was too loud, and it was more of a snapping that was echoing down the brick walls. Ethan wasn't sure what he was hearing. It would be dangerous for someone to actually try to climb down the shaft. Even if they squeezed past the ledges, most of the bottom levels had flooded with seeping water as soon as the pumps had quit running. It would be easy for someone to get trapped down there and drown.

Once he was back on solid floor, Ethan played his light around, looking for more prints. There were prints with boot tread, others from athletic shoes, but then there was something else: drag marks. Now he was really curious. He kept watching the floor as he approached the noise. The dust was really disturbed in this area. Maybe some vagrant had moved into Number Six. . . . Maybe a *crazy* vagrant . . . Ethan suddenly realized how dark it was outside of his flashlight beam, and since company policy forbid security guards to have guns, all he had was a nightstick. Maybe he needed to just back out of here and call the sheriff's department and let them deal with it.

There was a whiff of something rotten. Ethan saw something that made him wonder if the cold medicine was making him hallucinate. It was a paw print, only it was about the length of his size-ten shoe. He turned in a slow circle. There were paw prints everywhere. And then he saw the strangest track of all. It looked like a bird's track, with three long toes and a spur on the back like a chicken. Only it was ten inches wide and two feet long.

The beam of light rose, shaking, and he saw what was making the crunching noise.

Bones. They glistened red in the beam of light. There were big living *things* in the shadows, and they were cracking bones.

"Oh, dear God," he whispered.

The whisper that came over his shoulder almost made the night watchman leap out of his skin.

"He can't help you here."

⊰ Chapter 5 ⊱

The padre was the kind of man who kept his cards close to the vest. He didn't say too much about this supposed job, except that my odds of living through it were infinitesimally small, and who better to fight a monster than a monster? He would not say how he'd found me, how he had managed to avoid being detected while he'd watched me, or how he even knew what I was to begin with.

The last night of the full moon had passed. I had time. I had nothing better planned except catching the express train to hell, so why not go along for the ride?

We traveled across the big island. There was a small fishing boat waiting on the south coast. It took us to a little island named Cayos de Tiburon.

"There is a village on the other side of the island. My church is there. My people have been terrorized by something from the sea. It has carried off many of us. We are a simple folk, who make our living from the ocean, but since the creature has come, the fishermen are afraid to go out. It is slowly killing our village."

"Why don't you just get a few men with rifles and wait for it to show up?" I asked.

"We've tried. It is too clever. It only comes onto dry land when it can attack the unarmed and helpless. Apparently it has felt the sting of bullets before and does not appear when we are ready. It looks like a dumb beast, but it is very clever. It is huge, with the head of a shark and the tentacles of a squid. It is savage and pulls its victims apart before *devouring their flesh, unless it carries them off to its underwater caves. The Indians call it the* luska."

"So, you want me to wait on the beach for this luska thing to show up to eat me, and I kill it with my bare hands, or at least injure it enough while it's eating me so that it don't come back?"

"That would be most helpful."

That silver bullet was sounding better and better.

The beach was tranquil. For the first time in what felt like forever, I was totally at peace. I was about to die, but it was with a purpose. The moon was bright overhead, just a sliver off of full, but enough that the Hum was only background noise. I took off my boots and my shirt, and crouched on the edge of the surf, crunching sand between my toes and waiting. I'd left my revolver with the padre before he'd sailed away. We'd see how smart this critter was. My heightened survival instincts were balanced with that burning desire for the challenge of the hunt. I'd found balance.

It didn't take long for the luska to spot me, a single, helpless meal. I could sense it in the waves, studying me. I was alone and seemed feeble. My nose picked it up first, just a hint of ocean rot, a bit stronger than its surroundings. It was old and terrible. It watched me for half an hour, recognizing that I wasn't the same as its regular prey but not understanding just what a werewolf was capable of, even in man form.

Finally the luska made the decision that I was food. It hurled itself out of the surf and onto the sand, a giant black glistening mass. The front end was that of a giant shark, mouth chock-full of gleaming teeth and a little red eye on each side of its great big head. Its rear half was a mass of squid tentacles. The two longest tentacles ended in jagged barbs that looked almost like long-fingered hands. The hands were used to pull its huge weight forward, while several of the smaller tentacles shot back and forth, propelling it up the beach right at me.

Now that was a death worthy of a Hunter.

Heather had only been on her shift for a few minutes, still preoccupied with thoughts of the strange Mr. Peterson, when a big, black, jacked-up Ford truck had blown past her, doing at least forty-five in a twenty-five and ran right through a stop sign without even a flicker of brake lights. *Back to work.* She'd automatically turned on the siren and pulled out behind the truck.

It had started snowing. Gently so far, but the thick sky told her that it was going to be a real dumper. The roads were still okay, but it was always the assholes in the biggest trucks who assumed that four-wheel drive gave them the magical power to drive too fast on slick roads, physics be damned. The truck had Alabama plates, of all places, so it was probably somebody who had no comprehension of how to drive on ice, either. Damned tourists. It was either ticket the jackass now or pull him out of a ditch later.

She'd already called in the plate number by the time the driver saw the red and blues flashing in his mirror. The truck pulled over at the corner of Quinn and Red Jacket. She got out and approached the driver's side window cautiously. Copper Lake was a quiet town, but she prided herself on being a professional.

The window was already down. Somebody must like the cold. The driver was an average-looking guy. Caucasian. Early forties. Light-colored hair, groomed short from what she could see sticking out from under his hat. Average build. Beat-up leather jacket. Hands on the steering wheel. The truck put him up rather high, but if he had gotten out she was willing to bet that he would stand just over six foot. She'd been doing this a long time. He turned his head toward her with a polite nod. A few days of stubble. Some gray in there. Hard jaw. Not much fat on this one. Lean. Impression of a tough guy. Eyes an odd shade of blue. Mildly annoyed expression. "Evening, officer. Was I going a little fast?"

He even sounded like he was from Alabama, nothing overt, but the accent was there. Heather kept her tone firm. "Yes, you were. Are there any drugs or weapons in the vehicle you need to inform me about?"

"Negative, ma'am."

"License and proof of insurance, please. Did you even see that stop sign you just ran?"

The man sighed. "No, ma'am." His hat had a green happy face with horns on it. Probably some Alabama sports team she'd never heard of, but the only sport she ever watched was hockey, and she doubted very much that Alabama had hockey. After a moment of rummaging through the center console, he passed over the paperwork and his license. "I suppose I was a bit distracted."

"Well, Mr."—she glanced at the license—"Harbinger, you need to slow it down and pay more attention." Thanksgiving had only been a couple of days ago. People were still eating leftover turkey. Since she knew just about everyone in the county, she probably knew whom he'd been visiting. "What brings you to Copper Lake?"

He had a real strange look on his face when he responded. "I'm passin' through. Never seen this part of the country before."

"Uh-huh . . . Wait here." Heather returned to her car to run the stupid tourist's license.

"Damn it," Earl muttered to himself after the lady cop sauntered off. He'd been driving around, sniffing the air, trying to pick up a trail. The falling snow was damping the multiple scents, plus the wolfsbane in his pockets wasn't making it any easier to get a fix. He'd let himself get distracted.

But one thing was for sure . . . He watched the cop in his mirror. She was certainly human, but she had the smell of werewolves on her. One was stronger but unfamiliar, but the other . . . She'd been near Nikolai earlier. It was really faint, but it was there. He hadn't touched her—it would have been stronger then—but he'd been close recently. The scent brought back memories. It felt like there should have been a flood of memories, but because of Rocky, it was only a trickle and a sense of absence, loss, and a burning desire to tear Nikolai's throat out.

He watched the cop car in the mirror until snow covered the glass. Not a bad-looking woman as far as he could tell, with her so bundled up against the cold. He did have to chuckle at the stupid question about if there were any drugs or guns in the vehicle. Were criminals dumb enough to actually answer that truthfully? Earl had brought plenty of both. Out of view under the camper shell he had enough weapons to overthrow a Third-World nation and narcotics sufficient to knock out an elephant. The tranquilizers were in case he was out around the full moon and couldn't make it into the time-locked steel cage that took up half the truck's bed. Neither option was as nice as his cell back at the compound, but the portable cage beat the hangover from the sedatives.

The cop came back a minute later and handed over his license and a yellow carbon copy that read "Violation" in big black letters across the top. "So much for getting off with a warning."

Her uniform coat was a giant puffy green monstrosity with an embroidered yellow badge. A black knit cap hid her hair, and her cheeks were rosy from the cold. She was already coated in falling snow. "I only cited you for the stop sign. You're lucky you caught me in a good mood. I can throw the speeding on there too if you want. Twenty over is a pretty hefty fine," she stated flatly. The cop had fine features, a nose that was a little too big to be perfect, green eyes, and the hair that had strayed out from under the cap was a dark red. He decided that she could be pretty if she actually smiled, but she didn't strike him as the smiling type. Human scents always told a story. She wore the smell of workaholic stress, was healthy despite a lack of sleep, lived alone, had a dog, and had eaten Oreos and Diet Mountain Dew for dinner.

Asking where she'd bumped into a former KGB assassin was out of the question. Nikolai could be masquerading as anyone. By most standards, Nikolai spoke better English than Earl did. "You get many strangers in these parts?" he asked.

"Not usually, until it's good snowmobile weather, but lately we seem to be swimming in them."

"Really . . . What for?" *Where did you meet him?*

But apparently she wasn't the small-town type that liked to gossip about strangers. The cop just shrugged. "Just slow it down. You'd better be more careful. Your behavior could hurt somebody."

That was the general idea. But he just nodded politely. Knowing where she'd met his enemy could be a real advantage, so he tried one last time before she had a chance to walk away. "What do you say I buy you some dinner and you tell me more about your lovely town?"

She paused, incredulous. "You realize that *never* works, right?" Then the deputy surprised him with the barest hint of a wry smile. "And you're not my type. Good night, sir."

"Type?" Earl muttered to himself after she was gone. "Hell, girl. I ain't your species. . . ." Earl stuck the new ticket in the center console with the others. Owen got mad when he didn't save his receipts. Brushing the snow off the mirror, he watched her walk back to the cop car. At least she made those uniform pants look good. Must work out a lot. He waited for her to drive away and even waved as she went by before putting it in gear and heading back to the main street.

The last hour had been spent getting a feel for the area, but now he was starving, and Earl wasn't inclined to hunt down his nemesis on an empty stomach. Plus, he wanted to talk to more of the residents. There were definitely strange things going down in Copper Lake. The presence of multiple werewolves suggested that Nikolai was up to something unexpected.

The Russian had always been like Earl, a loner. It wasn't like him to run with a pack. Task-force intelligence had believed that Nikolai had gone so far as to refuse to create others of his kind for his controllers. Stalin had been the last leader that Nikolai had held enough respect for to bow to that command. Not that having fewer werewolves was a particular loss for the Soviet war machine, since the vast majority of them turned out just as dangerous to friend as to foe.

Kirk Conover had always felt that Nikolai had avoided creating others because he liked being special, being the only werewolf that the KGB could count on. Earl had known it was because Nikolai simply hadn't wanted the competition. It had been a long time since the USSR had collapsed and Nikolai had gone missing, but Earl had just assumed that some things wouldn't have changed. It smelled like he had been mistaken.

There was an open-late diner down the road a short distance from the hospital. It looked like it had been around for a while, the kind of small-town place where crusty old locals would sit and smoke and talk to whoever was willing to listen about anything that was new or out of place. It was exactly the kind of establishment where a Hunter could grab a cold beer and a hot steak, shoot the bull, leave a huge tip, and get some intel on what was actually going on. In other words, it was Earl's kind of place.

Which was probably why the sight of the Suburban with the government plates in the parking lot immediately made him mad. Earl swore to himself as he parked the MHI truck behind the black vehicle. It might have been from some innocuous federal agency, but the number of extra antennas and dark window tint in a town teeming with werewolves just screamed Monster Control Bureau. "Well, ain't that my luck?"

If the Feds were here because they knew about Nikolai, they'd surely screw it up. The Russian would go to ground and disappear for another decade. Earl took his time deciding on a course of action. He could get back on the road and drive around looking for werewolves or he could go inside and try to listen in on the Feds. Odds were that it wouldn't be anyone who'd recognize him, and if that were the case, he might actually be able to overhear something useful from them. His sense of hearing was better than a normal man's, so it was worth a shot.

Worst-case scenario, if it turned out to be a familiar Fed, he could try to pick an argument with them to see if they might slip up and say something they shouldn't. MCB loved to throw their weight around, and one of his favorite hobbies was provoking the easily provoked MCB agents. The thought of confrontation was so tempting that Earl almost left his MHI hat on. Discretion finally won out, and he left it in the truck.

The diner was warm and smelled of good cooking inside. The place was relatively busy for how late it was, but it was a Friday night. Earl took a spot at the bar with a few older gentlemen who were busy complaining about politics. A teenage waiter with hair covering his eyes had a menu in front of Earl a minute later. The Feds were easy enough to spot in a corner booth, being the only customers wearing ties. Ties stand out even more when almost everyone else is wearing flannel. The younger of the pair was unfamiliar but had that typical MCB look, being an intense, muscle-bound, square-jawed specimen of ass-kicking and witness intimidation. The senior one had his back toward the bar, but that raspy bass voice was familiar. The senior agent was a thickset man, totally bald, with jowls and a big nose. *What was it? Storm? Stork? He'd been Franks' partner years ago. . . . Sam had punched his lights out once at some Navy thing. . . . Stark.* That was it. Stark was a prick. So much for not being recognized.

The Feds were talking. Like most men who'd spent a lifetime around gunfire, Agent Stark spoke with the unconsciously raised volume of someone with some hearing loss. He was complaining about the weather, the locals, and the audacity of Copper Lake for not being Chicago, but nothing of any use to Earl. The waiter came back, and Earl surprised the kid by ordering two sixteen-ounce T-bone dinners, extra rare, extra everything. The waiter asked if he was expecting a guest. He just smiled, said that he'd been blessed with a fast metabolism, and went back to listening.

It wasn't the Feds' conversation that caught his attention, though. It was one of the locals.

"The thing must'a been a monster. I heard it was bad. Like it clawed him to bits."

"Damn straight. I never seen the like. It *ate* part of Joe's stomach. That boy's lucky to be alive."

Earl turned toward the two men sharing the bar to his left. "Sorry to interrupt . . . But did you say that somebody got *eaten*?"

"By a *bear*," the first man replied. "Can you believe that?"

Earl whistled. "That happen a lot around these parts?"

"Only never, far as I know," said the second, who seemed all too eager to share the story. "Everybody in town's talking about it. My nephew works at the hospital, told me all about it."

"Where you from?" asked the first suspiciously. Earl recognized the accent from when he'd worked a case in Finland. "You're not from around here. You talk funny."

"Alabama. Where bears don't eat people, it don't usually snow, and it's customary for the new guy getting told the tale to buy the drinks for the men doing the telling." Earl knew from experience that you couldn't ask for a better bunch than the Finns, once they warmed up to you and decided you weren't in need of a stabbing, at least. Tough climates bred tough temperaments. "Name's Earl."

"That's a fine tradition there, sonny," nodded the first approvingly, and he held up three fingers for the waiter. "I'm Aino. That's Henry. Up on Cliff Road, one of the local deputies, Joe Buckley, was in his car, bear came along and pulled him out the window and ate part of him."

"He was where the Randalls keep their horses," supplied Henry. "Other side of the hill from the old Quinn Mine. I used to work down there, ya know, back 'fore the big cave-in."

"Dark day for Copper Lake," Aino muttered.

Earl didn't know if the old immigrant was talking about the bear or the mine collapsing. "Did they catch the bear?" he asked, and he had a sneaking suspicion on what the answer would be. Both of the old timers shook their heads in the negative. "I'm a professional hunter by trade. Maybe I could help."

"Maybe." Aino scratched his grizzled chin. "They looked for it, didn't see nothing. Joe Buckley's a good boy though, so you see any bears, stranger, you do us a favor and pop it dead."

The waiter came back with three beers. "I got a few rifles in my truck," Earl responded, and *few* was an understatement. He took a bottle and tilted it toward the gentlemen. "And I'm a fair shot."

The waiter snorted derisively and blew the hair away from his eyes. "People like you put guns on our streets."

Earl looked at the teenager in disbelief. "And people like you put the fries on my plate." He waved toward the kitchen dismissively. "So hop to it, boy."

The waiter stomped away. Aino gave him a big grin. That was a new record for Earl befriending a Finn. Apparently living in America took the edge off.

Stark couldn't believe his eyes, but who should be sitting there at the bar other than the head contractor scumbag himself, Earl Harbinger.

The entire time he'd been eating his chicken-fried steak and talking with Agent Mosher, Stark had kept checking the test vial under the table. Once it turned blue, he'd told Mosher he needed to take a leak, and he'd gotten up with the plan of calling Briarwood to get their butts up here to make them all some cash. Seeing that pain-in-the-ass Harbinger joking and drinking with some old bastards floored him.

MHI is here. Stark let loose with a long string of profanity under his breath. Those jerks would swoop in, kill the werewolves before Briarwood could, steal the PUFF bounty, and, worst of all, there wasn't a damn thing he could do about it. He couldn't even pull jurisdiction and toss MHI out, because that required paperwork, and he sure as hell couldn't justify that if his official story was that the test kit had come back negative.

He hated Harbinger. Not only was he rich and successful beyond any public servant's wildest imagination—the guy kept senators in his pocket like most people kept change—he was also a balls-out fighter. Rumor in the MCB was that Harbinger had actually kicked the snot out of several members of Director Myers's strike team and gotten away with it. Which was another example of why Myers needed to be replaced. If Stark was running the show, there was no way that any MCB would ever be disrespected by a filthy werewolf.

That was the crux of it. Harbinger was a werewolf, a disgusting, stinking lycanthrope, no better than the trash that Stark had devoted his life to destroying. All the Special Agents in Charge knew about him. Those yokels were unwittingly sitting there next to a vicious animal, and Stark wasn't even allowed to do the sensible thing and go pump a silver bullet into the monster's head. Non-PUFF applicable creatures were out of his jurisdiction unless they went off the reservation and were caught up to no good. Sure, the second somebody like Harbinger screwed up, MCB owned their ass, but in the meantime his hands were tied. Nobody in the MCB knew exactly why Harbinger was declared off-limits, but Stark was sure that it had something to do with Monster Hunter International throwing big bags of money at spineless politicians.

He had to do something and quick. Harbinger would go to talk to the bitten deputy. That's how he got his new recruits, after all: sweet-talking survivors. Being a werewolf, Harbinger would definitely recognize that the deputy was infected, probably smell it or something, and then MHI would get that bounty instead of him.

Stark made it around the corner to where the bathrooms were without being seen. Luckily for him, the place still had a pay phone installed—good thing that all these backwoods types got bad cell reception—which meant that he didn't have to use his government-issued cell to call Briarwood. You couldn't be too careful in this business.

The sultry European sex goddess picked up on the fourth ring. "Briarwood."

He cut right to the chase. "If your boys can get here in time, you've got *two* bounties. But they had better hurry. There's been a complication. Some of your competitors are here."

"Competitors?"

"The boys from Alabama, if you get who I mean. One bounty is at the hospital. He won't turn until the full moon, but if you get him early, the blood test will justify the PUFF." Stark neglected to mention that the place was crawling with cops. That was Briarwood's problem. "The one that bit him is around here somewhere. How soon can you be on-site?"

There was a long pause, like she was covering the phone and asking someone a question. "Our team is almost there."

Stark glanced at his watch and swore. It was going to be close. "Head straight for the hospital." He slammed the phone back into the cradle.

When Stark came around the corner from the bathrooms,

Harbinger, who didn't seem surprised in the least, was staring right at him. Stark froze. From across the room, the Hunter actually had the nerve to raise his beer like he was giving Stark a toast. So much for getting out without being seen. Stark walked up to the bar to confront the obnoxious Hunter.

Earl Harbinger didn't look like anything special up close, just average. But there was something intimidating about the way he watched you, like he was trying to decide whether to eat you or not. But Stark was MCB, and MCB wasn't easily intimidated, even by a werewolf.

"Hey, Agent Stork. Been a long time," Harbinger said, sounding friendly as could be. That redneck-Confederate-illiterate-goat-molester-country-music accent made Stark even angrier.

"Stark," he corrected. "What're you doing here, Harbinger?"

"Vacation. These gentlemen were just telling me about the quality fishing they've got in these parts. Damn fine steaks here, by the way. You?"

"Official business. And you better stay out of it."

Harbinger smiled. "I'd have to take a significant pay cut to make your business worth my time."

"Screw you," he said automatically, but then Stark felt a brief touch of panic. Had Harbinger heard him talking to Briarwood? He paused, thinking it through; there was no way he could have, but it was still a sore spot for the agent. "Listen up, asshole. You want to—"

"Whoa there," interrupted one of the yokels. "What's your problem?"

"Shut your face, old-timer," Stark snapped. "This doesn't concern you."

"Damn, Earl. Who's this dickhead?" asked the other local.

"Somebody who's about to get his ass beat," said the first old bastard in a thick accent. He got off his stool but only came up to about Stark's neck. "You got a problem, fatso?"

"Easy, Aino," Harbinger said, putting one hand on the man's arm. The guy had to be in his sixties, and he was ready to throw down at the perceived insult, but at least the grizzled old man returned to his seat, glaring the whole time. "Me and Stork here have met before. He's just a little high-strung is all. . . . So, how's life been since you were released as Franks's jockstrap carrier?"

Mosher had heard the raised voices and come over. The junior agent had no idea what was going on. Stark pointed one thick finger right between Harbinger's eyes. "Funny guy, huh? Well, funny guy, one of these days you'll screw up, and then we own you."

"Uh-huh . . ." Harbinger took a long, nonchalant drink. "And when that day comes, I'll make sure that whatever I did was absolutely worth it."

Stark may have been angry, but he was smart enough to know that Harbinger was just goading him. Besides, slugging Harbinger's drunk hillbilly friend in front of witnesses would probably cause him some trouble. "Come on, Mosher. Let's get out of this dump. Remember, Harbinger, stay out of my way, or you'll regret it."

"See ya' round, Stork."

"Better keep walking," said the one with the accent.

Fists clenched, Stark made it back to the Suburban, Mosher asking him the whole time what that was all about. Stark was fuming, but the sudden cold air had helped clear his head. He'd made up his mind. "Get us back to the hospital," he snapped. Briarwood better get here soon, because he'd shoot the deputy himself and deal with the paperwork before he gave MHI the satisfaction of stealing *his* money.

⊰ **Chapter 6** ⊱

Since I had been bitten, I had learned about the obvious physical changes. I was stronger, faster, more agile, though at that early stage I hadn't realized just how much better I'd become. My hearing and sense of smell were more acute. I could see better at night. But the main difference was that I could heal at a phenomenal rate.

It made sense. Since my body was now capable of completely breaking itself down and reforming into a new shape in a matter of minutes (it was minutes then; it is seconds now), reforming broken pieces of my anatomy was an excellent side effect. Though exhausting, injuries caused by anything other than silver mended themselves almost instantly. Though it wasn't until I fought that luska *that I really discovered what I was capable of.*

I grabbed the first tentacle hand as it snaked in close. The fingers had the consistency of a thick crab leg. I snapped one off and stabbed the luska *with its own claw. For some reason I laughed as it tried to bite me in half, but I moved out of the way faster than the* luska *could react. It followed me up the beach, farther onto the sand, tentacles swinging like crazy past its big shark head, cracking like bullwhips. Each time a barb hit, it cut right through my skin. Regardless of how fast my skin knitted back together, it still hurt like a son of a bitch, every single time. But once I caught one of the big tentacles, I ripped it right off and beat the monster over the head with it.*

For being so damn heavy, luskas *are lightning quick. It finally caught up and overwhelmed me beneath its body, crushing me right into the* sand. I can still smell the rotting fish. Dragging me out with a tentacle around my leg, it swung me around to its jaws and bit me. Teeth punctured halfway through my body, from my shoulders, through my ribs, through one lung, through my stomach, and cracked my pelvis in half. It shook me back and forth like a terrier with a rat until my spine broke. When I finally hung limp, it slithered back down the beach for the black water.

Then I got really mad.

That was back in the days before I'd learned how to hold off the change. Now I only change when I let the Hum take over, or on the full moon when I have no choice. Back then, if I was in enough pain or anger, I couldn't help but change.

The luska had just reached the crashing surf when it realized that the thing in its mouth had suddenly gotten a whole lot fiercer. My spine popped back together as every fiber of my body twisted toward a new shape. I reached up with one rapidly lengthening thumbnail and scratched one of that luska's little red eyes in half. The jaws unlocked, and the teeth pulled free of my body.

The next few minutes were blurry, but as I changed, I managed to reach down the luska's throat to tear out great bloody chunks of meat. That disoriented it. I shoved its jaws apart until the bones broke. I ripped into it, spraying monster all over the beach. I bit and tore and clawed until the monster flopped and rolled away, trying to escape. So I grabbed on to one of the big tentacles and dragged the thing that was at least five times my size back up the sand. Confused and losing blood, it sprayed me with ink, but that just pissed me off more.

The holes in my flesh sealed. The blood loss weakened me, but fury filled the gaps. The holes in the luska squirted red blood, and that just egged me on. The beast was terrified now, bellowing in pitches that human ears could never hear, warning the others of its kind to avoid this island.

Finally I remember crouching on top of the mighty body, dripping black ink from my fur, claws sunk deep into blubber, as I howled at the moon in triumph. I ripped the creature apart, needing to feed, to replace the mass and energy that I'd just burned.

Luska tastes kind of like ahi tuna, only chewier.

✛ ✛ ✛

After Jo Ann had gotten the call from Agent Stark, Horst had told Lins to step on it. They were already speeding, but Horst wasn't going to pass up a free shot at a werewolf.

"I don't know. The roads are getting nasty," Lins said.

The driver was right. The snow was getting heavier. But they were in a Cadillac Escalade with good tires, were almost there, and he wasn't about to let those Alabama pricks come into his neck of the woods and start moving in on his business. Not that this part of the country was anything at all like the Chicago streets he was used to. All those trees made him uncomfortable. There was something wrong about all that land, just sitting there, completely unpaved.

"Don't be such a punk, Larry," said Kelley from the backseat, where he had been loading magazines the entire time. By this point Horst wasn't even sure how many mags he had stacked back there, but whatever kept the bearded brute distracted was fine by him, because he was hard to shut up once he got going. "Have faith, and put the hammer down." Kelley was a strange combo, a devoutly religious hooligan criminal. Horst's first clue was when he'd noted the many prison tattoos on Kelley's thick arms were all biblical verses, but he had come highly recommend.

"Jesus isn't going to tow us out of a ditch, Robb." Jo Ann was looking for a fight, as usual.

"Zip it, cow."

Horst just held up his hand, indicating he wasn't in the mood. They both shut up. Robb Kelley might have spent a lot of time breaking the knees of people who'd picked the wrong people to owe money to, but Horst knew that Jo Ann Schneider actually had more useful experience than anyone on the crew except for Horst himself. She had served the most time, run every con imaginable, probably offed the most people, and she was certainly fine in a voluptuous kind of way, which came in handy when working with the public.

Loco was in the front passenger seat, staring quietly out the window as usual. As talkative as Kelley was, Loco was quiet. They didn't call him Loco because he was crazy, though Horst thought he might be, at least a little. Loco was just short for Lococo. Jason Lococo was huge, ugly, with a shaved head and one glass eye that never pointed in *quite* the same direction as the other. The giant also bench-pressed close to five hundred pounds and had served five years of hard time for killing someone by accident. He'd punched the dude *once*. The reason Horst had hired him was pretty obvious.

"Hey, it's slick," Lins insisted. "I'm doing my best."

He didn't have time for this. Lawrence J. Lins, or Larry to his friends, was the oldest man on the Briarwood team and had been a major hitter for some gangs out of Cleveland. His uncle had also recommended Lins because of his reputation. He looked like a gray-haired biker, no-nonsense-take-care-of business type, and was not the sort to get jumpy just because they were facing something supernatural.

Horst hadn't been at MHI very long, but long enough to see that the kind of people they recruited were too soft for this kind of business. Sure, they'd survived a monster attack, and got all high and mighty, but they weren't nearly as bad as they thought they were. MHI's Hunters were just regular Joes pretending to be heroes. After monsters ate the wannabes, they were left with a decent-enough crew as far as he could tell, but the core of MHI was still soft. Instead, Horst had surrounded himself with hard cases. This bunch would kill anything without hesitation. He was the only one on the team without a record, and that was only because he was smart enough not to get caught.

But right now Lin's caution was going to cost Briarwood a bunch of money, so it was time to take charge. Horst's response was cold. "Listen. This is our shot at the big time. Killing a werewolf gives us money, a name, and a line of clients a mile long. I told you about those people I used to work for. They own fucking *helicopters*. Helicopters! That's the kind of scratch I'm talking about. You want to go back to knocking over liquor stores?"

"No. I'm done with that," Lins said.

"Then quit being a bitch and drive *faster*," Horst ordered.

Lins just grunted and gave it more gas. Horst prided himself on his management skills.

The hospital was one of the newer buildings in Copper Lake. It wasn't the biggest in the region, but it was a decently capable, bland, two-story concrete square, and it served all major needs of the many small towns in the rural area. They'd decided that Buckley had been too injured to risk transporting him to the bigger facility in Houghton until he'd stabilized, which everyone doubted would actually happen.

Then Buckley had surprised everyone by not dying. Word around the office was that Dr. Glenn had been speechless when he'd seen how well Buckley was doing. Heather figured that the initial severity of his injuries must have been exaggerated.

Heather decided to poke her head in for a visit. Buckley was single, no girlfriend, no close family. They had actually eaten Thanksgiving dinner together just a few days ago in the station's break room. As usual, the *unattached* had volunteered to work on the holiday so their coworkers could be with their families. He was an affable guy, but kind of a loner. Heather had always liked him. He was a straight shooter, friendly to everyone, and an all-around good guy you could count on in a tough situation. It broke her heart to come here.

There was a waiting area for friends and family on the second floor. Heather knew it all too well. She'd slept many nights on that couch right there. Her mom had died here, sick but never alone. Then her grandpa had spent his last days here after his stroke. Shortly after that her dad had ended up here. She'd gotten to know this particular couch during all their stays. Yep, she and that couch were old friends.

It was late, and there was no one else in the waiting room. The nurse on staff recognized Heather and waved her through to go straight to Buckley's room. Sure, it was after normal visiting hours, but small towns could appreciate when rules needed to be applied and when they needed to be overlooked. Buckley had gone through another surgery this morning, and normally they wouldn't have let anybody other than immediate family stay with him, but they were making an exception for the sheriff's department.

Buckley was lying there, covered in bandages, looking terrible. His normally handsome face seemed sunken, and his broken skull was wreathed in white. His torso was covered, but one arm was wrapped in a giant bundle where they'd tried to piece his hand back together. There were flowers everywhere. The people of Copper Lake loved Joe and had tried to show their support the best way they could. Heather had debated picking up some flowers but had decided that it seemed kind of silly. It wasn't like Joe was the kind who appreciated flowers. Anything else at this point would have just been a waste. They would all be wilted and dead by the time he woke up anyway.

There was nothing official about it, but the entire department had rallied to make sure that there was always somebody with Buckley, and the sheriff, being a good and kind-hearted man, had decided that one of his people had better damn well be there when Buckley woke up. Tonight it was Chase Temple sitting in his regular clothes on the recliner in the corner of Joe's room.

Temple put down his political science textbook and stretched. "Hey, Kerkonen."

"How's he doing?" she asked quietly.

"Same. Hard to tell . . . I don't know." Temple stood. "If you're going to be here a minute, I need to step out and grab a smoke. That smell's killing me."

"Smell?" Heather asked. "The flowers?"

"No, the hospital antiseptic. Can't you smell that? This place smells like sick people."

She shrugged. It was a familiar smell. She hadn't noticed. "You hungry?"

"Cafeteria's closed."

"They usually leave some sandwiches out behind the counter. There's a coffee can for you to put money in. It's on the honor system. Bring me a doughnut if you don't mind."

"You and your junk food . . ." Temple cracked a smile. "That stuff will kill you."

Ethan Pedde huddled in terror on the floor as the thing that looked just like a petite, young, naked woman squatted next to him sucking the marrow out of the end of a human femur. His flashlight had rolled across the floor, and in the shadows her eyes seemed gold.

The girl was half his size, but her grip had been like iron. She had backhanded him to the ground, tossed him around like he weighed nothing, and dragged him screaming by one leg down to the bone and meat pile, and left him there, quivering. The things in the shadows were hairy. The steam rising from their bodies warmed the space. They didn't bother to look up from their meal. The naked girl seemed at home with the terrifying animals. Ethan turned his head far enough to see that what was left of the body was wearing jeans and running shoes.

It smelled of musk. He was surrounded by huge carnivorous animals. He knew that if he tried to get up they'd attack. Two of them began to wrestle and snap at each other over a severed arm. That made the girl smile.

"Who . . . who are you?" he managed to whisper.

"The pack," she answered simply, then went back to gnawing on the bone.

Since it was dark, and the girl was coated in dried blood, her hair a matted tangle of dust and filth, it took him a minute to recognize her as one of the checkout girls from the Value Sense Grocery. She had always been friendly as could be, with a ready smile and a good attitude. If he remembered right, she'd even been a Copper Lake cheerleader a few years back. "You're the Langleys' girl, aren't you?"

"Not anymore."

Ethan understood that the thing squatting there amongst the terrifying beasts wasn't the friendly local girl he'd known. No longer human, she was something wild, feral, and dangerous. "What're you going to do to me?"

"If it were up to me, you'd already be in my belly," she replied. "So shut up. The witch's things are still searching. They don't need to breathe like we do down there, but don't you worry, we'll be gone soon. The Alpha said they almost had it."

The girl was talking crazy. "Please, I've got a wife and kids. Let me go," Ethan begged.

"Humans are such whiny little bitches." There was a clanking noise from the shaft. Her head snapped around, and she peered into the darkness of the entrance. "He's coming. You better not piss him off, or you'll regret it." The girl took a few fearful steps back and disappeared into the darkness.

Ethan tried to make himself look as small and nonthreatening as possible. The closest animal was sitting only a few feet away, crouched on its hind legs, its torso upright. One of its hairy forearms was sitting in the beam of light, and Ethan realized that it had fingers with pointed nails like black claws, but they were *fingers*. Not a paw. Fingers.

Every creature in the room moved, long heads shifting toward the shaft entrance at the same time. Their heads dipped submissively. Ethan couldn't see what they were looking at, but suddenly there was a man's voice in the darkness.

"The diggers have found it."

All of the animals howled in unison. The sound reverberated through Number Six. Ethan curled into the fetal position.

The man got close enough to the light that Ethan could just make out his silhouette. He was wearing a big black coat and wide-brimmed hat. His face remained in shadows, but his eyes seemed to glow like the girl's. He had a mud-caked box in this hands. The man got closer, put the box down, and then sat cross-legged on the dusty floor behind it.

"Who are you?" the man asked, noticing Ethan for the first time.

His mouth was so dry it hurt to talk. "The night watchman," he managed to answer.

"Oh . . . I thought I recognized you. I took the tour once." There was a long sound of inhalation. The stranger was smelling him. "You've been down below. You left your fear down there before, during the cave-in. I could taste it on the walls. You knew Kerkonen?"

"I knew him," Ethan croaked. What did old Aksel have to do with this?

The big black hat nodded up and down. One hand came to rest on the box. "It can't be destroyed. I know he must have tried. Can't break it, burn it, or melt it. They don't build things like this anymore. That's why he tried to hide it. He was scared of someone like me coming along. He thought if he buried it deep enough, I wouldn't find it. He buried it in the deepest hole on Earth and then filled it with water. It was a brilliant try. I'll give him that. It took me years to find this place."

It was a stainless-steel lockbox. The stranger broke the clasp and rusty padlock off with one hand. The box creaked as it opened for the first time in years. The creatures all crowded in closer to see. Ethan could feel their body heat.

The stranger lifted a rotting cloth from the box. Water drizzled out to puddle with the blood on the floor. "Behold, my children . . ." The stranger was eager. The rags fell apart. Something silver gleamed in the light; a chain spilled away from it and swung. The man's smile was visible in the dark. His teeth were too sharp. "The amulet of Koschei the Deathless."

The excitement could be felt coming from the horrible creatures as the man removed his hat and placed the chain over his head. He shuddered when the amulet hit his chest. The golden eyes closed. The pack drew even closer. It was almost as if the animals were holding their breath, waiting to see what would happen.

The man began to mutter under his breath, as if reciting a memorized prayer. The guttural language was unfamiliar. The prayer grew in intensity. The creatures let out fearful whimpers and dipped their heads further. The air seemed to bend around them. The light from the flashlight flickered and died.

The terrifying stranger finished in English. "Let the heavens cry their tears of ice. Let the rivers flow with blood." He exhaled slowly and reopened his eyes. Gold had turned to bright, glowing red. "Let the great hunt begin."

Ethan Pedde's screams died in his throat as several sets of jaws ripped him apart.

The Hum came out of nowhere.

Earl had to grab the bar to keep from falling off the stool. One hand convulsively knocked his dinner onto the floor. The plate shattered. The sudden clatter got the other patrons' attention.

Something was wrong. Terribly wrong. For a split second he thought the change had come on him. Visions of blood; he'd kill everyone there. They'd never have a chance.

Aino's hand landed on his shoulder. "You all right, buddy?"

Teeth gritted together, Earl tried to steady himself while his ears rang and all the hair on his arms stood on end. He shrugged the hand off. It was like the days leading up to the full moon had been compressed into a single moment with the density of a brick and then smashed over his head.

Luckily, the sensation was already passing. The Hum was fading to normal levels.

"I'm okay. Give me a second." He took a deep breath. *What the hell was that?* Earl shoved himself away from the bar and took a few halting steps, swaying, dizzy. The other patrons were staring at him. Beads of sweat were rolling down his clammy skin.

The annoying waiter approached. "Everything okay, mister?"

"You need a doctor?" Henry asked.

"Naw . . . I'm good. Gotta go clear my head. Fresh air." Earl got his wallet out, pulled out two hundreds and stuffed them into the waiter's shirt pocket. "Sorry about the mess." Head still swimming, Earl staggered for the exit.

Outside, the sky broke open and snow thundered down. The howling of wolves could just be heard over the howling of the wind.

✢ ✢ ✢

Heather started to form a response to Temple about how she wasn't going to get lectured to by a guy in his twenties about her doughnut addiction, when Joe Buckley groaned loudly and startled them both. The machines by the bed beeped wildly. Buckley suddenly jerked, his face contorting in a grimace of pain. "Get the nurse," Heather ordered. Buckley gasped and opened his eyes. He appeared to be in terrible pain. He looked around in confusion, then let out a blood-curdling scream. "Go!"

Temple sped from the room. Heather went to Buckley's side. "Joe, can you hear me?" Buckley began thrashing, his hands curled into fists and drawn up to his chest. He tried to sit up, but screamed again and fell back, only to try to rise again. There was a cracking noise, and Heather had no idea where it came from, but she could have sworn that it had come from *inside* of him. Scared that he was going to rip open his stitches, Heather put her hands on Buckley's shoulders and tried to restrain him. "Joe! Calm down!"

Suddenly, Buckley fell limp. The heart monitor began to sound a high-pitched alarm.

Buckley was looking right through her. Dead.

"Oh God. Not you, too, Joe . . ."

Then he blinked.

Veins grew large beneath the skin of his forehead and neck. A sudden heat emanated from his body, so intense that it felt like his flesh was about to burst into flames. Beads of sweat materialized and flowed freely down Joe's face. He screamed and kept screaming until he ran out of air; then he gulped more in and screamed again. Saliva flew from his lips and hit her in the face, but she still tried to hold him down. She'd never seen someone in so much pain. "Help! We need a doctor!" she shouted out the doorway.

When she looked back down, the whites of Joe's eyes had seemingly filled with blood from broken vessels. His pupils had turned a metallic gold. The screaming stopped, but then it was replaced with desperate panting. With a shock, she realized that his skin was actually burning her hands. She gasped and let go, backing away as Buckley's back arched, lifting most of his body off the bed. Other machines began squealing madly as tubes and sensors were ripped out. He kicked violently, the blankets flew across the room, there were more crackling noises, like bones breaking, and Buckley's body slammed back down.

Buckley looked at her, panting, foam coming from his lips, and gasped, "Kill me, please. Hurry." His voice was too deep. His gums were bleeding.

Temple returned with Dr. Glenn and a nurse right at his heels. The doctor was shouting orders. Heather raised her hands and covered her mouth, backing away slowly until her back met the wall. Mad with pain, Buckley's fists unclenched, and he began tearing at his gown with fingernails that were far too long.

Nikolai was driving down the snowy highway, cursing his bad luck and planning his next move, when the surge struck. It rolled over him, through him, like a tidal wave. It was as if the moon was suddenly there, not just calling him but screaming in his ear. He managed to gasp "No!" as his blood ignited.

Yes! Yes! the Tvar screamed inside.

He tried to fight the transformation. His muscles locked up and he helplessly jammed the accelerator to the floor. A spastic twitch cranked the wheel to the side. The BMW spun directly into the oncoming headlights of the other lane. An orange shape was hurtling at them in a billowing plume of dirty snow.

"*Govno*," Nikolai muttered as his body unclenched.

The snowplow's blade slammed into the car with a thunderous bang. The front end crumpled in two directions. Glass and metal filled the compartment as the world shifted into a sudden reverse and the BMW was lifted from the road. Nikolai, not wearing his seat belt, was hurled through the windshield.

Earl stood in the parking lot, face lifted toward the sky, eyes closed, open mouth filling with whipping snow, and he breathed it in, filling his lungs with ice. The cold cleansed him, cooled his burning skin. Something was terribly wrong. In all the years since he'd been cursed, he'd never felt anything like that.

The moon's humming was still there. It was always there. He could feel it to the core of his soul. It waxed and waned, more regular than clockwork. But now there was another Hum, an unnatural vibration, and it was coming from something other than the moon. Earl lowered his arms and opened his eyes. The wind ripped at his coat. A full-on blizzard had sprung out of nowhere. He turned in a slow circle, watching as the lights of the town were blotted out of existence by the shielding snow.

The new Hum, the false moon, it called to him. He could feel it. He could follow it like a beacon. There was something else that he could sense, too, much closer. He turned toward the squat concrete shape of the nearby hospital. *An awakening* . . . In a crowded public building packed with innocents. "Damn you to hell, Nikolai. What've you done?"

Investigating the new false moon would have to wait. Earl reached under his coat for the comforting shape of the Smith & Wesson 625 holstered on his right hip. The .45 was loaded with 230-grain MHI-issue silver bullets, and he guessed that he'd be needing them real quick. He set off at a run.

⇥ **Chapter 7** ⇤

"*Impressive,*" *the padre told me the next morning. "Even for a werewolf. Especially for one so young.*"

I woke up inside the luska carcass, using its liver as a pillow. I was absolutely stuffed, stunk like fish blood and oil, was extremely sore, and human. I stumbled out of the canopy of ribs to go wash off in the surf. The priest followed me. I asked him if he was an expert on werewolves as I used sand to scour the ink from my skin.

"Why, yes, actually. I am."

I paused and sniffed the air. He wasn't like me. That was obvious. "Keep talking."

"My name is Father Santiago. I was not always a simple parish priest. As a young man, I held a special assignment at the Vatican. Were you aware that the church has its own group of Hunters?"

For the record, I was raised Southern Baptist at my mother's insistence, but me and religion hadn't ever paid each other much mind. There were other rival organizations, even back then, but we'd never run into any churchy ones. Everybody we'd ever competed with had been in it for the money, same as us. "Makes sense, I suppose."

"Your organization started in 1895. Ours started in the twelfth century," he continued. "I was an archivist, so I know a few things about werewolves."

I betrayed my lack of schooling. "What's an archivist?"

"Someone who keeps records. But as I was saying, I know werewolves. For example, I know that you are certainly an oddity."

"Why's that?"

71

"*Most would be sitting in that* luska's *belly, but not quite so comfortably as you were. I do believe that* luska *should be digesting you, not the other way around. Also, most young werewolves are extremely erratic and easily provoked into rages, and you have not even attempted to kill me once.*"

"*Eh . . . I've been busy. I figured I'd get around to it.*"

Father Santiago was carrying his shoes to keep from filling them with sand. He put his toes in the water. "*What if I were to tell you that I know of a few cases in history where a lycanthrope with similar strength of character was able to control their curse enough to live a long and productive life?*"

Nobody had ever accused me of being a quitter. "*I'd say I'm listening.*"

⁜ ⁜ ⁜

The cell phone had lost its signal. Agent Stark glared at the display. He had managed to call his office and do his mandatory check-in for the night, but it had cut off when he'd tried to get his wife. She always got bitchy when he didn't check in. She said it was because she worried, but he knew it was because she was a control freak who wasn't happy unless she was nagging him to death.

"Probably interference from the storm," Agent Mosher supplied helpfully.

"Think so, Einstein?" Stark gestured out the front window of the Suburban. The snow was pounding down. The other cars in the hospital parking lot were quickly beginning to resemble white lumps. He would have sworn that it had dumped two inches in the last ten minutes. The wipers were going full blast just so he could still keep an eye on the parking lot. Stark tried his phone again, but it had gone from three bars to a big fat blinking *No Signal*.

A minute of uncomfortable silence passed. The junior agent could tell that his boss was in a bad mood. "Shouldn't we head to the hotel?" Mosher suggested. "Why'd we come back here? You said the test was negative."

"Intuition," Stark lied. He was just waiting for Briarwood or MHI to show up. If it was Briarwood, he could go get some sleep. If it was Harbinger, he was going to go shoot himself a deputy. "Trust me, kid. I've been doing this a long time. Sometimes an agent just has to trust his gut."

Mosher just nodded. The junior agent knew that Stark had been trained by the legendary Agent Franks, so if Stark said that was how it was, then you'd better believe that was how it was. There were certain bragging rights in the MCB that came from serving with Franks. That dude had killed *everything*. The new rumor was that he'd actually used some gizmo built by Isaac Newton to blow up an actual Great Old One, but Myers was keeping the details of the New Zealand op top secret.

The deputy was on the top floor. Some of the lights were on up there. Stark could see a few people moving around, but overall the place seemed pretty quiet. This might not be so bad after all. Maybe the cops would have gone home for the night. Hospital staff were far easier to deal with, and there wouldn't be too many of them. Stark scowled. However, there did seem to be some activity in the room directly above them. The blinds were partially open, and there was definitely movement. If he was remembering the layout correctly, that would have been the deputy's room.

Stark checked his phone. Still no signal.

Mosher managed to stifle a yawn. "So, we're here. What do you think is going to happen?"

"Something . . . I guess." Stark returned his attention to the window just in time to watch it explode outward in a shower of sparkling glass as a man wearing blue scrubs was launched through. He tumbled wildly through the air, face-planting onto a car parked in the front row. The body came to a sudden stop hard enough to bend the roof.

"Did you see that?" Mosher shouted.

"Kind of hard to miss." There was no way. It was too early. The full moon wasn't for a few days, but the limp body staring at him upside down, turning the snow pink, wasn't lying. "Come on," Stark ordered as he opened his door.

"Damn, sir, you *are* good," Mosher exclaimed as he followed.

Heather couldn't back any farther into the corner, but she wished that she could. The doctor had tried to do something to Buckley, but Buckley had just swung at him and the doctor had just been *gone*. She looked up, following the trail of blood splattered across the ceiling, and tracked the trail with her eyes to where it terminated at the shattered window. The blinds were hanging in tatters and a freezing wind pushed snow into the room. He'd swatted poor Dr. Glenn right out the window.

Buckley was sitting up in bed. The screaming had ceased. He was still panting, but he seemed calmer somehow. His golden eyes locked on hers as tears of blood rolled down his cheeks. "Kill me . . . please." It was as if his tongue was too big and he had a hard time forming the words. His hospital gown was torn, and his body was covered in hair. Buckley looked down at his hand. It was dripping, and each of his fingers ended in a red point. "Please . . ." His mouth opened too wide, as if it was hinging farther back.

Deputy Temple was too shocked to move. The nurse took two steps back, tripped over something, and fell on her rear. Heather drew her pistol. "Joe?"

"Do it!" he roared. Another wave of pain hit Buckley, only instead of a normal human scream, out came a terrible howl. His entire body was rippling, skin pulsing. Heather couldn't believe her eyes. The howl tapered off. Then the lights flickered twice, and they were plunged into darkness. The wailing of the machines stopped. An ominous silence fell as the background noises of the hospital died.

The only light was an eerie reflected white from the broken window. Heather raised her gun. Buckley's bed rattled hard. "Joe?"

There was no answer, only heavy breathing. Heather had a painful knot in her stomach. It took all of her conscious effort to take a step away from the wall. A few seconds later, the emergency generator turned over. The fluorescents flickered to life at half strength. The light was dim and twitchy.

Buckley was gone. Something had taken his place in the bed. He— it—was staring at her. Her mouth tried to form words, but no sound came out. It was still Buckley, sort of . . . Skull cracking, his face had twisted into a horrific snout. Yet as he looked at her again, she somehow knew that it was no longer Joe inside there. Joe was gone. He rose from the bed, twisting and gasping, his gums stretching past his splitting lips.

The nurse cried out and started crawling for the door. The noise caught Buckley's attention. His lengthening head whipped around, attention fixed on the woman. The attempted flight set something off. He leapt from the bed.

"Stop!" Heather cried, but she was already pulling the trigger. She didn't even remember aiming the Beretta or flicking the safety off, but the glowing front sight was right there on his center of mass, just like she'd been trained. She pulled the trigger again as his feet hit the floor and then again as he pounced on the nurse. The woman screamed as Buckley's teeth sank into her chest and his fingers into her neck. Buckley shook his head back and forth. The nurse was flung about helplessly, limbs flailing, crying, as Heather kept on shooting.

Buckley jerked as Heather shot him repeatedly in the back. He released the nurse, head rising, mouth spraying blood in a wide arc, and Heather shot him in the throat. Buckley got up, made it a few steps toward the exit, and then collapsed in a heap into the hallway.

Heather was shaking. The slide was locked back on her pistol. The Beretta 96 held eleven rounds in the magazine. Somehow she'd fired them all. The adrenaline had made the gunshots sound like insignificant pops. She realized she'd been holding her breath.

Focus, Kerkonen. Buckley wasn't moving. His feet and legs were still in the room, only they weren't shaped like feet anymore. She broke out of the tunnel vision. The nurse was coughing up blood. Her collarbone was visible. Temple was frozen. Heather reached for another magazine as she moved to the injured woman. It took her two tries with her suddenly clumsy fingers to get the new mag seated in her gun.

Heather squatted next to the nurse. The wound looked like she'd been hit with a chainsaw. Blood was pumping down her shirt. Buckley had bitten a *chunk* out of her. Terrified, the woman was trying to speak. "It's okay," Heather lied. Thumbing the safety down, she reholstered her pistol, just like she'd been trained. "Just stay calm. We'll get you some help." That's what they'd taught her. Tell the injured that everything was going to be okay, even if you knew they were screwed. Freak out in front of them with a bunch of *Oh man, you're all messed up, you're gonna die,* and it was just like you'd killed them yourself. However, this was so far beyond Heather's first-aid knowledge that she had no clue what to do. She tried to put direct pressure on the biggest hole. Blood came spurting between her fingers. But it didn't matter. The flow dropped in intensity, then stopped. The nurse was dead. Heather didn't know her name. She must have been new here.

Scrambling back, blood up to her elbows, Heather tried her radio, but there was no response, only static. She moved to the phone at the bedside, but it was dead, too. She needed help. People were gathering in the hall, a couple of mobile patients roused by the gunfire, and the final member of the skeleton crew of the night shift on this floor, and all of them were stopping and staring at Buckley's mutated hairy body, facedown, bleeding out on the carpet.

Finally another nurse stepped gingerly over Buckley's body and came to help his coworker. Heather recognized this one. Bailey Something, and he'd been nice enough while her grandfather had been dying here. "What happened?"

"Buckley . . . *ate* her," Heather tried to explain.

"Where's Doc Glenn?"

She awkwardly pointed at the window. Some weird shit had just gone down. Bailey went to work, though Heather knew it was too late. Heather tried to stay cool. *Need help.* "Chase?" The other deputy was still standing there, mouth agape. The young man didn't respond. "Deputy Temple!" she shouted. "Draw your fucking sidearm!"

He jumped. "Yes, sir," he finally responded, coming back to reality.

"Watch Buckley. If he moves, shoot him in the brain. Do you understand?"

"Yes, sir."

Cringing, she passed over Buckley's body while trying hard not to look at him, pushed past the patients, and made it around the corner to the nurse's station, keying her radio the entire way, getting nothing but static, and found that the main phone was dead as well. Not even a dial tone. The power, phones, and radio were all down. "Damn it all to hell." What else could go wrong?

Then the people behind her began to scream as Temple started shooting.

Luckily the power went off right before Agent Stark stepped into the elevator. Being trapped in an elevator with the power out while a werewolf was eating people would have been really embarrassing, the kind of thing that would become MCB lore. The other agents would never have let him live it down.

Mosher had his flashlight out in a split second. The brilliant Streamlight lit the entire lobby area. "Stairs?"

"Stairs," Stark responded as he drew his Glock 20. "Go." He'd gotten his own tac-light off his belt and clamped on to the dustcover of his 10mm by the time they found the stairwell, but by then the power had come back on. He jerked the door open and was greeted by the echo of gunfire.

They surprised a janitor on the stairs. The man just stared at the two armed men in suits. "Evacuate the building," Stark ordered. "You've got a . . . uhm . . ." He paused, not having thought the cover through yet. He'd figured he had plenty of time until the full moon. Cleaning this up was going to be a royal pain in the ass. "There's an escaped lunatic ax murderer upstairs. Run for your life!"

A patient hopped past her, one leg in a cast, crutch forgotten somewhere. He was terrified. Heather counterintuitively ran toward the danger. An older woman in a bathrobe was right behind the hopper. She screamed something incoherent, hobbled back into her room, and slammed the heavy door. Heather rounded the corner and skidded to a halt. She bit back a cry.

It was a bloodbath.

The hallway had been painted red. She'd only been gone for a few seconds. It looked like the scene of an industrial accident. *Is that one body? Two?* She wasn't sure, and she couldn't really tell now. There was just a jumbled mass of limbs in a pile. Unconsciously she started walking backward, toward safety.

Someone screamed inside Buckley's room.

Her boot clicked on the linoleum, and Heather realized that she'd been retreating. She stopped. Despite her best judgment, all reason, and logic, Heather knew her job, and nobody had ever accused her of not doing her job. "Crap, crap, crap." Drawing her Beretta, she flicked the safety off and raised it in both shaking hands, walking toward Buckley's room.

Temple flopped into the hallway, slipping onto his hands and knees, scrambling madly through the blood. Shirt rent open, he was bleeding from several deep lacerations. "Help me!" He had made it a few feet toward her when a black mass of hair bounded into the hall at his heels. It was unbelievably fast, and it certainly wasn't human. The animal grabbed Temple by the foot and in one smooth motion dragged him back into Buckley's room. Her fellow deputy disappeared, a look of shocked disbelief on his face.

There was a drag trail through the blood. It had happened so

quickly that Heather hadn't even fired a shot. *What was that?*
"Buckley?" Temple bellowed in agony. Heather forced herself forward.
"Hang on, Chase! I'm coming!"

Then the beast moved back into the hall. It came so quickly that it
just seemed to materialize. It saw her, and there was no hesitation.
Growling, it charged on all fours. Heather yanked the trigger
repeatedly. It covered the distance in a split second. The creature leapt
high. There was no time to dodge. She shut her eyes before impact.

There was a bone-jarring bang, but the expected hit never arrived.

Heather opened her eyes. The creature was sliding down the floor
away from her, wearing what she could have sworn was a too-human
look of surprise on its awful canine face.

A man in a leather jacket had come out of nowhere and was
standing protectively in front of her. He was shaking his right hand
loose as if he'd just struck something hard. "Stay behind me."

"Did you . . . Did you just *punch* that thing?"

"Seemed like the thing to do," the stranger grinned, winked, and
that's when she recognized the annoying Southerner from the traffic
stop earlier. "Any chance I can get you to rip up that ticket now?"

The animal came off the floor, roaring, and charged. "Look out!"

Nonchalant, the man turned back as a big stainless revolver
appeared in his hand. He fired so quickly that the shots sounded like
a continuous crackle. Every bullet struck home, right into the animal's
head. Blood and fur splattered the walls. It collapsed, limp, forward
momentum sliding it onward. The man opened the cylinder of his
revolver, punched out the spent casings, and slammed in a bundle of
six more so fast that his gun was reloaded by the time the creature
reached them. He casually raised one boot and put it down on the
body, stopping it in place.

"How? *What?* How?" Heather stammered. The thing under the
stranger's boot was bizarre, unnatural. One of its claws had come to a
stop only inches from her foot. "Ack!" She kicked the hand aside.

Taking his time, he put one last shot right between the animal's
eyes. Heather flinched. "Silver bullets," he explained. He stuck his gun
back into his holster, then took a cigarette out of his coat and put it in
his mouth. "Your regular ones won't do shit to a werewolf. I'll give
you a B for effort, though."

Heather was stunned. The fearless weirdo showed up, punched a giant animal down the hall, shot the hell out of it, and now he was talking about *werewolves*. "Huh?"

"Grading on a curve, obviously. I've got to reserve the A for this kid that works for me, killed a werewolf with his bare hands one time. Got another with a pool cue."

"Werewolf?"

"Yup. That there's one dead-ass werewolf," he explained, gesturing at the body. A Zippo appeared in his other hand, and he lit up. He took a long drag then blew out a cloud of smoke. "Name's Earl. Earl Harbinger."

She was still staring at the animal. "Uh. Yeah."

The new guy was completely calm, not even bothered that there were fresh brains on his boot. "That would normally be the part where you tell me your name, Deputy . . ."

"Kerkonen." Could that thing really be Joe Buckley? Harbinger had called it a werewolf, but that was just absurd.

"Talkative, ain't ya? Well, Deputy Kerkonen. Congratulations. You just survived a monster attack. Welcome to big-boy town. Now, how about we go see if there are any other survivors?"

"Temple!" She stepped over the animal's arm. Heather refused to think of it as a werewolf or Joe Buckley. She couldn't think of that thing as Buckley without endangering her sanity. "There were others in that room."

"Let's go then," he said, removing his boot from the animal.

She took one last look at the dead body. It had been mere inches from pouncing on her. "Thank you," Heather stammered as she realized just how close she'd come to being torn apart. Pistol in hand, she started for Buckley's room.

The two of them had only gone a few feet when the beast rose up behind them like a great black shadow and sunk its fangs into Heather's shoulder.

Deputy Kerkonen looked at Earl with an expression of complete surprise as the teeth pierced her. The disbelief turned into realization, and she cried out as the pain hit. The werewolf lifted her off the floor, shook her, then hurled her down the hall. The cop hit hard and went skidding away. The werewolf turned toward Earl, bloody jaws wide.

Earl reacted and slammed his fist into the werewolf's snout. Bones cracked. Teeth went flying. He slugged the werewolf again with a blow that would have surely killed any human, and then, as the werewolf staggered back, Earl kicked it in the stomach hard enough to knock the werewolf through a heavy wooden door and into the room beyond.

Impossible. He'd put multiple silver bullets into the new werewolf's skull. There was absolutely no way that it could be alive. *None.* All werewolves were vulnerable to silver. Earl followed it into the room. There was an old lady on the bed, watching the creature on her floor in surprise. She took the oxygen mask away from her face to point and screech incoherently about wild animals waking her up.

"Excuse me, ma'am," Earl said politely. The new werewolf was rising. Earl slammed his boot into the back of its head and put it back down, holding it there. He drew his Smith, then paused. "Would you kindly cover your ears?" He waited for the old lady to comply. Then he pumped the remaining five rounds into the werewolf's head. It made a ghastly mess on the floor. The patient began mashing her button to summon a nurse. "I don't think anybody's coming, ma'am."

"What kind of lousy hospital is this?" she wheezed. Grumbling, she got out of bed, grabbed a cane, and headed for the door.

As the patient slowly fled the room, Earl watched the bullet wounds pull themselves closed. He took a moon-clip from his belt and checked it before reloading. Sure enough, it was standard MHI ammo; a silver ball sealed into a regular jacketed lead hollow point. The werewolf should be assuming room temperature, not twitching its way back up to ruin his day. "Well, I'll be damned."

The regeneration time was remarkable, faster this time than the first go around, almost like it was adapting on the spot. It was already rising. Strong, too . . . Earl was shoved back as the muscled beast forced itself from the floor.

Claws lashed out. Earl barely moved aside as they cleaved the air where his head had been. *Too fast.* Jaws flashed, and Earl calmly fed the werewolf his right arm. Teeth clamped down on his jacket and shook him from side to side. He could feel the intense pressure through the leather, but hardly anything on Earth could pierce minotaur hide. He kept a small Entrek fixed-blade knife at the small of his back for just this sort of occasion. Calmly, Earl pulled the blade free with his left hand and drove it between the werewolf's ribs.

The werewolf let go, surprised. Earl moved in a blur, slashing the blade across his enemy's throat. The werewolf stumbled, gurgling, brain temporarily deprived of air, but Earl was already doing the math. The kid was too fast, too strong, and already healing. Earl wouldn't be able to outfight him in human form, and it was too dangerous to invite a change with all these bystanders around. Unexpectedly, he had a real fight on his hands, and this kid needed to be put down before he hurt anyone else. The bigger weapons were in the truck, and he hadn't thought to stick a hand grenade in his coat before dinner.

Then Earl spied the abandoned oxygen bottle and had an idea. As his daddy, Bubba Shackleford, the greatest Monster Hunter who'd ever lived, had always taught: when all else fails, kill it with fire.

Heather came to, flat on her back, looking at the dimly buzzing florescent lights. Her head throbbed from the impact. There was a warm slickness coating her chest. *I'm bleeding.* Disoriented, she reached up, pulled open her ruined shirt, and felt around her shoulder. The strap of her vest had stopped most of the damage, but there were several ghastly punctures in her skin, trickling slowly. It hurt, but nothing felt broken. Mostly her head ached from bouncing off the floor. *Lucky.* She could have ended up like the nurse. A wave of nausea hit as she stood. There was crashing and banging coming from a nearby room, probably that Harbinger dude getting killed, but Heather was focused on Buckley's room. Chase Temple was injured and needed help. She had to get him out of here.

There was a path of giant red paw prints leading back to Buckley's room. The blood on the floor made it slippery. She had to use the door frame to steady herself.

There was a man standing in the center of the hospital room. He was tall, broad-shouldered, wearing a black suit, and had his back toward her. There was a pistol in his hands, and something about his demeanor just screamed law enforcement. Help had arrived. *Thank God.*

Temple was on the floor, alive but hurt bad. Bailey was upside down in the far corner, obviously dead, nearly decapitated. The man was standing over Chase and asking, "Were you bitten? Did the creature bite you?"

"On my leg," Chase answered through gritted teeth. "It's bad. Help me, please."

Heather caught the man's profile as he shook his head sadly. He was young, beefy, with a buzz cut. "I'm really sorry, man."

"What?" Chase reached out plaintively. "Just get me out of—"

The suit raised his pistol and coldly shot Chase twice in the chest and then once in the forehead.

The world dropped out from under Heather. Her mouth fell open in shocked disbelief, but no sound came out.

The murderer lowered his weapon and shouted, "Clear!"

Heather stumbled back, reaching for her Beretta, but her holster was empty. Her gun was somewhere back where she'd landed. Still dizzy, she tripped over a severed arm, slipped in the blood, and fell. The killer heard her and came into the hall, pistol trained on her face, finger on the trigger. "Don't move! Agent Stark. Hallway. I've got another survivor."

A different man appeared from a side room, also in a suit, also pointing a gun at her. This one was even bigger than the first, older, bald, and looked like he meant business. "Shit. Local cop . . . This is gonna mean a lot of paperwork. Where's the creature, lady?"

Scared to death, she tried to keep her voice composed. These bastards had just executed poor Chase. She was next. "Back that way. Please. Don't shoot."

"Were you bitten? Did it bite you?" the murderer demanded.

He must not have realized that she'd witnessed what happened when he'd asked Chase that same question. "No! I'm fine," Heather exclaimed. *They're going to kill me.* She knew that if she made a sudden move they'd shoot, but she had to do something. She wished that she'd worn her backup gun, but the little .380 she'd bought for that purpose was sitting in her sock drawer because she'd gotten lazy.

She had other tools on her belt though. . . . *Steady.*

The older man got closer, gun still carefully trained on her, grabbed the tattered remains of her coat and pulled it back. She cringed as the fabric pulled at the wound. Biting his lip, he studied her bloody shoulder for a moment and then turned to his partner, shook his head, and stepped out of the way.

"Wait! I'm fine! What're you doing?"

"I'm sorry. This is for the best," Deputy Temple's executioner apologized as he aimed at her heart.

"She's wearing a vest," corrected the older one.

"Oh, yeah." He shrugged. "Didn't think of that." The muzzle rose toward Heather's forehead.

Then the hospital exploded.

⊰ Chapter 8 ⊱

My new home was a tiny black rock in the middle of the ocean. There were some trees, a beach, and a shack. I could walk across the whole island in two minutes.

"Nice place," I said, glancing around the shack that had been tied together out of the remains of an old shipwreck. "How's the neighbors?"

Santiago chuckled. "Far enough away that you won't be sorely tempted to devour them."

It took a while to help move the supplies ashore. He would return to visit once a month.

"There was once a knight commander of the Order of Christ by the name of Bartolomeu Zarco Cabral. He was bitten by a lycanthrope, but after spending some time cloistered in meditation on top of a mountain, he was eventually able to control his nature and became a fearsome warrior for good. He even protected Prince Henry the Navigator from a master vampire once. He was a fascinating man."

I wasn't sure if he was talking about the knight or the navigator. "Uh-huh . . . And how much time did he spend meditating on that mountain?"

"Twenty years before he was able to not fly into berserker rages," Santiago said but then tried to reassure me. "But you strike me as a fast learner."

✛ ✛ ✛

Nikolai saw the fireball rise in the distance. It was barely visible as a flash of orange through the haze of windblown snow, but he'd seen many explosions in the snow over his long life, dating back to Stalingrad during the Great Patriotic War, and he knew immediately just from the sound and color that it had been small, and from the time for the sound to travel exactly how far away it had been. Considering the strange events that were culminating in this small town, it was certainly no accident.

Assessing the explosion was the first coherent thought he'd had since the accident. It took a moment for the Tvar to return direct control to him. It was jealous, but it knew that now was the time for careful strategy. Ruthless savagery would surely have its turn, but for now Nikolai needed to be the one in the driver's seat.

A poor analogy.

"Silence," Nikolai wheezed.

The lights along the road were out. In fact, most of the lights in town were dark. The taillights from the snowplow were visible fifty yards away. He realized that he had struck a tree. Three ribs were broken. One lung was punctured and had subsequently collapsed. Pressure was building in the cavity as blood filled the space. That was the most pressing injury. Compound fracture of the femur. Left tibia broken. Armani coat, absolutely ruined.

Nikolai grimaced as he drove his thumb into his side and pulled out the rib. He palmed the jutting bone back into his leg. Impediment removed, the flesh immediately began to reform as the cells burned energy to return themselves to their normal station. Nikolai understood the science. A werewolf had two separate biological settings. Through horrendous amounts of physical energy, it was able to rapidly change between the two patterns. As a side effect, any deviation from those sets was quickly corrected.

Nikolai understood that, but even after eighty years, watching his flesh reseal before his eyes still seemed like magic.

What was that?

There was only one thing that could have that kind of powerful effect upon them. "The amulet is free," Nikolai explained to the Tvar. The false moon was still there, but not as strong now. The direction was unclear. He sniffed the air. "But . . . No *vulkodlak* yet. There's still time."

Harbinger must have it.

"Do not be a fool." Nikolai stood, bent over, and hacked up a great clot of blood. His breathing slowly returned to normal. He felt much better already. "Do not let your hate make you stupid. If that *nye kulturny svoloch'* had it, we would already be dead. One of Harbinger's minions must have retrieved it. We have to intercept him before he can activate it." He then noticed the dead body cooling in the snow. "What's all this?"

Driver of the snowplow. He came to help us. I struck him to protect us. We should eat him now.

Regeneration took fearsome energy. Nikolai's stomach rumbled, but he knew that human flesh would only inflame the Tvar and make it intolerable. "There is not time for your foolishness." Nikolai limped away. By the time he reached the remains of the BMW, the limp had corrected itself and he walked with purpose.

The rental vehicle's boot was crushed, but he was able to get his fingers into the crack, break the hinge, and pry the lid open. Fortunately the rifle he'd picked up at the safe-drop was undamaged. The suppressed Val was a favorite of Russian monster exterminators. It stood to reason that they knew what they were doing. The crash had shattered the glass in the Cobra optic, so he pulled the locking lever, slid it off, and tossed the scope away. The iron sights were robust and would be sufficient for his needs. He put on the blue camouflage vest full of spare twenty-round 9×39 magazines, then folded the Val's metal stock and slung the weapon under one arm. He found a spare overcoat and put it on, not that he desired protection from the cold, but just in case there was a need to be discreet.

I think the time for that is past.

Nikolai ignored the Tvar. The rest of his baggage could be left behind. Everything was clean and untraceable. The car had been rented under a false identity. The time for careful investigation was past. He had to find and neutralize Harbinger before it was too late. Now he just needed new transportation. Nearby, the snowplow's engine was still running. It would do.

The hunt begins.

The pack had gathered in the trees. The darkened town stretched before them, defenseless, soft, and ready to be harvested. The power had been cut. The witch assured him that all electronic communications with the outside world were blocked. The storm was upon them. He had placed teams on each of the roads out of town. To all intents and purposes, the humans of Copper Lake had been cut off from the safety of their herd. By the time the rest of mankind knew what happened here, it would be too late.

The amulet of the Deathless was a warm weight against his bare chest. It had been asleep for a long time, but it had been dreaming, and the dreams had led him here to fulfill his mission in life. It seethed with power, but it hungered for more. There were two others like him here, worthy enough to satisfy the needs of the amulet, drawn like moths to the flame, slaves to their own instincts, directed here through treachery and deceit.

He turned to the pack. Most of them had only been turned in recent months and were therefore expendable. The core of the pack had been with him for some time. He had turned them, taught them, and kept them under control; a difficult task to do in utmost secrecy. It was exciting to think of what they could do when given such absolute freedom. "There are two strong werewolves here tonight. Either one will do, but I absolutely must have one alive. Everyone else, turn them, devour them, or harvest them for the *vulkodlak* as you see fit." Studying the fearsome predators crouched in the snow, he could almost taste the coming slaughter. "Run free, my children. Run free."

The werewolves let forth a triumphant howl and leapt from the tree line, loping downhill to where the unsuspecting humans were waiting. The prey would never see them coming. He watched his children go, anxious for them, as any good father should be.

The witch was observing quietly. She was bundled in a fur coat, which made her slight form seem far larger than it was, only her gleaming eyes visible under the hood and scarf. She was flanked by her two diggers; giant, gangly, unnatural things that stood with perfect stillness. Their abnormal forms were difficult to make out in the blowing snow. The witch stank of excitement, with just a touch of apprehension. "You really believe that your children will be able to bring you Harbinger or Petrov?"

"Bring them? Of course not . . ." Already he could hear the sounds of breaking windows as the pack reached the houses on the periphery. "My children will slaughter the sheep of this town, but none of them is a match for the hunter or the assassin. I expect the pack will flush them out, force their little game, bring them to each other's attention. The survivor will be weakened. Ready to harvest."

The witch fidgeted inside her massive coat. Now there was nervousness in her scent, nearly as strong as her regular smell of fanaticism. Maybe now that the moment of truth was upon them, the fearsome nature of their adversaries had fully sunk in.

He chuckled. "You really don't need to worry. I could have taken either of them before. With this"—he gestured at the amulet—"they won't be able to touch me."

"They're bloody unpredictable," the witch insisted.

Unlike your father, I'm not enough of a fool to underestimate Harbinger. The thought went unspoken. It would only anger the already sensitive witch, and he needed her focused. "I have it under control."

There was a long, icy silence before she responded. "Very well."

His children howled from below. Prey had been cornered. It made him want to change, to glory in the hunt himself, but he had other responsibilities to attend to. Years of preparation came down to this one night. "Just be ready."

"Don't worry about me." The witch was as dedicated to this mission as he was, but for entirely different reasons.

The screams of the dying haunted the wind. He clutched the amulet tightly.

Stark realized that with Briarwood almost here, Agent Mosher was about to cost him a whole bunch of money by plugging the injured cop. That was one easy bounty, and he wished he'd caught Mosher before he'd popped the other one. He was just forming the words when the whole hospital shook. Orange fire spilled from a room down the hall as Stark hurled himself to the floor. Most of the flames disappeared quickly, rising into the ceiling tiles, leaving only smoke and choking dust. It had been a small explosion, but it had certainly gotten his attention.

"What the hell?" Mosher shouted as he uncovered his head.

Stark coughed as the dust settled on them. He rolled over and got up. "I don't kn—" There was a small pain in his shoulder and another in his side, and then he nearly bit his tongue off as a horrible, jittery, twisting bolt of white-hot pain surged through his entire body. His muscles involuntarily clenched as he collapsed back to the floor. Except for a buzzing twitch, he couldn't move, couldn't even scream.

Then as quickly as the pain had come, it was gone. "What the hell?"

There was the injured cop, sitting there, pointing something at his chest, and then Agent Stark realized there were skinny little wires leading from his body back to the thing in the cop's right hand. "Son of a—" But then she hit him with the Taser again.

Mosher bellowed incoherently and grabbed his face, rolling and thrashing across the bloody floor as the cop jumped up and ran for her life. She disappeared into the smoke just as Stark regained enough coordination to raise his Glock and crank off several wild shots after her. With disgust he reached down and yanked the Taser barbs out of his body, wincing as the little fish-hooks tore skin. "Mosher!"

"My eyes!" Mosher shouted. "I can't see a thing!" Then Mosher began coughing uncontrollably as his mucus membranes kicked into massive overdrive. There was enough residual pepper spray in the air that Stark nearly choked. Even looking at Agent Mosher made his eyes water. The cop had hosed his partner good, coating his face in sticky orange-dyed foam.

How dare you? Enraged, Stark got up and ran after her. He reached the burning room and turned quickly, looking down both hallways. The cop was nowhere to be seen. "Come back here!" he shouted.

"Hey, Agent Stark," someone said from behind him. He turned to see the outline of a man walking through the smoke. "You've got a crispy werewolf in there." Earl Harbinger jerked his thumb at the fire. "He was immune to silver, I shit you not, so I roasted his ass. I think all the surviving patients have hightailed it outta here. You see a fire extinguisher around here, anywhere? Figure I better put that out."

The filthy, stinking werewolf had the audacity to stop there, right in Stark's face, and pull out a pack of smokes. Harbinger paused after putting one in his mouth. He held out the pack. "Want one?"

Stark clenched his teeth together. MHI was here. Harbinger had stolen his kill. He was going to ruin everything. The MCB agent was so furious that he could feel his face turning red. He'd just been embarrassed, tasered by a Yooper cop, and now he was getting mocked by a bloodthirsty monster. Stark lifted his Glock in one big hand and pointed it right at Harbinger's smug werewolf face.

"So . . . You don't smoke?"

"You're under arrest," Stark spat.

Unfazed, Harbinger raised an eyebrow as he lit the cigarette. "What for now?"

"You had something to do with this! You damn werewolves stick together."

"Well, that sure explains why I just burned one to death." The smoke from the fire finally activated the emergency sprinklers around the fiery room. Harbinger glanced up in annoyance and took the now-sodden cigarette from his mouth. "It never fails . . ."

The water must have been sitting in the pipes for a long time, since it was as dark and foul as Stark's temper. The agent blinked as it got in his eyes, but he kept the gun on the sneaky werewolf. "You're coming with me. You've got some questions to answer."

"Listen, Stark." Harbinger seemed a little perturbed. "I ain't got time for your MCB power-trip nonsense. There's something weird going on here, something bad, and I need to figure it out before any more innocent folks get hurt." The two of them stayed there, glaring at each other in the artificial rain. "All right, let me try this again. We just had somebody turn into a werewolf for the first time, and not on the full moon. That don't happen. It can't happen. *And* he was immune to silver. Doesn't that strike you as odd? The lights are out all over town, and I can hear more werewolves howling for blood. There's something else out there, something evil, and I can feel it coming. We ain't got much time." The Glock didn't move. Harbinger sighed. "So I suggest you lower that heater 'fore I cram it up your ass sideways."

Stark's eyes narrowed. "You . . . You're threatening me?"

"Well, I ain't asking you to the prom," Harbinger answered impatiently. "What's it gonna be, Agent? Let me do my job, or we gonna have us a problem?"

Stark was shocked that Harbinger had the audacity to threaten him. The MCB agent had been intimidating people for so long, and never the other way around, that it took the words a moment to sink in. "Who do you think you are?" he sputtered.

Harbinger moved faster than Stark could possibly react. He smacked the gun aside. His other hand wrapped around Stark's thick neck and slammed him hard into the wall. Stark's shoes left the floor as Harbinger hoisted him into the air.

"Who do *I* think I am?" the Hunter snapped as he yanked the Glock away. He held two hundred and fifty pounds of Stark several inches off the ground without so much as a muscle tremor. "I've been kicking monster ass longer than you've been alive. I've *eaten* men that would make you look like a pussy on your best day. I'm Earl Harbinger, motherfucker." Stark gasped for air. Harbinger let go of his neck, dropping the MCB agent. Harbinger released the mag from Stark's pistol, racked the slide to eject the chambered round, and then tossed the pistol down the hall with a clatter. "And you damn well better not forget it."

Stark went to his knees. Harbinger had absolutely manhandled him. There were a few things that Special Agent Doug Stark of the Monster Control Bureau just couldn't handle, and one of them was being pushed around. He was far more angry than afraid. "You just signed your death warrant," he rasped.

Water was pouring down Harbinger's face as he growled at the agent. "Take it up with Myers." He spun on his boot and walked away through the forming puddles. "Just keep out of my way. This one is way out of your league."

By the time the half-blind Mosher found Stark sitting on the floor, cursing in the sprinklers and rubbing his bruised throat, Harbinger was gone.

There was no cellular signal and no dial tone at the hospital, so Earl had started back for his truck. Originally he'd planned on playing this alone, figuring that it was just his old nemesis Nikolai here for some personal business, but this was something entirely different. Earl prided himself on being stubborn, but he wasn't stupid—well, except for when his temper got the better of him around bullies. Something strange was afoot, but a man had to know his limitations, and a whole pack of werewolves and some sort of dark magic certainly fell into that category. He'd use the satellite phone to contact Julie. She could have the closest teams rolling in no time, and knowing her, the Cazador team wouldn't be far behind.

Stark would probably have the place crawling in MCB as well now. They'd been especially jumpy since the photos of the Arbmunep incident had hit the Internet. That, combined with the Five Minutes, had really shaken up the status quo. Lucky for the MCB, most of the conspiracy types were saying that the Arbmunep had been an alien spaceship, and it was old hat for the government to make the UFO people sound crazy. But there were cracks in the wall now. It seemed like it was getting harder every year for them to keep the lid on the secrets. Earl didn't mind that at all. If the truth actually got out, it would make his job that much easier. Just imagine how much business MHI could do if they were actually allowed to *advertise*? As a bonus, maybe Dwayne Myers would have a heart attack from the stress.

Earl understood the MCB. That didn't make him hate them any less, but he could see the reason behind their tactics. They were utterly ruthless when it came to protecting the country. For example, that cute deputy that he'd tried to help, Kerkonen, she was as good as dead. She'd be found by MCB and exterminated. Nothing he could do about that. He'd failed her by underestimating that young werewolf, though he knew there was no way he could have guessed that he'd be immune to silver, but he'd do his best to protect everyone else.

The storm had grown in intensity. Visibility was down to a few feet. Ice crystals in the wind rubbed his skin like frozen sandpaper. It was enough to put a chill on even a werewolf's hyper metabolism. He'd heard that this part of the country had terrible winters but suspected that this particular storm was related to the strange phenomenon from earlier. His suspicions were confirmed when he tried the sat phone in his truck and couldn't get anything on it. Earl had paid top dollar for that unit. It had been developed for Delta Force and should have been able to pick up a satellite from the dark side of the moon. The regular radio turned up nothing, either. He was on his own.

Earl sat in the cab and listened to the blizzard pound the windows and rock the truck around. He could now safely add the power outage and communications blackout to the list of oddness. Nikolai had really opened up a can of worms this time. Without reinforcements, that meant that he needed to stick with his original plan. Find Nikolai and kill the shit out of him.

But where to start? He took the wolfsbane from his pocket, sealed it back into a plastic bag, and put it in the center console. It would make him a bigger target for Nikolai, but he had to take the risk. His own senses needed to be uninhibited—well, besides the smokes, obviously. He wasn't about to give those up. Earl rolled down the window and was instantly pelted with stinging ice. He breathed deeply, taking in the smells of the town.

Blood's been spilled.

It wasn't from the hospital, either, but it was close. Earl put the truck into four-wheel drive and set out after the scent of death.

⊰ **Chapter 9** ⊱

I told time by the strength of the Hum.

No one knows why the phase of the moon has the effect on us, but it does. We can hear it. It is always there. When it becomes too much, we change.

When I change while the Hum is weak, I still possess some measure of control over my actions. But when the Hum becomes too strong, I'm at its mercy. It is like there is another thing that lives inside me, a whole different being, and on the full moon, it takes charge. During the nights of the full moon, I become something else. I become the animal.

Every month spent on the island, I got a little better, a little stronger. I missed my wife. I missed my children. I dreamed about them every night. I wondered if they'd moved on. Part of me wished for their sake that they had, but the selfish part of me hoped that they were waiting for me. I promised that I would do this for them, so that I would return as the man they'd loved.

It sounds crazy, but I'd hurt myself on purpose, exposing my body to ever greater stress, until even the most unbearable pain wasn't enough to force a change. I flung myself from the cliffs, over and over, to land on the rocks below. A werewolf can fall pretty far and live. The worst part was that regeneration uses up calories, which meant I spent a lot of time hungry. I ate so damn much fish that I couldn't stand the sight of one for about thirty years afterward.

Santiago was as reliable as the tides. Every month he would come with supplies and stay on the island for a few days. Mostly he taught me the things he'd learned from the libraries that he missed so much. He was well read and extremely well educated. I had only three years of schooling, but I did know how to read. I was relatively uneducated, but that didn't mean I was stupid. Quite the contrary. It was just that most of my education had been on the finer points of monster killing.

I was terrible at chess, but Santiago was worse at checkers. I think I seriously unnerved him the time that I showed I could drive a filet knife through the palm of my hand and out the other side, held it up, and said, "See? Not even twitching." He was a crafty one, though. I noted that he'd kept that last silver bullet, just in case I turned out to be a failed experiment.

Santiago had not been able to take the old scrolls and books with him when he left Europe, but it didn't matter. If he didn't have a photographic memory, then it was damn close enough. He had learned every story pertaining to lycanthropy there was, and he passed on that knowledge to me.

We started at the beginning. No one knew for sure where the curse had begun. There were theories, some of them branching into the downright absurd. There were myths and legends, half of which I knew to be false just from personal experience. From Romans eating their own kids to deals with the devil, it was all a bunch of bunk.

But there were some nuggets of truth in the old stories. I found out how Santiago had managed to avoid detection in Havana as he'd followed me. A small bit of wolfsbane worn on your person can mask your scent from a lycanthrope. You can smell the wolfsbane, but it distorts everything else around it. I'd learned that he'd been told of my presence by a Haitian diviner who knew of Santiago's past life. Apparently a diviner with actual talent could sense when one of my kind was near. This was information that would prove useful many times over the ensuing years.

One day the two of us were in the shack, perched over a game of checkers. I was beating him soundly, but he'd gotten better over the last year. He was telling me about how in any given region there was always a supreme lycanthrope.

"Well, I ain't met him yet."

"How do you know it is a male?"

"It just is," I answered truthfully.

"Interesting . . ." he said, pondering on my answer. "We know there is a hierarchy. There is an order. This is something that we've learned over time. Anywhere there are many lycanthropes, they will naturally form groups—packs, if you will. One will always become the leader. And yes, every time this has been encountered, it has been a male."

"The most dangerous will be in charge," I said, not knowing why.

"Apparently. But there are others, like the men that I've told you about, like Sir Cabral, or Monsignor Ratton. They, too, shared the curse, but by not giving into their beastly natures, they were packless, lone wolves. Often they were attacked by other lycanthropes. They are despised with that special hatred reserved for traitors. When you return to the real world, you must be prepared for this. You will be on your own, and therefore, you will be a threat."

✛ ✛ ✛

"Power must be out." Kelley stated the obvious from the back of the Caddy. "Place looks like a ghost town."

It was true. The emptiness of the roads was expected, since it was nearing midnight and snowing like crazy, but all the street lights were dark. Even the businesses' signs were dead. Everything was coated in white. Drifts had piled up on nearly every wall. When it snowed in the Upper Peninsula of Michigan, it really *snowed*.

"Anybody with any sense is going to be inside trying to stay warm," Lins said. "Like we should be."

"Yoopers don't feel cold." Jo Ann snorted when she laughed. "They're too dumb."

Horst had to wonder about the chick with the strongest Wisconsin accent he'd ever heard insulting the locals from one region over, but he was a city boy. They all seemed backwoods to him. "Everybody zip it," he ordered. "You're giving me a headache. Where's this stupid hospital, already?"

"I don't know. The GPS lost signal a few miles ago," Lins said, reaching over to tap the box that was showing nothing but a blue screen.

Horst swore under his breath. He'd disabled the OnStar, so they couldn't even fall back on that. He hadn't liked the idea of the government being able to listen in on his conversations whenever they felt like it—or shutting the engine off, for that matter. His cousin was serving some serious time after the FBI had gotten a warrant and used his OnStar to listen in while he'd been having a conversation about dumping a body in a Jersey landfill.

Horst reasoned that if he ever did anything that would cause him to float to the FBI's attention, they should at least have to do the work of putting an actual bug on his car. Not that he had to worry about that anymore, since he was a fully legitimate businessman now, which was sort of hilarious since he'd never had this kind of hardware when he'd been running errands for his uncle. And by errands, he meant putting a bullet in someone's ear or hitting them with a bat until they were smart enough to not want to blab to the authorities anymore.

"There," Loco said softly. That made Horst do a double take. It was the first time he could recall that the big man had spoken since they'd left Chicago. The hospital had lights, the only sign of life since they'd hit the city limits. There were emergency vehicles in the parking lot, including a single fire truck, its red flashers barely visible through the caked-on slush.

Lins visibly hesitated when he saw a parked police car, barely even visible under the collected snow, but then he relaxed. Instinct would've told him to avoid the police when driving around with a car full of machine guns, but it was like Horst said. It was hard to come to terms with the idea that this kind of awesome shit was actually *legal*. They slid to a stop behind the fire truck that had COPPER COUNTY VOLUNTEER FIRE DEPARTMENT painted on it in big letters. A few windows on the top floor of the hospital were broken and blackened, like there'd been a fire.

"I think we might be a little late," Jo Ann said. "Too bad Larry drove so slow."

Lins turned around. "You better shut your mouth, Jo, or I'll shut it for you."

Horst scowled. "You guys stay here. I'm gonna check it out." He zipped his coat up to his throat and got out, leaving his crew free to yell at each other. If he was lucky, nobody would get stabbed or shot while he was gone.

It was so unbelievably cold that he almost jumped back inside. Ice crystals instantly flowed up his sleeves, down his neck, and cut right through his jeans. He was shocked that anyone was tough or crazy enough to live here. This made the Windy City feel like Maui. Horst hurried for the front door, but slipped on some ice and fell on his side.

Getting up and dusting himself off, he glanced back toward the Caddy, because if he saw anybody laughing at his expense, he was going to cut their face off. Lucky for them, nobody was laughing.

It appeared that everyone in the hospital had been evacuated to the lobby. Most of them were dressed like they were patients, in bathrobes or wrapped in blankets. Some, in scrubs or sweaters, looked like they worked here, and there were a couple of guys in black-and-yellow rubber fireman's coats. Two men stood right in the entrance, like they were trying not to be overheard by everyone else. One of the firemen was arguing with a tough-looking, big, bald man, dripping wet, in a suit and tie. Horst came through the door partway through the disagreement.

The fireman noted Horst's arrival. The sudden blast of freezing air was hard to miss. He turned back and continued his argument. "I'm not moving those bodies anywhere until the sheriff says so."

The dude in the dirty suit poked the fireman in the chest with one meaty finger. "Listen very carefully, asswipe. See this?" He pointed at the ID pinned to his lapel. "That says Department of Homeland Security, and we've got ourselves a terrorist incident. I *am* the law, and I say I want all those bodies stacked in one room. I want the door locked, and nobody messes with them until my people get here, or I will make it my personal mission in life to ruin you in ways that your little brain can't even comprehend. You hearing me, dickhead?"

The fireman was obviously ticked off, but also unsure of himself. "I want to talk to somebody from the sheriff's department first."

"Well, feel free to try and find one," the government man answered. "They aren't exactly picking up the phone. Until then, get your ass up there and start stacking bodies, and I want all the pieces kept together, too. I don't want so much as a toenail missing or I'll toss you headfirst in a jail so deep and dark that your lawyer will need a spelunking expedition just to find you. You will not talk to anyone about what you see. You say one word about anything, and I will descend down on your head with the full weight and authority of a giant government that fully does not give a shit and will crush you like a bug. Capisce?"

Defeated, the fireman stomped off toward the stairs. Looking smug, the dude in the suit turned to Horst. "Who the hell are you?" he asked.

Horst put on his most professional business-type smile, crossed the distance, and stuck out his hand. It was all about authority and presentation, or at least that's what the self-help books said. "Agent Stark, I presume? Ryan Horst, Briarwood Eradication Services."

Stark nodded, looking at the proffered hand, but didn't extend his own. "You're late."

"Better late than never." Horst kept his hand out, still smiling. The Fed was annoyed, but grudgingly shook Horst's hand anyway. Stark had hands the size of boxing gloves, but Horst wasn't the type that was intimidated about such things.

Agent Stark released Horst's hand and glanced over to make sure the firemen had gone upstairs like he'd ordered. "Somebody saw the explosion and ran over and woke them up. Local PD is missing. Some of them are dead upstairs, and it wasn't like they had too many to begin with."

"What've we got here?" Horst asked, because that sounded like the logical thing for a professional monster hunter to ask.

"A real mess. Multiple casualties, infected running free, no comms, no idea where the creature that started all this is, and . . ." His head swiveled on his pot-roast neck, checking for listeners. "I've got another issue you might be able to help me with. I'd prefer for my partner not to know you're here. It's a *sensitive* issue. Walk with me, Mr. Horst."

Horst followed Stark to a side room, which turned out to be a large storage closet. Stark closed the door behind them. Horst realized that the lights must be on emergency juice, because the lone lightbulb in the narrow space was remarkably dim. Stark was sweating. "How high up are you in Briarwood, Mr. Horst?"

I own it, stupid, he thought, but Stark didn't need to know how small they were. "Management. I'm a team commander. I'm authorized to make any necessary decisions or business arrangements, if that's what you're wondering."

"You're younger than I expected."

Horst was twenty-six, but it wasn't the age, it was the mileage, and he'd done things that would curdle the blood of men twice his age. "Let's just say that I've been promoted because of my exemplary record. I get results, Agent Stark."

"Good." Stark leaned on a shelf and took a deep breath. Once past his hesitation, the agent plowed ahead. "I've got a business idea for you. Way beyond my previous arrangement with your company. I'm talking about something *big*. Something that could make both of us a ton of money. What I'm about to suggest doesn't leave this room, you got me?"

"I'm listening," Horst answered. He knew that Stark was dirty, completely untrustworthy, and if it wasn't for the extremity of their circumstances he would have assumed that this was some kind of elaborate setup. It was doubtful that Stark was wearing a wire.

"Do you know what the PUFF would be for a werewolf over a hundred years old?"

The Perpetual Unearthly Forces Fund bounty tables cut off way before that. The amount would be astronomical. "Is that a joke?"

"What if I told you there was a century-old werewolf here in Copper Lake, right this minute?"

Horst played it cool. Stark had gone mad. "If I was talking to anyone other than a respected senior MCB agent . . ." *I'd call you a liar and curb-stomp your head in.* "I'd say you might be exaggerating."

Stark smiled. "You think I'm full of it, huh? Understandable. I had the same reaction the first time I heard about him. He's only alive because he's been granted PUFF immunity for some top-secret reason."

"If he's got immunity, then where do I come in?" Horst folded his arms. This sounded like a load of garbage. He'd pulled sharper cons before he'd hit puberty.

"He's only immune if he obeys the rules, which means acting like a regular human and no crazy werewolf shit. But I'm afraid that our werewolf has gone on a rampage. He's the cause of tonight's troubles. He created another werewolf, and who knows how many others. He attacked me and escaped before I could apprehend him. If I could get word to the rest of the MCB they'd come down on him like a ton of bricks. We've been itching to get the green light to take him out forever, but our hands have been tied . . . If somebody were to take him while I was unable to get hold of the MCB, they'd be heroes."

There was no such thing as hundred-year-old werewolves. That was ridiculous. Werewolves were just too crazy and violent to live a fraction of that time. They didn't exactly have a lifestyle well suited to longevity. "Well, why don't you just point me at this super werewolf, and we'll take care of him for you?"

Stark paused, fidgeting, as if he was scared to continue. His beady eyes shifted nervously in his jowly face. Finally he blurted, "I want half!"

This whole trip had been a waste. Stark was an idiot. At best, he was looking at a normal werewolf, at worst a new one or a barely infected, and there was no way he was going to split that fifty-fifty. "Forget about it."

"But the PUFF would be in the millions!" Stark insisted. "There would be plenty to go around."

Putting his hand on the doorknob to leave, Horst addressed Stark as politely as his growing temper would allow. "Millions, assuming that this superwolf actually exists. If that were the case, you'd get half. Regular creature, regular cut."

"Trust me. He exists." Stark reached out and grabbed Horst's coat sleeve, pulling him conspiratorially close. "His name is Earl Harbinger."

Harbinger... Horst froze. He knew that name all too well. "Chain-smoking redneck, sounds like he should've been in *Deliverance*?"

"So you've met."

"Oh, we've met. Hang on. You're trying to tell me the leader of Monster Hunter International is a *werewolf*?"

Stark nodded. "Yes, and he's here."

"Dude . . ." Horst trailed off, but it made a certain kind of sense. Harbinger's exploits were legendary. Even the seasoned MHI members he'd met had talked about Harbinger like he was some sort of supernatural monster-smashing demigod. Some of the things they'd attributed to him had sounded far-fetched, like the kind of BS stories guys from the old neighborhood had spread about themselves to build street cred, but the MHI bunch had seemed too jaded to believe tall tales.

The stories of impossible battles would be a little more plausible if he was a werewolf. Plus, Harbinger had stood by Paxton's decision to kick Horst out of training, just because Horst had the balls to do what needed to be done. Harbinger had been a right smug bastard when he'd called Horst into his office that last time. They only talked a big game about their *flexible* minds, but when it came down to it, they were just as weak as any other regular mark.

Come to think of it, if Briarwood took down the baddest Hunter ever, what did that make Briarwood? He'd be a legend, able to write his own ticket. Why hire those fags at MHI when you could hire Briarwood, the company that smoked MHI's top gun like a cheap cigar? Buckets of money, plus the satisfaction of seeing the look on Harbinger's mug when one of his former Newbies took him out? *Perfect*.

"He's the oldest known werewolf in the world. It's like winning the lottery. I'll handle the MCB. They'll know that it was a legit kill. You get PUFF. Everybody wins."

"Except Earl Harbinger." Horst felt the beginnings of a honest grin form on his frozen face. This was going to be righteous. "You've got a deal, Stark."

Horst returned to the Caddy and briefed his team on the new mission parameters, telling them about the new primary target but leaving out the part about Harbinger supposedly being over a hundred. First off, Horst had no idea if that was even possible, and secondly, if it was, there was no reason he needed to share that kind of ridiculous bounty with his crew. An adult werewolf with a mess of kills was still worth a considerable sum, so they'd still get paid more than expected. The infected redhead cop chick was a bonus. Stark said that he didn't even care about getting his regular cut on that one, just as long as she died.

They were eager. Kelley and Lins were in this for the money, and this was more cash than either of them had ever come close to earning in their lives of violent crime. Jo Ann was a danger junkie, and as long as Horst kept buying her shiny things and nice clothes in addition to letting her kill things, she was happy. Everyone except for Loco was pumped. The big man just sat there, quiet as always, as he seemed to mull the new information over. Loco was so quiet that sometimes Horst wondered if he was all right in the head. He knew that after Loco had gotten out of prison, he'd gotten his skull caved in during some super-illegal pit fight. That was the same fight that had cost Loco his eye, and considering how scary Loco was, Horst couldn't even imagine what the other behemoth must've looked like. But it didn't matter if the guy that had broken Loco's skull had given him brain damage, too. Horst had hired Loco for his brawn.

Stark had somehow gotten the idea that silver might not work on some of this town's werewolves. Personally, Horst thought that sounded like more paranoid nonsense, as even the MHI people had sworn up and down in their fancy classes that silver *always* worked on lycanthropes, but he shared it with his crew anyway. If only he had MHI's budget, he'd have some of those fancy flamethrowers and flaming chemical grenades on hand. Briarwood would someday, but right now they'd have to improvise. Buying a single case of a thousand composite silver 5.56 rounds that an MCB agent had "misplaced" had already cost him an arm and a leg.

"So, our silver bullets might not work, but you said that Stark burned one to death in there?" Kelley asked.

"Sure did. Place smelled like burnt hair," Horst said. "Sounds like you got an idea."

Kelley's face lit up like it was Christmas. "There was a little convenience store back that way. Lots of glass bottles, and we can siphon gas out of some of the cars, if you get my drift."

"Way to go, firebug," Horst answered, having forgotten that Kelley had once made his living as an arsonist, terrorizing Boston industrial sites that didn't pay their protection money. "Good thinking—" The front passenger door opened, letting in a sudden blast of freezing air. Loco got out. His hulking form headed straight for the fire truck.

"What's that moron doing?" Jo Ann asked. "Close the door! I'm freezing."

Loco was quickly covered in snow and took on the appearance of a yeti. He rummaged around the back of the fire truck and returned a moment later, the wicked fire ax looking comparatively tiny in his massive hands. His eyes were too small for his big round head, but he met Horst's gaze squarely. Horst gave the ax one look and nodded in approval. The big man got back in the Caddy.

Old Earl Harbinger would never even know what hit him.

⊰ Chapter 10 ⊱

There are a few psychological changes that go hand in hand with the physical change of becoming a lycanthrope. Unfortunately for most of us, one of those changes is that it will turn even the most saintly personality into a bloodthirsty killer. Maybe it was because I was such an effective killer already that I was able to keep those instincts in better check than most. For me, the desire to kill wasn't really anything new. I had killed my first monster when I was ten years old, and had just kept on ever since. I took a break from monster killing for a few years when I'd volunteered to fight in the Great War, as we called it then. Though I did manage to squeeze in some monster killing in France when General Pershing found out that he had someone in the ranks who knew how to smoke out the ghouls that were attracted to the mass graves.

After the war I'd gone back to Hunting. It was all I had ever known. All I'd ever been good at, and I was really good at it. For most folks, the new super-honed predatory instinct of the lycanthrope pushes them into straight-up bug-nuts crazy territory. For me, it was a natural fit. It was like putting brass knuckles on a boxer.

The other immediately noticeable change is a drastic increase to your survival instincts. Werewolves are survivors. Usually by the time someone realizes what they've become, by then it is nearly impossible to find the will to end the curse yourself. The urge to live overcomes everything else.

You feel stronger, faster, smarter, healthier, tougher, sexier, everything. Basically, it feels good to be a werewolf. But at the same *time, there is always this glimmer of smugness, a dangerous feeling of being better than humans. You exist with them, but separate. It is real easy to start gloating in your superiority, and from there it's a real short trip for most of us to start looking at them as objects instead of people, weak things to be used for our amusement . . . as food, as prey.*

Combine unbelievable physical power with a new sense of ruthless superiority and a burning, insatiable desire to hunt and kill and you've got a recipe for disaster.

The key is being greater than your urges. I spent the next few years living on that little island in the Caribbean learning to understand and control my new nature. Rocky took many of those days away from me— the quiet reflection and meditation, watching sunsets, swimming in the ocean, sleeping on the sand, hours of reflection and study. But Rocky had planned on eating my most painful and brutal memories last, and had been stopped before he could finish his meal. So my most important lessons remained.

Santiago had given me hope.

❖ ❖ ❖

The sheriff's department was quiet. The lights were off here as well, and Earl could barely see the squat little concrete building from the street. This was the source of the blood scent. Though it wasn't the only one in the air tonight, just the closest.

"This ain't gonna end well," he muttered to himself. The power, the communications, and apparently the authorities, all neutralized simultaneously. This wasn't following the pattern of a leadership challenge; this was more like a coordinated attack. Nikolai was more than capable of that. Earl had seen that up close and personal across Southeast Asia, but it made no sense to do it here. The only thing a werewolf gained through this kind of action was attention, and attention brought Hunters.

Like any good Boy Scout or Monster Hunter, Earl had come prepared. He'd stopped long enough to change out of his wet clothes into his MHI-issued body armor. Milo had just gotten him a new suit, since the last one had been ruined by the acid saliva from a nasty flock of helicopter-spiders they'd found in Albuquerque. As always, the brilliant Milo had listened to Earl's feedback and made improvements. Earl's personal kit was a little less bulky than the standard suit, utilizing material that wasn't quite as loud when he moved. Earl reasoned that he valued speed, mobility, and stealth a bit more than the average Hunter and could afford to sacrifice some protection.

Plus, Milo had thought ahead and put some quick-release buckles on the side so that Earl wouldn't inadvertently ruin anything should he change in a hurry. Milo said he was tired of ordering replacements, and Owen kept bugging him about *budgets*. Even the boots had a zipper down the side so he could kick them off in a hurry, though he found himself regretting that neat feature as cold slush leaked through onto his socks. The new armor material was a mottled gray, which Earl had to admit he found aesthetically pleasing.

The snow was past his ankles as he trudged toward the front door. The drifts to the side were already far taller. His breath came out in clouds of steam, freezing his lips, before it was ripped away by the howling wind. It had crossed the point of discomfort, and for the first time in many years, Earl was actually cold.

Pausing at the entrance, he cupped his gloved hands over his eyes and peered through the glass. The place was still. He had a seventy-year-old Thompson submachine gun in hand and a few grenades wrapped in silver-wire on his vest and other assorted goodies in pouches. If there were any more cops in here, they might be a touch jumpy about seeing someone so heavily armed looking in the window, but the blood and viscera smell he kept catching on the wind suggested that wouldn't be an issue. The stencil on the door told him that it was past regular business hours and to dial 911 if there was an emergency. Luckily the door was unlocked.

He kept the Thompson at his shoulder as he entered. It was an antique, weighed a ton, and some of the younger Hunters gave him crap for choosing something so archaic, but he'd first shot one clear back when that jerk Woodrow Wilson was president, and the .45 caliber M1 Thompson ran like the proverbial sewing machine. Hunting monsters was hard on guns, but Earl was in no danger of running out of spares despite the fact they hadn't built any new ones in decades. In 1946, he'd found a navy chief petty officer who owed him a favor, charged with disposing of surplus war weapons by pushing them overboard into the Atlantic. Several pallets of weapons had been pushed overboard all right, onto the deck of a boat chartered by MHI. Earl had always hated government waste.

The death smell was stronger in here, as was the stink of werewolf.

A male had marked his territory toward the back of the building. The scent battered his senses and offended him on an instinctive level. There were several overturned metal benches in the waiting area. There was a reception desk. Blood was splattered on the darkened monitor, but the body that had been there had been dragged to the back to be consumed in privacy. He moved forward, silent as a ghost.

It was pitch black inside the station. Unlike the new guns that most of his Hunters used, which were covered in rails for everything from flashlights to lasers to wind socks and cheese graters, the Thompson was utilitarian bare wood and Parkerized steel. But then again, most of those Hunters couldn't see in the dark, either. Unless he was at the bottom of a really deep hole, Earl didn't need a flashlight to see. When his eyes adjusted to the dark, the world turned into a gray place where the tiniest bit of motion screamed for attention.

Past the reception desk was a semi-open area with a few workspaces. There were dozens of spent shell casings littering the hardwood and bullet holes puncturing the walls. Kneeling, he picked up a case. It was .40 S&W, a pretty standard police caliber. Whoever had been manning the night shift hadn't gone out without a fight.

There was a hallway at the back of the main room leading to the jail cells. It didn't take Earl's sensitive hearing to pick up the sound of eating. Apparently the werewolf hadn't heard him yet. *Amateur.* This was his opportunity to get some answers, so Earl quietly slung his Thompson and stuck one hand into his medical pouch.

There was movement at the corner of his eye, a reflection against a window. There was a flashlight moving along the outside wall of the building, probably somebody heading for the back door. The wind was taking the smell away from him, but he sure hoped it wasn't Stark coming to interfere. He really didn't have time for that, and if a senior MCB agent got eaten, Myers would probably become extra meddlesome.

The chewing noise stopped. Earl froze. But the werewolf hadn't heard him; it had seen the gleam of the newcomer's flashlight. Earl swore to himself. Now he had to hurry before the werewolf ripped apart their visitor. Still crouching, Earl moved between the desks and took cover.

There was a noise as the knob was tested. The side door was locked. A low growl came from the darkness near the cells in response. Within seconds a shadow moved along the floor, low-crawling on its belly, approaching the door. The deadbolt rattled as someone inserted a key.

As soon as the door opened, the werewolf would leap on whoever it was. They'd be dead before they even knew what had hit them. Earl removed the hypodermic from the pouch and pulled the plastic cap off the needle with his teeth. It would still take some time for the horse tranquilizer to knock out a charged-up werewolf, and during that time he was going to have one hell of a wrestling match. He might as well take advantage of the distraction.

There was a sliver of white and a sudden gust of freezing wind as the door cracked open. The werewolf surged from the floor just as Earl let out a roar, stepped onto a desk, and launched himself across the room.

Earl hit the surprised werewolf with his shoulder. Momentum sent them crashing into a vending machine, shattering the heavy glass. Earl ended up on top, briefly, before a hairy claw struck him in the chest and sent him sailing back. Earl hit a chalkboard hard enough to crack it and the wall behind, but he'd gotten what he wanted.

Roaring, the werewolf knocked the empty syringe out of its neck. The drugs would act rapidly. Earl had an idea and was already covering the distance when the side door opened with a bang. Howling wind flooded the room with snow, flinging every loose bit of paper chaotically across the office. Not having time to see who the newcomer was, Earl grabbed the vending machine and tugged hard. A toe claw caught him in the calf, and he grimaced at the hit, but the armor protected him.

The vending machine toppled over as Earl jumped back. The werewolf let out a painful squeal as the vending machine landed on it with a terrible crash. Candy bars and packages of doughnuts spilled across the floor.

The werewolf howled and thrashed but couldn't get out from under the vending machine. "That should hold you," Earl said as he stepped away. All four limbs were hanging out the edges, clawing wildly. By the time he got out from under there, the drugs should have kicked in. Earl turned to see who was at the door and had to shield his dark-adapted eyes from the sudden scalding light.

The bitten deputy, Kerkonen, was standing in the billowing snow with a 12-gauge shotgun with a big flashlight on it aimed right at his head. Wearing an angry expression, she pumped a round into the chamber.

"Whoa there," Earl said, raising his hands.

"Down!" she ordered.

Earl heard the rustle of fur and felt the flash of warmth as a second werewolf rushed from the cells. He threw himself aside as Kerkonen pulled the trigger. The shotgun thundered in the enclosed space. She pumped the shotgun and fired again. The werewolf shrieked but kept coming. She shot it a third time as Earl quickly drew his 625 and shot the werewolf right through the brain.

He managed to hit it five more times, had risen, reloaded, and reholstered, before the werewolf hit the ground. Sure enough, it was already healing. Not taking any chances, and only needing one prisoner to question, Earl landed on the werewolf's back, heavy Bowie knife already in hand. He drove it through the beast's neck so hard the blade struck the tile. He started slicing. "Hold still, damn it!" Hot blood sprayed up his arms.

"Oh, that's nasty," the deputy said, gagging.

A few seconds later the head came free in a great pumping mass. Earl rolled off the body and sat on the floor. Still illuminated by the shotgun's flashlight, he looked down at the red mess on his brand-new armor and asked, "You got any paper towels around here?"

"Who's Marsters?" Harbinger asked as he came out of the jail-cell area. He tossed a gold name tag on Heather's desk.

With one giant animal with a severed head on the floor, an unconscious one squished under the vending machine, and the bodies of two more of her coworkers dismembered in the back, Heather had needed to take a seat. She'd picked her regular desk. It was familiar, and therefore slightly comforting.

"Bill Marsters was one of our deputies." She picked up the name tag. It was splattered with blood. "They got Bill, too?"

"More like Bill got them," he answered. She'd found one of their battery-powered camping lanterns, and that gave an even measure of light. The unnerving man who fought like something out of a superhero movie stepped from the shadows in front of her desk and pointed at the decapitated animal. "That *is* Bill."

"Bullshit," she stated, opening her bottom drawer and taking out a box of shotgun shells. She furiously thumbed more slugs into her Winchester. "Absolute bullshit."

"You'll see in a minute." He pulled up a rolling chair and took a seat. His strange armor creaked as he put his boots up on a desk. She was about to tell him not to do that, but what did it matter? That desk had belonged to Chase, and he was dead, just like everybody else.

"Why? What'll I see? Is it like the wolfman movies? Once they die they turn right back into people?" She laughed angrily.

"Naw. That'd be silly. It takes a bit. Well, unless you mortally wound one, and it has time to calm down. Then it'll return to human form before kicking the bucket. But that's pretty rare. Sure, as the body cools off it'll start to look human. That's one reason they can keep lycanthropes secret. No forensic evidence. But we ain't got all night. I'm talking about this other guy." He jerked his thumb at the unconscious creature under the vending machine. "Judging by the way the cell door was smashed out from the inside, I'm guessing this dude was locked up."

"We had one crazy prisoner. State troopers found him wandering around a campsite preaching about Armageddon." She had just assumed that he'd gotten eaten like the others when the strange creatures had invaded, but then she chided herself for being in denial. She'd seen Buckley change. *Girl, you don't know what you've seen.*

"He was planted here," Harbinger stated, looking thoughtfully at the ceiling. "Interesting."

She got her older Beretta 96 out of the bottom drawer along with a few spare magazines and a box of .40 Speer Gold Dots. Loading magazines was therapeutic. "What the hell are you?" she asked finally.

"Mind if I smoke?" he didn't wait for her to respond before he'd already lit up. "Well, I'm with a company called Monster Hunter International," he replied. "I kill supernatural critters for a living."

"So this is all in a day's work for you."

He shrugged. "It's got its perks."

That didn't explain how he moved twice as fast as anyone else she'd ever seen. He sat there smoking, which was an obnoxious habit, but he didn't offer any further explanation. Once her mags were loaded, she stood. "I need a doughnut." Luckily there were a few packages that had spilled clear of the unconscious creature, because even as much as she needed sugar, she didn't need it bad enough to get close to that thing, sleeping or not. She found some old-fashioned crumbly doughnuts and returned to her desk.

"How's your shoulder?" he asked finally.

After running from the hospital, she'd gone into a gas-station bathroom, rinsed it out, and taped a bandage over the punctures. It itched and felt unnaturally hot. The sensible thing to do would be to get tested for rabies, but then sensible didn't take into account the strange men with guns trying to murder her. She could still see the little red hole appearing in Chase's forehead and how the back of his head had come off every time she closed her eyes. She didn't trust this Harbinger. For all she knew, he was with the same outfit as the murderers. "None of your damn business."

"I'm not gonna hurt you," he said softly. "I ain't your problem. Those men were from the government, and I'm afraid they won't stop looking for you until you're dead. They're very persistent. I'll give them that."

"Screw them," she said as she shoved a doughnut in her mouth and crunched the wonderful staleness. She was terribly hungry all of a sudden. "Why?" she asked with an impolite mouthful. "Why did they try to kill me? Why'd they shoot Chase?"

Harbinger took his feet off the desk and placed his hands on his knees. Talking about this seemed to pain him. "I'll be straight with you. You've been bitten by a werewolf. Which means you're cursed. You're gonna turn into one of them."

"That's probably the stupidest thing I've ever heard."

"I'm telling the truth." He let out a long sigh. "At the next full moon, you'll turn into a werewolf. You'll be completely out of control, and you'll kill anyone unlucky enough to get in your way. But odds are that you'll descend into a homicidal psychosis before that, though. It ain't pretty."

Heather laughed—until she began to choke on the doughnut. Then she couldn't help but start to cry a bit, because the men who'd shot Chase sure believed it. "You actually believe that?"

"Sorry," he answered sincerely. "It's on my head. If I'd been a little faster, you wouldn't be in this predicament."

Get a hold of yourself. She hurriedly wiped her eyes and strengthened her resolve. She was not going to cry in front of this weirdo. "Look, Harbinger, is it? This town's in danger. Somebody needs to warn everyone about these *things*. I'm going back out to do my job. If I see those assholes, I'll deal with them."

"You'll feel it soon. The hunger first, then the strength, then the urges." He shook his head sadly. "Your injury will be gone soon. By then, the change is in full swing. You don't believe me. I suppose it'll take some time for this to sink in . . ." He trailed off, looking at her strangely.

"Oh, what the hell now?" she asked.

"*Time* . . . Hey, your buddy at the hospital, how long ago was he mauled?"

"His name was Joe Buckley." Time seemed so compressed. It seemed like forever. "Just over twenty-four hours ago."

"And Bill, did he get injured recently? A bite or a scratch?"

"Not that I know of." She paused mid-doughnut, thinking of the crazy prisoner biting him during their wrestling match. "Wait. The prisoner did take a chunk out of his hand yesterday."

"Yesterday? Impossible." Harbinger scowled. "And he must have been in human form . . . Holy shit. That's bad news."

"Why?" she asked, but Harbinger was distracted, looking toward the vending machine. He got up and walked to the now-stirring monster. "Is he awake?" She didn't realize that she'd switched from *it* to *he*.

"Sorta," Harbinger said, slinging his stubby weapon, then bending over and picking up the vending machine. It had to weigh a couple hundred pounds, but he didn't so much as grunt as he put it back upright. *Crap, he's strong.* Snack foods cascaded down onto the hairy form.

Heather picked up her shotgun as she got up. "Careful."

There was a crinkle of cellophane wrappers as the pile of snacks seemed to compress, only Heather realized that it wasn't the plastic moving: it was the body under it seemingly shrinking. She watched one twitching paw. The fur didn't seem so thick now. When she blinked, it seemed more like the hair on a man's arm. The long black claws seemed to retract. Their color lightened, turning white. The skin around the nails seemed *moist*, pliable, almost squishy.

The head was obscured by wrappers. Heather was nauseous, but she had to see. "His face. I need to see his face." Harbinger nodded, then squatted down, knocking away the packages. She recoiled in disgust.

The head wasn't exactly canine, but it was similar. The animal had long jaws, but instead of a nose like a pad, it was more like the nostrils on the end of the snout were holes in the skin stretched tight over the bone. The skull wasn't low and flat like a wolf, but rounder, like a *human.* As the covering mask of dark hair receded, individual hairs crawling back into the skin for their proteins to be reabsorbed, the skin beneath went from gray to sick pink. Heather shuddered at the sound of cracking bone.

The flesh was covered in beads of sweat. Lips peeled back in an unconscious grimace of pain as the jaws seemed to shrink, finally disappearing into the skull, leaving a cartilaginous lump where a human nose would be. The skin was loose, dangling and wet. It slowly retracted until the nostril holes were in the right place, and the thing sucked in a great pained breath.

Heather stepped back, biting a knuckle. The worst part was the terrible grinding noise and the moans of suffering. The nearly human parody of a face opened its eyes. One was gold. One was brown. He looked around, terrified, his mouth open, teeth still sharp. *They're real.* Heather felt a sudden urge to vomit.

Harbinger drew his revolver and placed it against the werewolf's forehead. "Easy there, partner. No need to make this awkward."

She could recognize him easily now. The prisoner's voice was horribly slurred, far too deep. "What've you done to me?"

"Pumped enough drugs into your system to date-rape a yak. We're gonna have us a chat."

The eyes closed as the prisoner continued panting. There was a horrid scraping noise from his teeth, like fingernails on a chalkboard, that made Heather shiver. Gradually his breathing slowed. His glistening skin turned to a normal shade. When his eyes reopened, they were both brown. "You're the Harbinger," he stated, voice at near human tones.

"One and the same," he answered, cigarette dangling from the edge of his mouth. "Let me in on a little secret, friend. What's Nikolai here for?"

The prisoner tried to sit up, but was too drugged. He collapsed back into a heap. He began to laugh. It was a horribly distorted noise. "Nikolai's here for the same reason you are."

"I want straight answers, or I start hurting you. Trust me. You can torture something that regenerates *forever*."

"You're both fools, slaves to the old ways. You're slaves to your instincts."

Harbinger frowned. "That ain't a very nice way to talk about your leader."

The prisoner growled. "Nikolai's no more worthy to lead our pack than you are, traitor. We answer the call of the Alpha. He doesn't lock himself in a cage like a coward or keep part of himself chained inside his own head! My father is the king of all werewolves!"

Harbinger glanced at Heather. "Hmm . . . I must've missed that memo." He went back to the prisoner. "Tell me about this Alpha. I'd love to meet him sometime."

"Oh, you will." The prisoner giggled madly. It was an unnerving sound. "He's coming to take your soul. He'll use it to give life to the *vulkodlak*." The word was guttural, slurred.

"What's a vulk-odd-lack?" Harbinger asked. His pronunciation wasn't even close.

"Oh, you'll see!" he exclaimed with glee. "They're beautiful angels. Just beautiful. They're going to usher in a new age. The one-handed witch has revealed the way! But for them to be born he needs a perfect soul to give them life!"

Harbinger rolled his eyes. "Metaphysical bullshit. I swear, it's always some sort of metaphysical bullshit with these guys. Plug your ears, Kerkonen," he told Heather. She barely had time to comply before he pointed his gun at the werewolf's kneecap and blasted it into shards of bone and meat. Screaming, the prisoner grabbed his leg. "Okay, now that I've got your attention, get all poetic on me again, and you lose the other one. Got it? Why's your pack in Copper Lake?"

Grimacing, he pointed one bloody hand at Heather. "We're here because of her blood!" Harbinger moved his gun to the other knee. "Wait! No, really! One of her ancestors, the Finn, he stole something valuable from our people. He hid it here."

"Grandpa?" Heather asked.

"He's a thief! He's just lucky he got the chance to die before the Alpha tracked him down. But this whole town will pay for his sins!"

"What?" Harbinger shouted, then punched the man in his damaged knee. "What did he steal?"

"All right, all right." The prisoner whimpered. "The amulet of Koschei the Deathless. Man, that hurts!"

"I *hate* magic. That must be the source of the surge. What's it do?"

"It makes our kind invincible. The bearer can't die, just like Koschei of old. The moon no longer matters! The wearer's children receive blessings, too. It makes us all stronger. The birth of the *vulkodlak* are another. The pack that has the amulet can never be defeated."

"Where's he hiding?" Harbinger's voice was a low growl. Heather took an unconscious step back.

The prisoner began to laugh. "You think he's hiding? You think he brought you here so that he could hide? To hide from the Russian? No! Our time living in the dark is over. We've been set free. Tonight the pack is going to feast and grow strong. He's coming for you! He's coming to take your soul!" The laughter continued, bubbling off into insanity.

"That's enough," Harbinger stated, and Heather could sense the grim finality in his voice.

"Harbinger, don't," Heather pleaded. This was wrong. She was a peace officer. This man was in her custody.

"What? Gonna lock him up? Figure enough blood's been shed already and let him go? You become the animal, you cross that line, you get no mercy. It don't work that way." Harbinger turned his attention back to the prisoner. "*I* don't work that way. Any last words, asshole?"

"The Alpha will take your soul!" the prisoner screamed. "All of your souls!"

This wasn't right, but she looked at the decapitated corpse that had been one of her friends, and she didn't say another word.

"Ears." Harbinger stated. Heather complied and this time Harbinger shot the prisoner in the chest. The insane laughter gurgled off into a long groan.

Harbinger stepped away, examining the wound he'd just inflicted. "Interesting. Silver still works on werewolves created before that surge just fine. It's only the new ones that are immune."

The prisoner was in obvious pain, but fearless in his devotion. "Fool. I'm of his pack. He'll sense my death and come for you." His voice trailed off.

Earl nodded. "Good. Let's hurry him along then," he said as he shot the dying man in the face.

✤ ✤ ✤

The sudden death of the child stung him. It was not a true physical pain, more of a sense of loss, an empty space in the bonds of the pack. The pack had just been made less. His child's blood called from the dust for vengeance.

"Your sacrifice was not in vain," he whispered to the wind, then turned to the witch. "One of the pack has fallen."

"Which one got him?" She didn't seem surprised. "Harbinger or Petrov?"

"What does it matter? Come on. It is almost time."

The witch's nod was barely perceptible inside her great fur hood. He set out through the deep snow at a speed her weak human legs could never possibly match. One of her diggers gently extended a metal hand, and she gratefully climbed into its arms. The digger held her close, like a mother would hold a child, only in this case the reverse was true. The diggers set out after the running Alpha.

Disgusted, Earl holstered his revolver and stomped away from the corpse. This was a nightmare scenario. An entire pack of werewolves had declared war on mankind.

Packs formed occasionally, and when they did, they'd often hunt, but always on the sly. They'd kidnap runaways and homeless, take them out to the sticks and chase them down, then melt away to do it again later. Every time he'd discovered this, he'd made sure that MHI had tracked them down and eliminated the rogue pack. This was different. This pack were assaulting an entire community. The town was cut off from the outside. People were isolated in their homes, unaware of what was coming. It would be a slaughter.

Werewolves lived on the periphery. Outright war with mankind was insanity. It would take an incredibly strong leader to force this kind of counter-instinctual behavior onto his followers. That level of suicidal loyalty was bizarre. This was unnatural, a perversion of the natural order of things. It broke *his* rules.

And that really pissed him off.

The deputy was still staring at the body, probably just now realizing that he hadn't been lying, and that she was destined to that same fate. "Kerkonen," he said. It took her a second to focus. "You said you were gonna warn everyone. What's your plan?"

"I hadn't thought that far ahead."

"The pack will work its way inward, probably from multiple directions. They'll kill the ones they think are threats first, while they're not expecting it. Like this." He gestured around the damaged station. "They'll save the remainder for when they've got the time."

She went back to staring at the body. "How do you know all this?"

"Because that's how I'd do it. Wake everyone you can. Reliable folks first. Have them start spreading the word. Get into groups. There's safety in numbers. Individuals and stragglers are easy to pick off. Is there a secure building in town? Something you can fortify?"

"A couple of the churches are pretty solid . . ." she began.

"Too flammable. They look like animals, but they ain't stupid. They'll burn you out."

"The high school. The population used to be a lot bigger before the mines went away, so they built a giant gymnasium."

"Why? That doesn't sound very good."

"Not this thing. It's huge, its solid, and the windows are all up high. There's even an old civil-defense bunker under it, because it was built back in the Sixties, and there used to be an Air Force base down the road back then. They still use the bomb shelter under the gym for storage. There's only one way in, and it's all concrete. Even the roof is metal. It'd be hard to set on fire."

Earl nodded. That was good thinking. "Start moving people there. If space is limited get the women and kids inside and lock it up tight. And if anybody has a bite or a scratch, or you even suspect that they've got one, don't you dare put them in that vault. I've got cases of silver ammo in three calibers in my truck you can have. Regular ammo will work, but they'll heal quick, so hit them again while they're down. Cut their heads off, remove their hearts, or set them on fire. No mercy."

"We can do that," she promised. Earl nodded approvingly. These U.P. folks had spine. "Where will you be?"

"Doing what I do best. I'm going on the offensive. The most effective thing I can do for your town is to start picking them off. The more I kill, the less your people have to worry about."

"How many of these things are we talking about?"

"Unknown," he answered truthfully. That probably would have been a good question to ask the dead guy, but it was a touch late for that. But from the complicated smells when he'd first arrived in town . . . "At least a dozen, maybe twice that."

The more troubling question was, what about the new ones? Normally it took weeks for the metamorphosis to take place and the power of the full moon to unleash it. He'd already seen two cases of the change happening in less than a day, and they had both been set off because of that unnatural surge.

He glanced at Kerkonen suspiciously. She was a ticking bomb and didn't even realize it yet.

He'd tried to help others who'd been cursed, but Santiago had been right. It was almost impossible to learn to control the curse. It wasn't just a physical mutation, it was a change at the most fundamental of psychological and philosophical levels. Over the years he'd had several of his Hunters end up bitten. They had each been a warrior, tough, hard as nails, but in the end every last one of them had failed. He'd tried to help dozens of the survivors that he'd met over the years. He'd had young werewolves instinctively seek him out, looking for guidance. . . . All of them were dead now. Most eventually by their own hand, or if they lacked the strength, by Earl's.

Mastering the curse took more than locking yourself behind impenetrable walls a few nights a month. It made you into a perfect killer every single day. And it made you *want* it.

This was the hard part. "I need you to listen to me very carefully, Deputy Kerkonen. What I'm about to say is gonna be difficult. You're infected. I need you to deal with that. These people need you right now."

"Infected?" she asked incredulously. "Like a disease? What do we do?"

"There's no cure. There never has been. Believe me, a lot of really smart folks have tried. Bites are always infectious. If you start to change, you're gonna become part of the problem." He drew his backup gun, a snub-nosed 625, spun it around in his hand and held it out to her, butt first. "This is the solution."

"I don't understand," she said, her voice barely a whisper.

"It's loaded with silver bullets. If you start to change, stick this in your mouth and pull the trigger."

"That's—"

"Necessary," he stated coldly. "Otherwise when you change, you'll murder everyone around you. You'll kill, and kill, and kill again, until you're bloated on blood, and then you'll puke it up and go back for more. The first time is always the worst."

"I don't believe you," she insisted, louder this time.

"Yes. Yes, you do." The Smith & Wesson stayed there, between them. "Take this. I've got a spare."

Finally, she asked, "Is there any other way?"

He had the portable time-lock cage in the truck, brought specifically just in case he was stuck out during the full moon. . . . But he'd brought that for himself. It barely fit one. If that surge came back any stronger, it was his life insurance.

Kerkonen was terrified, but trying not to show it. She put on a tough act. Earl could only tell because he could smell the fear on her skin. Her hand closed around the gun, and she took it from him hesitantly.

At least he would have a chance of controlling himself if the surge came again. She didn't. The drugs were unreliable and a safe dose might not work fast enough. Enough to knock her out for sure was enough to kill her. Silver bullets hadn't worked on the other new werewolf, so they might not on her, either, and he really didn't want to kill the poor scared girl himself. He wasn't some heartless MCB executioner.

Damn it . . . He made up his mind. "There is something. If you can secure yourself, you can wait it out. It's got to be extremely solid, though. You saw what he did to your jail cell. Your strength goes through the roof. But I've got a box in the back of my truck that'll hold a werewolf." He pulled out his key ring and passed them over. "Take my truck. Get in there if you need to. Pull the lid shut behind you, and it'll lock."

"How do I get out?" she asked suspiciously. "Because that sounds like some creepy serial killer-type implement to just have in your truck there, Harry Houdini."

"It'll open automatically in eight hours." He smiled. "So I'd suggest going to the bathroom first."

She groaned. "I still think you're full of shit . . . but assuming, just assuming that you're not completely insane, how will I know it's time?"

When the burning gets so bad that eating that .45 sounds like a great idea. "Oh, believe me, you'll know. . . . We better move out. Good luck out there, Kerkonen."

"Heather," she stated flatly as she tried to stuff the big revolver into her coat pocket. "My name's Heather, and if you're lying to me, you'll regret it. See you at the bomb shelter."

⇥ **Chapter 11** ⇤

Santiago's last regular visit came in the spring of 1929, my third year on the island.

"How long have you known?" he asked me as we sat on the rocks with our fishing poles.

"Months ago," I answered truthfully. I'd been tipped off by some of the tonics Santiago had started taking. The cancer was in his bones. I could smell the sick from a mile away. It was natural for a predator to sense weakness. "I figured you'd talk when you were ready."

"Sic transit gloria mundi . . ." He saw my confused expression. "Latin. It means the glory of man is fleeting. Such is life, my friend. The church has already sent a replacement, and he seems like a good enough man. My people will be cared for. I suppose my work here is done. I have done my best, and I go to the Lord with a heart that is free in that knowledge. Are you ready to return to life?"

I wasn't sure. I asked what he thought.

"You've sat on top of this rock and let hurricanes buffet you. I've seen you do your very best to torture yourself into changing inadvertently. You have read the Bible seven times, absorbed everything I know about werewolves, and have spent many hours in quiet contemplation. I do not know what else you can do here. My opinion is that it is time to move on. Your curse could be a powerful tool in accomplishing the Lord's work. Besides, I won't be around to bring you supplies for much longer, and you are a terrible fisherman." He reached around his back and drew a familiar revolver. He opened *the cylinder and ejected a single cartridge before handing it over. "I believe this belongs to you."*

I took the silver bullet, all alone in its half-moon clip. "You know, I could give you the curse. You'd be healed immediately. Werewolves don't get sick. You're a strong man. You could learn to control it, better than me for sure."

"Do not tempt me, Raymond. I am less afraid of dying than I am of failure. . . . Do you know why I was exiled here?" When I didn't respond, Santiago continued. "My best friend was a Hunter as well, recruited to our group because of his bravery against the devil's legions. One day, he was bitten by a werewolf. I was ordered by our knight-commander to end his suffering, but I lied and hid him instead. I tried to help him much as I have tried to help you. I studied everything in the Vatican about lycanthropy. I became our leading expert. However, I still failed. My brother could never control himself. He was eventually consumed with evil. Many innocents died. I was forced to take his life. I was shamed, an outcast to the order, and was banished to live out my days here in a place where I could cause no more trouble." He turned to look at me, and his sad eyes cut through me harder than my sharpest knife. "I am counting on you to make my life's work mean something."

I gave him my word.

✛ ✛ ✛

Nikolai maneuvered the snowplow through the empty streets of Copper Lake. It was actually a rather beneficial vehicle, considering the present conditions. It was huge, the cab sat up high, and a dump-truck bed full of sand added significant weight, and therefore traction. The amulet was out there, somewhere, but he couldn't pinpoint its direction. The false moon was maddening, always just beyond the reach of his senses, and it felt like it was moving.

The storm was hurting his concentration. The scents were muddled and confused, quickly buried under pounds of snow. Past the plow's rapidly beating wipers, the town had taken on a surreal form. They were on a suburban street, nearing the center of town. The only lights from the windows were from battery-powered lights or flickering candles, but almost everyone was asleep. Every edge and straight line constructed by man had been rounded; several feet of snow had already piled up against the small homes. Even the street signs looked like giant white lollipops. There was nothing soft about this snowfall.

It was icy and brutal, harsh and unforgiving. Winter had come to smother the life from this place.

Reminds me of home.

"Shut up," Nikolai said. "I need to concentrate."

However, the Tvar was right. It was just like home. Their early years together had been spent in the Siberian woods, hiding by day, hunting by night, always staying one step ahead of the NKVD Hunters that had so ruthlessly pursued them. They'd raided the small villages, usually eating livestock or, if the Tvar was in control, people, often children. The Tvar preferred children, said they tasted better. Sometimes the lines blurred and he could not remember which one of them had committed the latest atrocities.

It had been a hard time for Nikolai, the idealistic young man whose life had been destroyed after he'd been mauled by a werewolf, but he'd come to understand the new part of himself and had brokered a peace between the two entities that lived inside the same body. They had come to terms, and that had made them truly dangerous.

Many of Stalin's finest Hunters had died after underestimating them. Eventually, after a chase that had taken them across the most unforgiving terrain in the motherland to a valley high in the Altay Krai, the NKVD had finally cornered them.

Strangely, rather than a silver bullet, they had been offered a pardon. Impressed by reports of the chase, Stalin himself had decided that young Nikolai Petrov would be a remarkable asset to the cause. The man of steel had a fearsome old werewolf serving him and had decided that Nikolai was to be his protégé. In one fell swoop, Nikolai had been given a mission, a mentor, and a purpose.

You miss it.

"Sometimes," Nikolai answered truthfully. The mission had ultimately been a failure, their mentor a madman. Yet Stalin had given him something greater than himself to believe in. The loss of the Soviet Union and its subsequent desecration had left him empty and selling his abilities to the highest bidders in a world without purpose. Nikolai was a fatalistic man without a bit of optimism in his soul.

Yet, surprisingly, he had found a purpose again, a reason to live. He'd found a human girl who did not fear him. It had seemed so impossible. *Lila.* She'd demanded the best from him and loved him despite the things he had done. So he'd silenced the Tvar. Oh, how it had fought, but in the end, Nikolai had won. They had built a life. Nikolai had lived as a man. They had been happy, for a time. . . . Before Harbinger had recently ruined everything.

So Nikolai had chosen to set his other half free. It had become so much more demanding since then. It made it difficult to think clearly.

I smell killing.

He stomped on the brakes as a figure ran into the street ahead and fell. The giant vehicle weighed many tons and slid to a gritty stop, inches from crushing the man beneath the plow.

Nikolai took the Val rifle in hand and stepped out of the truck. He dropped into the snow and walked around the front. The man was already scrambling to his feet and had put one hand on the ice-crusted plow blade to steady himself. Clad only in a pair of blue coveralls, he was shivering uncontrollably and stunk of fear so badly that Nikolai could actually taste it on his tongue.

"We've got to get out of here!" the man cried, looking back over his shoulder, terrified.

Nikolai's nostrils twitched. Another werewolf was closing fast. She had been tracking this man, and it was easy to understand how, since his fear stink was like a beacon. Nikolai could not hear the female's approach over the rumble of the truck's diesel engine and the howl of the wind. The headlights illuminated only a small patch of road, and the snow was so thick that it was as if the air was filled with hissing static. Nikolai put the Val's stock to his shoulder and deactivated the safety. The metal was ice cold against his cheek. It gave him clarity.

The werewolf hurled herself through the static. The man-prey screamed and fell against the plow as Nikolai calmly lined up the sights and pulled the trigger of the suppressed rifle. The only sound was the metallic *clack* of the action flying back and forth and the sharp *thwack* of the bullet's impact. The werewolf stumbled as the heavy projectile pierced her leg, just as he'd intended. She kept coming, but Nikolai stepped forward and slammed his palm into the inferior creature's snout.

She squealed like a pup and landed on her back. Rolling through the snow, she retreated on all fours, crying, leaving a bright red trail behind.

Finish her!

"I know what I'm doing," Nikolai said.

A hand fell on his coat. "Oh, thank you! Thank you!" the prey cried pathetically, as he got out of the snow. "You saved my life. That thing tore Bud apart. It ripped his throat right out, and then it came after me! There's more of them there, a whole bunch! We're all gonna die!"

The human's sobs sickened him. It was hard to imagine that he'd once been that soft and pathetic himself.

You were. Until I came along.

"Control yourself," Nikolai ordered. "Where are the creatures?"

Still shaking uncontrollably, he wiped his eyes. His name tag read STEVENSON. Besides fear, he smelled of petrol and cigarettes. "At the grocery store. Bud was unloading his ice-cream truck. I went in to fire up the generator. Power's out," he explained as Nikolai cocked his head to the side. The young werewolves would have been attracted to the noise and activity. "Have to keep the heat on or the veggies wilt." Shivering, he folded his arms in a vain attempt to stay warm. "Thanks, buddy. My name's Justin. You saved my bacon. We better get out of here, though. There were at least two more of tho—"

Nikolai reached up, grabbed a handful of hair, and brutally drove Justin's face into the thick metal at the top of the plow blade. There was a sickening crack as teeth shattered. Nikolai let him flop limply into the snow.

Excellent.

For a moment he wasn't sure if that impulsive action had been his, or the Tvar within. Sometimes it was hard to tell. Nikolai decided to accept responsibility. "His whining annoyed me."

He walked over to where the other werewolf had fallen. The blood splatter was bright and easy to spot on the snow. He got on his knees and drank in the scent, then picked up a handful of slush and put it in his mouth, rolling it around, savoring the arterial blood and the smoky taste of bone marrow. She was young and had not been one of them for long, a few months perhaps, but long enough to be a valued member of the enemy pack. Particles of silver began to burn his gums, so he spit the blood out.

Badly wounded, unable to regenerate from the poisonous silver, she would surely retreat to her Alpha to die amongst her pack.

Clever and ruthless. I like this side of us.

Justin moaned incoherently as he returned to the truck. Nikolai climbed back into the cab, ground it into gear, and drove, trapping and dragging the weak human beneath the plow blade. The body was dislodged within half a block and crushed beneath the tires. The bump barely registered. Nikolai rolled the window down as he drove slowly, savoring the painful cold and following the scent of blood.

Not knowing who else in her small department was still alive, Heather had tried Sheriff Hintze's home first. It was near the station, by itself at the end of a long driveway, but Harbinger's truck was barely sufficient to get even that far without chains. No one who lived in Copper County was a stranger to snow, but this storm was absurd, even by Michigan standards. The only reason the roads were still passable at all was because the howling wind was pushing most of the accumulation off the flat spots. There had to have been two feet in the last hour.

The lack of radio and phone was infuriating. Help was as close as the next county over, but there was no way to reach them. As soon as she had some help, she'd send somebody on a snowmobile, but until then she was on her own. She had left a note at the station, just in case somebody else came in, but she doubted that anyone would. Copper County was a relatively unpopulated place and had a correspondingly small sheriff's department. There weren't that many deputies to begin with, and she knew that almost half of them had been killed in the last few hours. Heather had a bad feeling about the others.

Heather knew that she was too late as soon as she arrived at the sheriff's house. His front door was wide open, already lodged in place by a fresh drift. The beam of her flashlight found what was left of Sheriff Hintze right inside the front hall, wearing pajamas and missing most of his neck.

A few hours ago, that sight would have scared her, perhaps even made her nauseous. Now she just felt anger. She crouched next to the body, with her Winchester 1300 ready to blast anything that moved, but the house was quiet except for the creaking of old boards. The thing that had done this was long gone. She caught herself sniffing the air, shook her head, and retreated to the porch.

Harbinger had said that it was a coordinated attack. Of course they had eliminated the sheriff. Her boss had been a sharp man and would have stood in their way. Yet why did she believe Harbinger? He was a mystery. And if she were to believe what Harbinger told her about the attack, then why shouldn't she believe him about the other things he had said? Her shoulder itched, but it didn't even hurt in the slightest. She was scared to look at it.

The night had already been so emotionally draining that the sight of her dead boss hadn't even disturbed her. Heather simply returned to the still-running pickup truck and set out for her next destination. She was so hungry it hurt. Heather could smell the food in the backseat and dragged Harbinger's cooler around. Barely slowing to rip the packaging off, she started stuffing her face, not even caring what it was, as she drove back down the sheriff's driveway. Regardless of what Harbinger told her, she still had responsibilities to attend to. She'd taken an oath to protect and serve, and she took that oath very seriously.

A few lights were on at the corner grocery.

It was a relatively small building. The kind of locally owned, overpriced, but convenient place that managed to hang on despite competition from big chain stores. It had already been decorated for Christmas. The signs said this place was called Value Sense Grocery, six-packs of Dr. Pepper were on sale, and there was a werewolf noisily devouring the contents of some poor sucker's chest cavity right inside the front door by the shopping carts.

Earl crouched behind the oblong block of ice that he suspected was concealing a mailbox and watched the windows. He was downwind, and even if it suddenly shifted, as it kept on doing, he'd put the wolfsbane back into a pocket. Other than the one visible target, there was at least one other member of the pack in there. He wanted to make sure he got as many as possible, as fast as possible. Anything that ran meant he would have to chase them down, and that would take time. Time spent chasing was time that could be better spent proactively killing these upstart punks before they murdered too many innocents.

The dark brown fur of a second enemy was briefly visible as it moved past the cash registers and a plastic Santa Claus. It joined the first, lighter-colored werewolf over the human remains. The two began to snap at each other, competing playfully for the tastier bits. The lighter-colored one was dominant, and the newcomer moved to the other end and started chewing on a leg.

"Enjoy that last meal, boys," Earl said to himself as he came out of the snow and walked for the front door. Lifting the Thompson, he waited until he was just on the other side of the heavy glass door and couldn't possibly miss.

Seeing those two there, just having a good old time, really irked him. He'd worked hard for over eighty years to make up for his own early mistakes, and these youngsters thought that they could come along and do whatever the hell they felt like. Earl realized he was grinding his teeth together. Wanting them to see their punishment coming, Earl raised the muzzle of the Thompson and banged it hard on the glass. "Hey!"

The two heads snapped up instantly, dripping blood and chunks of flesh, glaring at him.

The Tommy gun roared as Earl mowed them down. He worked the subgun back and forth, emptying an entire stick magazine of silver .45 bullets into the two werewolves, a continuous stream of hot brass flying out the side. A row of soda bottles behind them exploded as the monsters jerked and twitched. The werewolves fell as Earl ducked under the door rail and through the broken glass, already yanking the spent mag from the Thompson.

The light one was dead. The dark male was trying to crawl away, its body perforated multiple times. The wounds were closing. "Oh, a new guy, huh?" Earl shouted as he pulled the bolt back on a fresh mag. "I guess nobody told you about the two rules?" The werewolf had reached the checkout stand and was using it to pull himself up. Earl let the hot subgun hang by its sling as he drew his Bowie knife.

The werewolf turned, snarling. Earl swung the heavy blade, cleaving through half the throat in one mighty swing. The werewolf fell back, blood squirting everywhere. "And rule number one is no killing"— Earl raised the blade again and slashed it through the other side; the werewolf's head spun free and landed, bouncing down the rubber belt of the check stand—"innocent people!" The body tottered for a second before falling. It hit the floor with a dull thud, one leg kicking spastically.

Earl lowered his dripping knife. He could hear a generator running in back. The lights over the check stands were on, giving him a good look. The now-headless body still had the tattered remains of a red grocery apron tied around the midsection. Another poor sap, turned today. Earl spat on the floor.

"What's rule number two?"

Raising the Bowie, Earl turned toward the voice. It had come from the middle of the store, somewhere between the aisles, but he couldn't see anyone. Most of the store's lights were still off. "Who're you supposed to be?" Earl asked evenly.

The voice was calm, almost friendly, and oozed confidence. "I'm the one you're looking for."

It wasn't Nikolai's voice, that much was certain. Earl wiped his knife off on his leg and returned it to the sheath on his belt. He took up the Thompson. "You the leader of this pack?"

There was a jovial laugh. "I'm the leader of all werewolves."

"Uh-huh. And if I had a nickel for every asshole that told me that . . ." Walking to the side, Earl peered down the next shadowed aisle. They were perpendicular to the check stands. Even in the dark, he'd be easy enough to spot. He'd find this guy, shoot him full of holes, and finish this.

"Those were mistaken. I don't make mistakes. I'm the king of werewolves, the next step in our evolution. The future, if you will. I am the Alpha."

The voice seemed to be coming from the left side of the store. Earl kept walking, gun up. He had to keep him talking. "Why are you doing this? Seems kind of stupid to pick a fight you can't win with humanity." Next aisle. *Clear.*

"Don't assume man will win this one. Perhaps, the better question is, why are you here, Harbinger?"

Next aisle. *Clear.* "I came here looking to finish Nikolai Petrov. I figure once I clean your clock, I'll go kill him and be back in Alabama before supper." There were only a few aisles left.

Oddly, Earl's superior hearing couldn't pin down exactly where the voice was coming from. "Yet you don't know why Nikolai's here, either, do you?"

Clear. "Can't say that I do. . . . Something about a magic necklace, I gather."

"Amulet," the voice corrected. "Of Koschei the Deathless, to be exact. It's why I lured you both here. Only the soul of the most powerful of werewolves can awaken the amulet. Lesser souls gets lesser results. Only the fiercest will do. That would either be you or Petrov."

Clear. "That'd be me." One last aisle. Earl's hand tightened around the Thompson's grip. "Obviously."

"Historically, it would seem to be a draw. Your truce was inconvenient to me. Ideally, I wanted the two of you to meet to decide the victor before I harvested his soul. I wanted only the best of the best for this moment." His voice had an almost youthful pitch to it, but it was hard to tell with a werewolf. Earl didn't sound like a smoker. "But with both of you murdering all my children . . ."

Last aisle. Earl swept around. *Damn it.* The aisle was empty except for another mutilated human corpse spread from one end to the other. He had to be hiding behind one of the endcaps. Earl moved quickly, silently, down the aisle toward the back of the store. His wet boots barely made a sound.

"I've had to expedite matters."

Earl reached the other end and peered around the corner. Nothing was moving in the shadows of the meat and dairy section. He sniffed the air. The intruder had to be wearing wolfsbane as well. Earl couldn't pick up anything over the delicious smell of all that raw meat. "You want to challenge me? Let's go then."

It was impossible to isolate the source of the voice. *Magic?* "One doesn't challenge his inferiors, Harbinger."

"How about you come out and face me? King of the werewolves and all that, or you just talking a big game?"

"I'm more than a werewolf, more than you can comprehend. And either way, as I've said, I've had to expedite matters. I'm afraid you have another challenge to face first. Then I'll deal with whichever of you proves worthy."

Earl froze. The doors on the dairy cabinet had started to vibrate. Something was coming.

"Before I go, though, you've piqued my curiosity. What's rule number two?"

The front of the grocery store lit up as headlights flashed through the glass. The vibration turned into a rumble as a powerful engine revved. The lights grew in intensity as the vehicle rapidly approached.

"Stay off my bad side," Earl muttered as the giant truck's steel snowplow blade crashed through the front of the store.

The truck exploded through the wall in a shower of glass and cinder block fragments, barely even slowing as its heavy steel plow obliterated several checkout stands, displays of food, and three rows of tall shelves. Seemingly unstoppable, it came right down the center of the store. Cans, bags, and boxes were flung in every direction as the truck plowed everything aside. More shelves collapsed, causing a domino effect, in a cascading wave of destruction.

Earl moved quickly, dodging to the side, heading for the back corner, swearing the whole way but unable to hear himself over the terrible racket of breaking tile, shattering glass, and roaring engine. He dove to safety just as the orange snowplow collided with the back wall of the meat department with a thunderous crash. The plow caught a heavy steel pillar, causing the truck to lurch to a stop so suddenly that the dump-truck bed lifted a foot off the ground, spraying sand everywhere. The truck's impact tore the steel support beams right out of their concrete foundation. The entire building shook at the hit, and twenty feet of ceiling collapsed into the interior.

The Value Sense was a wreck. Dozens of jugs of milk had been knocked out of the dairy case and popped open on the floor. The center of the store had a furrow dug through it, and only a few outer aisles still had their shelves standing. The big diesel engine was still running hard, but it was stuck, plow driven halfway through the back wall.

"Son of a bitch," Earl muttered as he picked himself off the floor. The unbroken lights were flickering, and sparks shot from a crushed electrical box on the back wall. Fresh snow came flooding through the hole in the roof. Lifting his Thompson, he focused in on the cab of the truck. "Nikolai . . ."

Better safe than sorry. Earl fired a magazine of .45 ammo into the cab of the truck, puckering bullet holes through the door as he approached. Earl replaced the stick magazine in the Thompson as he ran up the side of a collapsed shelf, kicking bags of chips out of the way. He stuck the barrel through the driver's side window. *Empty.* Something had been jammed down on the accelerator. "Shit."

He glanced toward the ruined front of the store but could see nothing out there in the swirling storm. The engine was so obnoxious indoors that he could barely hear himself think, and the exhaust was pumping out a noxious cloud. Annoyed, he jerked the door open and reached down for the knife that had been used to wedge down the gas pedal.

Surprisingly, the blade had been stabbed through one of his own MHI patches. *What's that doing here?* He pulled the familiar happy face with horns off, noting that the patch was an old one, stained with dried blood. There was a backpack sitting on the seat, unzipped. Something wrapped in black electrical tape was visible inside the pack. Then Earl knew what a colossal mistake he'd made. "Shit!" he exclaimed, diving away from the bomb.

He didn't quite make it.

⧉ Chapter 12 ⧉

I spent that last full moon free on the island. It was a frustrating place for the animal to be let free. There was nothing interesting to hunt. No animals larger than a seagull to kill. My other half was frustrated, angry, and, if I had my way, it was going to remain that way forever.

That next morning, I had sat on the rocks of my nameless island, waiting for Santiago's boat to arrive to take me back to Cayos de Tiburon with all of my earthly possessions, which consisted of a satchel of worn-out clothes, the books Santiago had given me, a few supplies, and my Smith & Wesson .45.

Something was wrong. Different. There was a sensation in the air. I could feel it, but I couldn't describe it. At the time I chalked it up to the excitement of returning to the world.

It was the same boat as usual. They were downwind, so I saw before I smelled it, and immediately I knew something wasn't right. Instead of one passenger, there were three. By the time I recognized the other werewolves' scents over the diesel stink of the engine, it was too late.

The male was far taller than me, African, wearing a loose cotton vest over a torso made of solid muscle. He actually grinned when he saw me coming down the sand. The female was strikingly beautiful, Latina, with long black hair and a nice shape under her formless white shirt, but then again I hadn't seen a woman in three years.

Then I saw Santiago crumpled on the bow. Dried blood coated half his face, and fresh blood was still leaking from his nose and mouth. He'd been beaten to a pulp. Hemp ropes had been tied around his arms. He looked up at me through swollen eyes and mouthed the words I'm sorry.

The African, huge and intimidating, effortlessly hoisted Santiago by the back of the neck to better show him off. "Greetings, my son." The werewolf's voice boomed, and somehow I knew that this was the leader. "I've come a long way to find you. I've sensed you for some time."

"Let go of my friend," I ordered as I pulled the Smith from behind me. I cocked the hammer and aimed at the stranger's face. I only had one silver bullet. "Let him go right now."

"Now, you know that isn't how it's done," the stranger said, his accent thick. "What foolish lies did this old priest put in your head?"

"Kill him!" the female shrieked. "Kill him like he killed my sister!"

I turned the gun on her. Her sister? "Lady, I don't know who're you're even talking about."

"The one that made you. I made her. So that makes you mine. You are of my pack, upstart," the stranger said as he passed Santiago over to the girl. She immediately put a long knife to my friend's throat. The male hopped out of the boat and onto the sand. "I am Seamus. This"—he gestured at the island and the ocean—"is all mine. I lead. Many follow."

"Kill him," the girl said again. Santiago grimaced as the blade cut into his neck. "For Maria!"

"Hush, girl," he ordered, not even bothering to look back. He was getting closer. "You can feel it, can't you? You know that I am the father."

I could see now that his eyes were wrong. Too bright, an almost luminescent shade of gold, and I realized that I didn't know what mine looked like when I was about to change. It wasn't like I had spent much time looking in the mirror lately.

"My children must do as I say. Live as I would have them live. Let me teach you. Not the lies of this priest. Let me show you real freedom, what it is to run free, to join the hunt, to live as gods."

I hadn't shot a gun in a very long time, but I'd gotten plenty of practice in my life and some things you don't forget. The front-sight blade barely quivered as I spoke. "Let him go or you'll regret it."

Seamus laughed at my folly. "You will not best me, upstart. That's not the way. Join the pack or die. Which one will it be?"

Nobody had ever accused a Shackleford of being the hesitating type. I pulled the trigger.

⁜ ⁜ ⁜

The huge explosion rocked the grocery store, blowing out every remaining window inside, and most of those in the surrounding buildings as well. Car alarms went off on nearby streets. The town may not have heard the evening's gunshots over the noise of the storm, but that certainly would wake them up.

"Not what I expected," the Alpha stated matter-of-factly. He, the witch, and her two servants were sitting unnoticed on the roof of a house across the street from the grocery store. They had the best seats in the house. The witch's magic assured that they would not be seen as Nikolai Petrov sprinted across the parking lot, following the tracks of the snowplow. "I'd assumed that this would be a more traditional contest. This is *cheating*."

"I told you they were unpredictable," the witch insisted. "You assumed these men would still be caught up in the old ways. They've evolved, just as you have. Petrov is far too ruthless to play games, even more so when it is personal. It appears he'll be the one whose soul we harvest."

"Perhaps you're right." The Alpha clutched the amulet of Koschei to his chest. Like him, it was hungry. It would have to be fed soon, regardless of the outcome of this battle. He watched as Nikolai took cover at the hole in the wall. The Russian risked a quick peek inside at the flaming chaos, raised his rifle, and entered. "But I wouldn't count the Hunter out so easily."

The witch smirked. "Ten quid says Petrov annihilates him."

The Alpha wasn't sure what a quid was in dollars, but he knew from secondhand experience that Harbinger was an extremely difficult man to kill. "You're on."

Heather had been going from house to house, waking people up, and had been trying to convince Mrs. Valikangas that she needed to grab her deer rifle and get to safety when the explosion rocked the town.

The retired elementary-school teacher had been incredulous and had told Heather that she didn't look well, that she needed to come inside to warm up by the fire, and that she was worried about her. Heather had grown more frustrated by the second. Her stomach was growling as badly as her disposition when she'd heard the concussion. They were quite a way down the street, but the shock wave had shaken the Valikangases' front porch hard enough to dislodge chunks of snow from the roof. It took a second for the rumble to subside.

She had run down the steps, head turned in the direction of the blast. Heather reasoned that the storm must be letting up, though it certainly didn't feel like it, because she could hear much better now. See farther, too.

"What was that?" Mrs. Valikangas screeched.

"The Value Sense just blew up," Heather snapped. It was obvious. "Are you blind?"

The woman just stared at the curtain of falling snow between them and Main. "How can you—"

"Be quiet," she hissed at the woman that had been her fifth-grade teacher. Heather had the sudden and uncharacteristic urge to smack the obstinate lady in her stupid mouth. A seething anger bubbled up inside, and Heather wanted nothing more than to jump up on that porch and—

Calm down. Heather forced herself to take a deep breath. The angry feeling passed. "I told you. We're under attack by a bunch of creatures." It sounded asinine, but Heather didn't have time to argue with every person in town. "Wake up your family and get your guns. Head for the bunker at the high school or stick around here and get eaten. I don't care."

Not waiting for Mrs. Valikangas's reaction, Heather stomped back to the truck, tossed her shotgun on the passenger seat, and climbed in. Mrs. Valikangas was shouting, but Heather ignored her; it was something about how Heather's eyes were *strange*. But then she slammed the door and cut off the old teacher's ramblings. The tires spun but found enough traction to get her moving toward the grocery store. The sight of multiple flashlights in her rearview mirror told her that at least somebody she'd contacted had listened.

She'd found the silver ammo that Harbinger had told her about, and one of the cans had been 12 gauge, so she'd loaded the Winchester 1300 with it. Strangely enough, Heather was no longer afraid. It was the weirdest thing, but she was actually looking forward to finding one of those monsters. She fantasized about blasting the creatures into bloody bits with her shotgun. They'd killed *her* friends, attacked *her* town. This was *her* territory. She'd blow their heads off. Rip their hearts out. Then she would eat them.

"What?" Heather hit the brakes and stopped in the middle of the street. "What are you doing?" Her gloves were on the steering wheel, vibrating uncontrollably, and it wasn't from the engine. She had just been daydreaming about killing a monster and eating its still-beating heart. She was breathing too fast. Her heart was pounding in her chest. "Keep it together. Keep it together."

Surely it was the stress. It was from seeing her friends die. It was from having the men from the government try to murder her. It was from being attacked. It was just stress.

The stress was making her hungry. "I'm starving." Harbinger had packed the cooler with food, and she hurriedly removed a package of lunch meat, yanked open the plastic, stuffed it in her mouth, and started chewing. "Crap. I'm starving and I'm talking to myself," she mumbled around a mouthful of roast beef. "I'm falling apart."

The protein calmed her down. She still had work to do. Heather got the truck moving again. Something was going down at the Value Sense, and it was her duty to help. Agitated, distracted, and increasingly erratic, Heather still had a purpose, and by the time she got to Main Street, she was focused on that.

There was only one thing that was still bugging her. *Where is that damn humming noise coming from?*

Now, that hurt.

Earl tried to roll over, but couldn't. Something was wedged against his side—correction—*in* his side. All he could see was a red haze. His eyes had been pulverized. He gasped in a partial lungful of dust, and that immediately set off a painful cough thick with blood. It took him a moment to remember where he was.

Nikolai, you sneaky son of a bitch.

Anger gave Earl purpose. He had to move quickly. The Russian would be coming for him. *What am I stuck on?* His limbs didn't want to respond at first. The bones in his right hand had been crushed and wouldn't close into a fist, but he was able to leverage his left around, though it caused a terrible pain to radiate up his side as he turned. He found the source of his problem: he'd landed on a broken piece of shelving, and a jagged chunk of metal had been driven through his armor. *Well . . . damn.*

Putting his hand flat against the shelf, he shoved himself up. Six inches of painted steel slid out from between his ribs. The pain was ridiculous. He was thankful for the ringing in his ears, because he was certain that pulling himself off that thing would have made an awful noise.

He flopped down the shelf, rolling onto the floor into a pile of broken glass bottles. *Vinegar?* At least he could still smell. He'd landed in the pickle aisle. Earl hated pickles.

Keep moving. Blind, he staggered upright. His body was already healing, reordering his cells back to one of its two distinct templates, but healing would take time that he didn't have. Instinct told him to give in to the pain and the anger, to let the wolf free. But Nikolai had just used a bomb, which meant that he'd mop up with a gun, which meant that Earl needed his brain more than he needed his ferocity. If he was going to change, he needed to find a safe place to do it.

Can't see. Explosive concussion was hell on the soft jelly of the human eyeball. *Hell.* Nikolai was coming. He had to get to cover. Despite bleeding freely from his eyes and ears, Earl was perfectly calm as he quickly ran through his predicament. *Smell.* He inhaled more dust. The truck was smoking, but it wasn't burning. It was a distraction, but under that . . . Milk. Meat. *Escape. That way. Hurry.* Coughing, Earl staggered for the back of the store. He made it three steps, tripped, fell, but forced himself back up again. His right ankle had snapped, so he dragged that boot along behind him.

The blast had crippled him. Earl could feel the blood gushing from his body in great hot rivulets. He'd been torn open in multiple places. Bones ground unnaturally against each other. The pain would have rendered a lesser man incoherent. Groping blindly, Earl smelled milk as his boot dragged through the puddle.

Earl fell against the coldness of the dairy case. The rips in his flesh burned as the skin pulled tight over them, pinching off the leaks. Clumsily, he touched his face and then cringed as he discovered that his cheek was hanging off, dangling slick and wet. He shoved it back over his exposed teeth. Nikolai would smell the blood and track him easily. Blind, he wouldn't stand a chance. Hiding was out of the question.

Use your head. Earl forced himself up, knowing what he had to do. He needed to be smart. He hit the back wall, smearing bloody handprints across the glass doors. By the time he found the swinging double doors of the stock room, the bones in his hands had reformed enough to make a fist.

Blood. Nikolai's nostrils flared. Beneath the smoke, thousands of competing food, chemical smells, and dust was the smell of fresh blood. There were dead werewolves and humans inside, and the plow blade had smeared at least one body across half the space, further confusing matters, but Nikolai could smell Harbinger, and the smell was one of injury and weakness.

No fear, though. Come to think of it, Nikolai had never smelled Harbinger's fear.

Got him. We got him! We've finally got him!

The Tvar was eager. Nikolai's pulse increased, his breathing came faster. The truck was in the back of the store, the dump bed full of sand barely visible beneath the collapsed ceiling tiles. He ran down the open path left by the plow, scanning back and forth, searching for Harbinger. The instant he saw him, Nikolai would put a silver round into his enemy's head.

It wasn't sporting. It wasn't fair. It certainly wasn't the way that instinct demanded, but there was no time for such niceties. The amulet had been freed, and such a potent device could never be allowed to fall into the hands of a monster like Harbinger.

Before he could even reach the back of the truck, the Tvar practically screamed inside his head. *There!*

His other half, with its simple animal cunning, often noticed things far quicker than his analytical human mind could. Then he understood the reason for the excitement. There was where Harbinger had landed. A massive smear of warm blood was on a broken shelf and a thick trail of droplets led away from it. Nikolai turned to the utterly demolished cab of the truck and noted how the sheet metal had been peeled and twisted by the explosive. The blast had hurled Harbinger twenty feet. He should have brought more explosives.

A jagged shaft of metal was coated in blood, bits of flesh still clinging to it. A handprint showed him where Harbinger had forced himself up. There were bloody boot prints, but only from one foot; the other was a drag mark. Nikolai couldn't tell if it was him or the Tvar, but one of them was extremely excited. Harbinger was vulnerable. Revenge was within his grasp. He lifted the Val and followed the trail.

Harbinger had fallen and stopped here for a moment. Nikolai crouched next to a waist-high refrigerator unit filled with butter, studying the signs quickly. So much blood had been lost that Harbinger would be extremely weak, but Harbinger had gotten back up, and the droplets were fewer and farther between. Now there were two boot prints instead of a drag mark. His foe's healing speed was impressive.

Hurry. Kill him! Kill him!

The Tvar was correct. He had to strike while Harbinger was weak. Nikolai moved faster; the trail was still easy to follow through the debris. Blood never lied. Harbinger had crashed into the glass doors of the dairy case, dragging himself along, and then he'd gone—

He's hiding in the back!

There were two bright red handprints, one on each of the swinging doors to the stock room, clear as day, as obvious a sign as could be given. Driven by the Tvar, Nikolai kicked the doors open and stepped through . . .

And saw nothing.

The lights were on. A large generator was in the rear, chugging away. There were rows of shelves on both sides, but the blood trail had just stopped. . . . Fragments were strewn everywhere, and part of the truck's plow was stuck through the wall, but there was no place for Harbinger to hide.

No! No! Where is he? You should have let me do it!

"Shut up!" Nikolai snapped. He knelt to smell the floor. Harbinger hadn't come in here. He'd left his smell on the door . . . and backtracked. The blatant handprints on the door had been a trick. The blood hadn't lied—Harbinger had. *"Yob tvoyu mat'!"* Nikolai stood, turning back to the store, just as a cloud of grit hit him right in the eyes.

Nikolai was blinded by the fistful of road sand. Earl could still barely see anything himself. His opponent was nothing but an angry red blur, but Earl could see well enough to know that the long tubular thing in Nikolai's hands was a rifle, so he knocked it away. The rifle clattered across the floor. With a roar, Earl grabbed Nikolai by the coat and hurled him out into the ruined grocery store.

Earl had needed time to regenerate, and that meant a place to hide. After touching the back doors, he'd leapt as far as he could manage toward the truck, hoping the spilling diesel smell would temporarily cover his tracks. He'd found the cold metal of the truck bed and, not seeing any alternative, had climbed in and buried himself in the sand. Most of his bones had knit back together, the bleeding had mostly stopped, and he could hear, and even see a little, but he was still terribly weak, disoriented, and now had sand stuck in every crevice of his body, and was therefore in a *really* bad mood.

Nikolai hit a shelf and went to the ground on his back. Earl was right behind. He landed on Nikolai and slugged him in the face. The Russian got his hands up, trying to shove Earl off, but Earl knocked the hands out of the way and hit him again. Then he got his weight onto Nikolai's chest, and Earl's fists were flying, one after another, slamming Nikolai's head over and over again, beating his face into a bloody mess.

"Cheatin' asshole!" Earl roared as he cocked back another right and tried to drive it *through* Nikolai's face. Nikolai's hand shot up, and he managed to hook his thumb into Earl's eye. The Hunter bellowed as Nikolai gouged it deep into the socket, but he didn't let up. Earl took Nikolai's head in both hands, raised it, and slammed it into the floor repeatedly. The second impact cracked the tile; the third, Nikolai's skull.

Gasping for breath, Earl raised his fist to strike again but stopped as a terrible pain shot up his side. He rolled off, cursing, reaching for the source of the agony, found the hilt of a folding knife sticking from his kidney, and jerked it out in a spray of blood. Nikolai raised one leg and kicked Earl in the chest, sending him crashing against the truck.

Blinking through the blood, Earl stepped forward. His opponent had already risen and had picked up a can of creamed corn. Earl threw the knife and missed. Nikolai threw the corn and didn't. The can smashed Earl's nose flat.

Nikolai used the moment to his advantage and charged, throwing his knee. He managed to hit Earl twice in the side while the Hunter's hands had involuntarily flown to his broken nose. Each hit lifted Earl off the ground before he was able to shove Nikolai away.

The two moved with incredible speed, striking, blocking, each impact sufficient to kill a normal man. Nikolai grabbed Earl by the straps of his armor and rolled, throwing him down the aisle. Earl landed hard on his shoulder, but his hand fell on a weapon. Nikolai came in fast, but Earl slammed the wine bottle over the Russian's head. The thump echoed through the entire store. Earl tried to club him again, but the bottle shattered across Nikolai's raised forearm. Wasting no time, Earl drove the jagged remains directly into Nikolai's abdomen. Nikolai's responding snap kick launched Earl through a snack display.

They met in the next aisle. The two circled, breathing hard as their bodies healed.

"You've gotten slow," Nikolai said, holding the contents of his stomach in with one hand.

"You've gotten sloppy," Earl snapped. "I can't believe you fell for that."

"You're the fool picking up booby traps. . . ." Nikolai wiped the blood and sand from his face. "You snuck up on me. You could have changed first. You could have torn me apart. Why didn't you?"

"I don't need to be a werewolf to kill a punk like you. We're in a town full of innocents," Earl answered, blinking as his eye popped back into place. Everything was much clearer now. "How dare you bring a challenge here?"

For a moment, Nikolai's expression changed. His voice was suddenly too deep. "*This is no challenge. You want a challenge? Let's—*" Then he grimaced, gnashing his teeth together. When he spoke again, his voice had returned to a normal pitch. "No . . . Not yet. You're a nuisance, Harbinger. A scourge."

"You ain't right," Earl said. The Russian was nuttier than he remembered.

"I'll never let you have it." Nikolai closed his eyes and shuddered. The other voice came back. "*Enough! We end this my way.*" Nikolai's eyes flashed gold. The transformation had begun.

"We can't do this here!" Earl took a step back. "You lunatic. You psychotic fucking lunatic. We're in a town. People *live* here."

"*Their mistake!*" Nikolai growled.

A transformation was incredibly risky, but he had no choice. Nikolai was changing, and if he didn't, he stood no chance. Earl knew that he'd just have to destroy Nikolai and then maintain enough control to get away from civilization until the blood lust died down. He unbuckled his armor. "You could've done this the old-fashioned way, and nobody else had to get hurt."

Nikolai's strange voice roared, his hands curling into fists, teeth visible, every vein in his neck standing out, as he fought . . . *something*. "You have no room to talk!" The first Nikolai shouted. "You killed her! She was innocent, defenseless!"

"I've killed a mess of folks. You're gonna need to be more specific."

"Lila!" Nikolai was enraged. Bloody spit flew from his lips. "You murdered her. You murdered my *wife*."

Earl paused, scowling. "I'm drawing a blank."

Nikolai screamed as he leapt.

"I told you we'd have a good fight," the Alpha said. The witch glowered at him, then went back to watching the battle. She didn't like being proven wrong.

He was pleased to see that he'd made the right choice. Harbinger and Petrov were both unbelievably fearsome while still in human form. He could only imagine what they would do in their purified state. Certainly, he could defeat either of them in a challenge, but he was beyond such things. No slave to the old ways, he would set his own path, forge a new way for all of their kind. Harbinger's foolish rules dictated that they were only men, nothing better, just different, and that they needed to live in humanity's bloated shadow. On the other hand, at least Petrov understood that they were superior beings, super predators, but even then, he was content to remain a mere tool for human ideologies and lacked the imagination to do what needed to be done. Petrov had a slave's mentality. Neither of them had the vision necessary to lead their kind into the future.

His superior senses told him that many humans were coming out of their homes. They'd heard Petrov's explosion. Some of them had realized that they were under attack and were spreading the word. The streets were coming alive. His children were confused. The magical storm had reached an unbelievable intensity. But none of that mattered. The important thing was which of the mighty werewolves below would be the one whose soul would power his ascension.

It was a perfect struggle. Nature had selected these two as the ultimate predators in their sphere. One would die. One would live to feed his hunger. Which would fuel his metamorphosis? The excitement was unbearable.

The witch pointed at the street below with her flesh hand. "We have visitors."

A black SUV was sliding into the parking lot of the Value Sense. The driver was clueless in the snow, and they gently collided with a light pole. The doors opened and five heavily armed humans got out. "MCB?" he asked. There should have been no way that they could have arrived through the storm. In fact, they wouldn't even know about the slaughter of Copper Lake until morning.

"Worse," the witch muttered. "Hunters." She held a very special hatred for monster hunters.

"Harbinger's men?" That seemed odd. His intelligence had said that Harbinger surely would have come alone. He would never involve his human pack in werewolf business.

"No . . . not even close. I'd know if they were. MHI has a certain . . . *swagger*. Nothing would make me happier than the arrival of MHI," the witch grumbled as she extricated herself from the thick snow of the roof. "Enjoy your show. I'll handle these intruders." She made a clicking noise, and one of her diggers stepped forward, ready to serve. Eight feet of armored monstrosity bowed before its witch. This time she pointed with her artificial hand. The steel gauntlet seemed disproportionately large sticking out from the sleeve of her fur coat. "Destroy those humans."

The massive digger leapt from the roof and fell silently to the ground two stories below. The Alpha nodded approvingly. The unnatural things were nothing if not efficient. It would eradicate those vermin. His attention returned to the grocery just as an ear-splitting howl rose into the night. The main event had just begun. "Beautiful."

"Look what you did to my Caddy!" Horst shuffled through the three feet of freshly accumulated snow to where the Escalade's front bumper was crunched into the light pole. It actually didn't look too bad, but Lins had screwed up. Sure, it was hard to drive through slush, but that was no excuse for scratching his ride. "Is that a dent? That's a dent. That's coming out of your pay, moron."

Lins was livid as he got out. "Screw you, Ryan. What do you expect in a blizzard?"

"Shoulda let me drive," Jo Ann said. "I'm at least—"

The sound that cut her off pierced all of the Briarwood team to their cores. It started as the cry of a man, filled with anger and pain, only impossibly loud, but as it went on the cry changed, becoming deeper, fiercer, seeming to linger far after any mortal lungs would have run out of breath, until it slowly mutated into a full-on animal howl. A primal, terrible cry, instinctively more terrifying than anything that could ever emanate from a natural creature. The storm had frozen Horst's skin, but that howl froze his blood.

The staff of Briarwood Eradication Services was actually quiet for once. Horst looked to his employees. Every one of them except for Loco was staring back at him with wide eyes. Their big man just grunted and went back to pulling his machine gun out of the Caddy, probably too dumb to be scared.

"I think I just pissed myself," Kelley said.

Jo Ann turned toward the grocery store. "What the *hell* was that?"

That was an actual monster. The other things they'd run into were nothing compared to that. The fear ran deep. It wasn't any sort of conscious, logical thought. It was deeper, coming from the lowest part of his brain, warning him that they needed to get away before that awful thing consumed them all. Horst forced himself to speak, and tried to sound as confident as possible. "That's the sound of money, baby."

Then there was a second howl, even louder than the first, and somehow Horst instinctively knew that this was a *different* werewolf. Lins jumped. "There's two of them? You didn't say nothing about two of them!"

They were chickening out. "Shut up!" he shouted. "Everybody shut your stupid mouths."

"This isn't nothing like those zombies we killed," Kelley exclaimed. "I'm outta here."

Jo Ann and Lins were babbling, too, as the three of them started getting back in the Caddy. His dreams were falling apart right in front of his eyes. His people were scared senseless. None of them were cowards, but they hadn't been expecting this. That howl was just wrong, and the answering one was even worse. He understood now that Stark had been telling the truth. This wasn't a normal werewolf; that thing in there was ancient, and therefore worth a huge PUFF bounty. They couldn't back out now. There was a reason the government had to pay such stupidly large bounties for this level of creature, because no sane person would willingly go looking for one.

Somehow, Horst found his courage. He was the leader of an elite company of monster hunters. If he walked away, it would be like all those stuck-up MHI chumps would be laughing at him. Ryan Horst had vowed that he was never going to be a nobody again.

He needed to do something quick. He thought back to his brief time with MHI. What would they have done? Those bozos were always motivated. What would Earl Harbinger have done? He would have gotten his crew fired up. *I can do that.* Horst reached into his coat, unsnapped his shoulder holster, and drew his FN Five-seveN® pistol. He hoisted it into the air and yanked the trigger.

The sudden bang got their attention. Horst realized how stupid that had been as soon as he'd done it, because the insides of his right ear suddenly felt like someone had hit it with a hammer. "Listen up!" he bellowed at the top of his lungs, waving his gun toward the giant hole in the grocery store. "This is what you signed up for. Pull yourselves together, damn it. Each one of those hairy bastards in there is worth at least fifty large. Fifty large! We came all this way to kill these things. We got guns. We got silver bullets. What do they got? Teeth? Shit. They got nothing! I am *not* going home until I got one of these bastards as a rug. You hear me? We're Briarwood, and we've come up here to show these animals who's boss."

The three mutinous members of his crew turned their heads sheepishly, afraid to look him in the eye. *Damn right.* Lowering his piece, Horst glared at them. After chewing them out, Earl Harbinger had always softened his voice when he was trying to make a point to the MHI Newbies, like they weren't worth raising his voice over, but it forced you to listen extra hard. So Horst tried it, speaking quietly, but firmly. "So get your shit together and let's go. We can *do* this."

They actually surprised him then. His people responded and went to work. There were a series of metallic *clacks* as weapons were readied. A smirk crossed Horst's face. *Damn. I'm good.*

Nikolai was on him in a flash, claws erupting from the ends of his fingers. Earl moved aside easily, the change pumping massive amounts of adrenaline through his system. His body was flushed with

heat. Despite the freezing wind blasting through the gaping wound in
the store, sweat rolled from every pore. Time slowed as Nikolai tore at
him, Earl swung with all his might, hand open, fingers wide, and was
rewarded with a spray of blood as his nails ripped through the
Russian's flesh.

His enemy stalked away, circling. Four lacerations crossed his
heaving chest, having cleanly sliced through his ammo pouches.
Nikolai ripped the canvas off and tossed it aside. "MURDERER,"
Nikolai roared, his jaw already distorting. *"I'll rip you apart for what
you did to her."* Nikolai leapt at him.

Earl caught his opponent in midair, using the momentum as a
weapon, and hurled Nikolai down the aisle. Earl got one ear sliced
nearly in half for the trouble.

Nikolai hit the floor, rolled, and slid on his knees to a gradual stop.
The change was fully upon him now. *"You die now,"* Nikolai gurgled.
He said more, but it was unrecognizable as he tore off his shredded
clothing. *"Die for thing you done."*

Earl had a hard time forming a response. His mind changed along
with his body. Words became hard to understand, even harder to use.
"Try me," he answered, his voice a distorted growl.

After the heat came the pain. It started in the bones and radiated
out from there. It was part fire, part grinding, all horrible. The pain in
his jaw grew as bones twisted, cracked, stretched, and reformed. Blood
leaked between his teeth as they changed, new sharp edges slicing
through gum tissue. Heart rate elevated, breath coming fast, Earl
cringed as his old skin ripped.

Nikolai was a mirror image as he went through the same process,
matching cracking bone for cracking bone. Dark gray hair grew
rapidly across the Russian's body.

Clothing. Constricting. Earl pulled off the rest of his armor and
kicked off his boots. The change wrenched through him, ten times
faster than when he'd first been cursed, but the pain was all still there,
just accelerated. *Burning. Twisting.*

Earl took a step forward. The soles of his feet were hard as leather,
but he screamed as they hit the floor, bones cracking, heel separating.
His toe claws dug through the garbage. Earl took another step, the
pain traveling up his leg, joints tearing, burning, reforming. Muscles
hardened, becoming tighter, and it was only because of long exposure

that he was able to keep moving. He fell onto all fours, but as the geometries changed, that didn't matter.

Earl scratched his claws into the floor and howled. The challenge had begun.

Earl was angry. Hungry.

Nikolai raised his face, showing his teeth in a vicious snarl. Earl wanted to eat that face.

As his mind descended into chaos and visions of cascading red, Earl's last rational thought was a desperate plea. *God. Help me now. Keep me sane. Kill enemy. Hurt no people. Amen.*

⫷ Chapter 13 ⫸

If I had used my one silver bullet on the Alpha, then Santiago would surely die with a knife through the neck. So I shot the girl. I was rusty, so it went right through the cheek, just under her left eye. It still killed her instantly though, and she went right over the side of the boat and took Santiago with her.

Seamus charged. He was already changing, faster than I could comprehend. He hit me harder than I'd ever been hit in my life. And I found myself halfway down the beach. I came up with a mouthful of sand, four lacerations that went clear to my rib cage, and a transforming werewolf coming right at me.

He called me a fool for challenging him. The voice had changed, the last word tapering off into a growl. He threw off the vest, and black hair was already growing across his body. His eyes were glowing, fingers were getting longer, bones were cracking. Within seconds the most fearsome werewolf imaginable was towering over me. It was unbelievably smooth compared to the clumsy twitching suffering I went through.

He could have torn my human head right off then, but instead he stopped and cocked his head while his fur rippled in the breeze, crouched on all fours, claws feeling the sand, while he waited for me to catch up. I was a challenge to his leadership. And though I didn't understand it at the time, a challenge was supposed to be met on equal terms. If it wasn't, then your victory didn't mean anything.

I could feel the animal inside, screaming to get out. It was angry. Angry at me. I had kept it locked up, only let it free when I had to. I'd mistreated it, but now I was calling on it to save my life. Furious, it could have denied me, left me to die, but it was part of me. And we both wanted to survive.

Let me tell you, the pain is fire. The jaw clenches spasmodically tight. Blood thunders in your eyes. Your muscles pulse with electric shocks of agony, clenching, unclenching, clenching again, so tight that at each surge you wish for death. You change. Down to the level of individual proteins, and you feel every single bit.

It hurts like a stone-cold motherfucker.

It didn't matter that there were no witnesses. He waited. That was the way it was done. To kill me unfairly would make his victory meaningless. We were werewolves, creatures of instinct and a strange tradition. One would die. One would live.

The pain ends, and then there is the euphoria. I was whole. Beast and man, one. I became We. Then the other werewolf attacked us with a ferocity that had never been imagined. Bigger, stronger, faster, more experienced, the enemy tore into us. Within seconds the sand was soaked red with our blood. We should have lost. Rolling, tearing, snapping, thrashing, and then our teeth were in his neck and hot arterial blood flooded our mouth.

He tried to shake us off. Claws opened our stomach, spilled the stinking bowels, but it was only pain. Pain was nothing compared to the blood in our mouth. We got a better angle and chomped harder, cracking vertebrae and slicing meat. The tearing continued as our enemy grew weaker and weaker, until the claws dropped away from our eviscerated stomach and lay twitching, grasping futilely.

Somehow, we'd defeated our better. Then the beast was gone, leaving me alone with the pain.

It was the first time I went through a challenge. It would not be the last.

❖ ❖ ❖

Lins held out his lighter, and the gas-soaked rag stuffed into the bottle caught fire. Kelley took that bottle and used it to light the one in his other hand. "Awesome!" the bearded firebug shouted as he started toward the grocery store, flaming Molotov in each hand. "I've got them now."

"Cover him," Horst ordered as he ground the butt of his rifle against his shoulder. The other three got their guns up, ready to shoot as Kelley hurried down the relatively cleared path left by the crashed plow, the dump-truck end of which was visible at the opposite end of the building. Kelley was cackling maniacally as he got within throwing range.

"What if there's some bystanders trapped in there?" Lins asked quickly, realizing that they hadn't talked through that possibility.

"Screw 'em," Jo Ann spat. "I'm not going in there."

Horst scowled, but his girlfriend had a point. They hadn't thought that far past "burn it down and shoot anything that comes out," but listening to the racket coming from in there, the idea of survivors was doubtful. "Sucks to be them, I guess."

Lins didn't seem to like that, but he went back to looking through the Aimpoint on his carbine and didn't speak up.

They'd divided up their one case of silver 5.56 ammo. Horst had bought everyone their own full-auto and then done just like that four-eyed geek Cooper had done during MHI training and yelled at them to only shoot semi-auto, and at ten bucks a pop for the Fed's "misplaced" ammo, he could understand why MHI only used the good stuff on missions. Horst had kept his FAL, along with a few mags full of silver .308 he'd managed to sneak out of Alabama when he'd left. Everyone except for Loco had gotten an M-4 carbine. He'd given him the M249 Squad Automatic Weapon, because it seemed logical to give the biggest dude the heaviest gun.

The plan was simple. Burn out super werewolf. Hose it down. What could possibly go wrong?

Their arsonist was in range. Kelley chucked the first Molotov squarely through the front of the store. The glass shattered, and gasoline ignited across the broken shelves. Kelley had said that if they had more time he would have made up a better mix with other petroleum products, because that would have really made it stick, but judging by how fast the fire spread, there was plenty of flammable material inside there already.

With a crazed gleam in his eyes, Kelley pumped one fist in the air, then switched the other Molotov to his throwing arm. He cocked back his arm to throw this one deeper inside, but then stopped, his head jerking to the side as something startled him. Trying to see what had distracted his man, Horst squinted, trying to figure out what the tall, narrow thing coming through the windblown snow was.

It was way too tall to be a person, and unless MHI had totally lied to him, it sure as hell wasn't a werewolf. Thin, its lump of a head bobbed rhythmically, and what looked like its baggy clothing swayed back and forth as it approached Kelley. Its pace would have seemed almost leisurely if each of its long, spindly steps hadn't covered such a massive distance.

"What is that?" Lins shouted.

Horst had no idea. He must have gotten kicked out of Newbie training before the day Paxton got around to giant, gray, metal, scarecrow robots. "Damn if I know." It caught up to the scrambling Kelley in three big steps. Screaming his head off, Kelley ran for it, flaming bottle sloshing dangerous and forgotten in his hand. The thing's arms were so long that they dragged through the snow. The creature lifted one arm, and Horst could see that the block that passed for a hand ended in three big points, like a mighty garden trowel. "Shoot it! Shoot it!"

The four of them opened fire. His earlier instructions about "rapid, aimed, semi-auto" went right out the window as everybody started shooting like mad. Holes puckered in the snow, sparks flashed off the monster, and Kelley looked down in disbelief as a plug of goose-down erupted from his coat as one of his teammates accidentally shot him through the chest.

"Don't shoot our guy!" Horst shouted, but it didn't matter. The creature swung its metal claw, striking Kelley in the arm. The bottle shattered as he went down, showering gas all over the burning rag and Kelley's coat. There was a flash as fire tore across their arsonist's body. Letting out an ungodly cry, Kelley thrashed and flailed away, flopping into the snow and rolling like mad as the fire melted clothing to skin. Within seconds he was engulfed in black smoke and orange flames. The tall creature stopped to watch.

"It killed Robb!" Jo Ann shrieked.

By the time Horst's gun was empty, Kelley had quit screaming. The monster watched for a moment, as if assessing whether Kelley was dead or not. When it was obvious that stop, drop, and roll hadn't worked out, its misshapen head swiveled up on its too-long neck and it emotionlessly started toward them.

Everyone else had run dry except for Loco, because he had a two-hundred-round belt in the SAW and was actually firing it in short, controlled bursts like he'd been told. Even with one eye, Loco was the only one that seemed to actually be hitting the monster. "Reload! Reload!" Horst shouted as he struggled to get another magazine out of his pocket.

The creature was closing fast. Its giant legs pumped methodically, leaving a trail of huge, three-toed, birdlike footprints behind it. Most of their panicked shots were missing, and the ones that did hit didn't seem to have much effect.

Closer now, its head was round, featureless. It had no eyes, no nostrils, just a long slit from one side to the other that had to be a mouth. The neck was abnormally long, and the front of its neck swung back and forth with a jiggling mass of loose skin. Parts of it seemed to be made of a rough metal shell, but the joints looked like gray meat. What he'd thought had been loose clothing was actually *skin*, swaying rhythmically. It was like an obese man that had lost tons of weight, way too fast, leaving a skeleton inside a sack of drooping skin, and then the devil had crammed the whole mess into a suit of rusting metal armor. "Slow down and aim!" he shouted. "Aim for the soft bits!"

Taking his own advice, he put the sights on the bulbous mass of a head. Horst had used guns his entire life, mostly cheap ones fired out car windows while driving past the homes of people who owed his uncle money, but it was MHI that had actually taught him to *aim*. Turns out that he was pretty decent at it.

The bullet hit the monster right between the eyes, or would have, if it'd had eyes. It stopped, a plug of meat dangling from its face, leaking green slime. Jo Ann stepped past him, shouting, "How you like that! Huh? How you like that!" as she shot at its head.

She got her answer a second later when the creature lumbered over to her, its gash of a mouth stretching wide open. Its two huge hands landed on her shoulders, trapping her. Jo Ann's head disappeared into its mouth as its metal hands scooped her up. "Holy fu—" she screamed as the creature lifted her and reared its head back. Her lower half was visible as it choked her down, her feet kicking wildly. The flap of loose skin under the monster's neck stretched, like a pelican eating a fish, as it swallowed her whole. Her shoes disappeared as she travelled down its long throat. The skin stretched in places, Jo Ann's body visible through the slick membrane as she rolled around and fought inside the pouch.

The creature lowered its head and closed its mouth gash. It rumbled around, towering over Horst. The skin stretched madly as Jo Ann kicked, like a kid playing under a blanket. Her muffled cries could barely be heard as the now-full pouch dangled across the front half of the creature's body.

A giant, chicken-footed, faceless scarecrow-robot-pelican monster had just *eaten* his girlfriend. "Fuck this. Retreat!" Horst said as he turned and ran like mad. Lins was already twenty feet ahead, sprinting for the road.

Fury boiled Earl's blood. Nikolai landed on him, teeth taking a chunk of meat and pale hair from his snout. Earl swatted him off, and one claw cut Nikolai's nose in two. They clashed again, both reaching for the other's throat, hind claws searching for soft guts to pull out, teeth snapping for jugulars.

They crashed through the human garbage, spilling blood. Earl was weak from before. His muscles quivered. His body was a furnace, burning itself to stay alive. Moving so fast. Apart again. Circling. Attacking again. Slashing. Earl's chest was torn open, but not deep through bone. Nikolai's claw flashed again, but Earl was ready. His teeth pierced flesh!

The taste of blood. Nikolai's arm ripped open, his wrist torn, and he retreated. Weak.

Nikolai attacked, his teeth grinding on bone, but it was shallow. Earl's claws opened Nikolai's guts. He retreated, fell. Earl bit again but missed the neck, snapping bones in Nikolai's shoulder. Claws raked Earl's back. Claws slipped on his guts. He could taste his own blood.

But the enemy was weak, trying to get away. No escape for him. Must kill. Only kill. Earl howled.

Nikolai was dying. Earl tore into him and blood sprayed. Meat filled Earl's mouth. Filled his belly. Earl's hunger cried out. Claws ripped. Ribs broke! There was Nikolai's beating heart.

Distraction. Glass shattered and fire spread.

FIRE.

It burned Earl, his hair on fire. Nikolai screamed as fire burned him, too. Earl pulled away, and the fire was between them. Human garbage burned black. Nickolai's heart still pumped. Red. So close. Earl tried to pass through, but the fire burned too hot.

Earl retreated, his body still on fire. *RAGE!* Nikolai fled. Ran. Nikolai's fear stink was strong. Earl *never* stank of fear. Earl howled so the world would know his anger.

Circle. Pounce. Nikolai couldn't escape. Earl moved away from the fire, to the safety of the cold. The snow melted as it hit the burning, and the water cooled.

There was movement outside the store: Guns. Humans in the snow. An unknown threat stalked them . . . *Hunters? My Hunters?*

The human Earl forced his way to the top. The moon was not here. The Hum was not loud. Earl could still think. He could smell nothing over his own burned hair, but Earl knew these were Hunters. Hunters were *his* pack. Nikolai was forgotten. *Hunters in danger. No one messes with my Hunters.* Earl hurled himself out into the snow.

The monster swallowed a human. That made Earl mad. He forgot about Nikolai. Closer now. He could see better. These were not *his* Hunters. But they were Hunters, and that was enough for Earl.

The monster smelled of deep earth. Of ground and mud. It stank of Old Ones. Rot. Corruption.

Earl covered the space in a few bounds. Tall. He hit it low, diving into its legs. Its shell was very hard. But Earl sensed flesh at the gaps, and flesh was weak. Slashing, he searched for tendons. The skin was thick, hard to cut. But Earl was mad, and the skin broke, blood-pus coming out. Tendon-meats snapped.

The monster fell. Earl was on it, ripping. He never stopped ripping. The top part had less metal, more soft, easy to hurt. It had a long neck, and that long neck was weak. Earl bit the weak neck. His mouth filled with the blood-pus. *POISON!*

Earl spat it out. It burned his mouth. He leaped away and gagged in snow.

The monster rose silently. One leg was crippled but there was no fear smell. Skin moved on monster's front. The human was still alive inside. Earl circled, chewing snow to clean poison from teeth.

The monster opened its slitted mouth and vomited the human into the snow. The human female moved weakly, covered in the blood-pus. She smelled like she'd live.

The monster was lighter with pouch empty. Faster now. Ready for Earl. Claws were metal, made to rend. Monster was old, grown strong, deep in the ground. Monster reeked of dark magic: Hood's magic. Earl was weak and his muscles quivered. He was cold and sluggish. Nikolai had hurt Earl. The monster was made of metal and death.

But Earl was mad.

"Ladies and gentlemen, we have our winner."

It was Harbinger that emerged from the burning grocery store. His lighter-colored fur was easier to identify, even scorched and soaked with blood. Despite the fight, he still moved with blinding speed, covering the length of the parking lot in a split second. The witch watched, fascinated, as Harbinger effortlessly took down her massive digger. "It appears you were right."

"I'm always right. Pay up," the Alpha said.

Harbinger made the mistake of biting the rancid flesh of the digger and had to back away from the vulnerable kill. The Alpha marveled as the digger rose and disgorged the woman. The Old Ones' servants were remarkably sturdy. Harbinger, on the other hand, was ragged. Nikolai had almost taken him, but almost wasn't good enough when dealing with a wily killer like Harbinger.

"Sorry. I left my purse at home. Are you ready to harvest his soul?"

The time had come to unleash the full power of the Deathless. His army of *vulkodlak* were begging to be born. It was time to finish the job that evolution had started. "Take him."

Earl was focused on killing the monster. He paid no attention to the large human male until the ax was planted between his shoulder blades.

The ax bit deep. Earl screamed.

The Hunter wrenched the ax out. Earl fell.

Confusion. Blood filled his lungs. The human thought he was enemy. The ax rose. Earl wanted to strike, but the Hum was weak. So Earl could think. *No.*

Earl spared the Hunter's life. The ax came down. Earl caught it in his claw. The Hunter was strong, but no match for Earl. Earl took the ax away, took it in both hands and snapped it like a twig. He swatted the Hunter down, careful not to lay him open. The big Hunter scrambled back, the fear stink present, but the smell of determination stronger. Earl tossed the ax bits aside, growling. The Hunter knew death had come, but stood to fight anyway.

"Loco . . . Help . . ." the female cried from the snow.

Fists raised, the Hunter hesitated. *Go.* Earl dipped his head at the Hunter, dismissing him, then turned to face the real threat.

The monster had not moved. Another monster approached. Two monsters faced him now. Earl coughed blood as he healed. His body burned, weak but full of hate. The big Hunter got close enough to the monsters to scoop up the female Hunter. The monsters ignored him. They'd come for Earl. Earl waited for the humans to flee. Then he charged.

FIRE!

But it was not fire. It was light. So bright it burned like fire. The light came through him. He saw his bones through his flesh. Weak, shaking, Earl roared as he pushed on.

"Impressive, isn't he?" Voice familiar. From before. The pretender. The false Alpha. "Hold him."

The light was a pillar, shooting straight into the sky. The snow melted. The air was thick. Earl could barely move, but he did. He would kill this challenger. Rip him apart. The light burned hotter, and Earl was blind. Cold metal hit him on both sides. Iron fingers locked together around his arms. Earl kicked and thrashed, snapping his jaws, but only filled his mouth with more of the poison blood-pus.

"I'm ready," a female said.

"Do it, Lucinda," the false Alpha shouted.

She began to chant. The sound of Old Ones' magic.

The human part of Earl forced itself to the top. *Concentrate. Get out of here. Can't fight dark magic.*

A human hand grabbed his throat. Earl tried to bite the arm off, but the other hand squeezed his jaws shut. The hands were *strong.* "I've waited for a long time for this, Harbinger." The chanting was louder. Louder than the wind. Louder than the light that burned. The pretender shouted in his ear. Earl could smell him now. It was *familiar.* Long ago, but not quite right. "I brought you both here because the two of you were the finest of our kind. Nikolai would have done just as well, but I want you to know I'm glad it's you. I'm glad you're the one."

Earl felt the light burning through him, pulling him apart. The pain was worse than changing. With his muzzle crushed closed, Earl choked on his screams of agony.

"You feel that? Do you *taste* it?" the pretender asked. "That's your power being consumed. You need to understand how much this means to me, how much this means for our people. From your soul will be born a mighty army. In future generations, when our people rule this world, your sacrifice will *never* be forgotten."

Something is wrong. Though his body was changed, Earl could think clearly.

Chaotic images flashed in his mind, one after the other, each one tearing through his head like the shuffling of cards. He could reason, he could remember everything, and he followed along as the magic cataloged his entire life. For one split second Earl's mind was complete, the werewolf and the human, truly one, and Earl *saw*. The werewolf spirit travelled across generations; each life appeared for an instant then vanished. The visions came faster and faster as the pain grew to a crescendo.

Then the visions stopped, and Earl witnessed the beginning of all werewolves.

The agony pulled Earl back to the present. Wracked with horrific pain, it was as if his body were being unraveled like a great rope by the burning light of Old Ones' magic. The rope split into cords. The cords split into smaller strings. Again and again, as he was spread through the light. The werewolf side broke away, and the ancestral memories disappeared with it. There was a sucking vortex on the pretender's chest, absorbing every other string. Leaving some, harvesting others.

The vortex ended in a three-fingered claw.

I'm dying. For the first time, Earl smelled his own fear.

The false Alpha drew close and whispered in Earl's ear. "Thank you, Father."

Earl felt his life end.

The chanting reached a fevered pitch. The light consumed everything. A sudden concussion rocked the world as the vortex was filled.

The pathetic human body hung between the two diggers. The Alpha rested his hand on the side of Harbinger's blood-soaked head. There was no pulse. No breath. The amulet of Koschei had been fed. A great man had fallen.

"It's done . . . ," the witch gasped. She took a few halting steps, then sank to the ground, exhausted. Her metal hand made a clanking noise as it hit the bare asphalt. The spell had blown the parking lot clear of snow.

He should have felt triumphant, but instead he was plagued with a sense of loss. It made sense, he supposed. For a new age to begin, an old one had to come to an end. The Alpha removed his hand from Harbinger's head and wiped the blood on his pants. "Release him," he ordered the diggers softly.

The witch made a clicking noise with her tongue. Her creatures immediately complied. The joints of their metal claws snapped apart, dumping Harbinger's body in an unceremonious heap. "Gently!" he bellowed, outraged at the lack of respect.

The snow had been temporarily burned from the sky by the amulet's power. It began to fall again. Softly this time. In the distance his children howled as they continued their assault on the town. They were answered by gunfire. The prey were fighting back.

The witch placed her human hand on his arm. "There's still much to do," she suggested. "Our time's short."

He took one look at Harbinger's still form, crumpled there. She was right. They needed to have everything in place by dawn. His mission depended on it. "I know," he answered as he walked away. The witch was a few steps behind. Her diggers, one walking, and one limping, followed silently.

If the MCB didn't slag this place with nuclear fire before the night was through, the Alpha promised that he would return to this spot someday and place a statue in Harbinger's memory. He had been a hero to the werewolf race.

As a young man, I'd often been accused of thinking I was invincible. I took risks that others found mad, but I kept on surviving. As a boy I disobeyed my daddy's orders and tagged along on all sorts of dangerous things. It was a game to me. I joined the AEF and survived bullets, disease, poison gas, and suicide charges across no-man's-land. I came home and killed things that sane men couldn't even comprehend. After a while, folks all said the same thing. I was either crazy or invincible or both. I suppose I even started to believe it myself. God had given me a mission, and that mission was to kill monsters. Becoming a werewolf was like God sending me a message.

"Yes, my son. You are invincible. Now get back to work."

"Twelve. Thirteen. Fourteen—"

So cold . . .

"Fifteen. Sixteen. Seventeen—"

There was pressure on his chest as someone pushed down in rhythm with the counting.

"Eighteen. Nineteen. Twenty—"

It was freezing. He was lying on the ice.

The counting stopped. Hands tilted his head back and opened his mouth. The soft lips that were placed against his were either feverishly hot or he was so cold that they just seemed that way in comparison. Breath was forced down his airway into his lungs. The warmth left him . . .

And returned to desperately pushing on his ribs. "One. Two. Three—"

I'm alive. Well, don't that beat all?

Earl gasped and began to cough. The pressure left his chest. He cracked open his eyes. A woman was hovering over him. The thick snow falling past her created the illusion of a halo around her flaming red hair. "Harbinger, can you hear me?"

Heather . . . Why couldn't he smell her? He tried to move. The blood splattered all over his naked body had frozen into slush, and his back was stuck to the pavement. He was dizzy. His hearing was muffled. Everything seemed dark, like his eyes were cloudy. Why was he so cold?

The Hum was gone.

"Harbinger." Heather waved a hand in front of his eyes. "Stay with me."

For the first time in over eighty years, the Hum was *gone.* The world had gone silent.

He was pretty sure that the moon hadn't exploded. It was impossible. There was no way that could happen.

"What? What're you saying?" she leaned closer and put her ear close enough to hear.

His voice was barely a whisper. "I'm human."

⁜ ⁜ ⁜

I was mostly human by the time I was coherent enough to shove my guts back in.

Silver isn't the only way to kill a werewolf, just the easiest. We heal at a remarkable pace, but it takes energy, and there is only so much available. Outpace that, and we die. Lose enough blood, and you shut down, or inflict enough damage, and we're done. Or you could end up like Seamus, his head only barely attached to his body by a handful of bloody fibers. Apparently that worked, too.

Despite having his hands tied behind his back, Santiago had somehow managed to struggle ashore. He was hurt bad from the beating, bones broken, bleeding internally, I could smell the death building up in his tissues.

Santiago was delirious by the time I got him back in the boat and we set out toward help, the pathetic little motor running as hard as it could.

His eyes were unfocused. "You're alive . . ."

"We're going to get you some help."

"I knew you could do it. I knew you could control the monster. God told me you would. He sent me to you."

He was incoherent. "Just hold on, Santiago."

"He has given you a gift. You—" He began to cough. I could hear the bones in his chest grating. "A great and terrible gift . . . Use it for good . . ."

Those were his last words. I was alone except for the sound of the motor and the noise of the tides. The ocean was a stark and endless blue that I'll never forget.

PART 2

The Hunter

⊰≾ **Chapter 14** ≽⊱

It was early spring when I arrived in Okinawa, only one month after being given the option of serving my country again or losing my PUFF exemption. It wasn't the first time I'd been drafted. Each time was the same. There was always some new government asshole who had to lord it over me that I was a werewolf, and therefore at their mercy. I would have gone if they'd just asked nice.

This wasn't like when the Axis had been dabbling in black magic and the OSS had created their first special task forces to deal with it. What better way to fight monsters than with monsters? They'd pulled me in early for those. Originally, I'd thought I was going to sit out Korea, but they'd brought me in as a "consultant" when the Chinese had starting dabbling in the supernatural. I had developed a reputation as a go-to guy in certain circles.

Over the last two years I had been hearing about some strange things the commies had been doing, and I was frankly surprised that it had taken this long for the government to put together another special task force. It only stood to reason that I'd eventually end up in Vietnam.

It was an Air Force captain that met me as I got off the chopper. As a "civilian consultant" I didn't merit a salute, and I'd only been a corporal in the AEF, but he gave me one anyway. I just scowled and asked what that was for.

His name tag read Conover, though I was certain that probably wasn't his real name. He was an athletic young man, wearing enough cologne to really grate on a werewolf's nose. "I was told about your OSS record. Very remarkable. North Africa, Paris, Berlin, and then all over the Pacific."

"Don't ever salute me again . . . Snipers, you know."

He looked around, confused. "We're in Okinawa."

"And it's much nicer than the last time I was here. No flaming samurai demons."

Captain Conover tried to be as welcoming as possible. He even attempted carry my bags, but he was only human and ended up having to drag one of them to the waiting jeep. We rode across the base until we came to a small concrete building. "Welcome to Special Task Force Unicorn."

"Unicorn? Really? What Pentagon dipshit makes this stuff up?"

"Everybody knows there's no such thing as unicorns, Mr. Wolf."

I hated the new code name.

⁂ ⁂ ⁂

His dreams were of the beginning. The fiercest beast in the world had been captured, chained, tortured, and mutilated. Then mankind made a terrible mistake, all in hope of making a weapon.

The dream broke and faded as conciseness returned. He couldn't remember how the dream ended, but it hadn't been pretty.

At first he thought the Hum was back, but it was just the buzzing noise of the big circular lights hanging from the ceiling. He woke up under a basketball hoop. A blue banner that read GO BULLDOGS was on the wall behind the hoop. The place was crowded, echoing with voices, some scared, some excited, nervous, angry, confused, and under that was that most common refugee sound of all: children crying.

He was so hungry that it bordered on nausea. Every spare ounce of fat on his body had been consumed to fuel the change. It took him a minute to piece together that he was lying on a blanket on a hardwood gymnasium floor, somehow alive, tired, weak, sore, in desperate need of a smoke, and by some miracle, not a werewolf.

I'm human. Thank you, Lord, I'm a man again.

Earl Harbinger was a big proponent of having a flexible mind and adapting quickly, but having an unbreakable curse broken was going to take a bit to sink in. He'd long ago accepted that he would die a werewolf. There was no cure, never had been. Yet the mystery Alpha's magic amulet had sucked the werewolf right out of him.

The amulet had been shaped like a claw, but with only three fingers and a thumb. Inside of it had been carved a normal human hand. Already, he couldn't remember the dream, but the amulet had been in it. It had been important way back then, and it was important now that this other Alpha had it.

As for the Alpha, he'd called Earl *father*. That made no sense. Earl knew his kids. He was a devoted family man, and even in the many long years since his wife had passed, he was pretty sure he'd have known if he'd sired any more. Earl might not have been as fundamentally devout as his saintly mother had wished, but he wasn't the kind of man that left a trail of bastard children behind, either.

That left one other possible use for the word. . . .

But first things first. He needed to assess the situation. Grimacing, Earl sat up, feeling a deep ache in his chest where Deputy Kerkonen had pummeled his ribs doing CPR. It had been a long time since he'd borne that type of pain for more than a few seconds. He'd forgotten about the concept of *lingering*. Other than the soreness and the hunger, everything seemed to be in one piece.

There were at least two hundred people milling around the gym. Most of them had taken the time to get dressed, but several had arrived in their PJs. At least half the adults were armed. The sight of so many guns, mostly deer rifles and duck guns but with a smattering of black rifles and riot shotguns, made him glad that this was going down in a rural area where people still had their heads screwed on right about personal defense.

There was a knot of people conversing a few feet away. A raven-haired woman in a red parka saw him watching and stomped over in a pair of giant snow boots. "You're awake. Good. About damn time. Deputy Heather said you knew what was going on." She was rather tall, probably in her mid-forties, and struck him as the kind of person used to being in charge. The men she'd been talking with followed her over. "Well, spill it, mister."

He would've gotten up, but realized that under the blanket he was buck naked, and there were children present. "Who're you?"

"Nancy Randall, Copper County Council." She glanced around the gym. "Only surviving member, as far as I can tell." The men flanking her regarded Earl with blatant suspicion. One had a Mossberg 500 and the other had an AR-15. Neither was overt enough to actually point their guns at him, but he could tell they thought about it. He couldn't particularly blame them, either. It had been a stressful night, and he was an outsider and therefore suspect. "And since I personally saw a hairy wolfman rip the mayor's head off, and Heather said the sheriff lost his neck, I suppose I'm sort of in charge of this mess. So, what's the deal?"

"Name's Harbinger. I'm a Monster Hunter." She seemed like the type to appreciate brevity, so Earl didn't beat around the bush. "Well, Nancy, your town's being attacked by a pack of werewolves. They've got you isolated, and I figure they plan on slaughtering everyone here by dawn."

The two men exchanged glances. The one with the Mossberg was fat, bald, and sweating. The one with the AR was thin, young, and nervous.

"That's insane," the thin one said.

"Zip it, Phillip," Nancy ordered. "Werewolves . . . That's exactly what Heather said you'd say."

"I shot one in the *head*. Point-blank," the fat one said. "I blew its brains out! Then it got back up and jumped out a second-story window and ran away like nothing had happened. I'll believe anything right now."

"Yes, Steve," Nancy said in the most patronizing manner possible. "We've all heard about the brains thing already. Blah, blah, blah. Give it a rest already." She turned back to Earl. "So, what do we do about these damn things?"

He could mount a defense against the werewolves with these people. They were a sturdy bunch, but wasn't so sure about the mystery Alpha, the Old One's minions, or the black magic. He needed a chance to ponder on what to do about those. "Any of you got a smoke?"

"There's no smoking on school grounds!" Phillip exclaimed.

Nancy rolled her eyes. "If you haven't noticed, it's the end of the world. Pull that stick out of your ass and go get this man some clothes."

"There should be a pack in the backseat of my truck. Is it here—big black Ford?"

"It's in the lot," Phillip grumbled and then stomped off. Nancy took a pack of Virginia Slims and a disposable lighter out of her coat pocket. "Forgive my friend. He's the principal of our fine high school. Phillip is normally a gentleman to a fault, but it's been a stressful night."

Earl took the proffered smokes. Kind of girly by his standards, but he knew that if you bit the filter off, they would do. "What's your status?"

"We lost a few folks on the way in. They're like ghosts in the snow. Invisible until they're on top of you. Then some tried to get in behind us, but we shot the hell out of them and they ran off. I've got people clearing out the old shelter so we can shove all the kiddies in if we need to, and I put ten men on the roof with rifles. And believe me, I picked everybody I ever suspected of doing a little poaching and spotlighting and stuck them up there."

Earl liked this town. "How many people do you have that can fight?"

Nancy looked at the fat man. "This is Steve, county controller. So I put him in charge of organizing. How many people do we have?"

The fat man shrugged. "I don't really know. A bunch, I guess."

"I'd suggest you go count them." Earl would gladly have traded this guy for his personal accountant right then, but Earl had been stupid and assumed that this was just about him and Nikolai. An MHI team would have made a great early Christmas, but if Earl couldn't have a group of professional Hunters, he'd put together some amateurs. "There's special .308, 12 gauge, and .45 ammo in my truck. See who's got guns in those calibers and divvy it up."

Nancy nodded quickly. "Heather already passed out the bullets, said that it would work better on these things."

"Good." The deputy was reliable, and she'd been busy since they'd split up. Alert and organized, this town might have a chance yet. "Where's Kerkonen at?"

Steve answered. "She got together a few groups she trusted, some to go house to house and one to secure the hospital."

"Lots of injured," Nancy said pointedly, like that was somehow Earl's fault. "It's a nightmare out there."

Earl scowled as he lit the cigarette. Dark magic and that stupid amulet were changing the natural order of things. People were changing too fast, immune to silver, and even unbreakable curses were getting broken. It was threatening his calm. Those injured could turn rapidly, but he couldn't worry about that now. Hopefully, Kerkonen had briefed the men she'd sent there to be ready for that possibility. . . . Hell, she *was* the same possibility. It was like everyone around here was a werewolf *except* him. Suddenly, he coughed. It turned into a hack as the cigarette smoke burned his lungs. "Damn it," he croaked.

"Those things will kill you," Steve pointed out.

Earl removed the smoke from his lips. "Shit . . . *Now* they *can.* Nuts!"

Nancy had no idea what he was talking about and just regarded Earl like he was simple.

You disgust me.

Nikolai had lain hidden in the shadows between the dumpsters, waiting, but for what, he was not sure. Exhausted, it had taken quite some time to crawl to safety. If Harbinger or even one of the lesser werewolves had found them in their current state, they wouldn't have stood a chance.

Failure. You're a failure. You are weak. Pathetic.

The berating had continued for quite some time. The sad thing was that Nikolai agreed with the Tvar's assessment. If it hadn't been for the distracting fire, Harbinger would have torn his heart out. Harbinger was stronger, faster, superior. Nikolai hated himself for failing to avenge his Lila.

That is twice. Twice you've let him win. You failed your unit. You failed your precious motherland. He embarrassed you once before. Mocked you like a dog. Coward. Imbecile. If it wasn't for me, you'd be dead. You should be dead. I should be in charge. I would've drunk his blood, ate his bones.

His body was wrecked. Ribs pressed through his skin. If he had not let the snow cover him, he would have appeared nothing more than an emaciated corpse lying there. The spare flesh had been burned away to feed the furnace of regeneration. He needed desperately to eat but lacked the strength to care anymore. Perhaps it would be better to just let the cold carry him into the bleak.

This is what you get for imprisoning me for so many moons. You weakened us. We should have been strong. Ready. But no, you tried to be a man. You are no man, Nikolai. You were deluded. All to please your little human bitch.

"Silence," Nikolai gasped. Snow fell between his lips as he spoke. The little bit of moisture cooled his parched throat. "Never speak of her."

We owned the night. Everything feared us, but you chained me. Chained me for her! You betrayed me, your one true friend, for a soft human girl! Then, when you need me, you come begging back. Look at us now. Are you happy? She deserved to die. She died because she made you weak.

"Enough." Finally provoked, his voice was louder that time.

I wonder what Harbinger did to her. I know what I would've done. How many ways did he hurt her first? Did she cry? Did she beg? I bet she begged for death. She'd have promised anything to make him stop. Anything.

It had been late when he'd returned from the hunt, where he'd banished the Tvar, only setting it free on the frozen tundra north of Sklad when the cycle of the moon required it. As had become his custom over the previous years, he had been gone for five days, one to travel, three to hunt, one to return, as far from humanity as possible. The Tvar had despised him for it, but Lila loved him even more for the sacrifice. His sweet wife was always there to welcome him back, yet when he'd returned for the final time, he'd found his home desecrated.

The safe had been blasted open. The files he'd taken from the disintegrating KGB had been scattered. Only one was missing, but it wasn't until later, when he realized which one it was, that he understood just how serious the break-in had been. The file contained everything they'd gleaned about Koschei's murderer, including the name of the American town he'd immigrated to.

They'd left his wife's body upstairs. Lila had been in the bedroom, tortured, executed. A small green patch had been left on her forehead as a calling card.

I could have protected her, but I was degraded to chasing reindeer. She's dead because you were weak.

A fist exploded from the snow. "I said *enough!*" Nikolai roared. He grabbed the cold metal of the dumpster and pulled himself up. Legs wobbling, he waited for the dizziness to pass. He'd lost too much blood. He needed energy to repair. Hearing movement, he flung open the lid of the dumpster. The rat never stood a chance. One hand shot out and snagged it before it could flee. The rodent managed to scratch his thumb before he crushed it and shoved the entire flea-ridden thing in his mouth and chewed. It was hot with blood and therefore delicious.

You listen to me—

"No." Nikolai choked down the rat and wiped his filthy face with one filthier forearm. He needed more energy. Then he needed his rifle. "You listen to me. You will not speak of Lila again, or so help me, I will end us both. Do you understand?"

You wouldn't dare.

"I dare . . . ," Nikolai whispered, recalling the message that had been left on his bedroom wall, scrawled in his wife's blood. It had read TRY TO STOP ME. Leaving notes for each other, just like old times. A monster like Harbinger could never be allowed to possess the amulet. "I only have one thing to live for now. Mark my words. He will die for what he's done. You will not stand in my way."

Agent Stark was running out of both ideas and places to stack bodies.

At first he'd decided to hang tight and let Briarwood make him some money, but that was before he realized just how badly this place was infested. As the night had gone on, more injured and dying had turned up at the hospital. Hit-and-run strikes were occurring all over town. The remaining staff were doing their best, but the situation was an absolute disaster. The volunteer firemen had placed the dead in rows with sheets thrown over them on the still-damp second floor, until they too had come to the realization that the town was under attack and had snuck out the back to get to their families.

Luckily the other bitten had all died soon after arriving, because if he started shooting survivors now, he doubted the Yoopers would let them out alive.

Mosher had fetched their armor and rifles from the Suburban. Comms were still down, there was no word from Briarwood, weather was still awful, and the number of people who were now aware that something paranormal was occurring was growing by the minute. The giant beam of light that had temporarily made the place look like noon shooting up from the center of town an hour ago hadn't helped matters, either.

"Anything yet?" Mosher asked as he approached. The kid was fully geared up with an F2000 with all the fixings, including a 40mm grenade launcher, and he was obviously antsy, ready to get out into the action. Stark was glad he had a hard charger to watch his back, but he was really wishing he'd brought a full team. He'd seen what a single werewolf could do. Taking on a whole pack of the bastards? Screw that.

Stark lowered the sat phone. "Nada. We're still on our own. By the time we get help we'll be at a full-on level-five containment. We haven't had one of those stateside since Myers's clusterfuck at that concert in Montgomery."

The junior agent's face was still stained orange, and he kept blinking away involuntary tears. Pepper spray was the gift that just kept on giving. Mosher took a long look down the hallway full of sheet-draped corpses. "Sir, we can't keep waiting for a signal. I've got Amy Lee ready to go." He patted his rifle. Stark had no idea why Mosher had named his firearm. "We've got to do something."

"I know," Stark answered. "Best bet is to snag some transportation out of this mess so we can alert headquarters to send in the cleaners. If we don't get them here before the power comes back on, these yokels will be blabbing all over the Internet, and I do *not* want a level-five break on my watch."

Mosher nodded slowly, still looking at the orderly row of bodies. It was obvious that the kid didn't like the idea of running. "Permission to speak freely, sir?" Stark grunted his assent, and Mosher continued. "These people are getting slaughtered. The monsters are just going door-to-door. By the time reinforcements show up, this town will be toast. We need to hit back, now. We need to protect them."

Stark had been afraid of this. Apparently young Agent Mosher had a conscience. He clucked approvingly and tried to speak like the wise mentor/father figure that he was. His own mentor, Agent Franks, would have agreed with Mosher, and would probably be out there snapping werewolves in half over his knee, but sadly, unlike Franks, he and Mosher were eminently mortal. "That's really brave of you, Gaige, thinking about these poor folks."

"Uh . . . thank you, sir."

"No, no. Thank you. You're keeping a moral perspective. That's valuable. But you're forgetting something important. The most important thing of all."

Mosher was confused. "What's that?"

Stark had a gift. He was a remarkably loud man, and he turned it up for effect. "That's not our *job*!" Mosher flinched. Stark closed in, still shouting. "MCB protocol is to *contain* first and foremost. You think one pissant town matters in the grand scheme of things? We've been commissioned by the highest authority in the land to keep a lid on this kind of shit. Men way smarter than you set that mission for a very specific reason, which I know you've been taught! What is the *First Reason*, Agent Mosher?"

The importance of the MCB's mission was absolutely beaten into every new recruit's head during training. "The more people who believe in the Old Ones, the more powerful they become!" Mosher stammered his response. "Sir!"

Stark had no idea if the First Reason was even true, but it was institutional doctrine, and every sane government in the world thought that the more people who knew about and therefore had faith in the Old Ones' existence, the more those aliens would be able to meddle in human affairs. Sure, it was unknown if lycanthropes were even related to the Old Ones, since no one actually knew where they'd come from originally, but the rules were there for a reason, so all monsters got lumped under the MCB's umbrella mission. "We go out there and get eaten, then who's going to be the ones to get word out first? These people talk before we get a wall up, and it'll spread like wildfire. Do you want to be the agent that failed his entire country? Do you want to be the agent that destroyed a hundred-year perfect track record?"

The junior agent stood at attention and stared straight ahead. "Negative, sir."

"Damn right, Agent Mosher!" Stark lowered his voice. No need to keep pushing when the kid had already fallen in line. "This is what we're gonna do. We're going for help. We'll head south until we get a signal or hit the next town. Once headquarters is warned, then I promise we come back and fight these bastards ourselves until reinforcements arrive," he lied. "But the mission has to come first."

"I understand, sir."

Good, because Stark didn't. He had no intention of throwing his life away for nothing.

✣ ✣ ✣

The sickness came upon him unexpectedly.

Fueled by the harvested energy of Harbinger's mighty werewolf soul, the Alpha had felt strong, triumphant. It was unknown exactly what effect Koschei's amulet would have on his body, except that all the legends spoke of virtual immortality and invincibility. By most reckoning, Koschei himself had been seven hundred years old before his pride had led to his downfall at the hands of the Finn.

The initial surge of power had left him near giddy. Every sense had improved, until he felt bombarded with new information. Vision had taken on a surreal quality as his eyes had adapted further into the infrared and ultraviolet spectrums. The smallest sounds were audible, and there were noises that he'd never heard before to interpret, and the smells . . . Every living thing for miles, every chemical, every mineral, every pheromone, they were all there, an endless stream of data.

It was too much to process. The Alpha was overwhelmed. He was blinded by too much sight. His skin burned at the slightest change in air pressure. Individual hairs tingled as they felt shifts in the Earth's electromagnetic field. It was not pain, yet it was. "What's happening to me?" he growled.

"You're changing," the witch explained patiently. "It will take time for your body to adapt. When the metamorphosis is complete, you'll have been purified. This is not unexpected."

It may have not been unexpected in the logical sense, but the actual experience was much worse than what he'd imagined. He had hoped to revel in the slaughter of this town and to bring about the birth of the *vulkodlak*. But he could barely control his own body, let alone hundreds of new soldiers as well. He needed time. Swaying, the Alpha made his decision. "I must rest."

The witch did not seem surprised. "Shall we return to your home?" She was exhausted. He needed to remember how draining the dark spells were, especially for someone so young. Lucinda Hood was talented in channeling the forces of her newly adopted dark god, but it would take time for her to harness even a fraction of the power her father had before MHI had ended his life. "I need to warm up."

The Alpha's new senses created a virtual live map of the entire town. His children were scattered, operating alone or—the younger—in pairs as they picked off stray humans. Meanwhile, the people of

Copper Lake had formed armed groups and were patrolling for other survivors, having, in a way, formed their own packs. One such pack was in his neighborhood, near his house. Despite the feeling of newfound strength flowing through his limbs, he was unsure of his abilities and not confident in testing them just yet. "No. The way isn't clear."

"Bloody hell . . ." She gave a long sigh. "Back to the mine, then? Very well. One of my diggers is injured. They'll be glad to return to the dirt. That's what gives them their strength."

The Alpha wasn't fond of retreating when his goals were so close at hand, but unlike the werewolves that had come before him, he was not a creature of instinct. He was a man of logic and planning, and he would do what it took to lead his people into the future.

⊰ **Chapter 15** ⊱

It was appropriate that the military acronym for my new unit was STFU. Because Shut The Fuck Up was also the primary directive in our security briefing. The task force was so beyond top secret that I didn't even know if there was a word for the level that we occupied.

There were two teams on Unicorn. One human, one not so much. Since I looked normal, I got to attend both briefings.

First squad consisted of a collection of mortal ass-kickers, loaned from regular units to MACV-SOG, and then loaned to us. Even though it was obvious who was in charge, they had no official rank hierarchy. There were a lot of people with the rank of Mister. Their names were whatever was assigned by Conover's unknown bosses or whatever nickname stuck. I was introduced as Mr. Wolf.

The most experienced man on first squad was a giant Polynesian that the others called Destroyer, or Augie to his friends, which I was not. He was ugly as sin, quietly judgmental, with a zero-tolerance policy for bullshit and arms that suggested he bench-pressed jeeps for fun. He smelled like a Green Beret NCO, and it was obvious he didn't like me from the second we met. Many years later I would end up hiring his son, so it is a small world after all.

They were to provide our security, transport, and any other duties as assigned. They were not to look too hard at anyone on second squad. They were not to speak to second squad unless spoken to, and they were definitely not allowed to ask questions. I think it was all that enforced secrecy that made Destroyer dislike my team. After that, Conover herded me out of the room. I was guessing he didn't want me to hear the *part about how they were supposed to kill anyone on second squad who didn't obey orders. There was no need. That had been standard operating procedure for this kind of unit since 1942.*

Even though there were only three of us, second squad got their own, separate briefing. It was the first time I'd meet the others that I would be working with for the next year. As soon as we entered, I could smell trouble. The girl stood out. It's hard not to when you're supernaturally beautiful. Her skin almost glowed. She was so unnaturally perfect that you ached just looking at her. I pegged as some sort of divine-human cross. She was introduced as Sharon Mangum, code name, Singer. She gave me a polite nod, but didn't speak.

It's a pretty strong comment on Sharon's looks that I noticed her before the thing sitting next to her. It had the head of a bull and the body of a man. It took me a moment to understand that it wasn't just some stuffed cow head on a really big dude wearing huge green fatigues. His fur was dark brown, and his black eyes studied me with obvious intelligence.

It was the first time I'd seen an actual minotaur. I'd heard of them, big-time PUFF bounties, but I'd never seen one before. They were supposed to be solitary, rare, and deadly berserkers. Since he didn't immediately charge and tear me into bits, they were obviously not as bestial as the stories indicated. "Howdy," the minotaur said. His voice was very deep. "You must be the werewolf."

"Yep. I've never met a minotaur before."

"Minotaur?" The monster stood suddenly. He was over seven feet tall, and his horns stuck out a foot on each side. The floor creaked under his weight. I took an unconscious step back. "Do I look Greek to you, asshole?"

It is always best to assert dominance in these kinds of situations. "You best take it easy, or you'll look like a steak dinner and a new pair of boots."

The minotaur bared his blunt white teeth. "Why, you little mother—"

"Easy, Travis," Sharon suggested, placing one hand on the minotaur's massive hairy arm. Her voice was like soothing music. Even I felt a sudden sense of peace.

"Apologies, Ms. Sharon." The minotaur slowly returned to his seat on the floor.

"No offense intended, friend," I said, shaking my head to clear it. "It was a long flight."

"And you didn't have to ride in cargo. . . . Look, buddy, minotaur's got all sorts of bad connotations." Travis snorted. It was a thunderous noise. "My tribe's from Texas, by God, and we prefer to be called Bullmen. I'm Travis Alamo Sam Houston of the East Texas Bullmen, and I've come to prove our loyalty to the US of A."

"Don't use your whole name," Conover pointed out.

"Yes, sir. Sorry, Captain," Travis responded. Looking back, that was kind of pointless. Were we worried spies might mistake him for a different six-hundred-pound bull-headed mythological monster? "I'm here to earn a PUFF exemption by putting hoof to commie ass for my country. It won't happen again, sir."

Conover just sighed. I kind of felt sorry for the kid. This was going to be a tough assignment.

✢ ✢ ✢

Earl had showered in the men's locker room, scrubbed off the blood, and gotten dressed, so he at least appeared semi-presentable to these people, even though he'd gone in three holes on his belt and probably looked like Famine from the Four Horsemen. He combed his hair and made sure his teeth weren't stained red with blood. It would help to not look like a complete lunatic before giving this particular pep talk to a town of regular folks.

He finished his speech on werewolves. It was a condensed version of what he'd usually say at Newbie training, but it would have to do. "Any questions?" About a dozen hands went up. Those were the polite ones. The others just started to shout questions at him.

There were fifty men and women sitting on the wooden bleachers in front of him. The gym was even more crowded and noisy than it had been when he'd first woken up. The generators were running full blast, so they had light, heat, and a continuous trickle of townsfolk. Nancy Randall had gathered those that she said "had a clue," and Phillip had taken a quick poll to find all the military veterans, gun nuts, and hunters; this being northern Michigan, that was a very healthy percentage. Heather Kerkonen had cherry-picked twenty people for her rescue patrols earlier, and they hadn't returned yet, and they had more shooters on the roof and around the windows and doors. Earl liked the numbers, he just didn't like the attitude.

"Are you nuts?" a burly man shouted from the highest row.

Earl shrugged. "Is that a question or a statement?"

"Both, asshole!"

He was used to dealing with Hunters. Even his greenest Newbie was a proven survivor who'd already made that leap of faith necessary to realize they didn't know crap about how the real world worked. There was more shouting as those that had seen the werewolves, loose-skinned armored creatures, or dark-magic beam of light argued with those that hadn't. Earl knew that he had to rein this in real quick if he was going to turn them into a coherent force. "*Zip it!*" he bellowed. His voice echoed through the entire gymnasium.

Turning human hadn't cost Earl's command voice any of its power. The crowd shut up.

Pacing back and forth across the half-court line, Earl kept his voice raised. "I don't care if you think I'm full of it. That don't matter. What does is that something's killing your town. You can all agree on that. If I'm right, then you need to work together to beat them. If I'm wrong, then you still need to work together to beat them." There was a general murmur of assent. The people who hadn't at least seen some mutilated bodies were a distinct minority. "If you want to live 'til dawn, you're gonna have to fight."

"Why don't we go out there now, then?" a young guy on the front row asked. Earl guessed from his out-of-season tan and the fact that he seemed to be in really good shape that this was one of their recently returned vets. "Let's go get them!"

"Because there's like a thousand of them and they move so fast you can't hardly see them and then it's too late!" someone called from behind. "I say we stay here and let them come to us."

Earl nodded. He had two distinct personalities here, offensive and defensive. Both were necessary. If they all went out there, just like in nature, the weak would be culled from the herd. If they all sat here, eventually they'd be surrounded, and then they were sitting ducks. "We do both. The creatures will mostly be working alone, but as the night goes on and they've got fewer targets of opportunity, the bloodlust will attract them to the survivors. We leave enough here to defend the women and children—"

"That's sexist!" a girl exclaimed.

"Figure of speech," Earl responded. "Grown-ups are talking, so cram the PC bullshit. The fallout shelter under this gym serves as the base. We hold it at all costs. We leave a force here to fend off the monsters. The rest of us form squads and take the fight to them. You go out there alone, they will pick you off." Before he'd started, Nancy had explained how several individuals had set out in search of their loved ones. None of those had come back yet. "It don't matter how tough you are. You can only look in one direction at a time, and they're faster than you."

"I saw one hop clear up to the roof of the bank!"

"Uh huh . . . ," Earl said as everyone else started babbling about what they'd seen. It wasn't the werewolves that they'd seen that he was really worried about. It was the other things that were out there in the storm. Their capabilities were a mystery. He let the group work itself up with anecdotes about their night. Hearing it from their neighbors would convince the doubters far better than anything Earl could say himself.

"What about the injured?" a lady half-way up the bleachers asked.

"You can't trust 'em," Earl stated coldly. "Bites for sure, and maybe scratches. They're infected and could turn on you." As expected, those words caused a terrible uproar from the crowd. This was exactly why he always let Julie handle the negotiations. He was always too blunt.

Nancy Randall especially didn't like it. "What?" The woman had enough of a reputation that as soon as she started speaking, the angry group quieted down. "Those are our friends, family. There's no way."

"Take my advice or leave it. Your call. I'd keep them isolated if I were you. If they start to change, do what you've got to do," Earl said. Already, he could tell that most of them didn't believe him. Sometimes the ugly truth was just too damn ugly.

Nancy scowled hard, mulling it over, but she held up her hand to silence the objections. "We'll talk about that more later. Deputy Kerkonen said that she saw you kill a few of these things and that you were some sort of professional. How'd you know they were coming?"

"And why didn't you warn us?" cried a different man. A friend put a comforting hand on his shoulder, but he kept on. "My wife might still be alive."

"Easy, Stan," Nancy cautioned. "Well, Harbinger, answer the man's question."

They already didn't believe him about werewolves, period; he wasn't going to try to educate them on the finer points of lycanthropic society and the fact that Nikolai had just needed a good murdering.

Luckily, before he could think of an answer, one of the guards at the main hall entrance shouted that they had movement in the parking lot. Everyone grabbed for their weapons but relaxed as word spread that it was one of the groups returning. Most of the doubters went back to cursing Earl.

The patrol came in brushing snow from their coats and stomping it from their boots. All of the scouts were shivering except for the one in the lead. Kerkonen was barely recognizable. She'd ditched her ragged sheriff's department coat and found a big black parka. When she flipped back the hood, the difference was shocking. His human senses were weak; he felt blurry, slow and hungover, but he could already tell that she was well along the change. Her eyes gleamed just a shade too metallic, her skin was flushed, her movements too fluid. The others might not be able to tell, and she probably didn't know it herself, but he recognized the signs from experience. Heather Kerkonen was a full-on werewolf.

And that change had occurred in a matter of *hours* . . . Normally it took weeks. Earl swallowed hard. *That ain't good.*

"What'd you find, deputy?" asked Nancy.

"A lot of dead people and even more empty houses. But we found a few more survivors. They're in the foyer getting checked for bites before I let them in," she said. "The werewolves are on the move out there. We don't need any in here." That statement struck Earl as particularly ironic.

This time it was Phillip, the high-school principal, that interjected. "Not more of this werewolf nonsense. There's got to be a rational explanation."

Deadly serious, Heather put her shotgun over one shoulder and scanned the crowd. "I figured you might be having this conversation. I've got something everyone needs to see. . . ." She motioned two men forward. Each was carrying one end of a tarp-wrapped object that was very clearly a body. "Show them."

"Heather, there's kids here," said the man supporting the narrower end of the tarp. "Maybe we should—"

"They need to see it, too. There's no time for doubt," Heather said as she pulled her gloves off and eyed Phillip coldly. Earl had seen that look before. She was probably wondering what he tasted like. "Unwrap her."

The two men dropped their burden. It hit the wood with a dull thud. As they pulled the blue tarp away, the crowd gasped. A few looked away.

"**Look** at *it*," Heather ordered.

The werewolf was female. Deprived of his sense of smell, estimating age was out of the question. Gold eyes open, the lips were pulled back over bloodstained teeth. The cause of death was obvious, since the ribcage had been broken open and the heart was gone. That would certainly do the deed. Even for the fiercest skeptics in the crowd, the mostly humanoid creature was a slap in the face.

"It must be some sort of undiscovered animal," Phillip sputtered. "A cryptid! Or some genetic experiment that escaped."

"Yep. There's lots of money in crossing gorillas and timber wolves." Earl snorted. "Those science types are downright full of wacky fun."

Heather squatted beside the corpse, roughly grabbed one wrist, and lifted it without saying a word. The braver members of the front row got up and approached. The young vet was the first to notice Heather's point. "It's wearing a wedding ring."

The skeptical faction turned to the principal, who had somehow gotten himself appointed as their leader in the last few seconds. "Somebody must have put a ring on the animal."

"Crap. *Why*, Phillip?" someone shouted. "Are you retarded?"

Heather glared at Phillip. Then she roughly dropped the limb and reached for the gaping chest wound. "I noticed this while I was cutting the heart out before it could regenerate."

There was a cluster of people around the werewolf now, looking almost like a football huddle. The soldier spoke again. "What are those bags?"

"Well, Matthew, those appear to be breast implants," said Nancy as she stepped away from the huddle, rubbing her eyes. "Well, apparently this thing had a boob job."

Phillip had no response to that revelation.

"There's more," Heather said. "Anybody recognize this?" There was a long moment of silence. The people in the circle all exchanged glances. The audience was struggling to see. Several of the witnesses began to swear.

"Rose Greer had that same tattoo, same place. We used to work together at the substation before she went to nights," said one of them.

It was Nancy that spoke up again, loudly. "Phillip, can you think of any reason somebody would stick a wedding ring on a wild animal, give it breast implants, and then tattoo a little rose on its neck?"

Phillip, obviously, had no response. Earl was about to make a comment about the kind of weird stuff you could find on the Internet, but now was not the time for sarcasm.

Heather walked away from the body and turned to the bleachers. Her voice echoed through the entire gym. "Look at it. Look at *her*. Yesterday that thing was Rose . . ." She let that sink in for a moment. "After she killed everyone at the power company and wrecked the place, she walked home. I caught her eating her husband. That is what we're facing. There's more of these out there right now. Some of them are strangers, like the man who tore up our jail. Some of them are our friends, or neighbors, or people you see at the store, or people you go to church with. But not anymore."

The huddle had broken up so that everyone could see the twisted corpse.

"Now they're something else." Heather walked over, angry, shotgun still over one shoulder, and kicked the dead werewolf, brutally hard, right in the snout. Blood flecks splattered down the tarp. Earl tensed a bit, but remarkably Heather seemed to be keeping it under control. "They're the enemy. And we have to destroy them before they get the rest of us."

The atmosphere in the room had changed. They were committed now. Heather, a local, had swayed them where he, an outsider, could not. Heather risked a quick glance Earl's way, as if to see how she'd done. He nodded approvingly. She looked away, almost embarrassed, but not before he caught the flash of gold in her eyes. Tough, to the point, Heather would have made one hell of a good Hunter.

Too bad he was probably going to have to put her down before the night was through.

The volunteers left ten minutes later. There were three smaller teams, one for each way out of Copper Lake. Earl had made sure that each team had some of his silver ammo and some MHI phone numbers. Using snowmobiles and moving quick, they might have a chance. He suspected that this Alpha would have set some impediments in their way, and would have loved to go with them, but he was needed on offense. Two bigger teams were heading out momentarily to cause trouble and find survivors.

Heather joined Earl as he was strapping into his older suit of armor. It was pocked with burn marks and holes, but he was glad that he'd packed the spare. His leather coat fit over it, too, and he needed the added warmth. Humans got cold really easy. They were in the shadows of the main hall; the lights were out to conserve the juice. Heather stopped, folded her arms, and leaned against the trophy case. She watched him for a while, but didn't speak.

"This suit has seen better days," Earl said, trying to make conversation. There was a holster on each hip, gunfighter style. He removed an S&W .45 Nightguard from the bag, checked to make sure the revolver was loaded, and stuffed it into the left holster. "I'm going back out there."

"I know. And by the way, saying thank you for me saving your life would be nice. You look pretty healthy for someone who didn't have a pulse an hour ago."

Actually, he was feeling all right. Clumsy, slow, less capable than he was used to, but healthy. He had a sneaking suspicion that he should be dead, but that either something had gone wrong, or that amulet had left him alive for some unknowable reason. "Thanks," Earl answered. "Seriously. Thank you."

She bit her lip as she summoned her courage. "Harbinger, level with me . . ."

He already knew what she was going to ask. "You've been cursed." He kept his voice low so it wouldn't carry into the auditorium.

"You sure?"

He took out the second .45, opened the cylinder, confirmed it was loaded, snapped it shut, and holstered. "I'm positive. Sorry."

She nodded slowly. "I just thought maybe . . . never mind." Tears welled up in her eyes. "It's not fair." Heather stepped away from the trophy case, hands curled into fists. "Shit!" She slammed her fist into the heavy cabinet. The wood splintered, the glass shattered, and trophies and plaques spilled out. It made a terrible racket. Heather drew her hand back, shocked at the hole she'd put through the case. "How—"

"You're gonna have to be a little more careful with your temper," Earl suggested. "Super strength and hitting stuff when you get angry don't go well together."

Half a dozen townsfolk led by the principal converged on the noise within seconds, ready to blast the intruders. Earl waved them off. "Sorry. Kicked your case," he explained while Heather hid her damaged hand behind her back. Phillip already didn't like him, so he wasn't out much taking the rap. "By accident . . . so back off."

"Well, when this is over, you owe us a new one," Phillip muttered as he stomped away.

When they were alone again, Earl went over to Heather. "Let me see your hand."

Reluctantly, she held it out. "I didn't hit it that hard." Sure enough, the scratches were already pulling closed. Her hand was quivering. "I can't believe this. This is just too much."

On a purely technical level, Earl was astounded by the regeneration rate of the werewolves created since the surge. On a strictly practical level, he was holding the injured hand of a woman whose eyes were welling up with tears because she'd just realized that her life was over. "It'll be okay."

"No, it won't."

"Yes, it can," he insisted. "You don't have to end up like them. It can be controlled." *And if you can't control it, I'll have to kill you.* Earl quickly dismissed that unpleasant thought.

"How do you know?" she sniffed.

He was not good at *comforting.* It was hard to say, but he didn't think it mattered now. "Because I'm a werewolf, too."

Surprised, Heather jerked her hand away. "What? Get away." Her nose crinkled as she instinctively smelled to see if he was telling the truth. "No. No, you're normal . . . Oh shit, what did I just do?" Her eyes widened. "I'm *smelling* people now! Oh God!"

Earl raised his hands apologetically. "Well, I *was* a werewolf. Up until that big magic light sucked it out of me."

"Why? How? And why the hell do I *believe* you?" Heather asked, taking another step back. She folded her arms defensively. "That's why you've got that cage in your truck. That's how you moved so fast back at the station. But, but why aren't you . . . *evil*?"

So she was getting the urges already. She was hiding it well. "Listen, Heather." He took a step closer. "I know what you're feeling right now. You aren't what you think, you're what you *do.* You can fight it."

"But I want to *kill* everybody!" she hissed, then looked around to make sure nobody could hear them. She lowered her voice. "I want to just tear their stupid faces off. I want to break their bones with my bare hands."

"That part doesn't ever really go away, but it does get easier to tune out. The guy that helped me learn this stuff suggested prayer and meditation. So I took up smoking. That seemed to help. Crap . . . I might have to be one of those annoying people that tries to quit and then whines about it," he muttered. "I *hate* those people."

"You said you were cured by magic." Heather's eyes narrowed suspiciously. It did sound ludicrous, even by Earl's standards. "Hell, why not? I didn't believe in werewolves, either, so why not magic, too? But you said at the station that there was no cure. You said that people have been looking forever!"

"What can I say?" Earl shrugged. "Up until an hour ago, I didn't think there was one."

She responded with a sad little laugh. "You know that running joke, about how when a girl talks about her problems, the man just wants to solve the problem, and the girl doesn't want it solved, she just wants to talk about it?" Heather wiped her eyes. "Screw that noise. How do I *solve* this?"

Earl hadn't thought of that as an option. A cure had always seemed like such a pipe dream, it was either endure or die, but now he was living proof that there was a way. Could that amulet actually cure other werewolves? The possibilities took his breath away. "That amulet, the one your prisoner talked about. That's the key. It cured me. We've got to find it."

Having been given some small bit of hope, Heather latched on with both hands. "I can kind of feel it, I think. It's like this weird buzzing noise that won't go away."

As a regular man, Earl could no longer sense the real Hum, let alone the false one. He was groping blind. The only way he was going to find that thing was with Heather's help. There was still the matter of the Alpha and his forces to deal with, but Earl had been a damn effective Hunter before he'd been cursed. He still had a few tricks up his sleeve. "We'll head out with the teams, then break off and follow the trail right to that amulet. We find it, and we find the asshole behind this."

"Cure me, waste him, save the town. Sounds like a plan."

⊰ **Chapter 16** ⊱

The Russians had started it this time.

Sure, there was a war going on. An awful one, by all accounts, but it was the Soviets that had to go and bring a supernatural element into a normal, shitty human conflict. Let's say that operations that didn't actually exist, conducted by hypothetical units, across the border into countries that may or may not have actually been involved, had been too successful. And the Soviets had loaned a specialist of their own to their allies to deal with it. As you may have guessed, there are certain specifics that I'm not allowed to ever get into, especially in a journal.

A lieutenant colonel with no name and an old man in a shirt and tie with no name gave us the final briefing during the flight into Vietnam. If the communists wanted to escalate on the supernatural front, we were supposed to respond in kind. STFU's mission was to be put into a location where Americans were not supposed to be, and then kill the shit out of the enemy. Move and repeat.

I did not like jobs like this. Not that I wasn't good at them. In fact, I was really good. I'd come to terms with the fact that I was a monster, but I had to be careful just how much I let the animal out to play. Even monsters have rules. Well, some of us anyway.

Ideally, our actions would attract the attention of the Russian "advisor." It was hoped that we would then be able to neutralize him. The men without names said that he was known as Nikolai.

So we went hunting.

⊹ ⊹ ⊹

After running from the monster, Horst and Lins had climbed over a chain-link fence and broken into a storage unit, where they hid, freezing, until they decided it was probably safe to return to their vehicle to make a run for it. Though scared, he was careful not to show it to Lins as the two huddled in stony silence and listened to the werewolves howl. This situation was so far out of Briarwood's league that it was depressing.

The walk back to the Caddy took forever. He'd gotten turned around while running, the snow wasn't helping matters, and he wouldn't admit that he was lost. Their odd route was explained away because walking down the open streets seemed like a great way to get picked off by werewolves, so they'd gone through the backyards. After twenty minutes of hopping fences, they'd reached the scorched grocery store and his Cadillac. Horst had been surprised to find that any other members of his crew had survived.

Jason Lococo was sitting on the hood, scanning for threats. Having burned through his share of silver ammo in the SAW, Loco had taken Jo Ann's M-4 carbine, which looked like a toy in his hands, to keep watch. Horst almost said something to him about scratching the paint, but the giant looked like he might just open fire, so he refrained.

"Loco, I'm happy to see you," Horst said, glad that their big man had been too dumb to flee. Loco just grunted an acknowledgment. "I thought you were toast."

"Whew. I'm just glad you didn't take the car!" Lins exclaimed.

It was obvious Loco wasn't happy. "You had the keys." He hopped off the Caddy, and the shocks sprang up in relief. "Let's go."

"Let's get out of this stinking town," Horst agreed.

"No. We've got to get to the hospital," Loco said as he went around and opened the rear door. "It puked her up."

"Jo?" Horst got yet another surprise to find that his girlfriend was still alive. Loco had put her in the back of the Escalade. With the third-row seats put away, there was just enough room for her to lie down. The big man had done his best to clean her up, all of their bottled waters had been emptied, and he had thrown a blanket over her.

The inside of the Caddy reeked. That new-car scent had been replaced by the stench of monster puke. Jo Ann was shivering. Her face had taken on a sickly grayish-yellow tone, and she was soaked with sweat. Clumps of her long hair had fallen out, leaving purple blotches on her exposed scalp.

"Ryan?" Jo Ann asked. Even her voice was scratchy. Her eyes were closed, and Horst cringed when he saw they were matted shut with a film of green boogers. "That you?"

His initial reaction was to tell her that she looked like death warmed over. "Yeah, baby, I came back for you," Horst said instead.

"I knew you would," she said. "Oh, I don't feel so good." Then she gagged and threw up all over the carpet. Horst took an involuntary step back.

"Oh, dude, she's messed up," Lins exclaimed, covering his mouth with his shirt. "She's got a disease from being in that scarecrow's stomach."

Jo Ann Schneider was *seriously* ill. Horst tried to remember back to Newbie training. That hot blonde, Holly Newcastle, had run them through a big lecture on all the horrible things you could catch from monsters and what to do about them. Unfortunately, he'd spent most of that lesson ogling Holly and not paying attention. That stuff had mostly been aimed at the eggheads destined to end up in support roles, and Horst had known that he was destined to be a team leader instead. Only now Jo Ann was like *melting* or something, and it might even be contagious.

"She's running a fever," Loco said. "I thought about carrying her, but figured the monsters would've smelled her and got us. She needs antibiotics or something."

"Antibiotics won't fix that, man. That's like Ebola or AIDS!" Lins insisted. "Bitch's got Ebola-AIDS. I'm not getting in there with her. No way. No fu—"

Lins flinched as Loco reacted with surprising speed. One huge hand encircled Lins's throat. He let out a pathetic squeaking noise as he was dragged eye to glass eye. "Then you can walk." Loco didn't so much as raise his voice, but it was obvious that Lins was seconds from getting his windpipe crushed. "Gimme the keys, Larry." Eyes wide, Lins reached into his coat and pulled out the jangling ring of keys. Loco snatched the keys away, then held him there for another second, like he was contemplating just squeezing a *bit* harder, but then let go. Lins stumbled away, coughing.

Loco looked at Horst next. "You got a problem, *boss*?" Those too-small, not-quite-pointing-in-the-same-direction eyes were crazy. He certainly lived up to his nickname.

Embarrassed that he was scared of his own henchman, Horst just shook his head.

"You getting anything?" Harbinger asked her for the third time in as many minutes.

Heather thought about it, but wasn't sure of how to answer. That buzzing noise had been stronger a little while ago, but it had faded out. "It's weird. It was strong, but then it tapered off. Now there's another one, like a background noise. It's not as loud, but it seems bigger, if that makes sense."

"That's the moon," Harbinger explained as they turned onto another familiar street. The snow chains were making a huge difference in traction, and despite her earlier assessment of Harbinger's status as another stupid tourist driver, he actually knew what he was doing.

"So I can actually hear the *moon*?"

"Sorta. It's complicated."

"Well, I should probably learn it, don't you think?" she replied. "Duh."

"No need for sarcasm. I can spend our limited amount of time teaching you about werewolf minutia that I learned from dusty old books that are probably wrong, or I can stick with the important bits about how not to turn into a complete raving cannibal. Entirely your call."

"Anybody ever tell you that you're not a very likable person?"

"Once or twice." Harbinger relented. "Well, near as I can figure, the Hum isn't actually the moon itself, but the lunar cycle causes whatever makes it. That's the Hum that we hear. It's a low-frequency sound, stronger in some places, though nobody knows why. Even some humans can hear it once in a while, but it doesn't affect them like it does us. Maybe it's magnetic fields, and we're just more sensitive. Maybe it's something magical. Hell if I know, but whatever it is will trip our internal switch, guaranteed, right along with the full moon. You've got three nights a month where you will not be able to control it."

"That doesn't sound too bad." She could deal with three lousy nights. Harbinger just scowled and watched the road. "What? There's a catch. There's always a catch."

"It's complicated . . . Three nights you have to change, but you're going to *want* to change all the time. Like a dog, when something runs, they want to chase it down. That's us, only worse. Something pisses you off, you want to kill it. You want something, you just take it. Something turns you on . . ." He stopped himself, glanced over at her, and began to blush. Heather was surprised, but Harbinger seemed downright old-fashioned. "Sorry."

"I'm a cop, Harbinger, not a nun. I started on a big-city department, and the attractive ones always get loaned out to vice on prostitution stings." Heather had never thought of herself as beautiful, but she knew that she at least qualified as pretty. "You've got assets, you work them. Thirty-six D, baby."

Harbinger coughed politely. "Gotcha."

Mr. Tough-guy-monster-slayer hadn't struck her as a prude. "I've seen things that would blow your mind. Just a word of advice: The hooker with all her teeth? That's the undercover cop."

"Ahem. Well, let's just say it can get ugly. New moon, with some practice, you can control yourself, even changed if you have to. The closer it is to the full moon, though, the harder it gets, and on the full moon, it's tough as a human, and changed, not a chance. I've had years of practice, and I still lock myself into a vault on those three nights. . . . Well, I did. I'm still not used to thinking I won't have to do that anymore."

Heather went back to looking out the window. They were covering a lot of ground, but it was all neighborhoods where the scouting parties had already checked. She'd taken a map and a marker and had split Copper Lake's tiny neighborhoods into sections for the other groups to check. Nobody had questioned her authority when she'd given out the assignments. Apparently, if you acted as if you were in charge, everyone just assumed you were. "Turn left up here."

Harbinger complied. "You getting something?" he asked hopefully.

"Confused. That's about it." Heather was feeling pretty good right then. The bouts of rampaging hunger had settled down, as had the out-of-nowhere anger. She didn't feel too different, though every light on the dash seemed too bright, the engine was too loud, the air flow from the heater was obnoxious against her exposed skin, and she was being assaulted with so many confusing smells that she could taste the air. "Level with me, Harbinger. How hard is this going to be?"

"That depends entirely on you," he answered, completely evading her question.

"Don't be such a chickenshit. Give it to me straight."

Harbinger didn't respond for a long time. This seemed really difficult for him. She started to say something else, but he cut her off. "You need to know I am, or was, I guess, a rare one. Honestly, there's only been a handful of us ever to control it. It takes an iron will. It gets easier, but I've worked at this for a *really* long time. Almost everyone turns pure evil. Most that keep it contained, it ain't because they want to. It's because they're afraid of someone like me coming along to take them out, so they keep it low key. I'd say ninety percent are dead within a few months of getting turned, another nine percent make a year, tops . . ." he trailed off. "That one percent left, though, they're the dangerous ones. Most of them don't give up the hunt—they're just clever enough to hide it."

"And then there's a few like you."

"I suppose. We're an odd breed."

Heather wasn't the quitting type. The trophy case she'd broken back at the school had held a bunch of items with her name etched on them. She'd made the boys' hockey team out of spite just because somebody had once told her girls couldn't play. It was similar reasoning that had caused her to become a police officer. Life had beat her down at every opportunity, but she still sucked it up and got along. There had been plenty of opportunities to give up. She'd lost so many people, so quickly. After the personal tragedies of the last few years, nobody would have batted an eye if she'd just given up, but having inherited an Irish temper and Finnish stubbornness, she was just too damned obstinate to let life win. So, if Harbinger could beat this curse, so could she.

"You said that you've been doing this a long time?"

He chuckled as he glanced over at her. "You wouldn't believe me if I told you. . . ." She didn't blink. "Hell. All right. I was born in 1900."

"And?"

"Nineteen and nothing. One-nine-zero-zero," he explained. Heather stared at him blankly. "Nineteen hundred A.D. You know, the one after 1899. I fought in World War One. I've got grandkids older than you. You'd like this one great-granddaughter of mine, though. I think you two would probably get along great. She don't take no crap off nobody, either."

Heather closed her eyes. If it wasn't for the fact that she'd watched a cut on her knuckles heal in four seconds in addition to a bunch of other weird supernatural goings-on, she would just have assumed that Harbinger was stoned, but at this point, anything seemed plausible. "So, werewolves don't age?"

"No. We still age. Just really slow. The transformation is a rejuvenating process, like a monthly tune-up. Plus, you heal faster and you don't get sick. I haven't had a cold since the Twenties. If it wasn't for the uncontrollable bloodlust, this curse does have its good side. I've smoked about a million cigarettes, but got fresh lungs every full moon. Oh, your fillings will fall out when your teeth change into fangs, but you don't have to worry about cavities ever again."

It was insane. "That's just so . . . Wow . . . Hell. I don't even know."

"Transformations burn calories like running a marathon. So we eat a ton. When we go to buffets, my team always teases that I don't get full, I just run out of time. I try to fatten up every month. Hell, I wouldn't be surprised after the beating I took earlier if I didn't lose thirty pounds today alone."

"Wait!" Heather came out of the seat so suddenly that Harbinger stepped on the brakes. The truck slid in the snow.

"What? Do you sense the amulet?" he asked quickly, scanning back and forth for threats.

"No. Not that. You mean that I can eat whatever I want, all that I want, and I can't ever get *fat*?"

Surprised, Harbinger stammered his response. "Well, of course."

It was a remarkably exciting idea. "Doughnuts, cookies, chocolate? Oh my God. Pie?" Heather asked. Harbinger just nodded along through the list. "Seriously . . . *Pie*?"

"Hell, you can do all that and wrap it in bacon if you feel like it." Harbinger waited for a further outburst, but none came.

Heather sat back, deep in thought, wearing a giant grin. They got moving. About half a block later, she spoke again. "If I'd known that, I would've gotten bit by a werewolf years ago."

"Well, there is all the murder," Harbinger pointed out.

"I know, but all-you-can-eat *pie!*" Heather chose to look on the bright side. Besides the temper, she'd also inherited her mother's sweet tooth. Unfortunately, Mom had gotten fat and developed type 2 diabetes by the time she was forty. Heather loved to eat and hated to work out but exercised religiously because she had vowed not to end up like her mom, fat and with amputated toes. "Pie, Harbinger. That's awesome."

Harbinger just shrugged. "If I said anything, I'd be a hypocrite. If R.J. Reynolds has a corporate jet, I probably paid for it."

They reached her street. It was eerily quiet, cloaked in fluffy white and completely dark. "Pull over up there. The blue one. That's my house." Not that the color mattered, since every house was plastered in snow. "I just thought of something."

"Snack run?" Harbinger asked, only partially in jest.

"We live until morning and I'm going to eat an entire birthday cake and wash it down with a Super Big Gulp. No. Something that the prisoner said about my grandpa earlier got me thinking." The truck stopped, and she hopped out quickly, dragging the Winchester along. Harbinger left the engine running and followed with another one of those old tommy guns of his. She had to shout to be heard over the wind. "Somebody else came by asking about my grandpa, too, looking for a necklace. He said his name was Peterson."

That got Harbinger's attention. "Handsome fella? Little shorter than me?"

"Yep. He seemed nice at first, but there was something off about him."

"That was Nikolai Petrov, Stalin's favorite werewolf."

"Friend of yours?"

"I've *almost* managed to kill him twice now. I caught his stink on your clothes earlier. You're lucky to be alive."

They started toward the house. Harbinger kept moving his head side to side, always searching. Heather couldn't explain it, but she knew that there were no werewolves near. They were close, but not close enough to be an immediate problem. The whole weird sense thing was kind of cool. She heard the other engine long before she saw the lights. "There's somebody coming." Heather pointed down the road.

Harbinger had to squint for a long time to even see it. He swore. "I feel like I'm blind."

It was an SUV, a Cadillac with all the extra chrome, spinning rims, and obnoxious *bling*. Heather immediately noted the Illinois plates. More tourists. Which meant that she needed to warn them. She started waving.

The roads were barely passable. Visibility was awful. Loco was driving. Lins was in the passenger seat with the window rolled down, more worried about catching whatever Jo Ann had than frostbite. Horst had the middle row to himself, trying to figure out how he could salvage what was left of his company, and Jo Ann was in the back, making strange wheezing noises. Risking one glance, Horst winced when he saw that she was faring even worse, her face a mottled purple and gray, like one big spreading bruise, and her sweat had taken on a thick, mucuslike sheen. Little bubbles formed on her nostrils and popped every time she exhaled.

After that, he kept a scarf over his nose and mouth, and his eyes forward.

Most people would think it strange that he felt not even the slightest bit of concern for Jo Ann's well-being. Sure, he liked her okay. She was easy on the eyes and helpful to have around, but Ryan Horst didn't really *like* anyone. People were just kind of *there*. Some benefited him, others didn't. If she died, it would be really inconvenient, but that was about it.

The thing that was really bugging him was that this job was a total failure. His company, and by extension, he personally, would look bad. Horst didn't really care about people, but he sure did care about what the important ones thought about *him*. Kelley was dead, Jo Ann was probably going to die, and he figured that Lins and Loco would bail on him now that he wasn't going to be able to pay them. At this rate, he would never make it big.

They were close to the hospital when he saw the headlights. It was the first active vehicle they'd seen since sliding out of the grocery-store parking lot. A large pickup was parked on the side of the road, lights on, the exhaust cloud indicating that it was still running. Two figures were clumping through the snow by the truck. Horst swiveled his head as they crunched past. It was a man and a woman, both bundled up, both carrying guns. The woman was trying to flag them down, probably to warn them that her stupid town was covered in monsters.

Loco just kept on driving. The man gave them a slow appraisal, then a cold nod as they passed on by.

Recognition slapped Horst right in the face. "That's Earl Harbinger," Horst said. He'd hit the jackpot. "Stop the car."

"We've got to get Jo help first," Loco stated.

"Stop the car, idiot. Harbinger's the werewolf," Horst exclaimed, but they didn't so much as slow down. "Loco, listen to me. He's worth a fortune." Horst spun around. Harbinger and the woman were already out of sight. By the time they got Jo Ann dropped off, they'd lose him.

And Horst would lose millions of dollars.

He turned back. "Stop the car. That's an order. We need to pop that guy, right now."

Loco didn't budge. He was too stupid to listen to reason. "She's dying. We don't have time."

Shit! "Harbinger's the oldest werewolf in the world. The PUFF on him is huge, and he's getting away."

Lins looked over the seat, suspicious. "Why didn't you tell us that before?"

Because I was going to keep most of it. "Because I didn't want you distracted. But I got the intel right from the government." *Well, Stark, anyway.* "Harbinger's head is worth at least a million bucks."

Lins' motives were easy to understand. He didn't even have to think about it for long. "You heard the man, Loco. Pull over."

"We'll go back for him once we get Jo some help," he insisted. "The hospital is just over there."

"Screw that!" Lins shouted. "I didn't come up here to get some disease, I came up here to get paid!"

"No," Loco said with more force.

Horst glanced out the back window. Harbinger was sure to drive off in the other direction, taking all that ridiculous PUFF with him, and there was no way he was going to admit defeat that easily. Loco was a moron. Horst reached into his coat and unsnapped the thumb break on his shoulder holster. He turned forward, voice low and deadly as the FN Five-seveN® cleared nylon. "Last chance. Stop this car or else."

"You gonna shoot me? Kill me and Jo both?"

"She'd want us to catch him. She was committed to this company."

Loco laughed. Horst had never heard him laugh before. It was a mirthless sound. "You're a real piece of work, Horst."

Decision made, Horst pushed the muzzle of the FN deep into the seat ahead of him and said, "Larry, grab the wheel," then pulled the trigger. The concussion of the 5.7mm was sharp in the enclosed space. Stuffing flew from the hole in the fabric. Loco bellowed as the bullet slammed into his back. Lins went for the steering wheel and tried to jam his foot over the brake. The big man was tough, though, and got a hold of Lins's shirt, so this time Horst lifted his gun and shot Loco in the back of the head.

Lins got control of the vehicle as Loco's heavy skull hit the steering wheel. They slid to a stop, sideways, in the middle of the road. The safety glass was broken, and there was blood on the dash. Loco moved slightly and groaned in pain. Horst must have only winged that big noggin and would gladly have pumped a few more rounds into it, but Lins was now blocking the shot. His only remaining employee reached over, found the door handle, and spilled Jason Lococo out into the snow.

⊰ **Chapter 17** ⊱

We owned the night.

The other side was tenacious and damn tough. The nefarious bastards were in it to win it. That just meant that we had to kill more of them before they got scared.

Travis was a wrecking ball. It turned out that Bullmen were extremely robust. Their hide is nearly impenetrable, and they heal at an astounding rate. Not as quick as a lycanthrope, mind you, but one day Travis could soak up half a mag from an AK-47, and the next he'd be anxious to go out again. He did get shot a lot, though, because he wasn't very fast and was too damn big to make very effective use of cover. We had to keep him way ahead of the vulnerable mortals of first squad, because Travis tended to fly into fits of rage. Charlie began to tell campfire stores about him, as something that translated roughly into "Furious Water Buffalo."

Sharon was a surprise. Singer was her assigned name, and she'd received it because of her talent. Her father had been a sailor. Her mother had been a siren. That particular relationship had worked out better than normal, with the sailor not being drowned then eaten, and Sharon had been the result, brought back to human civilization and raised to be a civilized young lady. That had mostly worked out, until the government had decided that a half-siren still belonged on the PUFF list.

Ironically, she'd never hurt a fly until the government had helped her find that side of herself. Though she was far stronger than a human, she *was not as tough as me or our Texas Longhorn Furious Water Buffalo, but the girl was a terror of a different kind. Her song haunted the jungle. She could get into a man's mind and twist it so that you couldn't see straight. Sentries were unaware, patrols got sloppy, and no man could withstand her interrogations. All she had to do was bat her eyelashes a few times, say a few words, and the prisoners would spill their guts. She didn't even speak the language.*

We had to bring on a local from the ARVN to translate. His name was Van. Destroyer had worked with him once before, and said he spoke just about every dialect in the region. His French was better than his English, and his English was better than mine. I was surprised how young he was, but he proved valuable, and the kid was hilarious.

We were very effective. The humans of first squad were as good a bunch of soldiers as I'd ever met. Destroyer was a consummate professional. Even while riding in the close confines of a chopper, sitting across from a hunched-over Travis, disguised only by being covered in a big blanket, the man didn't ask any questions. He got us in, covered our butts, and got us out. The two of us were never friendly. Destroyer obeyed orders and didn't talk much. I don't think he liked the assignment or me.

Conover was a far better leader than expected. He actually cared about everyone under his command. He was one of those rare leaders with real integrity, and after having been recruited for a few of these black operations over the decades, I was thankful we'd ended up with somebody like him. If he hadn't stayed with the government after the war, I would have loved to have recruited him to MHI. He would have made a superb team lead.

As for me . . . I led the actual missions in the field. Nobody had more experience than me. First squad thought of me as just another human, only one extraordinarily good at stealth and jungle fighting, though I think Destroyer suspected I was something more akin to the blanket-wearing giant and the nearly glowing goddess that forced them to wear earplugs. Three nights a month I was lowered into a pit, and then Travis covered the top with something heavy. Even in a war, there are certain things that shouldn't be done, not if you want to be able to tell yourself that you're the good guy.

That would soon change.

✢ ✢ ✢

Heather stopped at her front door to remove her heavy gloves in order to manipulate the keys. A lot of the older folks in Copper Lake didn't even bother to lock their doors, but she knew what the actual stats were. Even their small town had enough tweakers to really run up the property-crime numbers. Like every other rural part of the country, there were meth labs out there, and when there was meth, there was thievery. If she was lucky maybe the werewolves would eat some of those scumbags and OD from the chemical cocktail in their blood. It would be like killing two birds with one stone.

There was a series of pops. She froze, listening. "You hear that?"

Harbinger looked around. "Nope. I feel like I'm deaf." Despite having thrown an old leather coat over his weird armor suit, his teeth were chattering.

"Gunshots . . ." There was the slamming of a car door, the roar of an engine, the spinning of tires. "That SUV is turning around." A sudden fear hit. It must be the two government men. They'd murdered Chase earlier, and now they were coming back to finish her.

"Get inside," Harbinger ordered.

Heather found her house key and got the door open just as the returning headlights illuminated the front yard. Harbinger followed her inside and closed the door behind them.

Startled, Otto began barking in the kitchen. To his credit, the German shepherd was ready to repel intruders. Her dog was just a shadow as he moved through the living room, shoulders hunched, head low. "Easy, boy," Heather said. "It's just me." The barking ceased. Otto stopped, tilting his head, confused. It was like he didn't recognize her in the dark. He barred his teeth and growled. "Calm down, big dummy." The German shepherd got closer, snarling. Then Heather realized she could smell Otto's fear. He was scared of her.

Peeking through the blinds, Harbinger studied the road. "Hmm . . . I don't know who this is. You know 'em?"

Otto was her pet, her loyal companion, but right then he was prepared to go for her throat. Otto may have only had three legs, but he was still an intimidating eighty pounds of Purina-fed muscle. "Harbinger, my dog doesn't recognize me."

He didn't turn from the window. "I should've told you. Animals fear us. Dogs especially hate our guts. I hope you're not into horseback riding."

Not Otto. He'd been a loyal friend forever. She loved Otto. There was no way. She reached out one hand, but Otto's brave growl turned into a whimper, and he scrambled for the kitchen, tail between his legs. It broke her heart. "Otto?"

"What're these assholes doing? Wait. One fella is getting out. Guns. *Get down!*" Harbinger grabbed her by the sleeve and jerked her to the floor just as the window shattered. Heather hit the carpet hard. There was a crackling noise as a machine gun raked bullets through the walls. Splinters and drywall rained down on them as the gun thundered.

Harbinger rolled on top of her protectively, a purely instinctive move, but asinine since he was only human and therefore not much better than a meat sandbag. "Crawl! Get to cover!" he shouted in her ear before rolling off, raising his Thompson and firing back through the window. He was answered with even more fire, but Heather was already scrambling for the kitchen. She'd just reached the linoleum when the bullet struck. The impact hit like a baseball bat and took her leg right out from under her. Heather shouted in surprise and fell on her face.

It took a second to realize that she'd been hit. She'd never been shot before. It *burned.* Rolling over, she grabbed her calf and felt the blood pouring between her fingers. The kitchen cupboards were flying apart, so she tried to become one with the floor.

Harbinger had heard her cry. Rising, still shooting, he backpedaled until he reached the kitchen and took cover in the doorway. "You hit?"

"I'm okay," she responded, but as she spoke, the burning sensation mutated into the worst pain ever. "Oh shit! No, I'm not. My leg!"

Bullets still flying, Harbinger came to her, and Heather almost passed out when he touched her leg, grabbing it roughly in the dark. His hands were firm as he probed the wound. Heather shrieked as her severed nerve endings fired. The pain flipped a switch deep inside. Something deep within Heather *awoke.* She gasped, but it wasn't because of the gunshot wound.

"Artery ain't hit. Keep pressure on it," he ordered. "And stay down."

"No kidding!" Heather shouted as the microwave exploded.

Then Harbinger was just gone. He may have only been human, but he was *fast.*

Earl used his minotaur-hide coat to protect his face as he went through the side window. It was an old, solidly constructed house, and in the excitement, Earl had forgotten that he was no longer a werewolf. That fact was driven home as he slammed his shoulder through the wooden slats and tumbled into the snow in a cascade of broken glass.

"Damn," Earl croaked as he got up and concealed himself in the deep shadows of the wall. That had actually *hurt*. The gunfire stopped. Earl was up and moving instantly. Running through the deep snow was far harder than it should have been. His legs were too weak. Reaching the front corner of Kerkonen's house, Earl crouched and shuffled into the narrow space between the wall and a snow-covered bush. It was dark except for the headlights, which their attackers hadn't had the forethought to actually point at their target. The light reflected off the snow of the road, illuminating the yard but leaving everything else in deep shadows.

Earl peeked over the edge of the porch. There were two of them. A short white guy with a buzzed head was wrestling with the feed tray on a SAW, obviously not familiar with the weapon. An older man with a mane of gray hair and an M-4 carbine was going up the steps, heading for the blasted front door. The SUV's windows had been tinted, so he didn't know how many other targets he had, so he'd start with these two assholes.

It would have been easy to just mow both of the knuckleheads down, but Earl kind of wanted to know why they were shooting at him first. He'd long ago rigged all his Thompsons with single-point slings that clipped to his armor so he could just drop his gun to use his hands, and Earl had always been a hands-on kind of guy. He let the Thompson fall as the first shooter huffed his way to the front door.

"Come on, Ryan! Back me up."

"The damn gun's jammed," the one with the SAW responded, obviously frustrated. "Hang on, Larry. Wait for me."

The names meant nothing to him. Earl smiled. These two idiots had tunnel vision. They were so fixated on what was inside the house that they couldn't see the danger right under their noses. Focusing on a perceived threat while losing your peripheral vision was a common effect of an adrenaline rush. That's why Earl always told his Newbies to keep on scanning.

"Hell with it," Larry shouted as he raised one boot to straight-kick the door in. Earl reached under the porch railing, grabbed him by the other ankle, and yanked. He yelped in surprise as his grounded foot came out from under him, and then he was tumbling down the icy steps. Earl came around the porch in a flash. He kicked the M-4 carbine off into the snow, then brutally slammed his fist square into Larry's face, and Earl knew how to knock someone the hell out. Earl grimaced as the shock traveled up the bones of his hand, but Larry was down.

The one named Ryan looked up from trying to clear the malfunction and saw Earl coming right at him, wearing a look of predatory confidence. "Oh shit!" Ryan tossed the SAW, reached across his body, and stuck one hand into his coat. Shoulder holsters amused Earl. They were comfy, but they sucked when your target was right up in your face, which Earl promptly demonstrated by reaching over and easily trapping Ryan's hand inside his coat. "Shit!" Ryan shouted again, eyes widening, as he realized he couldn't get his pistol out. Earl smiled, then brutally head-butted the shorter man.

The sound of their skulls connecting made a terrible *thud* noise. Ryan hit the snow flat on his back. Dizzy, Earl staggered away, holding his forehead. That was another move that worked great as a werewolf, but not so much as a human. "Son of a bitch, that stings." Everyone loses with a head butt.

But like they say, if an idea's stupid, but it works, then it ain't stupid, and Ryan was neutralized, moaning and dazed. Earl crouched there, waiting to see if there were other would-be assassins. Cursing his lack of awareness and the general dullness of human senses, Earl decided that apparently it was just this pair of jackasses.

With headache rapidly forming, Earl removed the pistol from his fallen opponent's coat. It was one of those oversized Belgian plastic guns that carried half a box of those little tiny armor-piercing bullets. He threw it in the bushes. Larry was still out, but Earl patted him down just in case. This time he found a .50 Desert Eagle, which was probably the single most unwieldy pistol ever manufactured, and to make matters worse, this one was actually gold plated. Grimacing, Earl tossed the gaudy thing onto Kerkonen's roof, where it would be hidden until the snow melted. He dragged Larry by the leg back to his buddy and dropped him there. Ryan was stirring, so Earl helped wake him up with a swift kick to the ribs.

"Ohhh . . . My head . . ." Ryan came to, saw the Thompson pointed casually at his face, realized what was happening, and immediately began to whine. "Please don't kill me. I'm sorry. I'm really sorry, Harbinger. Please don't hurt me."

"You've got the advantage, then. You know who I am. So, who're you and why are you shooting at me?" It took Earl a moment to realize that Ryan looked familiar. "Hold on." Earl reached down, grabbed Ryan by the collar, and dragged him up. Sure enough, it was one of his old Newbies. "Horst? Ryan Horst?"

"Yeah. You remembered," Horst said, raising his hands defensively. It was obvious he hadn't been mentally prepared for Earl being the one with the upper hand. "Come on, man, careful where you point that thing."

"This?" Earl jiggled the Thompson under Horst's nose. "You're lucky I don't ram it up your ass. What're you doing here?"

"Hunting monsters, just like you taught me." His voice quaked.

"Taught you? Hell, boy, I *fired* you." Earl remembered that Horst had been a low-life hood, but that hadn't precluded him from being picked for a Newbie class. A couple of Earl's best Hunters were ex-cons. The important thing was that they were survivors. The problem with Horst wasn't that he'd survived, it was the *how*, and when MHI had found out the whole story, they'd immediately booted him. "And I can see I made the right choice, because no decent Hunter would've got snookered so easy. Why'd you shoot at me?"

Horst was nervous, his eyes kept flicking down to the .45 caliber hole at the end of the Thompson. Earl remembered that Horst was the kind of sleazeball, know-it-all bastard who thought he could talk his way out of anything. Blood was running pathetically from his nose, but he tried to stand straight and look Earl square in the eye. "I promise I won't tell anybody your secret if you let me go."

"How—what're you talking about?" That took him completely by surprise. He was always careful to make sure the Newbies didn't know about his condition. Larry groaned, dizzy, bleary-eyed, and tried to sit up, So Earl removed the Thompson from Horst's face long enough to whack the barrel over Larry's head. Larry cried out and covered his head protectively.

"You stay down there." The Thompson's muzzle returned to Horst's neck. "You talk."

He was an excellent liar. "I won't tell anybody you're a werewolf. Look, I can give you money. Lots of money. I've got a rich uncle. He'll—" He cringed when Earl slapped him upside the head.

It made Earl's hand sting in the cold. "Do I look stupid? Who told you I was a werewolf?"

"Agent Stark!" Horst exclaimed, hoping to turn Earl's wrath against someone else. "Stark told us about how big the PUFF was. He told us you were evil, and that all the killing tonight was your fault."

Stark. Earl scowled. If the MCB had turned loose on him, he had even bigger problems on his hands than Nikolai, the mystery Alpha, Old Ones, and a pack of werewolves to deal with. The MCB were an obnoxious but dedicated bunch. Ending up on their shit list meant that he was going to have to find a rock to hide under for the rest of his life. "Where's Stark?"

Horst seemed glad to give that up. It gave Earl somebody else to be mad at. "The hospital, last I saw."

Earl had an idea. "Stark lied to you. I don't know why. The guy's crazy. Watch this." He lowered the Thompson and pulled a folding knife from his pocket. Earl flicked it open. Horst flinched, surely imagining that Earl was going to carve him up, but instead Earl made a small cut on the back of his own hand. He held it right in Horst's face as it bled. "See that? It ain't healing. I'm no werewolf. I'm just a man." The blood kept on flowing. "You kill me, all you're getting is a murder charge, not a dime of PUFF."

"It's totally Stark's fault." Horst nodded his head at the blood. "I was just trying to help. You know, all that saving people, protecting the public, just like MHI. We're on the same side. It was all a big misunderstanding. I was just doing my job."

"Job?" Even if they were from a rival company, other Hunters could make a huge difference. MHI was the best, but some of the other companies were pretty damn good, too, and Copper Lake needed all the help it could get. "Who the hell hired the likes of you?"

"Briarwood Eradication Services," Horst answered quickly.

"Never heard of them."

"BES? Based out of Chicago?"

"Ain't ringing any bells," Earl said. Horst seemed somehow deflated. Larry started to get up again, so Earl kicked him on the shoulder. That time he seemed to get the hint and just stayed still.

These had to be the other Hunters he'd saved at the grocery store, where he'd been promptly rewarded by getting an ax to the back. "Where's your team leader?"

Horst was hesitant as he answered. "I'm the team lead—"

Earl snorted. It figured. Sure, some of the other companies were professionals, but for every one of them, there were five little fly-by-night outfits just trying to cash in on the PUFF. He wasn't going to get any help from these amateurs. If their attempt on him consisted of hosing half a neighborhood with a belt-fed, then they'd probably be even more of a danger to the locals than the werewolves. Earl leaned in close and gave Horst an order. His tone left no doubt that it was not a suggestion. "Get your team. Get out of town. If you make it, spread the word and get help."

Horst was wide-eyed and seemed glad to just get out of there with his life. Earl let go of his collar and gestured with the knife at Larry. Horst helped lift his dazed friend, and the two stumbled for their car. "Horst," Earl shouted after them. His former employee stopped. "As a professional courtesy, one hunter to another, you get *one* free pass. Cross me again, and I put you in the ground."

Horst gave him a nod of acknowledgment, but Earl could see the hate in his eyes. This one could be trouble. Earl briefly entertained the thought of just gunning them down and being done with it, but a terrible wail came from the house at his back. It was audible even over the wind. The Briarwood men scrambled for the perceived safety of their car. Earl turned and lifted his subgun. "Damn it, Heather, not now." He started up the icy steps as the Cadillac fled. He didn't want to execute Kerkonen, but it didn't sound like he was going to have much choice.

Where am I?

It took a moment. It was dark, but she could see okay. She was on the kitchen floor, which just raised other questions, like how she'd gotten there. Then she saw the damage. The fridge was open, and the power had to be out because no light was coming from it. The digital clock must be out on the microwave, too, since it was blank. Then, as the clarity of her vision improved, she saw that the microwave was broken open and the fridge door was puckered with holes. Cabinet doors were hanging from broken hinges. The window over the sink was shattered and snow was blowing in. The flimsy curtains around the window were billowing in the wind.

Why am I sticky? Ewww. What is this mess?

Something warm and wet was on her hands, on her face. It soaked her clothes, making them cling to her body. She felt nauseous and feverish.

I must have gotten really drunk.

Slowly the events of the night came trickling back. Buckley, the monsters, getting bitten, running, striking back . . . Then the trickle turned into a flood, and as the dam burst, Heather realized exactly how she'd ended up on her kitchen floor. Lifting one tattered pant leg, she checked, but her calf muscle was whole and smooth. She lay there, breathing hard, thankful to be alive and wishing that it was in fact all a bad dream but already knowing that it wasn't.

Her senses were too acute. There were voices in the front yard, two engines running. The kitchen smelled of broken containers, freshly disturbed dust, and . . . *death*? In a panic, she realized that she couldn't remember what had happened after she'd gotten shot. It had hurt. She'd been scared, but after that . . . What? What had she done? She remembered the inwardly directed fear turning into outwardly directed anger, and then *nothing*.

Chairs had been turned over. One was broken. There was a darker shape in the shadows under the kitchen table. These memories seemed alien, out of place, but she knew that it had just been hurled there. The blood on her clothing, on her face and hands, had come from it. Hurt, she had lashed out. She remembered instinctively eating so she could recover, and then a sudden shock and revulsion. The other set of memories had tapered off then, leaving her alone.

She crawled toward the table. "Otto?" There was no answer. The shape didn't move. It was him. Otto was dead. She reached her dog, pulled him into her lap, and started to sob, rocking back and forth. She'd killed her dog, her friend. Heather lifted her head and howled her sorrow with a voice that was more than human.

Otto had been murdered, and she barely even remembered doing it. Tears cut through the blood on her cheeks. This was what Harbinger had warned her about. She was a monster. She hadn't even changed physically, and she'd *eaten* her dog.

The steps were audible a long way away. Harbinger walked softly by anyone's standards, but each boot fall seemed like thunder in her ears. He stopped in the doorway. Her back was to him, but she didn't need to turn to know that he had a gun pointed at her. "Heather?" he asked hesitantly, surely ready for her to leap up, with golden eyes and fangs to attack him, so he could mow her down without remorse. "Heather?"

"I killed him," she whispered.

"What?" There was another step. A glass shard ground between his sole and the floor.

"Otto. I killed Otto." She held the cooling mass of blood-soaked fur tightly in her arms as she rocked back and forth. She'd pulled another one of his legs off. Had the evil part of her thought that was funny? "I killed him and I ate him."

The Hunter was quiet. Her mind's eye could see the old gun at his shoulder as he lined the sights up on the back of her head. She'd never see it coming. She deserved it. But instead of putting her out of her misery, he said, "It was an accident. You reined it in quick. That's a good thing."

"Shoot me, Harbinger."

"Only if I have to."

"Promise?"

"I promise." There was a metal-on-metal click as Harbinger put the safety on and a creak of a nylon strap as he set the weapon down. There were two more steps and then a gentle hand on her shoulder. His voice was soft. "Come on. Let's get you cleaned up."

⊰ **Chapter 18** ⊱

The memories are murky here. I'm missing days, and sometimes even weeks from this period. Rocky hurt me badly here.

STFU had been working well together for several months when we were sent to operate out of an area known as Salem House. During this time we may or may not have hypothetically entered another country, like say . . . Cambodia, for example. We were inserted by a CH-3, which is a huge and very handy helicopter. All of this riding in helicopters for the last few months had convinced me that MHI really needed a chopper, and I promised myself that when I got home, I was going to buy us one.

A long-range patrol had disappeared. It was believed to be the work of the mysterious Russian. Conover hoped to pin down if this Nikolai even existed, and if so, what he was and how we should best go about killing him.

We found the remains of the patrol in short order. They'd been wiped out so fast that they hadn't even tried to use the radio. Only two of them had time to fire their weapons. It hadn't done them any good. I could smell the other werewolf everywhere. He'd left me a note, written on the back of a map and pinned to a dead soldier with his own bayonet.

> You kill mine. I kill yours. It is a game. Who is
> better? Let us find out, brother.
>
> —Nikolai

That was the real beginning of our war.
STFU ambushed a supply train the following day. We killed ten men.
I left a note on the leader.

Come out and face me like a man.

Two days later we responded to a raid on a firebase. We were
requested by name, which Conover found embarrassing for a unit that
did not actually exist. Four men on guard duty had been killed silently,
before the intruder had made it all the way to the center of the camp,
where he'd left a note on the commanding officer's cot. He'd taken the
major's head with him. Nobody else had heard a sound.

Dear Mr. Wolf and Special Task Force Unicorn,
    You are not trying very hard to impress me. You
can do better than this.

—Nikolai

The next night was the full moon. I informed Conover that there
would be no need to dig a hole. I was going out alone. He pulled the
task force inside the perimeter and issued silver bullets.

✢ ✢ ✢

Saying that the bridge was out was an understatement. A better
description would be that the bridge had been blown to bits. Though
rusty, Stark knew his way around demolitions, and he could tell that
whoever had taken out the bridge had not known what they were
doing, so had made up for it with volume. A few well-placed small
charges would have dumped the whole thing into the river. Instead it
looked like one really big one had been set square in the middle and
detonated. It had worked, though. Nobody would be driving across
the scorched remains of that thing anytime soon.

Agent Mosher thumped the steering wheel in frustration. This was
the second bridge they'd checked. The first had been just as ruined.
"Not again!"

"At least there aren't any bodies at this one," Stark pointed out. There
had been a pair of snowmobiles abandoned at the last bridge. They'd
gotten out to investigate and found where the riders had gone
downstream a bit and attempted to cross the icy river at a low spot. The

werewolves had picked them off on the far side. A few bloody limbs sticking out of the snow had been the only evidence. Stark checked his watch. They'd be covered by now, probably invisible until spring.

There was one other route out, but Stark had no doubt that it, too, would be covered. Even sitting here, he could tell they were being watched. The trees were thick on each side of the road, surely crawling with werewolves. This was abnormal behavior. Werewolves never showed this kind of coordination or planning. Even the most organized packs the MCB had ever encountered hadn't shown nearly this level of sophistication.

"Maybe we should try to ford it. It doesn't look too deep," Mosher suggested.

The kid's desire to be the hero was coloring his judgment and making him stupid. "They'd like that, I bet. The river isn't frozen solid enough yet to walk across. We don't have wet suits. You fall in that water and you're in trouble, trust me. And they'll just be waiting on the other side to pounce, just like those assholes at the last place. Wet, freezing, you're an easy target."

Agent Mosher cursed under his breath. It took a while to get the Suburban turned around. Plows weren't running, and they'd be lucky to make it back to town without getting stuck. "Careful," Stark ordered. If they got trapped out here, he knew that they were as good as werewolf chow. "Nice and easy."

"I can drive in this, sir. I'll get us there. Map shows a third route," Mosher said. "The next town is to the southwest, and it's on the same side of the river, so no bridges. Let's try that next."

Stark's contrarian nature made him want to argue. They could easily get stuck or slide off the road, and then they could either walk out and get eaten by werewolves, or they could stay put in the Suburban until they ran out of gas to run the heater, in which case they could freeze to death or be eaten by werewolves. So he really didn't have any other ideas.

The drive was nerve-wracking. It was a black-and-white, wind-whipping, snow-hurling world outside their windshield. They passed a car abandoned on the side of the road. The doors were open, the interior filling with snow. There was no sign of the driver. Mosher knew better than to even ask about stopping to check. Slowly they made their way through the slippery countryside.

They drove for half an hour. The silence was uncomfortable. Stark missed the constant chatter of the radio. He needed to make conversation. "So, Mosher, how'd you get recruited?"

"Akkadian sand demon attacked my convoy heading out of Faluja." Mosher laughed nervously as their rear end slipped, but they straightened out and managed not to end up in a ditch. "Though none of us knew what an Akkadian sand demon was at the time. We just thought of it as a giant skeleton-mummy that sand-blasted people to death. Turns out they're all over the place in Iraq. Official story said we'd hit an IED. A couple of us survived, got recruited. How about you, sir?"

"Deep Ones," Stark said.

"I hear fish people are nasty," Mosher said. "We've been torpedoing their cities since, what, the Thirties?"

"You don't know the half of it." As deepwater imaging had gotten better, every country that could afford subs had gone to work eradicating those vermin. They were down to hiding in tiny settlements off the coast, and the last of their cities were too deep to reach. "Scaly bastards climbed up a cruise ship, ate the men, kidnapped the women. I had just joined SEAL Team Two. We were nearby on a training mission. Small team got inserted by chopper before the sardines could escape. Smoked them all, saved a few hostages, but lost some good men."

"That's too bad, sir," Mosher said.

It had worked out well for Stark's career, though. Sam Haven had been the senior surviving SEAL on that op. Haven had not been pleased with Stark's performance, even going so far as to accuse Stark of choking under pressure, but what did they expect? It wasn't like Stark had gone in there knowing there were fish monsters laying their eggs in tourists. However, Chief Haven had been too honest for his own good, and fought with the MCB over the necessary eradication of the survivors. Haven had been drummed out of the Navy, and Stark had become the official hero of the moment. The rest was history.

The last road out of Copper Lake was also history. Luckily, Stark realized what was going on before they drove into the kill zone. "Stop," he ordered. Mosher complied immediately. Thankfully, the bright white of the snow gave enough contrast that he could make out the multiple vehicles parked ahead. A truck had been stopped across a narrow, low point in the road, completely blocking it. Some of the cars had tried to go around the truck skirting the forest and had promptly gotten stuck. No one was visible. "It's a trap."

"Crap." Mosher put it in reverse, looked over his shoulder, and sped them back the way they'd come. The first bullet pierced the windshield and center console between them. Other rounds struck the Suburban, hitting with loud metallic *pings*. "Ambush!"

Stark couldn't see where the sniper fire was coming from, but he could see the shadows moving between the trees, paralleling them. *Werewolves.* "Keep driving!" Stark ordered as he rolled down his window, picked up his SCAR-H, and fired the rifle out the window. The stock was still folded, so he didn't hit anything, but it made the pursuing werewolves think twice, and they took cover.

Mosher got them around the bend, and the incoming fire stopped. The junior agent did a three-point turn, cutting deep new ruts in the snow, while Stark scanned for threats. *Don't get stuck. Don't get stuck.* The werewolves had hunkered down and were just watching now, their mission accomplished.

Stark swore and punched the dash. These things were everywhere.

They were half a mile from the ambush before Mosher spoke. He was flushed with excitement. "We should stop here, try to cut through the forest on foot."

"Negative. I saw at least two werewolves moving, plus the shooter, who had to be in human form. That's scary good coordination for these beasts. As thick as that forest is, in these conditions? We'd be dead in ten minutes and never even see them coming."

"We've got NVGs and thermal," Mosher said.

"And they've got a million years of evolution, and that—" Stark waved his hand at the frozen landscape outside the cracked windshield—"is their element. Stalking prey in the woods is *what* they do! Regulations say that facing lycanthropes in wooded environments requires at least a complete fire team."

"The next town is only a few klicks," Mosher insisted. "I could run that in no time. Let me out, you head back to town and I'll go for help."

And leave me alone? Oh, hell, no. The kid was brave but incredibly stupid. "Regulations say that we can't split up."

Agent Stark wasn't a coward. He'd done some remarkably brave things . . . when he was younger. This easy little job to earn some under-the-table PUFF had turned into a disaster, and he really didn't feel like getting eaten for nothing. He'd been like Mosher once, full of piss and vinegar, but years of pushing paper in a soulless bureaucracy had sapped that youthful naïveté. He'd long ago accepted that he wasn't a hero, he was a bureaucrat. The young guns like Mosher were the ones that got to risk their lives playing hero. Stark was *management* now.

His young partner must have taken Stark's lack of response as hesitation. "We need to do something. People are dying!"

Stark sighed. He needed to take a different tack. Mosher was too earnest for his own good. "You're right, Agent. And getting torn apart in the woods isn't going to help them. Get us back to the hospital. We'll do what you suggested earlier and protect these yokels."

He obviously didn't like it, and they drove on in stony silence, but like all good MCB agents, Gaige Mosher knew how to obey orders.

Earl Harbinger found himself in a tricky predicament. Normally he wouldn't be too concerned being around someone newly turned into a werewolf. Worst-case scenario, they'd flip their lid and he'd have to deal with it with some good old-fashioned violence. But he was no longer in a position of strength. Before, if there was a sudden change, and he caught a surprise claw, he'd just tear the upstart's head off and then heal up in short order. Now, if Heather wigged out on him, he'd probably be dead before he got his gun out. He wasn't the king of the werewolves anymore. Now he was just another fragile human, and therefore he should do what any sensible human would do in his situation and promptly shoot her dead as soon as her back was turned. Instead, he found himself trying to comfort the distraught young woman turned killing machine because she was upset she'd eaten her dog.

"I'm pretty sure Otto had already been shot before you got to him," Earl explained. "I'm sure that's what set you off. He probably never felt a thing."

Heather had managed to wipe off most of the blood, and she seemed *relatively* okay after spending the last ten minutes in the bathroom puking. She pushed past him and walked down the hall. "You think so?"

"Sure. Otherwise he would've just run from you. Dogs are smart like that. Besides, don't beat yourself up about it. The first time I changed I ate a family of five."

"That really doesn't help."

He followed her into the bedroom. Heather hadn't specified what she was looking for, except that it was related to the amulet and the fact that the prisoner had said her grandpa had stolen it. Heather immediately went to rummaging through the back of her closet. With the power out, it was extremely dark back there, but she didn't bother to turn on her flashlight, and Earl wasn't about to point that fact out because it would probably just disturb her more.

Now that his vision seemed pathetic, Earl had to use his own flashlight to scan the walls. The room was more *feminine* than he'd expected for some reason, with frilly pillows, pastel colors, and scented candles. Maybe it was because the entire time he'd known her he'd only seen the tough side of the girl, but it was a little surprising. Also humanizing, but that didn't exactly help along his thoughts about the potential need to hurry up and shoot her. His light fell on some portraits.

At first Earl thought the lady in the picture with Heather might have been the Queen of the Elves, since she was about the right size, as in morbidly obese, but she had bright red hair. The man standing next to her was dark and thin. "Your folks live around here?"

"Used to. They're dead," she answered, not looking.

"Sorry to hear that."

"It's been a rough couple years. Mom got sick first, not that she was exactly in good health before that. Dad wasn't exactly the nursemaid type and really couldn't handle it, so I ended up quitting my job and moving back here. I got a job at the sheriff's department. It was supposed to be temporary. Crap." There was a crash as Heather knocked something off a shelf. "Mom died, but then Grandpa got sick, so I ended up sticking around. . . . Then, right after Grandpa died, Dad . . . well . . . It's complicated."

"It's really none of my business."

"That's okay. After Grandpa died, my dad changed. They weren't close or anything, but Grandpa's death really did something to him. Messed Dad up. Mom was gone. He started having all sorts of psychological problems, insomnia, and it got worse. He wouldn't talk about it. He wouldn't get help. He got really depressed. . . . Shot himself last Christmas. So I guess it's been almost a year now."

That was a tough one. "My condolences."

"Really screwed it up, too. He was in the hospital in a coma for weeks before he slipped away. He really should've asked me for advice. Heaven knows I've responded to enough suicides to know how to do it right. . . . Wow. That's morbid. Sorry."

Earl didn't know how to respond to that.

"I guess I'm still a little angry at him. Sad, but bitter, too. Well, anyways, everybody is gone, but I don't know . . . After Dad died, I just felt like I should stay here. I can't explain what changed. You know, I moved away from Copper Lake as soon as I could when I was younger. I used to hate this place. But somehow I ended up right back where I started."

"Life's funny like that." He moved to the next picture. "This your grandpa?"

Her head popped out of the closet. Heather had discarded her skullcap, and her hair hung in front of one eye. "Yep. That's the famous Aksel Kerkonen."

He was a weathered old man, scowling hard at the camera with his wiry arms folded. A gangly teenage girl stood next to him, and it was only the hair color that tipped Earl off that it was a much younger Heather in the picture. "He don't look friendly."

"He wasn't." Heather went back to looking. "He was a morose, bitter drunk, with an awful temper. He was kind of a local legend, since he kicked the crap out of roughnecks a third his age, got into a few knife fights, and the only reason I think he never went to prison is because everybody in town was too scared of him to testify."

"You didn't like him, I take it."

She came out with a long wooden box and set it on the bed. "Oh, I didn't say that. I loved Grandpa Aksel. I was about the only person he liked. The guy was a real character." Heather opened the clasps and lifted the lid. "This was his. He was a sniper during the Winter War."

Earl shined his flashlight onto the bed. The rifle was an old Mosin-Nagant. "May I?" Heather nodded, and Earl lifted the long bolt-action from the case. The wood had been worn smooth by hands and much use. The bolt worked easily for a Nagant, probably polished by a good smith at some point. No scope, which was odd by American precision-rifle standards, but scopes hadn't been as good back then, and not nearly fog proof, which really mattered when you were fighting in the miserable cold, spitting distance from the Arctic circle. Earl knew his tools and could tell that this rifle had been used hard but well cared for. "M28." He moved the receiver into the light. "Sako. 1939. The Finnish ones are supposed to be more accurate, I hear."

Heather was removing items that had been stashed under the rifle and setting them on the bed. "You seem like somebody who knows guns."

Earl shrugged. "Eh. I got shot by one of these once. Right in the kisser. Pow! That hurt." She gave him a strange look. "It was a Russian version, though, back in '45. Race to loot Hitler's experimental occult bunker . . . Long story. Never mind. What're you looking for?"

Heather held up a small book. "This belonged to Grandpa, too." She flipped through the pages until she found what she was looking for. "I'd forgotten about this, but your Russian friend was asking about an amulet that Grandpa might have had. Check it out."

He traded her the rifle for the book. It wasn't that different than the little leather-bound journal in his own pocket. Earl held up his flashlight to the yellowed pages. The letters were rough, almost drawn rather than written. "I can't read Finnish."

"Me, either, and Grandpa was barely literate anyway, but look at the *picture*."

Earl found the little ink drawing she was talking about. Aksel Kerkonen hadn't been much of an artist, either. "It looks like a pointy blob with a hand in it."

"That's what I thought when I first found this after he died, but look at the line around the back. But if that's a claw, then it's what I was asked about earlier. Now I'm thinking that line means it's supposed to be a necklace." It could be the amulet. After all, Earl hadn't got the best look at it while it had been ripping him to pieces. The claw in the picture was also short a finger. "And check this out." She moved in close to him and turned the page. "What's that look like to you?"

There were a bunch of stick figures, one of which had a gun, a couple of directional arrows, more words in Finnish, and a very cartoonish picture of an explosion. It took him a second to realize what he was looking at. The stick figure's actions were *numbered*. "These are instructions."

"Bingo!" Heather said excitedly. "The prisoner said Grandpa stole their amulet, and I'm betting this is about how he did it. Maybe it can help us get it back, and I can get cured."

Earl realized that she was standing uncomfortably close, close enough to feel the feverish warmth coming from Heather's skin. Distracted by the book, she brushed against his chest. Her hip touched his leg. Earl stepped back politely.

Heather caught his uncomfortable reaction and frowned. "Chill out, Harbinger. I'm not going to eat you."

Though it was a possibility, it actually hadn't been what he'd been thinking about at that particular moment, but Earl Harbinger had been raised to be a gentlemen. He tried to get back on task. "Know anybody who reads Finnish?"

"A bunch of the old-timers will. We've got a pretty big immigrant community here. There were a few at the gym." Heather placed the archaic Mosin on her bed. "Let's get back."

Earl noticed something gleaming in the case. "Hang on a sec." There was a stripper clip loaded with five rounds of ammunition. He picked up the clip and examined it under his flashlight. It was 7.62×54R for the Mosin, but there was something extremely odd about the projectiles. "Strange. These are sabots."

"He had a box of those with the rifle. What's a sabot?"

"An undersized bullet that doesn't fit the rifling, so it's held in place by a cup that falls off in flight," he explained. Heather shrugged; that meant nothing to her. "Pure silver bullets are junk. Stuff's too light, too hard, and a pain in the ass to make right, so I've seen Hunters improvise things like this before. These are silver, but it doesn't look quite right. They're too shiny."

"Let me see," Heather said, the impatience obvious in her voice. She held out one hand and Earl dropped the stripper clip onto her palm. As one of the bullet tips touched her skin, there was a flash of orange sparks and an audible *snap*. Heather jerked away and cried out. The ammo went flying. She clutched her hand to her chest. "It shocked me!"

"Let me see," Earl said. Heather stuck out her injured hand hesitantly. There was an obvious burn mark where the bullet tip had touched her skin. Heather withdrew her hand and put it to her mouth, wincing. Earl picked up the old ammo. "That ain't normal. Just touching silver should irritate a werewolf, maybe burn a little, but nothing like that. It don't mess you up unless it's put *inside* you, usually at high velocities. What is this stuff?"

Heather took her hand away from her mouth long enough to say "Electric-shock death bullets."

Earl gathered up the strange ammo. It could come in handy. "You say that like it's a bad thing."

⊰ **Chapter 19** ⊱

It got dirty from then on. I would change and hunt. Nikolai would respond with a new challenge. I'd kill his side, and then he'd kill mine. The body count climbed. He'd hit a village on our side and arrange the bodies like they were posing for a portrait. I responded by crawling into a tunnel complex and painting it red. Months passed.

He was goading me, pushing me to dark places that I'd thought I'd long ago controlled. I was transforming constantly. It was beginning to change me, to affect my judgment. Santiago would have been very disappointed in my behavior.

But I had to stop him. Nikolai was terrifying. He was everything I was not. He had no reservations, no hesitation, no mercy. Nikolai had to be defeated; otherwise it was like saying that my way was wrong and his was right.

What drives such a man? One part logic and one part savagery. I could not catch him. I couldn't outwit him, and in order to match him, I found myself doing things that I'd never thought I'd allow myself to do.

I'd not let the animal out to play like this since the island jungles hunting the Japanese. I was enjoying myself far too much. I was free, and I felt justified. Pride made me stupid. I was walking too close to the edge. I would shortly pay the price.

✢ ✢ ✢

Look at those pathetic slugs. Let's kill them.

Nikolai crouched in the shadows behind a shed, dressed in clothing stolen from the dead, watching the civilians as they continued their search for survivors. "What would that accomplish?"

They just deserve it. You want a reason? You used to not need a reason. Look where your reasons have gotten us. Fine. They're weak, they're stupid, and they're made of delicious meat. We're the top of the food chain. It's our job to eat them.

The voice continued its rant as Nikolai concentrated on the potential threats. There were three trucks working as a convoy, with humans in the back of each and more in the cabs, all armed. Two groups of four were moving between the houses on both sides of the street. He could parallel those, take them out quietly as soon as they got out of view of the vehicles. Then they could pick off whoever they sent after the missing, then kill the remainder at his leisure. It wouldn't be very hard.

He shook his head to clear out the red fog. Feeling a burst of anger, he once again couldn't tell if it came from him or the Tvar. Reasoning was difficult. His other half was pushing, becoming more and more demanding. Nikolai knew from long experience that he had to put his foot down or risk losing everything. Killing these men would serve no purpose. "No."

We're weak. We're hungry. They're right there! Kill them! KILL THEM! DEVOUR THEM!

"Quit shouting at me." That further enraged the Tvar. Nikolai grimaced against the sudden pain in his head. It was fighting to assume control of their body. It took all of his will to resist the fresh bloodlust pounding in his veins. Three years in desolation had tamed the Tvar, or so Nikolai had thought. He'd been fully in charge for so long that he'd forgotten just how forceful his other half could be. The bones in his hands cracked, and he clumsily dropped his rifle into the snow. Fingernails lengthened into claws. Nikolai curled his hand into a fist and drove the sharp edges deep into his own flesh. "I *refuse*."

Don't deny me. You owe me. Get up. Get up and fight!

Shuddering against the pain, he concentrated, just as his mentor, Koschei, had taught him. Giving in to the Tvar made it stronger, and each time he let it take control he'd be that much more likely to lose himself forever. He never should have let it free, but he'd been so desperate after Harbinger had murdered his wife. Rage had overcome intellect and the Tvar had come back with a vengeance. Being chained had angered it. It would not be put away quietly this time.

The images flashing before his eyes were of slaughter. The Tvar was excited. The delicious hot taste of blood could coat his mouth and quench his thirst. Swallowing hard, Nikolai made himself picture Lila's face as he'd last seen her alive; eyes as blue as the summer sky. She stood in the doorway of their home, waving, until he was over the hill and out of sight, just as she did every month, proud of his sacrifice yet eager for his return. The image jerked violently to that of her torn corpse. Logically, Nikolai knew the Tvar had done that to anger him, to goad him into changing.

The mission came first. Nikolai's breath hissed out between his teeth. The cloud of steam clouded his vision just as the Tvar's anger had clouded his thoughts. He gathered all his strength and pushed the Tvar away from his conscious mind, but it was winning the battle for their body.

It had been a long time since he could think clearly—since Lila's death, in fact. Blood welled between Nikolai's clenched fingers. Twitching, he forced his hand open, grasped his rifle, and dragged it against his body. His jaw ached as it began to extend. Teeth ground and cut through gums as they sharpened and grew. He maneuvered the muzzle under his chin. "I warned you."

No. Wait. If you kill us now, you'll never have your revenge. Remember Harbinger. Remember what he did to her.

The muzzle of the Val was freezing cold against his throat. "You will be silent." He was not bluffing. He'd had enough. He would not live as an animal again. She would not have liked that. Lila would be disappointed. Nikolai's finger found the trigger.

You win for now, coward.

The bleeding claws slowly retracted as the ache in his jaw subsided. Nikolai let the rifle rest against the shed as he sagged, exhausted, into the snow. Bitter, the Tvar retreated from the front of his mind. For the first time since he'd found Lila's body, his head was clear. He was alone.

Lila had been torn to pieces. The smells had told a story of terrible violence. He'd found Harbinger's patch, he'd found Harbinger's message, and the place had reeked with Harbinger's scent. Enraged, he had broken his sacred promise to his beloved, freed the Tvar, and set out on the hunt.

Lying there in the snow, weakened, freezing, Nikolai thought back to that day. When not distracted by the roiling anger of his other half, Nikolai was a very analytical man, and now he forced himself to remember the details. Every time he'd tried to do that before, the Tvar had interrupted and steered his thoughts back toward revenge. The Tvar had hated his sweet Lila. It had begged him daily to be rid of her so that they could return to their old ways.

This was Harbinger's fault. Nikolai did not believe in God, and even if he did, he knew there could never be forgiveness for the things he'd done, but for the first time in his long life, Nikolai had found simple happiness. Then the Hunter had forced his hand.

Yet the bastard Harbinger had seemed confused before they had fought. Surely he would have known why Nikolai had come here. Harbinger had unearthed the probable location of Koschei's amulet and murdered the only person Nikolai loved. Why should he be confused? The purpose of Nikolai's presence should have been obvious. Perhaps it had been an act to enrage Nikolai before the fight, to distract him from his righteous purpose.

But Harbinger was no actor. Their war had taught him that Harbinger was straightforward, direct. If he'd killed Lila, he wouldn't have denied it: he would have bragged about it. Harbinger was not devious enough to try to confuse the issue. And despite all of their battles, Harbinger had always avoided harming the innocent. He had a strange respect for humanity that even Nikolai's human side could not fully comprehend.

The scent was there. The patch. The message. It was obvious. Nikolai shook his head, unsure again who was doing their thinking. Lila had been slaughtered, but Harbinger had not reveled in the slaughter during the war. Even Harbinger's bestial side had been direct, killing swiftly, without mercy, but then moving on. Perhaps he'd changed, but men like Harbinger didn't change. Their course was set in stone, and then seen through to their inevitable conclusion.

Why would Harbinger even want the amulet? He never cared for the traditions or the challenges. Harbinger was a king who'd abdicated his throne to live as a man. It made no sense.

The Tvar returned quietly, padding back into his thoughts, sniffing nervously at Nikolai's suspicions. *Enough of this, Nikolai. Please.*

It was not like the Tvar to ask. Normally, it only demanded. What did it not want him to know?

There is no time for weakness. There is only time for revenge. For killing. Doubt makes you weak.

"Doubt makes me human."

Another truck turned onto the road below. The wolfsbane in Nikolai's pocket threw off his sense of smell, but somehow he knew who had just arrived. Harbinger was here. Nikolai would have his suspicions confirmed, one way or the other. Rising, he took up his rifle and staggered through the snow.

"There," Heather said, pointing. Earl had to squint hard to even make out the tail lights. "That's Aino Haapasalo's bunch. His family immigrated when he was a teenager. He should be able to translate."

"Grumpy fella, used to be a miner?" Earl asked. "Met him. Nice guy."

There were a few men bundled up against the cold, huddled in the back of each truck, rifles at the ready, watching. "I *volunteered* him. He's a tough old cuss. Used to be Grandpa's hunting buddy. He's a good shot, at least when he's not liquored up."

Earl smiled. "Is that often?"

"Only at deer camp. Those old timers all loved Grandpa's homemade booze. It tasted like paint thinner and rusty nails, but it sure did clean out the sinuses."

She sounded a little better. Earl reasoned that eating your own dog could be rather traumatic. "How're you holding up?"

"I'm not a quitter, if that's what you're wondering. I took an oath to protect this town, and I'm going to keep it." The words came out with steely determination.

"I'm focused on stopping these monsters, getting that amulet and getting cured. That's it. Let's go."

It appeared the locals were doing as Earl had instructed: using multiple vehicles, keeping them in the center of the road as a kind of mobile firebase, providing cover as another group went door to door, knocking. The trucks had spotlights, but they weren't using them right now. They could actually see farther without the falling snow reflecting the light back into their eyes. The key to fighting something fast and stealthy was by not putting yourself somewhere it could get a line on you. There were at least two guns pointed at them as they parked. These people were scared, but they were ready to fight. Earl was impressed, and he didn't impress easily. MHI was going to be able to do a lot of good recruiting in this town, provided anybody survived the night. Copper Lake was keeping it together, but he also knew that if these men came up against the Alpha, they wouldn't stand a chance.

This street was on the outskirts of town. There were only a few big houses, and behind them was nothing but trees. The squads had probably covered the rest of the town by now. Earl got out, dragging along his Thompson and tugging his coat tight against the freezing cold.

A young man hopped over the tailgate of the nearest truck and headed toward them. "Deputy," the kid shouted to be heard over the wind. He seemed excited. "We found something! You've got to see this. Come on." Heather looked at Earl, shrugged, and followed. "This was the last house, but man, you won't believe what's inside."

Several sets of boots had crushed a path through an iron gate and up to a large dwelling. It was difficult to tell in the weather, but it seemed like one of the nicer homes Earl had seen in Copper Lake. If it wasn't considered a mansion, then it was real close. Their guide slipped his way up the path to where two other armed men were waiting at the bottom of the steps. They seemed nervous. The kid pointed them onward before settling in with the others. For whatever reason, he didn't want to enter the shelter of the home.

The door was open. There was one figure waiting in the shadows at the top of the stairs. Earl barely recognized Aino under his giant wool hat and the scarf that was covering the lower part of his face. The old man seemed huge under all the layers. "Happy to see nothin's ate ya yet, Heather." He gave Earl a curt nod. "And, Mr. Earl, glad to see you jump in. I guess this is more fun than huntin' bears, eh?"

Earl returned the nod. "What did you find?"

"Something *odd*." Aino leaned to the side and spit over the railing. "It's inside." He stomped his feet on the mat out of habit before entering, leading the way with the beam of his flashlight.

Earl started in, then realized that Heather was standing, frozen. Her eyes were wide, darting back and forth. Something had spooked her. "Werewolves?"

She looked around to make sure no one was close enough to

overhear. "Not now, but there was. One of them is *strong*. He lives here."

"Who lives here?" Earl asked, already suspecting the answer.

"I don't know. This is his . . ." Heather paused, smelling the air. "It's making my head swim. I can't believe you can't smell that. Musky. It's like really strong cologne."

Earl cursed his pathetic homo-sapiens senses. Conover's informant had said that Nikolai had just arrived in the country, so this had to be the Alpha's territory. Their mystery man was a local.

"Come on," Aino shouted from inside. "Sooner we're out of here, the better."

Earl entered, shining his Streamlight along the walls. The place was nice, but unadorned. No pictures, no decorations. It was too clean. Heather followed a moment later, her manner subconsciously meek. Earl recognized the behavior. An Alpha was incredibly intimidating to lesser werewolves, and they were entering his den without permission. He'd always been too stubborn to bow to any werewolf, but he remembered the feeling. Every instinct Heather had was probably telling her not to come inside. Earl understood how much courage that took, even if she didn't. "Who owns this place?"

His voice seemed to startle Heather back to reality. She swallowed hard. "Used to belong to the Quinn family. The mine owners, before they got sued into oblivion after the big cave-in." She was gripping her shotgun so hard that her gloves creaked on the forearm. "It was empty for a long time. Then this guy from out of town bought it last summer and fixed it up as a vacation home." She scowled as Earl shined his light around the mostly empty reception room. "I never met him. He keeps to himself when he is around, lives alone."

"He got a name?"

"Smith, I think," she answered as they tracked Aino's bobbing light around the corner and into the living room.

"Uh-huh. I bet it is."

"The local girls talked about him a lot. He was single, supposed to be good-looking, apparently rich, day trader or something from back East, but he wasn't the social type."

Earl was still thinking about how the Alpha had called him father, but for the life of him, Earl couldn't recall anyone that he'd ever spread the curse to without having dealt with the repercussions immediately.

It was possible that maybe Rocky would have damaged those memories, but there weren't any gaps in his journal sufficient to explain this. Maybe there would be something here that would clue him in as to who he was dealing with.

The living room was huge, with a vaulted ceiling that opened up to a second floor. Aino was waiting for them by the dead fireplace. "We came through here and spotted a couple of RVs parked round back. The plates were from out'a state, so I figured there'd be guests stayin' here. Nobody answered, so we broke down the door and came on in. That's when I saw this. . . ." Aino aimed his light at the far wall, illuminating a monstrosity. Heather gasped and took an involuntary step back.

"Damn." Earl whistled. "That ain't something you see every day."

The skeleton was massive. It would have been too tall to fit in any room with a regular ceiling. The shadow the dark bones cast made it appear even bigger. The teeth gleamed white. One clawed hand was held out, palm open, as if warning them to come no closer. Standing on its rear legs, it towered over them, ugly as sin.

"Mr. Smith had some weird tastes in home decor." Puzzled, Earl approached the bones cautiously, knowing from experience that just because something was dead didn't mean it might not try to murder you. Yet it was not some fierce undead, just a bunch of bones held together with stainless-steel rods. It was a museum-quality display. The skull leered at him, grinning with long teeth that, despite their condition, still appeared razor sharp.

"At first I thought this guy had hisself a dinosaur—you know rich folks. But that ain't no dinosaur, now, is it, eh? It's got a wolf's head. Poached and skinned enough of the things to tell," Aino said. "Oh, don't give me that look, Heather. What're you gonna do? Cite me? Look at the skull. That's a wolf's skull on a man-shaped body. Sound familiar?"

"It's a werewolf, all right." Earl circled the stand, studying how the bones came together. "Just not like any I've ever seen."

"Because it's the size of a moose."

"It ain't just the size. You should see a warg some time."

"What's a warg?" Aino asked.

"A real pain in the ass to potty train," Earl muttered. He lit a cigarette as he paced around the fossil, scowling at the oddity. You can't study monsters for a century and not learn a thing or two about biology. These looked like werewolf remains, but they were wrong in more ways than just the size. The claws were thicker and too curved. The jaws were longer. The joints were wrong. Though werewolves could run on all fours for short bursts, they were primarily bipeds. Though the stand had this thing upright, it appeared it would be much more comfortable with all four paws on the ground. "I've seen a lot of monsters in my day, but I don't have a clue what this thing is."

Heather spoke up for the first time. "It's old."

"Probably." Earl examined the creature's outstretched arm. The bones were remarkably thick. If it had the regenerative abilities of a werewolf, it would have been a nightmare to fight. "Hard to tell when it died."

"No, I mean it's really old. I can sm—" Heather glanced over at Aino. "I just can tell. This thing is *ancient*."

Earl knew her nose was telling her things far beyond her logical comprehension. "How old do you think?"

"Well, I don't actually *know*."

There was knowledge, and then there was instinct. "Give me your best guess."

Heather seemed embarrassed. "I've got a feeling this thing was hunting woolly mammoths, if you get my drift."

Not for the first time, Earl found himself missing his werewolf senses. He'd forgotten just how unaware humans were about the world around them. If only he could—Earl caught himself. *Don't be an idiot.* After longing to be free of the curse for a lifetime, now by some miracle he'd got his wish and only a few hours later he was whining about it. *Hypocrite.*

Turning his attention back to the task at hand, Earl followed the creature's forearm down to the extended claws. Just like a werewolf. This was no paw: it was a hand, fingers, and an opposable thumb. It took him a moment to realize what was wrong.

There were only three fingers. The pinky was missing. It wouldn't seem so odd, except that the skeleton was remarkably complete. The bone had been sheared off, but he couldn't tell if that had been before or after it had died.

A fragment of his dream broke loose. The cigarette fell forgotten from his lips. It was as if the dead bones were covered in muscle and sinew, skin and fur. It was a living, breathing monstrosity, thrashing against the thick ropes that bound it to heavy stones. A lone warrior stepped forward to chain the monster's soul, while an army of men pulled on the ropes, dragging the mighty claw up, for the warrior to place his own palm against it.

He blinked, and the vision was gone. Hesitantly, Earl extended his hand until his palm touched the cold bone and steel rods. It was the image of the amulet. It was the beginning.

"Holy shit . . ." Earl stepped away. He rubbed his face in his hands. This wasn't some mere museum decoration. This was a sacred object. For the Alpha, this was holy ground.

"What is it, Harbinger?" Heather asked quickly.

"It's the first one," he whispered. Just like the images from when the Alpha had torn the curse from his soul; *this* was the beginning. He turned toward Heather. "This is how the curse started!"

"So, it's a caveman werewolf?" Heather asked.

"No. This was never a human being. People think of werewolves as a cross between a man and a wolf, but they're not. The behavior is wrong. The features are wrong. It's a cross between man and something, all right, but something different from a wolf. Similar, but something older, stronger. Something extinct. Something *worse.* "

Aino scratched his stubbly face. "I don't get what you're saying."

Heather instinctively knew. "This thing started as a wolf, but got twisted. Corrupted somehow."

"There are other shapeshifters out there. All sorts. Man and animal combined, but none are near as savage as the werewolf." Earl finally stopped and stared right into the ocular cavity of the huge skull. "Look at it! It's—"

"Beautiful."

The voice had come from above. Earl spun around as Aino's light flickered up. Nikolai Petrov leaned over the upstairs railing, haggard, with dark circles under his wild eyes. Earl reached for his Thompson but knew it was too late. The Russian gave a small, fatalistic smile as he casually pointed his strange rifle at Earl's face. "Place your weapons on the ground. Slowly."

Nikolai had the drop on them. Earl complied, sliding the sling over his head and putting the Thompson on the carpet. *He must have snuck in an upstairs window.* Distracted by the bones, none of them had even heard him coming. Heather and Aino were hesitating, but Earl shook his head at them. With Nikolai's inhuman reaction times, they'd be dead before either could lift their guns.

"Sidearms as well." Nikolai was wearing a bloodstained coat and a shirt that had been torn to rags. The ribcage was visible through his too-pale skin. Nikolai was little more than a walking skeleton. Their battle had taken a fierce toll. "You should have finished me when you had the opportunity, Harbinger."

Cursing himself, Earl tossed his revolvers on the floor and slowly raised his hands to a position of surrender. "If somebody hadn't set me on fire, I would've."

"Yes. Fortunate. I should just shoot you now, but—" Nikolai suddenly grimaced, as if in terrible pain. Earl tensed, ready to go for his revolver, but Nikolai's gun did not waver. The Russian's face turned red as he rapidly blinked. "I have to know why. Why did you do it? After all these years, why did you break our truce?"

"I didn't do any—"

Nikolai jerked, the muscles of his face twitching hard. "Shut up!" he shouted, spit flying from his lips. "Shut up!"

"I was trying to answer your question."

"Not you, idiot," Nikolai snarled, steadying himself against the railing. "*Him.* I asked you a question, Harbinger. Answer me."

Nikolai's lost it. "Well, I will if you'd quit yelling," Earl said, using the calmest voice he had. "Make up your mind."

Nikolai moved the rifle slightly and blew a hole in the carpet a few inches in front of Earl's boot. The gun was suppressed, but the sound still made a resounding *THUMP* in the enclosed space. "No more games. Why did you kill her? She'd done nothing to you."

"I have no idea who you're talking about," Earl said.

"You came all the way to Sklad to rip her apart."

"Where the fuck is Sklad?"

"It was my home!" Nikolai roared. The next bullet winged Earl's leg, just barely creasing armor and scratching flesh. Earl flinched. Heather cried out. His minotaur-hide jacket might stop a rifle bullet, but regular Hunter armor wouldn't. Earl knew the next one was going through something vital. The scratch burned and let loose a thin trickle of blood.

"Never been there, never heard of the place, and I don't recall going out of my way to kill anybody recently."

A different sound came out of Nikolai, deep and guttural. "*He lies!*" Then his voice returned to normal. "I told you to shut up!" Then back to deep. "*He's a trickster. Destroy him!*" Nikolai shook his head. "First, I must know the truth."

Earl glanced toward Heather. She was more confused than he was. Aino mouthed the word *crazy*. Earl turned back to Nikolai. "I didn't come into your territory. You came into mine. I swear I don't know what you're talking about."

A scowl creased Nikolai's face. "He's telling the truth. But how . . . how did his scent—the patch. Wait . . . You wanted me to believe. You lied to me."

"I'm not lying!"

"I'm not talking to you, Harbinger!" Nikolai was growing increasingly frustrated. "It was a simple trick. I should have seen right through it, but you let me believe. All this time, you clouded my mind, all so you could run free."

The Russian was erratic, and the crazier he got, the odds of them getting shot grew. "You were lured here. I think we both were. Lower that gun, Nikolai. We've got a mutual enemy."

The Russian's face contorted. For a moment he appeared to be an entirely different person. Nikolai's strange, deep voice intruded. "*Harbinger lies! I would never betray you.*"

"I've been framed. Can't you see? We're both being used. Me, you, and . . . you. Both of you have been set up."

"Don't patronize me. I should kill you where you stand . . . but you're telling the truth. You do not have the amulet. I would be able to feel it. In fact . . ." Nikolai sniffed the air. "Impossible. The wolfsbane must be corrupting our senses. I can smell the female, but I can't smell you. It's as if you're just one of *them*."

He knows. Perhaps if he could get Nikolai off guard, he'd have a chance. "Your real enemy used that amulet to remove my curse. I'm only a man. I'm no longer any threat to you, but the other Alpha is. He's powerful, too powerful, and he's up to no good. He's got dark magic and minor Old Ones helping him. Help me stop him, Nikolai. He's the one that hurt your woman, not me."

Nikolai went quiet, deep in thought. Standing perfectly still, they waited for nearly a minute. Despite the cold, Earl felt a single bead of sweat roll down his forehead. His arms were starting to quiver from holding them up. Nikolai seemed to breathe again. His next words dripped with weariness. "I know now what I must do."

Then, with incredible speed, the Russian acted. The sudden movement surprised Earl, but rather than using the rifle, Nikolai tossed it aside as he leapt over the railing. He landed effortlessly, crouched in the living room. Earl's hands flew downward to snatch a revolver from the ground. Nikolai charged as the Smith & Wesson filled his hand, but Earl knew he was too late. His human reaction speeds were too slow. Nikolai was just too fast.

One skeletal hand locked around Earl's wrist like a vise. Nikolai's gold-flecked eyes were staring into Earl's, so close he could smell the Russian's breath. Yet Nikolai stopped, only inches away. Slowly, Nikolai released Earl's gun hand and took a step back. The two watched each other, Earl knowing that Nikolai could easily strike him down before he could raise his gun. *What's he doing?* Nikolai gave the slightest hint of a nod, like a gunfighter at high noon, and Earl tensed, waiting for the killing blow.

No attack came. Instead, Nikolai *bowed.*

Earl speed rocked the revolver into position. They were so close he didn't even need to aim. He drove the muzzle into the top of Nikolai's skull.

Nikolai spoke, calm for the first time since his arrival in the Alpha's home. "I yield."

Finger on the trigger, Earl hesitated. "Huh?"

The tone was humble. "You are the superior werewolf. I submit to the will of your pack."

"What?" A few more ounces of pressure and Earl would put a silver bullet through the top of his enemy's head. "What . . . What are you doing, Nikolai?"

"Surrendering. I challenged and failed. Do with me as you will."

Dumbfounded, Earl just stared at the man kneeling at his feet. "You miss the part where I'm not a werewolf anymore?"

"It doesn't matter," Nikolai said, lowering his forehead until it touched the floor. "I need you. I'm not strong enough to hold him much longer. The Tvar, the beast inside me, believes in the old ways. He *will* follow. He has to. Instinct demands it. You won. We lost.

I pledge myself to your pack. Do with me as you will . . . Kill me, but let me help you find the man that hurt Lila first."

Clack. Earl thumbed back the hammer of the Smith. Cocking a double-action was a totally unnecessary movement, but it made him feel more confident for some reason. "You're insane. You had me, and you do . . . whatever the hell this is?"

There was no response. Plea made, Nikolai waited patiently for his sentencing.

"What're you waitin' for?" Aino shouted. "Shoot him already!"

But for the first time in his life, Earl Harbinger was actually too surprised to kill someone.

⇥ **Chapter 20** ⇤

There are many gaps in my memory here, and for once I think I might actually be thankful to Rocky for taking something from me. Some things are better forgotten.

I'd changed and gone out alone, hoping to find his scent, but Nikolai was too clever for that. I happened on some Viet Cong setting booby traps. I killed them and then followed their trail back to their base. It wasn't an armed camp. It was a village.

I can try to justify what happened next. These were the enemy. This was where they lived. There were families here, but it was my enemy's fault for hiding behind them. This was war. Nikolai shouldn't have pushed me. . . . But the excuses are hollow. They're human excuses, human justifications. I was a werewolf, operating on instinct, and I was doing what came naturally.

We found a new note several days later.

> Mr. Wolf,
>   Playtime is over. Now we are getting down to serious business. I have been looking for a suitable challenge, and it seems I have finally found one. With respect.
>   —Nikolai

It seems all werewolves are searching for something.

✢ ✢ ✢

The Alpha awoke suddenly. Fevered dreams had haunted his sleep, plagued by visions of the lesser werewolves that had come before.

Strange energy hummed through his body. The *becoming* was complete.

He'd taken refuge inside Shaft Six. The witch had buried her two diggers at the entrance to guard as he'd slept, vulnerable. Lucinda was upstairs, resting next to a propane heater. His senses could pick her up easily through several floors. The prisoner he'd had Lucinda's minions gather was secured in another room to be dealt with later. A few members of his pack had returned to the relative safety of the mine building to lick their wounds. Two were sleeping on the ground nearby, having returned to human form, recuperating from multiple gunshot wounds.

The amulet of Koschei rested on his chest, burning with the heat of Earl Harbinger's werewolf spirit. Taking it in his hands, the Alpha could feel the spirit inside stir. It was powering him, giving him greater vitality and strength, just as the first of their kind had robbed the mighty forerunner to become so much more than human.

Since the time of his ascension was at hand, it was time to raise the *vulkodlak*. The whole thing was very exciting. They would be an unstoppable wave, crashing across the Earth. Koschei had been too frightened to set them free, but he had been a fool, an immortal with no ambition, which made for a remarkably sad creature. The Alpha, on the other hand, was a man of vision.

It was simple, really. The *vulkodlak* would spread like wildfire. This isolated town was just a practice run. The humans would probably be able to contain this first wave, but the Alpha had been planning for this moment for a long time.

The MCB would try to contain them in silence at first, but it would be too much. The *vulkodlak* reproduced far too rapidly. The Alpha knew exactly how the MCB would respond, because he had studied their doctrine. Copper Lake would be cut off from the world and burned clean. This place was just a test, and a deserving one at that, since it had unwittingly sheltered the man, Aksel Kerkonen, who'd dared to steal the birthright of an immortal.

The hiding place of the amulet was sparsely populated and about as isolated as anything in the continental United States could be. It seemed a waste to unleash the *vulkodlak* here. Copper Lake, the tiny community where he'd lived off and on for the last year while searching for the amulet, was just to get the bugs worked out without the MCB leadership getting too nervous. They'd cover it up and assume it was some sort of isolated event. Similar things had happened before and would probably happen again. It would be just another monster-related tragedy in a long list. By the time they figured out what had happened, he'd be ready to launch the second wave.

The big show would come later. He'd analyze the results of tonight's mission and adjust accordingly. There was a steep learning curve involved whenever ancient magic was utilized. He knew this, but he liked to dream big. The next wave would be far more impressive. He had children staged in huge, densely packed cities all across the country. He'd run the simulations himself using MCB-designed software. If everything worked as predicted, eighty percent of the population of Chicago would be overrun in eight hours. New York in six.

Humanity would not last under that onslaught. They were an evolutionary dead end. The select would become werewolves. Those that fought would be harvested for the *vulkodlak*. The remainder would be kept as prey. He reasoned that entire regions would become game preserves. The Alpha was going to hit the reset button for the world.

Harbinger's life was more than strong enough to raise the local *vulkodlak*, but the Alpha didn't want to squander such a spirit just yet. The amulet had been created with dark magic to enslave and bind the spirits of monsters. He understood that now. It burned life as fuel. Every use drained it. It would need constant replenishment: the stronger the werewolf, the better. If he'd realized that before, he never would have let Harbinger kill Petrov. He would have harvested both of them instead. He hated being wasteful.

There were others that he could use instead. They were his pack, but most of them were expendable.

Strange, the Alpha thought to himself as he selected his victims. He'd loved his pack once, but their lives no longer mattered. Only an hour ago, these had been his beloved children, but now they were just more fuel. The two here would suffice. For some reason, he could no longer remember their names.

He raised his voice and shouted for Lucinda. The entire shaft shook. He would need the witch's help for the awakening. The thunderous noise startled the other werewolves awake. Frightened, they tried to creep away, but he coaxed them back with a gentle word, using the full power of his voice, and they meekly returned. He reached out and took a female by the neck.

The harvest had begun.

Nikolai took a seat on the leather couch at the far end of the Alpha's living room. He seemed rational now, but Earl wasn't taking any chances. The Hunter stood at the far end of the room, his Thompson shouldered and trained on the Russian. The safety was off, and Earl's finger was already inside the trigger guard. At the slightest movement, Earl would hose him down.

The giant skeleton sat there, watching from the shadows. Heather had given her grandfather's journal to Aino to try and to decipher, and the miner had gone back to the relative safety of the convoy to read. Earl had asked Heather to explore the rest of the house to search for anything interesting. She was not a trained Hunter, and probably wouldn't know what to look for, but Earl had wanted to question Nikolai alone. Earl planned on killing Nikolai as soon as they were done talking. Witnesses seemed to cheapen that. Though evil, Nikolai was a warrior and deserved at least some dignity in death.

"I always suspected you would be the one that finally killed me," Nikolai began.

"I had that thought about you a few times myself," Earl answered. "I can't say I ever imagined you'd just up and commit suicide, though."

"I died the day I found Lila dead. The weeks since have been nothing but a bad dream."

"I didn't do that," Earl stated. "I give you my word."

"I know that now. Tvar has relented. I can see clearly again." Nikolai shook his head. "They must have had something of yours and used it to spread your scent at the scene. I should have seen right through the ruse, but he capitalized on my anger, confused me so that I would let him run free. . . . I don't know how you do it. . . . How do you keep yours chained so well? He is so demanding. Always interrupting, only letting me think when it suits his purposes."

It was the first time the two of them had actually had a conversation, and Earl was mildly surprised to discover that he didn't understand his old nemesis nearly as well as he'd thought. "That's not really how it works for me."

Nikolai's werewolf side had broken off and become a separate personality. Earl's was, or had been, just a shadow in his mind, jumbled urges and anger. He shuddered at the thought of it actually *talking*. If anything, Earl's inner werewolf had been the strong, silent type.

"Lucky you," Nikolai said. "I'd contained it. The longer I was strong, the quieter it became, until finally it was silent except for when the moon was full. Someone helped me find peace, but when I lost her, it came rushing back to fill the void. . . . But enough about that, comrade. Will you accept my service?"

"I've not come to a conclusion on that point just yet," Earl lied.

Nikolai knew the truth. "I understand. Do what you will, but just know this: until you pull that trigger, I am your man. I have sworn my loyalty to you. The Tvar was winning. I could not allow that. It must obey the instincts, and the instincts demand that the superior werewolf leads. It will follow."

"My distinct lack of werewolfhood might cause a bit of an issue there, when he decides to come out and eat me and all."

"You have my word that I'll deal with that should it arise."

"You were a KGB assassin. Forgive me if I don't get warm fuzzies about your personal integrity."

Nikolai smirked. "Believe what you will. I will answer your questions to the best of my ability until my time comes. The Tvar is confounded for now. All I ask is that you avenge Lila. The one who bears the amulet of Koschei must be stopped at all costs."

"Who is it that has the amulet?"

"I'd thought it was you, of course. I do not know his identity, but he must have been remarkably strong to even wield it. It doesn't matter now, though."

"And why's that?"

"The amulet will have changed him by now. Whoever he was before will have been erased. It is a powerful artifact."

Earl was getting tired of holding up the Thompson. Being a werewolf, he'd forgotten how darn heavy these things were, having been made back in the good old days when everything was made of solid wood and machined steel. "Tell me about it."

"Do you know of Koschei?" Nikolai asked. When Earl shook his head in the negative, Nikolai continued. "He was my mentor. The oldest of all werewolves. He'd pledged his loyalty to Lenin, and Stalin after that, though neither realized just how old he really was. They believed him to be just a mere werewolf, willing to serve in exchange for legitimacy and protection, which sounds a *bit* familiar. . . ."

Earl didn't let the jab upset him. "Man's gotta eat."

Nikolai continued. "Since Koschei wore the amulet, he was virtually immortal. He kept a low profile, doing their bidding but never rocking the boat. Before the Soviet Union, he had served the tsars, and before that the Rus. Before that, who knows? He was a follower, not a leader. Koschei was a figure of myth. They called him the Deathless, yet he rarely indulged in using the amulet's powers. I believe he was afraid of it. I had become like a son to him before he even revealed it to me. Not even he knew where it had come from, only that it was old, and that it granted terrible powers."

Earl nodded toward the skeleton. "This fancy amulet look like that thing's hand by chance?"

A moment passed as Nikolai silently studied the three-fingered claw. "In fact, yes. Though I do not know what this creature was, it calls to me. Can't you hear its song? No, of course not, I forget, your Tvar has been silenced. Believe me, Harbinger, these bones are special. This is a shrine."

"You mentioned terrible powers. What're we talking about here?"

"The amulet feeds on the life energy of werewolves and bestows it on the bearer. Koschei only used it sparingly to keep from aging. For someone who was supposedly a loyal Communist, he had an inordinate fear of the afterlife. However, near indestructibility is not the ability that worries me. Have you heard of *vulkodlak?*"

The prisoner in the county jail had spoken of them before Earl had put him out of his misery. "Only in passing."

"I first heard it from one of Stalin's Romanian necromancers. When Koschei learned that the Motherland was experimenting in such things, he became distressed. I suspect that he even sabotaged the project. Well, perhaps sabotage is the incorrect word, since the outright murder of several necromancers is a bit stronger than sabotage. Koschei had lived for seven centuries, and nothing caused him greater worry than the idea of the *vulkodlak.* I do not know the specifics of such beings, only that they are related to werewolves and death magic, and that they struck fear into the heart of an unstoppable man."

"Well, I'm guessing somebody stopped him, otherwise his fancy necklace wouldn't have ended up in Michigan." Earl finally gave up and sat on the carpet, leaning his sore back against the wall. He was careful to keep the subgun on Nikolai the entire time. "Do you know how he went down?"

"I was not there. Stalin sent him to fight in the Winter War. Koschei was lost in battle. Intelligence discovered who had been given credit for the kill, a young rifleman named Kerkonen. The amulet was never recovered, but since I was the only one aware of the amulet's significance, I did not pursue it."

"Why not?" Earl asked. "Something like that could have been mighty handy for you Commie bastards."

Nikolai's smile was unnerving. "If you knew my Tvar, you would understand. He could *never* be allowed such a toy. It was for the best, for all of us."

This confirmed what Earl had already learned. Heather's grandfather had somehow defeated an immortal werewolf and then brought its magic talisman to America. Why hadn't he just destroyed the damn thing? Why come here at all? Had he realized what he had? The rough pictures in the journal indicated that he had at least some idea of its significance.

"Who else knew about the amulet?" Earl wondered aloud. "It's no coincidence that a powerful werewolf who just happened to have the bones of the great-granddaddy of all werewolves moved into this house in the town where the amulet was hidden."

"Perhaps it was fate?" Nikolai suggested.

"Me and fate don't get along, and coincidence ain't exactly my friend, either." Earl kept his right hand on the Thompson's grip as he fished a cigarette out of his coat with his left. "Want a smoke?"

"Do I get a blindfold, too?"

Earl chuckled. "Like you'd want one. Don't worry, you'll see it coming. That's only fair. . . ." Earl lit up and took a long draw. He blew out a cloud. Hopefully the Alpha didn't smoke and Earl was at least stinking up his fancy living room. "So, how do I kill this asshole?"

"I do not know, but I would like to help. It helps when I have a purpose. If you order me to help, Tvar will have no choice but to obey."

"Nikolai, I'm afraid you're broken inside, and I don't trust you at all. I'm trying real hard to decide what to do with you right about now. I don't suspect you'll like what I've come up with."

"I can be of assistance."

"I'm sure you could. . . . One question?" Earl took another puff, savoring the smoke. He was going to miss those regenerating lungs. "How many innocent people have you killed? Not in total, because we both know it would take all night to make that list. How many have died just since you've gone on your latest rampage?"

Nikolai looked down at his hands. "Too many."

"One is too many, *comrade.*"

There was a polite cough as Heather came down the stairs. "Am I interrupting something?" she asked.

"Nothing of significance. Just my trial," Nikolai said, taking his eyes off Earl for a moment. "My, my, Deputy, aren't you the lovely specimen. The curse suits some of us more than others. I bet you feel simply wonderful right now. You're quite the butterfly compared to the little caterpillar I met this afternoon."

"Stuff it, weirdo." Heather walked as far around Nikolai as possible. "The place is mostly bare, Harbinger. Everything is neat as can be. Clothes are clean and folded. No ID, no papers, no personal effects, no decoration, nada. There's a Mac on the kitchen table. We can plug it in at the school and see if there's anything useful on it." She held out something to Earl. "This is the only thing out of place in the whole house, other than Mr. Bony, obviously. It was in the dresser drawer next to the bed."

"Cover him for me," Earl suggested as he took the photograph. Heather aimed her shotgun at Nikolai.

"I assure you, there's no need for that, my dear." Nikolai spread his hands innocently.

Heather cocked her head to the side. "I'm guessing people have probably told you you're a charming man, Mr. Peterson."

"Why, yes, they have."

"They lied. Now shut the fuck up."

The photo was crinkled and falling apart with age. Earl flicked open his Zippo and studied it with the light cast by the flame. It was yellowed and discolored to the point that it took him a moment to realize that he *knew* these people.

It can't be . . .

Suddenly, everything made sense.

He must have made a noise. "Harbinger?" Heather asked, the concern evident in her voice. "Are you okay?"

No. I'm not. The Alpha had called him father. He couldn't remember spreading the curse, but the evidence was here. Earl didn't understand how he'd been tricked, but with dark magic involved, there were ways to deceive the senses. The smell had been wrong, the voice had been wrong, but he and Nikolai had both been lured here, not just because of their strength, but because of their personal connections. Earl had been lied to by someone he'd considered a friend, and there was nothing he hated more.

Earl touched the photograph to the flame. It caught quickly. He held it out as the flames consumed the paper. Finally, as it began to sear his fingers, he tossed it to the carpet and watched it burn. It was sorely tempting to let the fire spread to the whole house, but he rubbed it to ashen bits with the toe of his boot. "Heather, wait for me outside."

"But—"

"*Now!*"

Heather hurried for the exit. Earl waited until she was gone before resignedly setting his Thompson on his legs. He closed his eyes, and for a moment didn't really care if Nikolai charged or not. Apparently, the werewolf meant to try and keep his promise, and stayed seated on the couch. Nikolai sensed the change in Earl's demeanor. "What is it?"

"It's just like the old days, Nikolai. . . . We've been used. Just like the old days." Tired, Earl rubbed his face in his hands. He should have been angry, but it just hurt. The last time he'd felt this way was when he'd learned about Martin Hood's betrayal. Earl was getting mighty sick of people lying to him. "Remember our war?"

"How could I forget?"

"I did. I forgot a bunch of it. Not by choice, but it was taken from me." Earl opened his eyes. "Apparently, I lost more than I'd thought."

"I do not understand," Nikolai said hesitantly.

"It don't matter. A lot of good men died fighting you."

"I did not hold a monopoly. Good men died on both sides."

"What can you tell me about the last time we met in Vietnam?"

"I led an assault on your base of operations. Both sides took heavy casualties. We severely injured each other, and both of us were evacuated."

"Did I . . . hurt, maybe give the curse to anyone on my side?"

Nikolai seemed confused by the question. "No. You were an honorable adversary."

Earl smiled as he stood. "Wish I could say the same for you, but you were surely the most dedicated son of a bitch I ever crossed." He reached to his belt and pulled out one of his Nightguard revolvers. He opened the cylinder and ejected the moon clip. "Scary, mean, downright ruthless, but dedicated." Earl put the moon clip in one pocket and rummaged around until he came out with another clip holding six rounds. Holding it up, he studied it, squinting in the dim light. Earl ran his thumb over the bullets and nodded. "I can respect that. So I'm giving you a chance."

"What's that for?"

"You want me to trust you? Well, after the things you've done, you've got to earn my trust." Earl pulled one cartridge's rim free of the sheet-metal moon clip and studied it. Apparently satisfied with the round of ammunition, Earl dropped it into the cylinder and gave it a hard spin before closing it. "You say your life's worth nothing and that you're willing to follow the old ways. Well"—Earl tossed the gun in a long arc across the room—"prove it."

By the time the revolver landed at Nikolai's feet, Earl had already lifted his Thompson to cover him. "Really? Russian roulette?"

"Appropriate, don't you think?" Earl gestured with his subgun. "Pick it up. . . . And you so much as twitch in my direction, I'll cut you in half with silver bullets. You're fast, but you ain't that fast."

Nikolai slowly lifted the Smith & Wesson. His expression was blank.

"Put it against your temple."

Hand quivering, Nikolai did as he was told. It took him a long time to respond. "The Tvar is not happy with this development."

"Your *ta-var* is a whiny little bitch. Tell him the king of werewolves says to quit his crying. This is how it's gonna work. I'll ask a question. Each time you answer wrong, you pull the trigger."

"I hope this is a short quiz."

⤞ Chapter 21 ⤝

Sharon was the first to speak to me. We'd been working together long enough that she knew me well. She approached me one day while I sat, exhausted, unshaven, and haggard, smoking and glaring at the jungle. Even my human hours were spent filled with anger. Conover's superiors had been pushing him, so he'd been pushing us. She told me that she was worried about me.

"I'm just doing my job," I told her.

"You're changing, Earl. There is a darkness growing. I can feel it in you."

It took everything I had not to lash out at her. She was right. I was having a hard time staying in control. "Don't read my mind. You really won't like what you find."

She had a lovely laugh. "That's not how it works, but I don't need magic to understand the emotions I can read right off your face. You are not him. He is not a reflection of you. Nikolai is a monster."

"Look around you. So are we," I snapped. She put a gentle hand on my shoulder. It was like all of a sudden my cares were less. Happy memories filled my head. Sirens have powerful magic. "Sorry. You're not. You're a decent girl with questionable parentage. Travis ain't a monster, either. Scariest damn thing you've ever seen, but he's basically a big hyperactive teenager. . . . But me, I'm something awful."

"You do what you have to. You don't enjoy it like Nikolai does. We've all seen what he leaves behind. You're starting to think that you two are the same."

"Not anymore. We are the same. Killing . . . It's all I want to do. It's all I can think about."

Sharon then asked something that has stuck with me ever since. "Why does it mean so much to be human when you're not?"

I didn't have an answer.

"Oh, Earl. Just think about it. You're far more human than most humans I know. You have to make a choice. You have to try. Let me help you," she offered. "I can soothe you. I can quiet the monster inside."

I laughed at her. "You coming on to me?"

Sharon blanched. "Ugh, no. Really, no offense, but I'm descended from Achelous. My nearly immortal mother fell for my father because he was the most perfect man she'd seen in hundreds of years. Once I get out from under this PUFF thing, I'll probably go be a model or marry somebody stupidly rich. I'm really, really, really out of your league. If I turn on the charm, men would commit suicide to be with me. You're kind of . . . plain. And, well, frankly you're very average. And you're not very tall. Your accent is horrid, too."

"Wow. Don't hold back, honey."

"And it would be like kissing an ashtray. No, Earl, what I meant was that I can calm you with my magic. I can help you find your focus again. Let me use my voice."

And she did. Let me tell you, there's a reason mariners drowned themselves trying to reach a siren.

It turns out that there really is something to that old adage about music soothing the savage beast. Santiago taught me that as well. There are different tools for different times, but the Lord always provides a way for man to control the beast inside. Sometimes, the only way left may be death, but even that is acceptable to the alternative.

✤ ✤ ✤

Get up! Get up and fight!

Despite the screams of desperation and the muzzle of the big American revolver pressed against his head, Nikolai was strangely calm. The Tvar was helpless. The voice was fainter, and he knew it would stay that way until the moon pushed it to the top. In the meantime, Nikolai was in control. It had no choice but to obey. It would fight, but now it was nothing more than a petulant child.

He's not even a werewolf anymore. Harbinger is a pathetic human! He's food. Food can't lead.

Stalin had only been human, too.

Silence.

The Tvar had no response to that. Nikolai smiled inside. After being captured by the NKVD Hunters, he'd declared his loyalty to the Soviet Union. It was strong. It had beat them, and therefore it had become his Alpha, and the Motherland, his pack. Instinct had been satisfied, and Nikolai had functioned well that way for a long time. Nikolai craved order. Despite its protests, the Tvar needed structure. Having someone else make the decisions for them gave them both purpose. It was only when they were on their own that they struggled to see who was in charge.

We always made a very good soldier. Nikolai was not sure which of them had thought that.

Harbinger was a man of convictions. There was no doubt that if Nikolai failed this test he would die. Death was a frightening prospect, as werewolves desired survival above all, but Nikolai was a man of his word, and he knew that Harbinger, despite his ruthlessness, was not without mercy. He'd thought of that as weakness before, but now he needed that mercy. They would prove themselves, then he would avenge Lila, and the Tvar's fury would be quenched in the blood of Harbinger's enemies.

"First question, did you kill Van Huong?"

Nikolai did not know that name. "Who?"

"Wrong answer," Harbinger stated. "Pull the trigger."

When not fighting for control, his human mind was extremely analytical under stress. One in six. A seventeen percent chance. It was a reasonable sacrifice to make for peace.

CLICK.

The hammer fell on an empty chamber. He slowly exhaled. His finger creeped forward, and the trigger reset.

"Van was my translator. Disappeared during your attack, was listed as MIA. Ringing any bells?"

Nikolai remembered now. They'd put together an extensive dossier on all of Special Task Force Unicorn, supernatural and normal, before the assault. "Yes. I did. I killed him myself."

Harbinger's eyes hardened behind the iron sights of the old Thompson. "He was a good kid."

"If it is any consolation, I snuck up on him and snapped his neck. It was quick. He never felt a thing."

"Neither will you. Wrong answer. Pull the trigger."

"But that wasn't even a question—"

"*Pull the trigger!*" Harbinger bellowed.

Two of six. Thirty-three percent. Or to look at it another way, one of five remaining chambers was loaded. Twenty percent. Nikolai held his breath.

"Pull the trigger," Harbinger ordered. "Or I will."

He could hear the cylinder rotate. *CLICK.*

Harbinger sounded grudgingly impressed. "Who betrayed us? How did you find the task force?"

It wasn't like it was a state secret any longer. "We brought in a Kazakh orc tracker. All orcs have a specialty, and nothing could elude this one. It took him some time to acclimatize to the terrain, but once he did, he led us right to you. "

"Orcs sure can be talented. I inherited a bunch of Uzbeks. Good folks."

"You still gave us quite the chase."

"That we did." Harbinger's lips turned up slightly, in a semblance of a smile. "It was a hell of a fight."

"Admit it, you enjoyed the challenge."

"A bit." Harbinger chuckled, then he grew deadly serious. "Oh, and by the way . . . wrong answer."

Third of six. Fifty percent. Even odds of death; flip a coin. Or one live round in the remaining four chambers. Only a twenty-five percent chance.

That is not helping.

Nikolai's voice cracked a bit. It made him ashamed. "I am beginning to believe there are no right answers in this test of yours."

Harbinger shrugged. "Maybe."

Enough of this. This is madness. Turn it on him! Kill Harbinger! Kill them all—

CLICK.

He was shaking badly. His mouth was dry. His stomach ached with nervous acid. Going back was not an option. Only Harbinger or the other Alpha could defeat them, and the other Alpha had murdered

Lila. Masterless, he was nothing but an animal. Death was preferable to failure. Nikolai forced himself to speak. "Next?"

The nub of Harbinger's cigarette dangled from his lip, forgotten. "Impressive. I want you to know that. You may be an evil man, Nikolai, but you're an impressive man. I've got one last question."

Four of six. Sixty-seven percent chance that this question would bring a silver bullet. Or one in three remaining possibilities. Thirty-three percent.

"What do you regret?"

It seemed an odd question, but not to someone like Harbinger. He was, above all, a creature of moral absolutes. He pondered on the answer. Nikolai Petrov had taken so many innocent lives over the decades that numbering them seemed like an impossibility. He'd committed atrocities, followed madmen, murdered, burned, tortured, destroyed, and wrecked his way across half the world. He'd fed the gulags, hammering down the nails that stuck out. He'd killed the dissidents, ripping them from their homes and leaving the half-eaten corpses in the streets as a warning to the others. A cog in the greatest death machine ever, he had lived a life free of mercy, compassion, or accountability. And most of that had been done with the full complicity of his human mind. He couldn't even blame it on the curse.

You named me Tvar, the word for feral beast, but which of us is the real animal?

There was only one true answer. "I regret only one thing. . . . I regret meeting Lila. She showed me a world that I never belonged in. I tried, oh, how I tried for her. I am a corrupter, but I was loved by an innocent. How many like her did I hurt throughout the years? I do not know, but one, just one good person forgave me. Only . . ." Nikolai's voice fell to a whisper. "Only, by becoming part of her life, I condemned her to death. It would have been better if she'd never known I existed, or perhaps it would have been better if I had never existed at all. . . ."

Nikolai did not wait for Harbinger's judgment. He pulled the trigger.

"I don't know what Aksel was goin' on about. I can read the first part, it's about being in the war, but this . . ." Aino gestured at the section about the amulet. "This is mostly gibberish. The words seem made up. Maybe it's a secret army code or something, eh?"

A gunshot rang out. Heather looked up from her grandfather's journal. The noise had come from inside the Alpha's house.

"You hear something?" Aino asked.

"Clear as day," she answered. It was hard to believe that he hadn't heard that, but Heather had to remind herself: she wasn't *normal* anymore. "I'll be back."

Heather took her shotgun, got out of the truck, and slammed the door too hard behind her. The biting wind felt refreshing after the artificial warmth of the laboring heater. Quickly, she went up the icy steps three at a time, not even realizing that she did so. The others had to lumber along, lifting each leg high to clear enough snow to walk. Heather forced herself to slow down so as to not look suspicious.

She found Harbinger standing in the living room, the giant skeleton looming behind him. Nikolai Petrov was still on the couch, only slouched forward, and for just a moment she thought that nothing had changed since she'd left. But the smell of exposed brains and blood told her a different story.

How do I even know what brains smell like? Go figure. "What're you doing?"

Harbinger walked over to the body and picked up one of his big snub-nosed revolvers from where it had fallen on the couch. "Looking for something to write with. I told you to wait outside."

Blood was leaking out the side of Nikolai's cracked skull, dripping down his face, and pooling on the carpet. She should have felt something—revulsion, maybe? But she didn't. It was more habit than any real feeling that made her speak. "You're a monster."

"Correction. Monster *Hunter*." Harbinger reloaded his revolver and stuck it back under his coat. "I'm only a monster when I have to be. You got a pen?"

The Alpha opened his eyes. He was standing in the center of the bottom level of the Shaft Six building. The walls were covered in blood. Confused, he studied his hands. They were red up to the elbow. He looked up to see Lucinda Hood standing at the top of the catwalk, her mouth agape. It must have been bad, because it took quite a bit to shock a necromancer. "What have you done?"

He looked down. Two of his pack were at his feet, so brutally mangled, more bone than flesh, that they were barely recognizable. The amulet burned even hotter against his chest. It had been fed. He had been fed. "It is time to free the *vulkodlak*," he explained.

The witch raised her artificial hand and covered her mouth. Her eyes were wide with fear as she nodded.

⊰ **Chapter 22** ⊱

I quit playing Nikolai's game. We just fulfilled our missions with precision and got back out. His notes kept coming, but I ignored them. Sharon had helped me put the animal back in its place. I would not let him draw it out. We continued fighting, and we accomplished much, all without a single casualty.

A few weeks passed with no communications left by Nikolai. Conover said intelligence from his chain of command suggested that the Russian had been called home. We were told to stand down and await further instructions.

A week later, it was confirmed. Nikolai had returned to Moscow. President Nixon had agreed to draw down any supernatural assets in country. Apparently we weren't alone, though we'd never met any of the other special task forces in operation. Preparations would be made. First squad would be returned to their regular units; second was going to be flown home with thanks that could never be talked about and a renewed exemption from PUFF. We celebrated.

Nikolai hit us the next evening. Werewolves are sneaky like that. They get you when you least expect it.

✢ ✢ ✢

Stark paced down the line of stacked bodies. There were far more at the hospital now than when they'd left to go for help. The senior MCB agent muttered and swore under his breath as he stepped between the heads.

"We started it, but the other survivors have been dropping bodies off here, too," Agent Mosher explained. "The guards posted downstairs said that the town has fortified the school and then formed patrols to fight the monsters and gather people. . . . Kind of like I suggested *hours* ago."

Mosher was still bitter. Stark knew that it was because he was too stupid to realize just how much trouble they were going to be in once headquarters found out just what a clusterfuck of a containment this was going to be. Stark was too old to recover from this. This line of bodies and the number of people that knew about them was a career-ending event.

"Don't get lippy with me, kid." Stark stopped his pacing at the last corpse in the line. It was the body of that first infected deputy, Joe Buckley. It was uneven from the rest. Stark knelt and pulled back the sheet. Burning to death was always unpleasant. The skin was all crispy and black, except for where it had split open to expose red muscle. This one was even worse, since he was all twisted up, mostly shaped like a werewolf but not quite all the way there. The unevenness was caused by one hand sticking up, like it was reaching for him, claws all curled up from the heat.

It bothered Stark quite a bit, like the stupid monster was still being defiant despite the fact that it was dead. Why wouldn't monsters just fall into line, like everybody else? Stark stood, put his boot on the forearm and pushed down. It wouldn't budge. Stark grunted and put more weight on it. Ash flaked off and the bones made a sick cracking noise, but the arm finally went down like it was supposed to. Stark nodded and covered the body back up. "That's more like it," he whispered.

Mosher sounded worried. "Are you feeling all right, sir?"

Stark walked away without responding. He wandered down the hallway, still muttering, bubbling with impotent rage. There was a strange noise, for just a split second. It was barely audible, kind of a *hum*, but then it was gone. It left his ears ringing and added to his growing headache.

"You hear that?" Mosher asked nervously.

"Probably nothing." Stark ignored his partner. He found a break room with a soda machine in it. At least the generators were running here. He pulled his wallet out from under his armor and thumbed through it.

Mosher had followed him in like a lost puppy. "Sir? What are we going to do now?"

"I'm going to get a Dr. Pepper. . . . You got any dollars? All I've got is a twenty."

This was just like the *Pacific Star*. One helicopter load of SEALs against an ocean liner full of Deep Ones. There had been so damned *many* of them. They came out of the walls, through the floor, through the ceiling. They climbed up the sides to slide their slimy heads through the portholes. Every time they'd turned around there were more fish men. All but two of them had been wiped out during the first contact. The fish men had numerical superiority and fucking Dagon on their side. Magic, claws, and ancient mutants against two SEALs? What had Chief Haven expected? Of course Stark had hid. . . . That was the smart thing to do. Hide, and wait for reinforcements.

But no. Not Sam Haven. Mr. Big Shot Hero. He had to go all balls out and kill ten dozen fish men all by himself and then poke an ancient deity in the eye. Well, who's dead now, asshole? Yeah. You, Sam. You're dead, and I'm management.

"No . . . I . . . I mean . . ." Mosher was so confused, he was beginning to stutter. It was unbecoming in an MCB agent. "What are we going to do about the *situation*?"

Stark was getting a headache. He was sick of Mosher's whining. He was starting to stick up like that crispy werewolf's arm. "I'll think of something. . . . But right now I've got other problems." He put his big hands on the soda machine and shook it. Stark had managed to fix other people's problems and always kept from getting into anything over his head. He was an ideal government employee. It wasn't his fault werewolves had taken over a whole town. He kicked the hell out of the soda machine, but it still wouldn't cooperate.

The door closed behind Mosher. "Sir, look at yourself. We've got more important things to worry about. People are dying out there!"

This was not an insurmountable problem. Special Agent Douglas Stark of the Monster Control Bureau was a professional. He would *get* his Dr. Pepper. Failure was not an option. Stark leaned his SCAR rifle in the corner. Studying the machine, he formulated a plan of attack. Drawing his thick SOG knife, he jammed the point in by the lock and began forcing it in, using it as a pry-bar. They'd just blame the property damage on the werewolves. Stark chuckled at his cleverness.

"Agent Stark? Stark! Are you kidding me?" Exasperated, Mosher slammed his fists down on a table. The noise barely distracted Stark from his important task. "What are we going to *do*?" A gloved hand landed on Stark's broad shoulder and spun him around. "Look at me, damn it—"

Stark lost it. He slammed his armored forearm into Mosher's chest and drove him back across the break room. Mosher crashed haphazardly into the wall. Stark pressed his elbow against Mosher's throat and the combat knife against his cheek. Mosher's face turned red as he struggled for air.

There are two distinctly different reports at the end of the mission. In the first, a group of SEALs is ambushed in a rescue attempt, until only two remain, a chief and a new officer on his very first assignment. The officer spends the night hiding in a laundry hamper while the chief goes on a one-man suicide mission to save as many hostages as possible from the amphibian servants of an elder god. Except, that lone warrior didn't like it when the responding MCB cleanup team unnecessarily torched the uninfected survivors. He caused quite a fuss. That makes the first narrative difficult for official channels to swallow.

"You listen to me, dipshit. I'm not going out there. I'm not getting eggs laid in me." Stark pushed the knife just enough to break the skin. "And you're not going out there, either. We stick together. Those are the orders. You hear me, Haven. No *eggs*!"

On the other hand, story two says that the SEAL team defeated the Deep Ones, but lost most of their men in the process. Afterward, an MCB cleanup team responded in a professional capacity, following regulations to the letter. One of the surviving SEALs acted in a very irrational manner and made unsubstantiated allegations that the MCB killed some uninfected survivors, probably due to post-traumatic stress.

Forcibly retire one. Recruit the other to the MCB. "I won." Stark smiled broadly. "And I'll win again, because only the survivors get to file the reports."

It took Stark a second to realize that it wasn't Sam Haven he was holding against the wall, they weren't on a cruise ship, and he couldn't smell fish. He was strangling Monster Control Bureau Special Agent Gaige Mosher, in a crap town filled with werewolves, and the cold thing pressed against his ear was Mosher's 10mm Glock 20. Mosher managed to hiss. "Let. Me. Go. *Asshole*."

Stark removed his elbow, withdrew the knife, and stepped back. Mosher lifted his pistol in one hand and kept it on Stark. "Easy, Gaige. That's insubordination." Stark carefully lowered the knife to his side. "Come on now—"

"Stay back," Mosher ordered. He put one hand on the doorknob. "You've gone insane. I can't believe this. You've cracked under stress."

Stark laughed. "That's absurd. I was just messing with you. We'll work through this *together*."

"Bullshit! I'm done with you, Stark. If this is how the MCB works, I'm done with it, too!" Mosher was furious. "I'm done sitting around with my thumb up my ass while people are dying. You chicken-shit, I can't believe you. We've got guns. We've got training. We're supposed to be the heroes. Not janitors. Our duty is to protect this country from monsters."

He'd be damned if he was going to get yelled at by some corn-fed Iowa junior jarhead. "Don't you dare lecture me on duty, boy. I was—"

"You're a bureaucrat. You're a lazy, washed-up, good-for-nothing hack. You push papers, go to meetings, sign the reports, but you've forgotten what the job was!"

"This is the end of your career."

"Career? You're still thinking about that? I'm talking about our *job*. Our job is to be heroes. That's what I signed up for. Ass-kicking, monster-killing *heroes*. You can sit here and dick around with your pop machine, I'm going to go do my job." Careful to keep the Glock on Stark, Mosher opened the door. "See you around, *Agent* Stark."

Stark's eyes flashed to what was standing in the doorway. "Oh shit."

Mosher frowned. "I'm not falling for that."

The charred, blackened, twisted form that had been Deputy Joe Buckley rose behind Mosher. The werewolf's hair had been burned off, exposing thick muscles that cracked and bled as he moved. Ruined lips parted in a snarl of jagged teeth, dripping a slurry of bloody ash. Mosher heard the sound and turned, armor creaking. The agent and the werewolf stood nose to nose.

And then Joe Buckley bit Mosher on the face.

Stark blinked as blood splattered him. Mosher screamed and kicked as Buckley dragged him into the hall. There was a series of loud *bangs* as Mosher ineffectually fired his pistol. Stark hurried and kicked the door shut, but not before he saw that all of his neatly stacked corpses in the hallway were getting up.

"You suck at this," Lins told Horst.

"Screw you," Horst muttered, lacking the energy to argue. Plus, it was taking all his attention to maneuver the Escalade without getting stuck.

"No, really, man. You need to go back to whatever it was you did before, because you're a really lousy monster hunter."

They'd gotten lost again. Sure, it was a really small town, but Harbinger had knocked him senseless, maybe even given him a minor concussion, which was making it hard to concentrate, and everything looked the same when it was covered in snow. This was what the stupid GPS was for, but according to it their car was in the middle of a giant blue field.

There was a terrible moan from the back of the Caddy. Horst cringed, wishing she'd just hurry up and die or something. Jo Ann sounded really bad. He hadn't checked on her for a while, since the last time he'd looked she'd been so *puffy* and *slimy*. She probably should've died already, but she was hanging on for some reason, being a pain in the ass.

"What if she mutates into one of those giant pelican robots?" Lins asked, risking a glance over his shoulder. The side of his head was swollen and purple from Harbinger's beating.

"Well, we don't know what those even are. I figure she'll either die, or maybe they can fix her. So if she does . . . *mutate* . . . then we collect the PUFF on her, I guess."

Lins stared at him. "Now that's some cold shit right there."

Horst had lost one employee, murdered another, and had another one poisoned. It had been a really tough night. Right then, he'd have collected PUFF on his own mother. "There's the hospital."

"Maybe we should just dump her and get out of here," Lins suggested.

"Who's cold now?"

"She's not my girlfriend."

"Trust me, Larry," Horst said. His only surviving employee snorted. "There's a method to my madness."

"Oh, what's your brilliant plan now? We're down to what, two guns? How much silver we got left? Your million-dollar werewolf isn't even a werewolf. What're we gonna do now, smart guy?"

Horst smiled. "Remember how I told you it smelled like burned hair when I went in there earlier? That's because they'd burned a werewolf upstairs. We know Harbinger's busy, so he probably hasn't collected it. All that PUFF money, just sitting there. . . ."

Lins nodded slowly, then grinned. "I take back what I said. That's good thinking. And we only have to split it *two* ways."

The smile on his face was forced now. "Yeah, totally." Maybe he should have shot Lococo *and* Lins at the same time. It wasn't like he'd been particularly useful.

How did MHI make this stuff look so easy?

The lights were on, which meant the generator was still running. At least it would be warm inside. This place was brain-numbingly cold. There were a bunch more cars this time, and he could see people standing in the entrance, and this time they had guns. They didn't look like Feds or Hunters, though, just regular people, probably standing guard over their injured. "Well, here we are."

"What's that?" Lins asked, pointing toward the second floor.

His eyes flicked over just in time to see the window slide open as a large man dressed in black crawled through. "What's that moron doing?" The man fell from the wall into the snow drift. It was a pretty significant drop. "Weird. Wonder what's got into him?" The man immediately popped up out of the snow and limped toward them. "Stark?"

"Who?" Lins asked.

"The MCB guy," Horst began to explain, but Stark turned, raised a pistol in one hand, and fired off several quick shots at the window he'd just jumped from. "Shit!"

Horst threw it into reverse. The tires began to spin on the ice. He looked over his shoulder, *clear,* and then spun back around. He nearly jumped out of his skin when Stark crashed face-first into the driver's side window. Stark banged on the glass. Another shape came out the window, only this one didn't even try to slow its descent. It just dived out, head-first, and disappeared into the drift.

They began to roll backward; Stark ran alongside. He was shouting something that looked like *Help me.* The black shape came out of the snow. Stark turned and fired several times. The shape went back down.

This time Horst could hear him clearly. "Let me in!" Stark reached the back door and began tugging on the handle, but it was locked. "Let me in, you pricks!" He began to fall behind. "*Pricks!*"

"Ryan, look!" Lins shouted.

The glass front doors of the hospital were now coated in red. . . . *But there'd been men standing there just a second ago. . . .* "Whoa." One door swung open, and a man in a big floppy wool hat spilled out, running for his life. He slipped and fell as a woman followed him out the door. She was moving *weird,* all crouched over, but fast. Her clothing was ripped apart and hanging off. She was on him in a second, raking him with her fingers, only they weren't fingers at all. They were black *claws.* The snow all around them turned pink. "Whoa," Horst repeated.

Fixated on the sight, he drove their back bumper right into the side of a parked truck. They lurched to a sudden halt. Horst whacked his chin on the steering wheel.

Agent Stark caught up. He shattered the backseat window with his pistol, and then reached through to unlock the door. He slid inside. "Drive! Drive, you idiot! Drive!" Horst put it in gear and gunned it. Unable to gain traction, the wheels just spun. "Not like that, damn it!" The thing that had been chasing Stark was up and coming after them. Stark shoved both hands out the window and started shooting. The gun was right behind Horst's left shoulder. It was extremely loud.

Lins was saying something. "—slow at first. Get it rolling."

More things were coming out the front of the hospital. One door was open, but they just crashed through the glass of the other and kept on running. They looked like people, but they weren't. Some of them appeared more like the werewolf pictures he'd been shown in Newbie training, but not quite. It was like they were stuck in between the two forms, all ungainly and messed up. They weren't hairy at all, though their skin seemed too tight, like you could see the color of their muscles through it, but they had *claws* and they had *fangs* and they were coming this way *fast.*

"Drive, or I'll kill you myself!" Stark shouted in Horst's ear while he reloaded his pistol.

It took all his self-control to do it correctly. He gently fed the Caddy gas. *Easy. Slowly.* Which was difficult when a horde of shrieking lunatics were heading right at you.

A tire caught, they started forward, and then they were gaining traction and speed. Horst began to laugh, but it turned into a shriek as one of the monsters landed on the hood. He was wearing a black armor suit and had a short rifle slung across his chest, though the thing seemed totally unaware of the fact it possessed a gun at all. Most of the face was missing except for a long strip of scalp dangling across the bright red skull. He still had both eyes, only they were impossibly wide, milky-white, and utterly *dead*. The thing opened a mouth full of long, pointy teeth but made no sound. The half-werewolf slammed a gloved fist into the windshield, shattering it right between the front seats and obscuring their view.

"Mosher!" Stark shouted. He leaned forward and stuck his pistol between Horst and Lins. He cranked off at least half a dozen deafening shots before the thing disappeared from the hood.

"What's a Mosher?" Lins cried.

"My partner." Stark was panting. "*Was* my partner. He already changed into one of them! Infection to transformation in seconds; death followed by almost instantaneous reanimation. . . . Oh, this is bad. This is bad."

They were on the road. Horst checked his mirror. The monsters were running along behind, and they were keeping *up*. The first man that had come out of the hospital was convulsing and twitching on the ground. A second later, he popped up and ran after the rest of the pack.

⊰ **Chapter 23** ⊱

We were in a supposedly safe area, farther to the south. It was an actual town, with paved roads and everything. I couldn't pronounce the name to save my life. Van had mocked me, and done a pretty good imitation of my accent in the process. There were a hundred marines stationed next door, so it was about as secure as we'd been in months. Unicorn was relaxed.

We'd picked an evacuated two-story hotel to stay in while awaiting new orders. It was ratty, but sleeping under a roof was a big improvement. As usual, the two squads had been broken up, with first being downstairs and us upstairs. It was rather silly at this point, because most of first had seen Travis, and as Destroyer pointed out to Conover, even when Travis was in "disguise" under a big blanket with eye holes cut out, he left giant hoofprints everywhere he went. But orders were orders, and Travis was honor-bound to impress the government enough to get his tribe taken off the PUFF list. Bullmen were big on the whole honor thing. I'd come to love the big shaggy goofball.

Despite Sharon's protests about average human males, I'd often caught her batting those big eyes at Conover. They'd been spending a lot of time alone together, and the scents didn't lie. He was a good-looking man, and unlike many of the people I'd gotten stuck serving under, I actually had a lot of respect for him. Half-siren or not, she could do a whole lot worse. Conover was a rising star in the intelligence community; for all I knew, he was just seeing if they wanted to keep working together. Uh-huh . . . My commanding officer had hooked up with our love-goddess. I was willing to bet that didn't make it into the official report.

Travis and I were talking that night. I had asked if he was offended that humans ate beef. He thought that was stupid, and asked if I would be offended if he ate a monkey. That of course led into an interesting discussion on theology, since I figured I had no particular relation to monkeys. I ended up asking about the biology of the Bullmen, particularly their females. Okay, so if they're like a half-girl, half-cow . . . the whole udder thing? How's that translate over? Up high like on a human, or down low, and if so how would they walk? And are we talking two or four? Travis had told me that I needed to head out to Texas for a visit, and that if I called his girlfriend a heifer at any point, he would be honor bound to duel me to the death.

We'd had a lot of conversations like that. Travis was like a younger brother to me. A giant, monstrous berserker younger brother, but you get the idea. He kept score. He said that I'd saved his life seven times. He'd only saved mine twice. He said that he would never rest until we were even. Bullmen are odd like that.

It hurts to remember what happened next. The first memory is clear, the rest not so much. I remember how it began, and I remember how it ended. Rok'hasna'wrath took much of the rest.

It began with an explosion.

I found out later that it had been a truck bomb. Several tons of explosives detonated between us and the Marine encampment. One moment I was playing cards with the Bullman, and the next the hotel collapsed on top of us.

⁜ ⁜ ⁜

Heather was just glad to get out of the Alpha's home. The place had reeked of him, and those bones had filled her with a terrible dread. It was like they were looking at her, angry, and declaring that she wasn't worthy. Harbinger was a few steps ahead, slipping and sliding his way down the icy steps.

He'd been so graceful earlier, it was a shame that now Harbinger was so slow, weak, and *human*. He was still a remarkable man, though. And if she'd met him in other circumstances, she might have been interested in getting to know him better.

Heather sucked at dating. Her track record was dismal. She knew she was one of the prettier girls around Copper Lake, but she'd had zero luck meeting anyone decent. She'd even tried Internet dating for a while, but had just felt dumb and lonely paying money to meet bozos from the next town over and had given up.

She'd not met anyone like Earl Harbinger before. Not that she would have thought to tell eHarmony to match her up with a chain-smoking Southern monster hunter. He had an iron will, but at the same time he was still a gentleman. Plus, he wasn't bad looking. Though he was wearing bulky armor, she could sense the muscles of his legs tighten as he tried to find his balance. Even if he wasn't a werewolf, he was still strong. She could totally mate with that.

Mate? Who actually used the word *mate?* Heather stopped herself. She was actually *lusting* after Harbinger. *What the hell? Focus, girl. Psycho werewolf chick or not, I've got standards.* She shook her head to clear it. It was just like he'd warned her. Fight the random impulses, stay calm, don't eat anybody, don't eat your dog, and don't rip anyone's clothes off. *I can do this.* She took a deep breath. *He's got to at least buy me dinner first.*

"You get anything from the journal yet?" Harbinger shouted at Aino as they reached the trucks. Aino started to respond, but Heather couldn't hear the rest because of the terrible humming noise that suddenly slammed into her head.

Hands clamped over her ears, she cried out as she went to her knees. It was like that background hum she'd been hearing all night, only a thousand times worse. Pain like a railroad spike pierced her skull. The sound was killing her.

Harbinger grabbed her by the coat and held her upright. "What's wrong?"

She tried to answer, but her jaw hurt too much to form words. Maybe she screamed; she couldn't tell. Heather grabbed the straps on the front of Harbinger's armor and clung to him. The pain got worse, radiating from her head down her spine and from there out to her bones. Something cracked inside her as a joint realigned, and this time she knew for sure that she screamed.

Harbinger's mouth was moving. He was yelling orders. She focused on her hands, curled around the fabric pouches on his chest. Blood was coming from around her fingernails. The pain moved down her face to her teeth. Closing her eyes tight, she tried to make it through the pain, but beyond the pain was terror, and the pain actually felt better than the terror.

When she opened her eyes, the world had changed. Colors were different, faded. Only life and shadows to hide in stood out. She could see the blood pumping in Harbinger's neck, and she wanted nothing more than to reach up and set it free. He was still shouting. "You, pop the tailgate on my truck. Unlatch the big stainless box. Move!" He turned back to her. "Come on, Kerkonen. This way. Hang in there."

"What's wrong with her eyes?" The voice sounded too slow, like when you play a video at half speed. The action of a gun was worked. "They're yellow. She's one of them."

"Calm down," Harbinger said, and it seemed to take forever. "Get out of my way."

"Shoot her!"

At some point, in addition to the pain in her bones, she must have caught on fire. Her hands were burning. Instinctively, she jerked them away from Harbinger. Bewildered, she watched them, turning them from back to palm. They weren't on fire at all, but her fingernails were so *long*. She bit her nails. It was a terrible habit, so she'd never had nice nails before. Too bad they were on fire and bleeding.

"I said, get out of my way," Harbinger growled at the unseen roadblock.

"Do what Earl says." Aino sounded scared.

A fresh wave of pain, somehow even bigger than the last, came, this time from her rib cage. The sound of breaking bones was audible even over the humming noise. It twisted her down. She had to drive her hands into the snow to keep from falling over.

"Step aside, stranger." Distantly, Heather recognized the voice. Something Prescott. She'd cited him for DUI once. He was a real asshole. He seemed really frightened, though; it was probably because of all that screaming. *Oh, wait, that's me.* "I'll shoot you both. I mean it."

"I ain't got time for nonsense." There was a sudden movement ahead of her, and a *thud*, but Heather couldn't focus enough to lift her head. Somebody hit the ground. "Any of you other slack-jawed idiots get in my way, you'll get the same," Harbinger said. "You, boy. Do what I told you. The rest of you, get out of here. *Now!*"

The fire spread. Now it was a competition between the skin fire and the bone pain to see which would rend her apart first. It was worse than anything she'd ever imagined. The fire was winning, though. The heat kept getting worse. She ripped her coat off and fell into the snow, but it didn't help. A hand wrapped around her duty belt, and suddenly she was being dragged through the snow.

"Hang in there, Heather. You can do this."

A tremor ran down her legs. The bones of both feet broke simultaneously. She kicked out involuntarily and collided with something. Harbinger went sprawling. The burning wouldn't stop. She began tearing off the rest of her clothes. Her belt buckle fought her. The complicated thing was too confusing, so she curled her hands around each side and ripped the leather in half. She tried to let the pain out through her mouth, but the screams weren't taking much pain along with them.

"The first one's always the hardest," Harbinger muttered in her ear as he lifted her from the snow.

He sounded like he was in pain. *I'm sorry!* she thought, but now, behind the pain, the burning, and the fear, was something else. *Excitement.* It beckoned to her. If she could make it past the first three, the last one called. Harbinger's hands felt like ice blocks on her naked shoulders. He was steering her toward something. It was a silver box. Inside was darkness.

Don't go into the hole. There is only death in the hole.

She shoved him away. Her push was enough to send him flying across the street. *I'm really sorry!* In horror, she looked down at her hand again. It was covered in red hair. Fire was red. The burning was leaking out of her skin. Her nails had turned into knives.

Harbinger sat up in the snow, ten feet away. There were new tears down the front of his armor. He winced as he felt the blood. He looked over at Heather and lifted his gun. "Aw, damn it."

I'm sorry! I'm so sorry! She reached out to him, but then her pelvis snapped. Her spine pushed her skin to the bounds of elasticity. Teeth sawed through her gums. She fell again, screaming. But the scream had changed, this was a new scream, and it let out much more of the pain. No, this was no scream. This was a *howl.*

Looking up, there was Harbinger, standing over her, bleeding. "I'm sorry," he said. She saw nothing but meat.

Now she understood why Joe Buckley had begged her for death.

She understood why Harbinger had given her the gun—forgotten in her coat—with the silver bullets. The change was starting to feel *good.*

Kill me! Please! Hurry.

Harbinger lifted his gun.

She lowered her head. *Kill me before I kill you.*

Everything went black.

A single tiny candle flickered on top of the pathetic little cupcake.

Happy birthday to me.

Happy birthday to me.

In a mine shaft with a bloody werewolf,

Happy birthday to me.

All across Copper Lake, dead bodies rose, powered by the waves emanating from the amulet of Koschei. Anyone that had been killed by one of the Alpha's pack was born again as one of the wretched *vulkodlak.* They were remarkable creations; undead lycanthropes, caught somewhere between man and werewolf, nearly mindless, driven only by a single instinct: the need to spread their curse. They would never tire. They would never stop. Smelling prey, the creatures were already surrounding the survivors clustered at the school.

They would kill, but not feed on the flesh. The *vulkodlak* were vampiric. They would rend the flesh, drink the blood, and within moments the deceased would become one of them. Once the last of the survivors was turned, the *vulkodlak* would set out in every direction. They were swift on foot and could cover many kilometers before the magic driving the storm died off.

Lucinda knew that the American government would never allow the *vulkodlak* to spread. Northern Michigan would be burned to ash before they'd let that happen. But the Alpha had thought ahead. Before the government bombs fell, she would use her magic to whisk herself and the Alpha to another prepared location. She had a portal rope tied around her waist, just waiting to be activated. Werewolf-killed corpses had already been prepped and hidden across the country. *Vulkodlak* would arise elsewhere. Chaos would ensue. Her new god would be pleased.

The plan was brutal and blunt. Her father would not have approved. Martin Hood had been discreet; he'd wielded magic like a surgeon's scalpel. He'd planned his every move years in advance. In contrast, the Alpha's plan was like a sledgehammer.

Martin Hood had served the Dread Overlord with the utmost devotion, but in the end, it had been for nothing. MHI had killed her father and her god. Her church had fallen apart, and her hand had been torn off by that super-bitch vampire. Alone, she'd built a new hand with magic and steel, and set about recovering much of her father's work. It had been a depressing time.

Then she'd found a new god, or rather, he had found her, and a world of new possibilities had opened. She had been the one to introduce the Alpha to her new god. The Alpha had already been working with the Sanctified Church of the Temporary Mortal Condition. They had even traded two of his pack for two of her father's diggers, to aid his quest to find the amulet of Koschei. The two werewolves had been lost in the assault against the MHI compound, killed by that damned Owen Pitt and the disgusting thing known as Agent Franks, but the Alpha had understood that their deaths had been for the greater good.

She had respected the Alpha at first. It was difficult to admit, but he'd almost become a father figure since Pitt's bayonet had ended up in her own father's heart. He was charming, not just because of the gifts he'd inherited from birth, but there was also a certain nobility to his purpose in protecting the werewolf race.

Only, the Alpha was becoming increasingly erratic as the night went on. The amulet was changing him. He had devoured several of his own children in the last hour and hadn't seemed to notice. Despite knowing that he needed her knowledge of magic to complete his plans, she was becoming frightened of the Alpha.

However, her new god seemed pleased by their progress, and she would do what he commanded. Her new god was not as ancient as the Dread Master; in fact, he'd only recently been awakened from millennia of slumber. But he was far more interested in the affairs of humanity than the distant Old Ones she'd grown up serving.

The new god felt that it was time for the defenses of man to be tested. The Alpha was to be his instrument, and she was to be his prophetess. Today was her nineteenth birthday. She'd packed a Hostess cupcake in her kit along with a single candle and a lighter, because it was a celebration, after all. She'd stuck the candle in the little snack and lit it. Singing to herself seemed a little odd, and everyone else at Shaft Six was either being eaten by the Alpha or hiding from him. The diggers weren't much for singing, or communicating in general. So, once again, she was on her own.

Lucinda Hood rested her tired head against the cold steel of her artificial hand and watched the snow falling beyond the double-paned glass of the window. There were only a few hours left until dawn. After making a wish, she blew the candle out.

I do not recall what happened next. Rocky destroyed the memory of my final confrontation with Nikolai. He ripped it apart and spread the fragments. All I got are glimpses.

When I began writing this journal, I already knew I was missing that part. The real first memory I have after the battle was stepping out of a chopper onto the deck of an aircraft carrier. Six men of first squad had been killed, and one was missing. Every other man had been injured.

The huge body of Travis Alamo Sam Houston was unmistakable under his blanket, now soaked with blood, as the corpsmen laid him on the deck. Conover and Sharon had both been injured, Conover not too badly, but Sharon had suffered a severe laceration and had been rushed away. We'd been left unsure as to her fate. Conover had cried on my shoulder.

The memories would have been blurry anyway, since I knew that we'd clashed as werewolves. I still know that there was a truce between us, but I don't know how we got it.

STFU was disbanded. We were instructed not to speak about it and not to contact each other. I was sent home. A few months later, I got a fancy letter stating that I was once again PUFF-exempt, along with an anonymous note telling me that Sharon had survived, but no other details.

A Bullman came to visit me in Cazador a year after I'd returned. My Hunters almost attacked him before I was able to get them to stand down. He was a holy man. He told me that Travis Alamo Sam Houston had earned a PUFF exemption for the Bullmen of East Texas, and that in his final message to his people, he'd spoken of how he'd declared a werewolf to be his brother, and therefore of his tribe. The shaman had brought me a gift. It was a leather hide.

I damn near blew a gasket when I found out it was Travis. The shaman explained. The greatest honor a Bullman could bestow was to give his body in the service of his tribe. It was their way. I suppose it was like Travis telling me that death wasn't about to keep him from watching my back. It would be a huge dishonor on all Bullmen not to use the gift. Plus, the shaman was Travis's father.

Turns out Travis's letters to his tribe had detailed how he still needed to save my life several times before we were even. The shaman explained that this was the only way that Travis's spirit could get a proper rest in Bullman heaven. Together, we crafted the hide into a coat—broke a mess of needles in the process—and the shaman enchanted it with the Bullmen's strongest medicine. I've used it ever since. It was the nicest gift anybody ever gave me.

I've not heard from Nikolai since Vietnam. He's out there. Waiting. I know there will come a time when we meet again. I can only pray that I'm stronger and wiser this time. I have to rise above.

Nikolai reminded me what a true werewolf was. It's not the claws or the fangs. It isn't just the physical manifestation. It is the darkness that lives inside us all, left free to roam. The Hum awakes the evil inside. The only difference between us and everyone else is that we can't keep our evil bottled up like everyone else. We have to face it. We have to overcome it. In Vietnam, I failed. I let myself become like him in order to fight him.

If I could have one wish, it would be to take this curse from me. I dream of being a man, and nothing more than a mortal man. How would it be? Freedom? I can't even remember what that was like. But even if somehow this curse was lifted tomorrow, I'd still have to pay for my sins. Besides, being cured? That can't ever be. It's stupid and vain to wish for the impossible. So instead I will live every day trying to atone for the things I've done. It's the best I can do.

Santiago was wrong. He thought I was a good man. I'm not. I can never be worthy of that title. My father was a good man. Santiago was a good man. Travis was a good man, though he'd be insulted if I called him a man. The men of first squad and the hundreds of Hunters I've helped set in the ground have been good men. No. Not me. The best that I can ever aspire to is kicking evil's ass at every opportunity, until eventually it wins and I die.

Then I can look God in the eye and say that I did the best I could with the hand I got dealt. A werewolf can't ask for much more than that.

PART 3

The Harbinger

STFU was operating out of a firebase in the highlands when I found my new name.

Let me explain. As a werewolf, you age very slowly. Having the same Shackleford running MHI for too long could get suspicious, so I'd started picking a new name every generation. I planned on restarting again after getting back from Vietnam, and Mr. Wolf certainly wouldn't do for a proper name.

One morning Van came and woke me up. He said that an important man had come to the village and wanted to speak with me. You've got to understand, we were in the middle of nowhere, so I wasn't sure what kind of important person would end up out here, but our young translator was adamant. So I followed him down to the Degar village.

I liked the Degar. Montagnards or "Mountain People," The French called them. So most of the Americans called them Yards for short. They were on our side, and they could fight like nobody's business. The locals had been guiding Destroyer and his boys and had been feeding intel to STFU.

Van took me to a hut on stilts with a really tall roof. It appeared that all of the local warriors had formed a perimeter around the hut. They were showing a lot of deference to whoever the mystery guest was. Inside the smoky, dark, hot dwelling was one of the oldest men that I'd ever laid eyes on. He was blind, wrinkled, could barely whisper, and was playing with a plate full of chicken entrails.

"What's the deal, Van?"

"He's a holy man, Mr. Wolf. He's come a very long way to find you."

"No. I mean with that chicken."

"He's telling the future."

Van was an earnest fellow, and I'd never known him to be the superstitious type. The old man whispered something. Van had to lean in real close to translate. "An animal gave its spirit to a man. The spirit was tricky and thought it could change the man. The spirit had always changed the man. But this man would not change. Instead, he made the animal spirit change its ways."

279

My condition was not to be spoken about. "I'm sure hoping you didn't tell him anything classified, Van."

"No, Mr. Wolf. I didn't tell him. He said the mountain spirits told him you were coming." *Flexible mind, I preferred to think that this old man's mountain spirits were whispering to him rather than my translator was talking about things that could get him in trouble. The old man kept on whispering.* "He says that the animal spirits have waited . . . I don't know the word . . . A very long time for one that could change them. The animal spirits will listen to you . . . the mountain spirits will help you . . . in the war."

"Tell him thanks. In a war, you'll take whatever help you can get."

Van told him. There were flies buzzing around the chicken, and the hut was so humid it made Alabama seem frosty. The old man kept on in a monotone whisper. Van looked confused. "Not this war. The big war."

"This one ain't big enough?"

"No. The coming war . . . Sorry, I don't understand. The mountain spirits told him it is coming. The war to end all things. You are one of the four."

"What's that mean? Four what?"

The creases of the old holy man's knuckles were filled with dried chicken blood. "The Mountain Spirits won't say. Before you can lead the animal spirits, you have to teach someone. Make them ready for the war that will end all things. You have to prepare the way. . . . There will be many battles. Many changes. If you fail, the animal spirits will fight on the enemy's side instead. When the time is right, you will announce the war, and all the spirits will follow you into the dark place."

"None of that makes a lick of sense."

"He says you are the one that prepares the way. . . . I don't know the word. One that prepares the way. . . . A harbinger? Yes. The mountain spirits say you are the harbinger."

The holy man fell silent. He scooped up the plate of guts and tossed it out the door to the dogs. He was done. He'd delivered the message from his mountain spirits. We were dismissed.

Harbinger. I liked the sound of that.

❖ ❖ ❖

⊰ **Chapter 24** ⊱

The Briarwood company Cadillac was stuck. "On three," Stark ordered. "One, two, *three!*" He threw all his weight against the bumper. The tires spun uselessly in the snow. "No! Damn idiot! You've got to rock it! Rock it!"

Ryan Horst stuck his head out the window. "I'm trying, okay? Quit yelling at me."

Stark stood up with a grunt. His back was killing him, having wrenched something during his jump from the hospital window. They'd managed to lose the zombie-werewolves right before Horst had spun them off the side of the road into a ditch. The other Briarwood Hunter, Lins, was trying to help push the front end of the truck out. It was hopeless. It would probably take a tractor to drag them out.

The two of them stopped to take a breath. Stark looked back the way they'd come. The monsters were bound to catch up any second, but he couldn't even see far enough through the snowfall to tell how much time they had left. "All this shit on here and you don't have a winch? You've got rims that spin, and no winch? Are you kidding me?"

Lins shrugged. "Weren't expecting none of this, man. This was supposed to be a cakewalk."

"No heavy weapons. No clue. It's amateur hour." Stark glanced around. His parka was back at the hospital, and the wind was cutting right through the seams of his armor. He needed to warm up, but if they hunkered down the monsters would tear them apart. There had to be something they could use, somewhere they could go. "I can't believe I trusted you idiots."

"Hey. Look at that." Lins pointed at something in the distance.

Squinting, Stark could barely make out the lights. "I think that's the high school. I drove by there earlier."

"You got a better place to be?"

Stark's face burned from the cold. His ears were probably going to turn black and fall off. Odds were there was nobody worth a damn at the high school, either, but if they had lights, then they had a generator, so at least he could die warm. "Better than being out here." He slammed his fist on the hood to get Horst's attention, then regretted it immediately as the impact stung his frozen hand. "Come on, stupid. Let's go."

Horst gave him a sullen glare as he got out, but he was smart enough not to say anything. Stark wasn't in the mood.

The three of them gathered around the back of the Cadillac so Stark could take stock of the situation. Horst and Lins both had rifles, but there were only a couple of mags left between them. Stark had his issue Glock and a combat knife; that was it. He had pouches full of SCAR mags filled with composite silver 7.62, but his rifle had been left leaning against the wall during his hasty escape from Deputy Buckley. To make matters even more embarrassing, there was a Suburban full of top-of-the-line MCB equipment sitting in the hospital parking lot surrounded by zombie-werewolves.

"Before we make a run for those lights, you guys have any more cold-weather gear you can spare?" Stark asked through chattering teeth.

"If we did, I'd be wearing it," Lins answered sharply as he sat on the Caddy's bumper. Balancing his M-4 carbine between his legs, Lins pulled his sweater up over his mouth and nose, then shoved his hands into his armpits. "What're we supposed to do about Jo?"

A slimy hand landed against the interior of the back window. A horrible visage rose behind the hand. The face was slack and pale, dripping sweat past bloodshot eyes. Drool spilled out as the mouth opened wide. The monster's face hit the glass with a wet thud.

"Threat!" Stark shouted as he went for his sidearm.

"No, wai—"

BANG.

A hole appeared in the glass. The horrible face disappeared.

Lins fell off the bumper. "Son of a bitch! You shot Jo!"

Stark slowly lowered his Glock as the hand slid down the glass until it also disappeared from view. "Jo?" He looked to Horst, but the lead Briarwood man was just standing there, mouth hanging open, apparently in shock. "Who's Jo?"

"*That* was Jo Schneider," Lins said as he got to his feet. "She's with us. She's Horst's girlfriend! Shit, man, you just capped our secretary!"

It took his numbed hand a few tries to get the Glock back into the holster. "The one with the sexy voice?" Stark mumbled. "Well . . . Huh. I pictured her as better looking."

"She was, before a giant scarecrow robot puked her up," Lins said.

Horst stepped forward without a word and opened the back of the Cadillac. Stark looked past Horst's shoulder. The woman had been wrapped in a blanket and appeared to have been in really rough shape even before the gunshot wound. He'd seen healthier looking zombies. "In my defense, she *looked* like a monster." Jo Ann was still alive, but probably not for long. Stark's bullet had punched through her shoulder, and from the amount of blood, he assumed that he'd severed the axillary artery. "Well . . . Shit. Sorry, I guess."

Jo Ann squinted at Horst. She was having a hard time focusing. "I . . . I was just gonna . . . tell you I was feeling . . . better."

Lins urgently tapped Stark on the shoulder. "We got company."

He turned around. There were dark shapes moving against the white backdrop down the block. The undead were back. They weren't running this way yet, but they would be soon. "Time to go, Horst . . . Horst?" He turned back to find Horst still staring at the woman. Stark leaned in and whispered, "We don't have time to be sentimental, kid. If you want to put her out of her misery, do it quick and don't make too much noise."

Shaking his head, Horst stepped back. "Naw. I'm cool."

"Ryan?" Jo Ann croaked.

"Nothing personal, baby, but my pop used to say that if you're being chased by a bear, you don't need to outrun the bear, just your slowest friend." Horst's expression was as cold as their surroundings.

Jo Ann reached out for Horst as he turned away. She managed to snag his coat sleeve and held on for dear life. "Don't leave me."

Horst jerked his arm out of her grasp without giving her so much as a glance. "If we're lucky, they'll slow down for a snack. Come on. Let's go."

Stark whistled. That was harsh, even by MCB standards.

Earl swung the locking bar shut on the stainless coffin before stumbling away, wincing at the pain. He could feel the burning of the fresh cut across the top of his chest. Heather had sliced him good. A little higher and he would have lost his throat, so he'd gotten lucky, but he still needed to tend to the injury quickly before it became an issue. He always kept an extensive first-aid kit on hand, though it was normally for his Hunters. It had been a real long time since he'd needed one for himself.

Earl addressed the only other person remaining in the street in front of the Alpha's house. "Everyone else had the sense to run. You're a stubborn one."

"I ain't seen nothing like that before." Aino had made the decision to help, and had even had the guts to help lift the unconscious Heather into the box. "Her grandpa saved my life, pulled me out of a collapsed mine. I thought you aimed to kill her; figured I owed Aksel to see that to the end. Surprised me when you picked her up instead. . . . You're bleeding. Let me see that cut."

Earl opened his coat. Heather had managed to tag him just above where it had been fastened, and one claw had made it through the Kevlar beneath. "Just a scratch," he lied.

It wasn't fair to blame Heather. It wasn't like she'd done it on purpose. Earl reasoned they were probably even, because he'd smashed the Thompson's steel butt-plate over her head until the stock had cracked. Just shooting her would've been the safe move, but she was a good girl. Even though the odds of her beating the curse were near zero, she deserved a chance. Santiago would have done the same for him. Though Heather was going to be mighty surly when she woke up inside that dark little prison box.

Once safely back in the truck, Earl turned on the interior dome light, found his first-aid kit, and unbuckled his armor. Heather had scored a solid laceration just over his collarbone. A flap of skin was dangling, loose, leaking blood in a wide circle. "Damn. That's ugly."

"Just a scratch, huh?" Aino grunted.

"It's wide, but shallow. It's the depth that gets you." Earl shoved the skin back into place, wiped it with iodine, and applied a pressure bandage. As soon as he had a spare minute, he'd give himself some stitches. It was too big to glue. The hard part would be keeping an eye on it at that angle. Since the last time he'd given himself stitches had been in the 1920s, he was a bit out of practice. "Turn up the heater, would you?" Earl asked as he closed his eyes and leaned back against the headrest. "Why do people live someplace this damn cold?"

"Keeps out the riff-raff. . . . This was a quiet town, 'til recently."

"Got me there." Earl lit a cigarette and got back to work, having decided that thirty seconds was too much sitting around. He could bleed later. "I need you to figure out what that journal says, and I need it fast."

"I can do that. What about Heather?"

"Through no fault of her own, she's one of them now. Locked up, she can't do no harm, but if she gets out . . . She's not the girl you knew before."

"Is there a cure?"

Surprisingly, there was. If that amulet could cure Earl, then it could cure anyone. He had a sneaking suspicion that it was the same device that had started the curse to begin with, so it reasoned that it could end it, too. Not just for Earl and Heather, but for all werewolves, everywhere. If he could get his hands on that amulet and figure out how the magic worked . . .

The truck lurched. A terrible grinding sound came from the back, claws against steel, followed by an enraged roar. Heather was awake, and not surprisingly, she was a fierce one.

"There's a cure," Earl said with renewed determination. He had accidentally created the monster that was terrorizing this town, but he could make that mistake right and in the process end the curse forever. "And I know who has it."

The storm was finally breaking up, having transitioned from blizzard to horrible snowfall in the last hour. That should have made Horst happy, but instead that just meant that the werewolves could see them better. Sadly, sacrificing Jo Ann hadn't seemed to slow them very much. The awkward creatures weren't much more agile in the deep snow than the Hunters they were chasing, but they didn't seem to be getting tired, whereas Horst thought his heart was about to explode. The monsters were gaining on them.

"We're almost there!" Lins shouted. The only other remaining Briarwood Hunter turned out to be the fastest on foot, and was a good twenty feet ahead of the other two when he stopped to urge them on. He raised his M-4 and popped off a pair of shots at their pursuers. "Come on."

Horst was gasping for breath as the frigid air scorched his lungs. Agent Stark wasn't doing too much better, since the MCB man looked a little too old to be sprinting through uphill snowdrifts, but the mass of undead werewolves behind them was one hell of a good motivator. It was tempting to shoot Stark in the leg to give the werewolves another distraction, but they still had a couple hundred yards to cover. He'd save that option for later.

There was a fence at the top of the hill. Passing Lins, Horst reached the chain link. It rattled as he struck, knocking snow from the metal. Horst had gotten a lot of practice clearing fences tonight, so it only took him a second to sling his FAL and clamber over. He landed softly on the other side and took off without waiting to see if the others needed help, but the *clank* from behind told him somebody was following. He made it down a narrow lane between concrete bleachers and onto a long white field. The vaguely goalpost-shaped blobs at each end told him they were running across the football field. The lights of the gym were on the other side. On the roof were the spotlights they'd seen earlier. One of them flashed over to blind him. Horst began waving his arms madly overhead, too out of breath to call for help.

Keep running. Almost there. You can do it. He'd despised all that running that MHI had made them do during their stupid Newbie training, but right then he was really wishing that he'd kept up the regimen. *I'm doing good. I can make it.* Then Lins passed him by again. *Shit!* Lins just had longer legs.

There was a horrible sound from behind. Horst was too terrified to look, but knew he had to. He craned his neck around to witness a sea of half-mutated bodies, some hairy, some naked, mottled red and black, crashing over the fence like an unstoppable wave. The first of them hit the ground running wildly. It was charred and twisted, like a burn victim.

Agent Stark raised his pistol and shot the burned monster

repeatedly. It slipped and crashed against the bleacher. Other monsters passed it by and didn't even slow. Stark emptied his gun into the crowd, but none of the creatures seemed to notice. Terror gave him renewed stamina as Horst turned back around and ran for his life.

There were harsh buzzing noises overhead. *Bullets!* The men on the roof of the gym were shooting at the monsters, too. Maybe it would buy them some time. There was another fence, but luckily there was an open gate. Lins reached the brick wall of the gym, but there was no door on this side, just drifts piled waist-deep against the wall, and windows that were far too high to reach. "What do we do now?"

"Get to the front!" Stark shouted as he caught up and slammed the gate shut. Furious, he reached over and snatched away Horst's rifle. "Give me that if you're not going to use it!" Stark shouldered it and began shooting across the football field. "Up yours, fish-men! You'll never take me alive!"

Horst had no idea what fish-men Stark was shouting about, but the monsters were closing in fast. Lins had run for the front corner of the building, so Horst followed. He'd made it another fifty yards after Lins before the other hunter came back around the corner, wildly firing his M-4 from the hip. "They're attacking the front door, too! Go back. Go back!"

"Back where?" Horst asked desperately. He started back the way they'd come, only to realize that Stark wasn't there. "What? How—"

"Up there!" Lins shouted, grabbing Horst by the arm and dragging him along. Somebody had opened one of the side windows and tossed out a rope. Stark was pulling himself up, boots pressed against the walls. The dude wasn't much of a runner, but he sure could climb fast. By the time they got close to the dangling rope, helping hands had reached out from the window, grabbed Stark, and hoisted him inside.

They had to get up that rope. It was their only chance. Monsters were crashing into the fence all around them, and others had followed Lins from the front corner. Others smashed down the gate and poured through. They were surrounded. Horst reached into his coat for his FN, having forgotten that Harbinger had stolen it. "I'm out of guns!"

"Get to the rope," Lins said as he stepped in front. "I'll hold 'em off. Go!"

Horst was actually impressed by the bravery. He hadn't thought Lawrence J. Lins had it in him.

A monster charged. This one was mostly werewolf but was wearing a fuzzy bathrobe and pink curlers in its hair. Dead white eyes bore into him as it opened its mouth in a soundless roar. Lins raised his gun and put a silver 5.56 round right through its nose. Another followed, and Lins cranked off four rounds before it fell. Horst jumped over the body and grabbed the fat nylon rope. Another monster was closing fast, but Lins stepped in the way and slammed the barrel of his carbine into its face and knocked it into the drift.

Horst climbed with a strength born of adrenaline and desperation. Then the unseen people above were hauling the rope in, and it was as if he were flying up the wall.

"Come on! Come on! Bring it!" Lins could be heard shouting between gunshots. The shooting stopped. Lins's gun was empty. Then he began to scream, but Horst was too scared to look down. There was a terrible snapping noise, and the scream trailed off into a gurgle.

There were knots tied in the rope every foot. It gave him something to hold on to. It had probably just been the rope for PE class that somebody had cut down and thought to dangle to them. Here he was, the leader of an elite group of monster hunters, and his only lifeline was a PE rope thrown to him by some country bumpkin. His entire team was dead. He was a failure. Everybody was going to laugh at him.

A monster leapt. The claw struck the side of his boot. Horst squealed and drew his knees up to his chest, squeezing his eyes closed extra-tight as the people above hauled him in. He was so terrified yet glad to be alive at the same time that tears were flowing freely to freeze on his cheeks.

Now he knew how that girl had felt.

He'd done what he'd had to do. He'd been trapped in a warehouse with a shipment of drugs and the ghoul had eaten almost everybody else. The girl had belonged to one of the mules. Maybe eight or so, she didn't even speak English. He needed to draw the thing out, so he'd done the logical thing and used bait. His Spanish was lousy, but he'd lied and told her he was tying the rope to her so he could lower her to safety. She'd been terrified but happy for a chance to escape. Happy . . . at first. Then he'd waited for the monster to show up so he could nail it.

That's why they'd fired him. Who was MHI to judge?

There was a blast of warm air as he reached the window. A hand latched onto his coat and pulled him tight. "Oh thank you. Thank you. Thank you. Thank you."

"Hey, *boss*."

Horst opened his eyes. He blinked away the tears. "You're dead."

Loco nodded slowly. There was a thick white bandage wrapped around his big head. It was stained bright red on the side where Horst's bullet had struck. "Not quite."

His heart was beating so hard that it was hard to talk. "I . . . I shot . . ."

"Man, this just isn't your night. Bullet grazed my skull. The other one tore a nasty little hole through my love handle. It hurt a *lot*, but didn't hit nothing important. These nice folks patched me up when they found me . . . where you left me to die."

The fabric on Horst's coat made a crinkling noise as Loco dragged him in nose to nose. Horst stared deep into those dark eyes, one glass, one just angry, and for the first time, he realized that he'd drastically underestimated some of his employees. "You got anything to say?"

Twenty feet below, the monsters snapped and howled as they fought over Lins. "I'm *sorry?*" Horst squeaked.

A woman called from inside the gym. "Any other survivors, Mr. Lococo?"

Loco shouted down to the floor below. "Afraid not, Mrs. Randall. They didn't make it."

"Wait—" But then Horst was falling backward through the air.

He hit the snow flat on his back. The drift cushioned the impact. Too scared to breathe, too scared to look, Horst lay still in a cloud of white. All that could be heard were the sounds of rending and chewing.

I'm dead. He slowly opened his eyes. The monsters surrounded him. Their bodies were cold. No breath clouds formed around their jagged mouths. Milky eyes studied him, curious about what had just fallen into their midst. Lins was lying off to the side. The monsters had torn off his lower jaw and eaten one ear. Lins opened his eyes, and they too were blank, white, and dead.

Horst did not want to end up like that. Lins's carbine was there in the snow. He just needed to get it long enough to shoot himself in the head. His hand slowly moved until it landed on the gun. He dragged the muzzle toward his chin.

A foot landed on the gun and pinned it down. Horst's eyes tracked slowly upward, across the familiar body, wrapped in a tattered, bloodstained blanket, across the slimy, dripping face, and into the dead eyes of the zombie-werewolf thing that had once been Briarwood Eradication Services' secretary, Jo Ann Schneider.

Horst managed to say "Karma's a bitch" before Jo leaned down to give him one final kiss.

⚍ **Chapter 25** ⚎

The MHI truck stopped just shy of the parking lot of the Copper Lake high school. Heather had begun to cry. It was an eerie sound, and one that Earl was certain he'd never heard a werewolf make before. Something was wrong. He'd left the interior lights on so Aino could read Aksel Kerkonen's journal. Reaching up, Earl shut off the dome light so he could see outside better.

"Hey, I need that. I just found where Aksel was talking about getting these magic words from a Baba Yaga to . . ." He looked up. Muzzle flashes indicated the shooters Nancy Randall had placed on the gym's roof were firing like mad. Their spotlights were bobbing back and forth, illuminating hundreds of shapes moving along the perimeter fence. "What the hell?" Aino asked, squinting. "All those werewolves?"

"Can't be. There's too many. There's no way they could turn that many people so fast." The snow had let up enough that Earl could actually see a fair distance, so he retrieved his binoculars from the center console and stepped out of the truck.

What he saw took his breath away. Some were more werewolf-like than others, but none of them were fully changed. It was like they were stuck mid-transformation. Their movements were jerky, and there were many obvious injuries, including missing limbs. Experience told him that these were some type of undead. Dozens of them were piled up against the front doors of the gym. It was a seething pile of fury. If they got inside . . . Earl hurried and got back in the truck. "I think these are the *vulkodlak* everybody's been talking about." He passed the binoculars over to Aino. "I've got to stop them before they break in."

"What're you gonna do?"

Walking in, guns blazing, would be a noble but futile gesture. The explosives he had in back would damage the gym, too, and probably create an opening for the surviving monsters to get through. "I don't know. I'm *only* human," Earl said bitterly.

"Those are my people in there, buddy. You better think of something fast."

The *vulkodlak*'s abilities and vulnerabilities were an unknown. Some undead were dumber than broccoli, like zombies, while others, like a lich or a vampire, were just as smart dead as they were alive. Some types had special abilities, like the paralyzing touch of a wight, the death wail of a banshee, or the crippling glance of a night-shade. Some were easy kills and others were walking tanks. . . .

A tank! Now that would be just the ticket. They were all clustered together tight, with plenty of room to maneuver a big, squishing vehicle back and forth. The entrance to the gym was even inset a bit, with walls on each side that would create a fatal funnel. "You guys got a National Guard armory around here. Maybe an army tank?"

"No. Why the hell would we have a tank? That's the stupidest—" Aino slowly lowered the binoculars. "Wait a sec . . . I get you. Hang a right up there. Come on! Drive. What're you waiting for! It's only half a block that way. We'll grab a county snow-cutter."

Earl didn't know what a snow-cutter was. He was, after all, from Alabama, where there were very few things with "snow" in their names, but it had better be good.

The inside of the gymnasium was pandemonium. The place was literally packed with people. They were crammed together, standing room only. A good portion of the town's population had survived to make it here. At the very back, a group of women was herding crying children downstairs into some sort of basement. The was a continuous echo of gunfire from the windows and through the roof, but audible even above that was the general noise of nervous chatter, rough swearing, and fervent prayer.

Special Agent Doug Stark's first thought was that this was going to be a very difficult event to contain, but then, after listening to the crashing noises coming from the barricades at the front of the gym, he realized they were probably all going to die anyway. Making containment sort of irrelevant.

At least it was warm. In fact, after the death run through the snow, it was stiflingly hot. This many bodies packed together, it was downright muggy. Stark took another, slower look at the packed crowd. Considering how fast Mosher had been turned, a single one of those creatures inside these walls could turn this place into a slaughterhouse.

He'd come down the ladder rather roughly, and it had taken him a few minutes to catch his breath. The run through the snow had taken a few years off of his life. Horst and Lins hadn't come up after him, so that was the end of Briarwood. He sure wouldn't be getting any under-the-table PUFF money off this trip! Stark kicked himself. If he'd followed procedure and brought a full unit, this never would have happened. This whole thing was . . . *his* fault. That caused Stark to pause. He wasn't used to blaming himself for anything.

Stark made his way through the people, trying to assess the situation. A little girl pointed at him and then at something high behind him, and she giggled. Stark turned to see what the deal was, and saw a banner of the school's mascot, a cartoon bulldog. It too, was bulky, jowly, and scowling. Strangely, it was a rather good caricature. "Fair enough," Stark told the kid.

"What're you supposed to be?" A tall lady in a parka stopped him. She gestured at his armor.

He pulled out his real ID; the time for pretending was over. "I'm from the government, and I'm here to help. Agent Stark, Monster Control Bureau, Department of Homeland Security. Who's in charge here?"

She seemed relieved. "I am. Unless you brought the Marines, then you're more than welcome to it. Nancy Randall. Copper County Council."

"Negative. Just me. I had a Marine, but he got his face eaten."

There was a small spark of hope. "Is help coming?"

He took her hope and stepped on it. "Probably not. Well . . . Eventually. I'm supposed to report in by oh-eight hundred. When I don't, they'll come looking."

Nancy checked her watch. "That's hours from now!"

It would actually be far more. All agents on assignment had a mandatory check-in to confirm their status, but just because they couldn't reach him didn't mean the cavalry would arrive immediately. MCB would eventually dispatch somebody, but the nearest other agents were hours away. "What's your status?"

Spark of hope extinguished, she sighed. The woman had been through a long night. Nancy pointed toward the front. "We're screwed. Question is, how long can we hold them?"

The interior bleachers had been hastily broken down, and the materials had been used to barricade the front doors. It was an impressive pile of jagged wood, but the monsters were relentlessly throwing themselves against it. Clawed limbs were flailing around every gap as the townsfolk hammered at them with axes, shovels, and hammers. Every window had someone perched on it shooting a gun. Luckily there were no windows at the ground-floor level. A bottle with a flaming rag stuck in it was shoved through the windows over the entrance. The resulting conflagration cast the shadows of the men manning the windows onto the ceiling. The flames only slowed the creatures' onslaught for a moment.

Stark had seen how many of the things were out there. He was guessing much of the local population had been turned, and whatever they were, these undead were extremely resilient. He'd already head-shot a few of them with only a momentary effect. "Yes. You're screwed."

Nancy's patience had run out. "You're certainly a big old help. I'm glad I pay my taxes." She kicked the floor. "We're running out of bullets, and these new things don't seem to ever die—it just slows them down. Setting them on fire only works for a minute, and the only gas we've got left is the little bit left in the generator's tank. No word from the hospital, either."

"Eh . . . They're already dead. That's where I came from," Stark said.

"When the ammo runs out, then they'll be coming in. The best we can do is put the children in the bomb shelter and hope these things can't get through its big steel door."

"Bomb shelter?" Stark felt a twinge of excitement. If there was a bomb shelter, then he might be able to survive this until the cavalry arrived. Heck, the MCB would probably just have the air force carpet bomb the place when they found out. That shelter was definitely the place to be.

"There's not enough room for everyone," Nancy explained. "The best we can do is protect the kids. And not even all of them. I've got some mad parents of older teens to deal with now."

"Yeah, sure," Stark agreed, barely listening. That sounded like a personal problem. He'd make sure that he got a spot in that shelter. *After all*, he reasoned, *somebody knowledgeable needed to survive to write the report*. But the earlier the monsters got in, the more time they'd have to break into the vault before the MCB could get here. He needed to help keep those things out as long as possible. It was time to get this defense running properly. "Okay, listen up, Mrs. Random."

"Randall," she corrected.

"Whatever. I'm running this show from now on. See that? That's *my* barricade. See those yokels with guns? Those are *my* yokels." Stark folded his broad arms and surveyed his kingdom with a slow nod. "Stick with me, and we'll get through this." Someone screamed at the barricade as a claw caught them. "Damn it!" Stark shouted toward the screamer. "Let me show you how to do it!" He strode off to inspect his defenses.

Nancy just watched him go. She was joined a moment later by Phillip, the school principal. "Somebody told me the government was here to take over," he exclaimed excitedly. "We're saved."

"*Saved* is a remarkably optimistic term," she muttered.

Stark reached the barricade. He hated to admit it, but these Yooper rednecks were doing a passable job considering their lousy logistical situation, but the monsters on the other side were going to get in, and very soon. Stark peered through one of the cracks. Through the waving limbs, at the very back of the silent pack, stood a creature that he recognized. This one was far more werewolf-shaped than the others, but the charred flesh was what gave him away.

"So we meet again, Deputy Buckley," Stark said. "You've been a pain in my ass all night. Well, come and get me, crispy."

Buckley and several of the other creatures at the back of the pack stopped and lifted their heads simultaneously, as if they'd heard something. Without making a sound, four of them broke off in a run heading away from the gym. They were going after something. Stark had no idea what, but that was a few less that he was going to have to worry about.

"After the mine collapsed, I got a job working for the county," Aino explained as he unlocked the padlock and pulled it from the latch. Earl hurried over and lifted the giant garage's door. He was careful not to make too much noise, but once it got out of his reach, it slid up the rest of the way automatically and made a considerable racket. Earl cringed and looked around the county vehicle yard. There were several school buses, snowplows, and tractors parked inside the fence, but there was nothing moving between them.

Aino ignored the noise. "Only worked part-time, ya know, but I work on these here things. This one was all prepped and ready to go for the storm. It would be out clearing the roads now, except, lucky for us, the safety on the augers is broke. Meaning the blades won't automatically stop when they hit something solid. Which considering what we're gonna do with her, I see as a bonus." He let his flashlight play over the big orange vehicle in the shop.

"It's a tractor," Earl pointed out. Earl didn't know much about farm equipment, but it just looked like a big orange tractor to him.

Aino snorted. "Tractor? This ain't no tractor, boy. This is a custom-built, top-of-the-line snow cutter. . . . Snow cutter?" Earl shrugged. "No? Guess they don't have these where you're from." The diminutive man walked around one huge, chain-clad tire. "We're talking two *thousand* horsepower. She can tear through anything. When snow's as wet and heavy as around these parts, you need *power*."

"And what's to keep the monsters from climbing into that little *glass* cab with us?"

"Well, it's your job to keep them off with all your fancy machine guns." Aino stopped at the front of the vast machine. He grabbed one edge of a blue tarp and yanked it off. "While I give the bastards this!"

Earl whistled when he saw the wall of blades. There were three vast steel screws, each one reflecting light from the ground-sharp edges. The blades filled a giant scoop that covered the entire front of the tractor. A small car could fit in there.

"She can throw tons of snow an hour, and with no safety I can feed trees into it." Aino put his light beam on the blades. "Werewolves go in here"—he let the light climb up to a two-foot-wide spigot coming out the top—"and come out here. Only in itty-bitty pieces."

"Your secret weapon is a really big snow-blower."

"The *biggest*," Aino corrected. "Biggest fucking snow-blower *ever* in the world."

"I'd been hoping for an armored vehicle, but we're out of time, and I don't have any better ideas. Fire it up, my fine Finnish friend. I'll go grab some more guns from my truck. Then let's go rescue your town." Aino gave him a lopsided, homicidal grin, then went to work.

Earl ran back outside and opened the tailgate of his truck. There was a thump as Heather rammed herself against the lid of the box. The heavy latch barely even budged. There was no way the werewolf inside could get enough momentum to break out unless somebody lifted that bar. Otherwise, it meant waiting for the time lock to open. "Sorry, Heather, but you'll thank me later." He patted the box then began pulling out cases.

There wouldn't be room to use the sniper rifle, so Earl left the .300 Winchester Magnum behind. He made sure he had a revolver on each side and more moonclips than he could count. Chest pouches filled with Thompson mags. *Check.* Might as well bring some 50-round drums, too. He'd had Milo modify them to work in the old GI-issue Thompsons. And since he was going to be riding, rather than walking . . . He slung the Thompson around his back so he could use both hands to pull out the biggest nylon bag of all.

The Carl Gustav was just in case those freakish creatures that stunk like the Old Ones or the other Alpha turned up. Maybe that amulet granted immortality, and then again, maybe nobody had ever bothered to shoot the son of a bitch wearing it with an 84mm high-explosive round from a recoilless rifle before. Immortality was a relative term in this business.

Heather made a sad whine through the wall of the container. "Yep, I know. I won't blow him up until I get that amulet for you. I promise."

Earl grunted under the weight as he got the big nylon bag slung over his other shoulder. It was easy for a werewolf to forget how much good armament weighed, but not so easy for a man. He almost left Aksel Kerkonen's old Mosin Nagant rifle behind, but decided against it. There was something special about that odd silver ammunition, and it was related to that journal. He might need it. Aksel had defeated the bearer of the amulet once before, and it would be foolish to discount that.

What else? He had pouches for hand grenades. Might as well fill those, too. Inside the shop, the snow cutter's engine turned over with a roar and a belch of diesel smoke. There was a sudden howl from the box, and Heather began to thrash. "Easy. You'll be fine here. I'll be back . . . Probably." She made the same noise. It sounded *familiar*. Earl was no longer in touch with his instincts. They were buried too deep on a human. Then she growled, so low and dangerous he could barely hear it over the tractor.

Heather was trying to communicate. She was trying to *warn* him.

Earl turned just as the *vulkodlak* swung. Ducking, the claws parted the air where his head had been. He stumbled back, raising the Mosin as it struck again. Claws tore a divot from the wooden stock. Earl retreated as fast as he could without tripping over his own feet.

The *vulkodlak* had been a young man. He was dressed like he'd been killed in bed. The bites were obvious on his neck and chest. It was as if he'd been brought back to life, and partially twisted into a werewolf, but left trapped in between and awkward. One arm ended in a werewolf's claw and the other ended in a human hand. His limbs were misshapen and clumsy, and it was only that distorted nature that allowed Earl to avoid being torn apart.

It struck again. The rifle blocked the hit but was torn from Earl's hands and sent sailing into the night. Before another attack could land, Earl swept his hands down and grasped both revolvers. The twin Smith & Wessons came up spitting flame. The *vulkodlak* stumbled back as he stitched bullets through its naked chest and into its face, but it didn't go down. Extending an arm, Earl drove the muzzle right into one of the creature's eye sockets, squishing the white orb back into its skull, and fired. The expanding gasses of the muzzle blast actually blew the other eye out in a white spray.

It tottered for a long second before dropping into the snow. "Tough bastards," Earl noted, not that anyone could hear him over the tractor as it came rolling far too fast out of the shop. It was too far to one side, and the edge of the scoop ripped through the wall. Earl had to step away to keep from being run down. The engine roared as it was given too much throttle. The blades began churning with a terrible metallic roar. He couldn't figure out what Aino was doing, but then he realized that the driver was distracted by the two *vulkodlak* that were trying to smash their way into the tractor's cab. Earl couldn't hear the words Aino was shouting but could recognize that he was angrily cursing the monsters that were trying to eat him.

Shrugging out from under the heavy Carl Gustav, Earl stuck his partially empty revolvers back into the holsters and ran after the tractor. The tractor spun around in the county yard, sucking up snow in the whirling blades and spraying it in a magnificent arc across the sky. Earl swung his Thompson around and took it in both hands.

The snow cutter clipped the side of a school bus hard enough to shove the entire thing a few feet. Yellow metal was torn apart in a shower of sparks as soon as the blades touched. The tractor veered to the right as a *vulkodlak* drove its fist through the window of the cab. Aino threw himself to the floor to avoid the claws, but the creature forced itself against the spreading safety glass. Aino would be dead in seconds.

Earl shouldered his Thompson and took careful aim. Blood puckered up the *vulkodlak*'s side, forming pink mist clouds before the tractor's lights. It lost its grip and tumbled down the moving tractor, only to disappear under the rear tires with a sick crunch. The tire kept on turning, painting the snow red behind it.

One more. But it was on the other side of the cab, and Earl didn't have a shot. The wheel had been turned. Aino was no longer steering, and the snow cutter turned back toward the shop, scraping and tearing its way along the county vehicles. Earl ran, trying to position himself for a clean shot. The snow-cutter continued doing a doughnut around the yard in a widening arc, and Earl realized it was heading right for his truck.

"No!" It slammed the edge of its scoop directly into the Ford, T-boning it with a wall of spinning blades. "Not my truck!" The MHI truck didn't even slow the snow cutter. The truck was lifted and shoved sideways, then crushed and scraped along the garage building, slowly levered upward until it rolled free onto its side. "Awww! Son of a bitch!"

The edge of the snow scoop hit the cinder-block wall of the county garage. The tractor lurched to a violent stop, and the other *vulkodlak* was dislodged from the cab and flung into the snow. Earl opened fire on the run. The creature didn't even have time to rise before he'd nearly decapitated it with a long burst of silver bullets. He stopped long enough to shoot an additional five or six more rounds through the *vulkodlak*'s head. "I was fond of that truck!"

The tractor was stopped, but still running. His truck was toast. There was no movement inside the cab. "Aino! Are you ok—" Earl didn't see the final *vulkodlak* until it was too late. It crashed into him, shoulder-checking him to the ground. He hit hard enough to punch through the cushion of snow to impact the hard pavement beneath.

It was on him in a second, claws flashing. He raised his forearm and felt the bone-jarring impact as the claws struck minotaur hide. His other hand raised the Thompson into the beast's belly and force-fed it a string of .45 slugs. The *vulkodlak* swatted the muzzle aside as it rolled away.

Struggling to his feet, Earl tried to lift the Thompson, but the creature circled back and hit him again. Claws struck his side, bouncing off the coat, but the impact staggered him back. The monster darted away.

Disoriented, Earl searched for the target. This one was quicker than the others. *There!* It was coming around, another shadow flickering in the darkness. This *vulkodlak* was different from the others, more like a werewolf that had died and been partially twisted back into a human. Its skin was burned to charcoal, and red flesh twisted beneath where the black split open to weep congealed blood. Earl recognized him immediately, because he'd already killed him once before.

Buckley charged. Earl fired from the hip. The bullets took the *vulkodlak*'s legs out from under it, but it still reached him, taking them both to the ground. Buckley sunk his teeth into Earl's shoulder. The pressure was unbearable, and Earl shouted as he was shaken. The teeth didn't penetrate the hide. *That's another one, Travis.* Gun trapped between them, Earl drew his Bowie knife and slammed it between Buckley's ribs, again and again, as Buckley gnashed and ripped with his fangs.

Realizing that he didn't have a killing grip, Buckley released his jaws and leapt aside. Earl clambered to his feet. It was a rematch, only now Buckley was the strong one and Earl was the weak. Buckley looked down at the new gashes through its torso, then back at Earl, understanding that this prey could bite back. Buckley began to circle.

Earl lifted the knife protectively. The Thompson was dangling against his chest, but the bolt was forward. It was empty. There was no time to reload. Steam hissed from Earl's mouth as he shouted to be heard over the roaring blades. "So, Buckley, how many times does somebody have to kill you before you stay dead?"

Arms spread wide, Buckley leapt. Earl stepped aside as he lashed out. The thick Bowie sliced Buckley's bicep to the bone. The *vulkodlak* didn't seem to feel the steel. Buckley's momentum carried him away, but he immediately turned back to charge again.

He'd been tagged. Earl blinked as he felt the sudden burn where a claw had sliced across his cheek. Blood rolled down his face. "That the best you can do?" Earl wiped it away. He moved a few feet, trying to get the blades directly behind him. They were close enough that he could feel their artificial wind. *Vulkodlak* were tough, but hopefully they weren't very bright. "Better monsters than you have tried to take me, boy. Come on!"

Buckley charged. Earl sidestepped as he stabbed, hoping to get Buckley closer to the snow cutter, but the *vulkodlak* had anticipated the move and adjusted. One solid forearm caught Earl's chest, and both of them went down hard. The side of Earl's skull slammed into the steel edge of the snow cutter's scoop.

The impact nearly knocked him out. Earl was facedown in the snow. Head swimming, only a foot from the whirling death blades of a tractor that was only not rolling forward because one corner was jammed into a building. Groaning, he rolled over. The animated corpse of Deputy Joe Buckley was standing over him. The hilt of the Bowie knife was sticking out of Buckley's neck. Blood ran down the *vulkodlak*'s cracked chest and splattered onto Earl.

Buckley's claw wrapped around the knife handle. Blood leaking sluggishly, he jerked it out and tossed it into the snow. Buckley cocked his head to the side, white eyes gleaming. This time it was going to bite something unarmored, and that would be the end. Earl got ready. The least he could do would be to shove them both into the blades while it was distracted eating him. "Nobody eats me and gets away with it."

Something moved in Earl's peripheral vision. It took a moment to focus past Buckley's gleaming teeth to see that the stainless-steel lid of the prison-coffin was dangling, broken and open inside the rolled-over pickup. Earl had never seen a red werewolf before.

Buckley didn't know she was there until it was too late. Claws flashed from the right, from the left, flaying Buckley's back open. He turned, stepping off Earl, as Heather cleaved him twice more, crossing an X of lacerated flesh clear through his ribs. He raised one arm, and she batted it down. The other came up, and she took it off cleanly at the elbow. Buckley's hand spun off into the night.

A *vulkodlak* was no match for a *real* werewolf.

Heather lashed out, spraying blood across the yard. Buckley was crumbling, falling, but that wasn't enough. Heather was out for *murder*. She slashed his throat clear to vertebrae, then sunk her fingers into his neck, down, until she caught his sternum, and using it like a handle, hurled the *vulkodlak* into the roaring blades. Buckley simply exploded. One instant he was there; the next he was replaced with a rapidly expanding cloud of meat. A second later blood belched out the top spout, spreading a fine mist of Buckley into the air.

The werewolf stood, heaving, a dark red that was visually striking against the snow. No longer recognizably human at all, Heather turned toward Earl and bared her teeth.

Earl went for his gun.

She effortlessly caught his wrist, claws curling around it, *hard*. Her fangs were inches from his neck. His other hand was pinned beneath his body. She had him. Earl sighed. "Better to die by your hands than some filthy undead."

Her nose pressed against his bloody cheek. He knew that she was smelling him, checking for the fear smell of prey.

But Earl Harbinger had no fear, just acceptance, as he closed his eyes and waited for death. There would be no reasoning, no begging. He'd be gone, but hopefully he'd made a difference. He was dying as a man, free of the curse, which was far more than he'd ever dreamed of.

Hopefully, she'd do better than he had. He spoke as clearly as possible. "Listen, Heather, you might remember my words later. No matter what happens. I know you can beat the curse. There's a journal in my pocket. I want you to have it. It's what I've learned. Maybe it'll help you. If you remember, come back and get it off my body when you're you again."

Her breath was hot against his neck. The coarse hair abraded his skin. It would be over soon. Lips peeled back, and he could feel the teeth against his neck.

She licked his cheek.

Uncertain, Earl cracked open his eyes. Heather stepped back and growled. Her eyes were shining gold, the same as his would have, only there was something different there that he'd not ever seen in another werewolf. Something surprising.

Reason.

"I'll be damned." He could have sworn that the terrifying werewolf actually nodded. Heather took another few steps back, lifted her head, and howled in triumph. She'd destroyed Buckley, so she'd earned that.

"Earl, look out!" Aino shouted.

Earl turned to see Aino aiming down the sights of the old Finnish rifle. "Wait!" Earl cried, but it was too late. Aino fired. "No!"

Heather studied him quizzically and seemed to shrug. Then she turned and ran from the yard, barely even slowing to leap over the fence to disappear into the snow.

Aino hadn't shot Heather? Earl rolled over. So what had . . . *Oh.* His target had been the first *vulkodlak* that Earl had shot in the eye. It had gotten back up, and he hadn't even heard it coming over the tractor. Judging from what that odd silver bullet had done to the *vulkodlak,* the projectiles had to be magic. Fully half of the creature's torso was gone, spread across ten feet of the shop's wall.

His head was throbbing as he got up, but being close to those moving blades was just plain unnerving. "I thought you were going to shoot Heather."

"Why would I do that? She seemed friendly enough. Did you see that shot?" Aino asked, limping up. "*Voi kyrpa!* Son of a bitch blew up!"

Earl stumbled over. "Nifty. Gimme that rifle. We've got a town to save."

⊰ Chapter 26 ⊱

There was blood on the carpet. He stared at the floor and the congealing puddle between his feet before he realized that the blood had come from the interior of his skull. The pain had subsided, but he could only vaguely recall the sensation of his head coming apart. There was something hard in his mouth, crunching and rolling between his teeth. Clumsily, he spit it into his hand. It was bone and lead fragments.

What happened?

Fully awake now, Nikolai took stock of the situation. They were in the living room, sitting on the Alpha's couch. Harbinger was gone. His nose told him the house was empty except for the stink of the Alpha and the unnatural stink of the tar-soaked skeleton. He remembered pulling the trigger, the sudden flash, then nothing.

Why aren't we dead? And why did you shoot us? Fool!

"Now you know I mean business. Do not question me again." That silenced the Tvar. Nikolai could sense its fear. "Cower. I've shown what will happen if you disobey me."

But why *were* they alive? He had played Harbinger's game and lost. Nikolai lifted the bullet fragments to his nose. *Lead.* It hadn't been a silver bullet.

But you thought . . . You would have killed us. . . .

"Lying to me, tricking me. You deceived me. That will *not* be tolerated again."

Standing took a moment; he was weak with hunger. His body had stripped itself of every spare molecule in order to heal. A folded piece of paper had been shoved into the remains of his shirt. The edges were jagged from where it had been ripped from a small notebook. Aching eyes were barely able to make out the handwriting in the darkness.

> *Nikolai,*
>
> *I used a frangible lead round. They make a real mess and take a while to regenerate from, but you'll live. I needed to know if you were telling me the truth. Nothing personal. I think I understand you better now. I'm impressed. That could have been silver, but you did it anyway. There are only two ways for this to go from here. If you changed your mind, you got one chance to walk away. But if you're a man of your word, help me find this Alpha and kill him. Help me save this town. This is not their fight. They were dragged into this because of our kind. Help me make this right. Either way, know that I'm sorry about your woman. I swear to you that I had nothing to do with her murder. We were both lured here by him. He needs to pay. He needs to be stopped.*

Harbinger had shown him an unexpected mercy. The quest to silence the Tvar should have killed them both. His Val rifle had been left on the floor. There was food in the kitchen. It would not take too long to heal enough to hunt.

What do we do now?

The Tvar was actually *asking* for direction, and meekly at that. It was not shouting at him, nor telling him what to do. Nikolai was not used to such a tone.

"I have won," Nikolai whispered. He'd begged Harbinger for assistance, but it had been Nikolai who'd demonstrated that he had the courage to take control. Harbinger was a trickster, but he was no longer the king of the werewolves. Nikolai did not need a master. Harbinger was not nearly as clever as he believed himself to be. Nikolai had just demonstrated to the Tvar who was the master. Harbinger's continued existence was nothing more than a liability.

"We came here for revenge. That has not changed. We find the Alpha werewolf and destroy him."

What of our nemesis?

"First we avenge Lila. *Then* we settle old scores."

The snow cutter was faster than it looked and they reached the perimeter of the Copper Lake school grounds in three minutes. Aino stopped the tractor so Earl could survey the scene. "Think they heard us coming?" Even though the driver's seat was only a foot away, Aino still had to shout to be heard.

Between the two of them and all the extra guns crammed into the cab, it made for a tight fit. Earl had smashed out the rest of the side window for a place to sit, straddling the edge, with one leg dangling over the tire, and the windchill had damn near froze him.

"Just 'cause they're dead don't make them deaf." Earl lowered his binoculars. Some of the *vulkodlak* were already moving to intercept, but the vast majority were still concentrating on attacking the gym. "Here they come. Head straight for the front door while they're still bunched up." Aino let out the clutch, and the tractor crept forward. Both men put on safety glasses taken from the shop. This was about to get extremely messy. "Remember, if you see somebody out there that you know, it's not them anymore. Run them down and try not to look at the faces."

"Eh . . ." Aino shifted gears. "I don't really *like* most folks anyway. Like 'em even less when they're trying to eat me." They were about to use the devil's personal blender to make an undead smoothie, but Aino did not strike Earl as the type of man destined to end up in Appleton in need of psychiatric care afterward.

Earl adjusted so that he could lean farther out the window. Several *vulkodlak* were running right toward the tractor. Aino and Earl weren't in danger of breaking any speed limits, even in a school zone, but they were going fast enough that it would be difficult for the *vulkodlak* to simply climb onboard. His job was to make sure that didn't happen.

The fifty-round drum made the Thompson feel ponderous in his hands. Snow puckered around the *vulkodlak* as Earl struck the first few down with a burst of .45 ammo. Earl stuck his head back into the cab. "Fire it up!"

Aino pulled a lever, and the blades began to turn with an ominous series of clanks. Within seconds the noise had grown into a roar. The first of the *vulkodlak* he'd shot came out of the snow just in time to hit the blades. They were yanked in, thrashing until they disappeared. The ones on the outside edge were clipped, instantly dismembered, and launched spinning through the air.

"Hot damn!" Earl exclaimed as a severed leg flew over the scoop to strike the windshield. "That would even impress Milo." Aino just spat on the floor and turned the windshield-wiper speed up a level. Earl stuck his head back out the window and started shooting at anything that moved.

The *vulkodlak* at the back of the crowd surged toward them in a wave. Earl mowed them down until the bolt flew forward on an empty chamber, so he automatically yanked the cumbersome drum and slid in another. The drums were much slower to get into place, and by the time he was ready they were in the midst of the creatures. Aino jerked the wheel to the side and caught another *vulkodlak* in the scoop.

"Head for the big group!" Earl shouted as he pulled the safety pin from a frag grenade. "I'll get the stragglers." He chucked the grenade out the opposite window. It detonated a few second later, ripping the *vulkodlak* with prefragmented silver wire.

They were moving too slowly. Now that the creatures knew what was going on, they were dodging the blades and swarming up the sides. Earl kept shooting. Putting a distracting burst into one target before quickly switching to another. His second drum was finished too quickly and he threw another grenade. Before it had even exploded he'd had to draw a revolver and shoot a *vulkodlak* off the back of the tractor. "Can't this thing go any faster?"

Aino shifted gears again. Black smoke belched from the exhaust as Earl locked in another drum. A *vulkodlak* made it between the tires and came up the side. Earl barely had time to cock the Thompson before it was onto the hood. Earl fired through the cab and shattered the front windshield. The *vulkodlak* flipped over the side.

"Well, now I can't see nothing!" Aino shouted.

Earl knocked the rest of the glass out with the butt of his gun. "Better?"

"Much. Thanks."

They were surrounded. Some of the creatures were more damaged than others—those ended up in the blades or under the tires—but many of them were nearly werewolf-fast, and those were a severe problem. Earl knocked off another two with his Thompson, emptied a revolver into one coming up the side ladder, and, with his Bowie knife, struck the hand clean off an arm that came reaching through the back window, but there were more coming.

Knife in one hand, Thompson in the other, Earl kept on fighting as the tractor's cab was covered in bodies and reaching claws. He moved from window to window, continuously shooting or reloading, on a violent reactionary autopilot. Their course had been set, Aino had aimed them right for the entrance, and now with his hands free he took up Heather's shotgun and opened fire. They were a raft floating in a sea of undead monsters. The tommy gun was smoking hot as Earl dropped his final drum and switched to stick mags. The cab floor was filled with spent brass.

Antifreeze and oil were spilling from punctures along the engine cover. Claws ripped through their tires. A particularly agile *vulkodlak* grabbed the rotating tread and rode the tire up to the cab's level. It had been a girl, once. She latched on to the driver's seat and pulled herself inside. A split second before she reached Aino, Earl drove his knife through her head, grabbed a handful of ponytail, and hurled the *vulkodlak* back out the window.

They crashed into the main crowd with an incomprehensible ripping sound. Earl looked up just in time to see the blades impact the packed-in mass of the *vulkodlak* pressed against the gymnasium entryway. A sea of white eyes and snapping teeth was fed into the tearing blades, but with walls on both sides, there was nowhere for the *vulkodlak* to escape. The scoop barely fit between the brick walls. Hundreds of the monsters were trapped.

It was disturbing, even by professional Monster Hunter standards. Earl couldn't look away. The *vulkodlak* were simply consumed, like wheat in front of a combine. Some made it over the top of the steel scoop, usually missing their legs, only to flip over to end up under the tires.

The tractor lurched and groaned as the scoop was packed with *vulkodlak*. "Gotta put her in low." Aino dropped the shotgun and got back into the driver's seat. The snow cutter engine groaned as gallons of red material and rags were pumped out the spout and sprayed against the gym walls. It came splashing through the broken windows.

"That is . . . *amazing*," Earl said as his safety glasses were hit with spatter. A claw slashed wildly through the bottom of the door, forcing

Earl to turn his attention back to keeping them alive. He stomped it with his boot until he was positive that every bone was broken.

It was a painful, gradual approach as the tractor inched forward. The *vulkodlak* ahead of them scrambled, pushing themselves up the walls to escape, only to be sucked back down as the creatures below them turned into hamburger and were belched out the spout. The ones in the front tried to break through the barricades with renewed frenzy, but they were ineffectual under the crush of bodies behind them.

At the rear of the tractor, the remaining creatures were gathering, slashing at the already shredded tires and scrambling up the bumper. Earl wasted a dozen rounds on one before he realized it was wearing MCB armor and switched to carving its head apart. The dead MCB agent went over the side, but there were too many others at the rear to drop with small-arms fire alone. "Fire in the hole!" Earl shouted as he threw a pair of grenades out the back window. The twin explosions shredded many of the remaining creatures.

The *vulkodlak* were as savage as any undead Earl had ever encountered, but they weren't stupid. They knew when to regroup. The crowd behind the tractor broke and fled.

At the front, the last of the trapped *vulkodlak* was sucked into the blades. The barricade was clear. Aino stood up for a better view over the scoop. "That's all of 'em." And not a second too soon, because their engine was spitting and hissing, and several warning lights were flashing on the dash.

The cab was entirely filled with cold, wet gore. The air tasted like blood, and Earl coughed as he tried to breathe against the haze. "Throw her in reverse," he ordered.

They backed over the crunchy remains behind them. Earl scanned for threats but couldn't spot anything that seemed worth shooting. Aino put the clutch in, and they rolled to a wet stop, engine rumbling, blades slowing and coming to a stop. The only movement came from the continued twitching of the many severed limbs. Blood dripped from the cab's ceiling, covered every surface, and formed shell-casing-filled puddles on the floor. The brick corridor leading to the front door was greased with a substance that could best be described as *mush*. Everything in a large circle around them had been painted a sloppy red, and the snow was a discolored pink for another hundred feet past that.

Earl tried to find some part of his body that was not covered in blood to wipe the safety glasses on but finally gave up and tossed the glasses out the window. Aino shut off the engine, and the tractor gurgled its last. After the mechanical noise and the gunfire, the night seemed abnormally quiet. The only sound was the hissing of air escaping from their punctured tires. Even the snow had stopped falling.

"You know, I've been doing this kind of thing a *long* time. . . ." Earl pulled out a cigarette and lit up. Thankfully, at least it wasn't red. "I've got to say that this is the single nastiest thing I've ever seen. And trust me, brother, I've seen some crazy shit in my day. Smoke?"

"Yup." Aino surveyed the carnage. Earl was impressed that the old man didn't need to puke. They built them tough up here in the frozen north. "So, this is what saving the day feels like, eh?"

"Something like that. Welcome to the exciting world of professional monster hunting. Usually not quite so . . . messy. Well, it's always messy, but we've reached a whole 'nother level on this one."

It would be dawn soon. The storm was wearing off. The energy used to disrupt local communications was weakening. It was only a matter of time before the MCB found out what they'd done here, and there would be hell to pay. It had been nearly twenty years since this level of supernatural carnage had been inflicted on American soil. The MCB would surely react with overwhelming force.

Yet, the Alpha wasn't even slightly worried.

Lucinda Hood had mustered her courage and had descended into Shaft Six. The Alpha had been surprised to see her come down into the dark. The witch stank with fear, and it wasn't the nervous anxiety of earlier: it was actual terror, and it was because of him. "Somehow they've killed most of your bloody *vulkodlak*. It's stupid to stick around," she shouted. "This is madness!"

"Fulfilling a destiny isn't madness," the Alpha corrected. There was no way he could be upset with her. Her pathetic senses couldn't see what his could. Even her new god was less than what he was becoming. "We'll leave in plenty of time, but there's one last thing to do. He's coming for me."

"Who?" Lucinda asked, confused. "Who's coming for you?"

The amulet had whispered that there was one last challenge to be faced before he was complete. It had become more aware as he'd fed it souls, until it had begun to communicate freely. The spirit of the forerunner was restless, but after being kept dormant by Koschei for so long, it had to know that he was worthy of all its gifts. "I don't know," he said simply. "But he'll be here soon. I'll prove myself worthy. Then we'll go."

"Worthy? Harbinger killed Petrov. You killed Harbinger. Who else is there? There are only a handful of other werewolves of their caliber, and none anywhere near here."

"Petrov is alive. I can smell him. Maybe he's the one, maybe not." Despite the fact that his senses were ridiculously acute, the clues were more confusing about Harbinger. He would surely know if there was another Alpha out there, and he'd seen Harbinger die, the spirit ripped right out of his body, and used to feed the amulet. . . . Yet there was a strangeness in the air, almost like a shadow of Harbinger was lingering.

There was only one other werewolf in range that didn't belong to the pack, but created by one of his line just this very night, an anomaly caused by the mad fluctuations of the amulet. A woman, and she had the blood of the thieving Finn, but also something else, something odd about her scent. *Could it be her?* The idea was absurd; she was too inexperienced to be a threat.

At this very moment the female was watching this place from the shelter of the forest, thinking that her presence was unknown. The Alpha had assumed that she had been driven by instinct to come begging for a place in the pack, but instead she'd just stayed there, observing. Perhaps she was frightened to come down. Maybe she understood how he'd fed on his own pack earlier, but he was satisfied now. With the bloodlust past, she would have been safe enough. He was feeling merciful. Yet, though there was a hint of fear on the mystery woman, there was far more resolve.

Lucinda continued to plead with him, but the witch could never hope to comprehend what the amulet wanted. Since putting it on, his understanding had continually increased. He knew now for sure that this was the item used to create the very first of his kind. It was not alive, it was not intelligent, but it had been programmed to search for someone worthy. Now it was telling him all that remained was to confirm he was truly the one. That meant facing one last unknown challenger.

The Alpha had learned about the amulet from intel gathered by the original Operation Unicorn during the Second World War. It had been far before his time, but he had read the OSS reports detailing the mysterious Koschei and his mysterious abilities. It wasn't until archeologists had uncovered the bones of the forerunner that he'd come to understand his mission in life. The MCB had seized the forerunner's remains, but not before word had spread to his own organization. The first time he'd touched the bones, he'd known. The spirit of the forerunner had filled his mind with images. The dreams had begun shortly after, and finding the lost amulet had become his sole purpose in life.

Of course it was fate. He was a werewolf, but he'd also started as so much more than a human. It was obvious why the forerunner had chosen him. It was still far beyond his comprehension how or why the amulet had been fashioned through human alchemy and the Old Ones' lore, and then used to rip the spirit from the fiercest of all monsters to be bonded to a man, but he knew with all his heart that he was the one they had built it for. He was the true Alpha, the one who would prepare the way.

As the Alpha listened to the witch's protests, the unknown female werewolf left the tree line and loped back toward town. Running her down would have been easy, but the amulet told him to let her go. Apparently, it thought she had some part to play.

⊰ **Chapter 27** ⊱

The good people of Copper Lake came out of the gym to check for survivors, then promptly took an ax to any *vulkodlak* that was still moving.

"I'll be damned, Mr. Harbinger. I do believe you've made an unholy mess of things out here," Nancy Randall said after she climbed through the barricade. She looked down at the organic slurry under her boots in disgust and then back at Earl with only slightly less disgust. Earl stood his ground. His armor was still dripping blood. She cracked a smile. "If you weren't so damn gross, I'd give you a hug."

"Thank you kindly, ma'am," Earl said as Aino approached. "But the wood-chipper on wheels was Aino's idea. I do believe the county owes him one hell of a Christmas bonus."

Nancy looked over Aino, who wasn't much cleaner than Earl. "I'll make sure he gets a parade and the keys to the city."

"Forget the keys. I'll take paid vacation," Aino said. "Someplace with no werewolves."

There was cheering and shouting from inside the gym as word spread about the *vulkodlak*. "Don't get too excited just yet," Earl warned. "They'll be back. This isn't enough to account for every dead body in town. The ones I hurt ran, but they'll be back. The tractor's toast, but we can use it to shore up your barricade, which should make it tougher to break in. But we've still got bigger problems."

"You've got no idea," Nancy muttered as a large figure ducked under the barricade to join them outside.

Earl frowned. "Agent Stork?"

"Stark," the MCB man corrected automatically before launching into a spittle-flecked tirade. "Damn you, Harbinger. The only reason I don't shoot you on the spot is because of all the rednecks with guns in there who think you're some sort of . . ." He searched for the word.

"Hero?" Earl pointedly looked at the splattered walls and spread his hands. "Well . . . duh."

Stark's face was flushed and angry. "Let me tell you something. When we get back to civilization, you're going down. I'll make sure—"

"Cram it, fatty," Nancy said. "Come on inside, boys. It really stinks out here." She led the way back through the hole.

It was obvious Stark wasn't used to being told what to do by civilians. He just glared as Earl casually bumped into him, staining Stark's armor red, but the agent held his tongue. The original doors had been torn to splinters and then replaced with the boards from the bleachers, bathroom stalls, and everything short of the kitchen sink. Judging from the looks of things, they'd gotten there just in the nick of time.

It was much warmer inside, so warm in fact that Earl's frozen face began to tingle like it was being stabbed with dozens of tiny needles. Despite the blood on his clothing, complete strangers manning the barricade slapped him on the back. Earl was not used to so many people looking at him like that. MHI tried to keep a much lower profile. Frankly, the attention made him uncomfortable. Someone passed him a gym towel, and he used it to scrub his face clean.

"Shoo! Give these men some room." Nancy ordered. The crowd drew back automatically. She'd obviously established herself as the leader during the night. "You said we've got more problems. What else can go wrong?"

There was enough background noise that he wasn't worried about anyone overhearing anything they shouldn't. "The man that started this is still out there. I need to find him. If I don't, he'll just do this again someplace else."

"I can send some people with you," Nancy said. "You'll need—"

Earl raised his hand. He was going after an Alpha; a mob would just get in his way, and most of them would probably get killed in the process. These people had guts, but they didn't have training. He needed Hunters. "It's not safe yet. There will be more *vulkodlak* coming, and they're fast and tough to kill. Plus, he's still got some other critters he could throw your way. You need every shooter you've got here."

"I'm coming," Aino stated. "There's nobody to miss me."

Earl didn't know how to respond to that. Aino was a sturdy fellow in a fight, that was for sure, but he had to be about the age of Earl's kids, as in too damn old to be fighting monsters. "You did real good back there, but you—"

Aino raised his voice. "Just mulched half the people I know."

"No doubting that, my friend. We'll talk about it, but I need you to translate Aksel's journal for me first."

The curmudgeon obviously didn't like it, but he understood. Aino nodded his blood-matted head once and walked off, determined to get to work.

Stark had to butt in again. "I don't think you're going after anybody. I think you're the one behind this, and I think you're going to run off to cover your ass. How do I know you're not going to go destroy the evidence?"

Despite the sheer stupidity of that assertion and the sudden desire to slug Stark in the mouth, Earl just smiled and said, "Well, then, Agent. How about you come along to keep an eye on me? You are, after all, a highly trained professional."

That caught Stark by surprise. "Well . . . I . . . I'm needed here for . . . command and control."

"Not really," Nancy pointed out. "We had that handled just fine before you showed up."

"But . . . somebody needs to get in contact with MCB head-quarters . . . in case the lines open up."

Nancy put her hands on her hips. "Don't forget your phone then. You'll get better reception outside anyway. I'll be sure, when the rest of your people show up, to tell them how brave you were to try and protect us *poor* defenseless types from all those horrible monsters. That sounds much nicer than me telling them about how you were basically useless and spent your time trying to boss yourself into a spot in the basement."

Earl looked between them. He didn't know what had transpired, but apparently it was making Stark uncomfortable, and therefore Earl approved. Stark spoke very slowly. "You wouldn't . . ."

"Whatever you are, you're still a government employee. And I know government employees, since I myself am a politician. From the way you're used to throwing your weight around, I'm guessing you've got a pretty high-level job, but I'm also assuming a tragedy like this will bring out some even higher-level scrutiny. Regardless of who you work for, I bet they won't like the fact that you were trying to throw some children out of the bomb shelter to get murdered to make space for your ugly ass."

"I . . . well, I . . . I mean . . ." Stark looked at Earl and sighed. "Shit." He'd just been deftly outmaneuvered. "I'll go round up some cold-weather gear." Dejected, Stark stomped off.

"You know, I didn't really want him along," Earl pointed out as he watched the agent retreat. "I was just trying to shut him up."

"Better you than me. If he gives you any lip, maybe you could *accidentally* push him into the snow cutter?"

"Tempting. Well, at least MCB are usually handy in a fight. I could use some real Hunters."

A very deep voice intruded on their conversation. "Mr. Harbinger?"

Earl turned, and then had to look up. *Way* up. The man was huge, bigger than Pitt or Gregorius, bigger than his largest Hunters. The man had to be nearly seven feet tall and was built like an NFL lineman. His enormous shaved head was wrapped in a bandage. He had one lazy eye and the facial scarring of someone who'd once suffered a severe cranial injury. Despite the fact that he was an extremely memorable specimen, and Earl was positive they'd never spoken, there was something oddly familiar about the man. "Do I know you?"

"I believe I hit you in the back with an ax earlier. Just wanted to say sorry about that."

Earl nodded. *The other Hunters.* "Briarwood, wasn't it?"

"Yes, sir. I'm the last, though. Name's Jason Lococo. Most people just call me Loco."

"Most people are stupid, too. What do you prefer?"

"I . . . Well, Jason would be fine, sir."

There was no sign of the other Briarwood men that had shot up Heather's house earlier. "What happened to Horst?"

"Gone." Jason gave a grim little smile, leaving the impression that it was *gone* as in *dead,* as opposed to *gone* as in *left.* "Turns out he wasn't as clever as he thought he was. Is MHI hiring?"

"MHI is always hiring."

"I don't have a resume handy, but I can provide references."

"You managed to hit me with an *ax*," Earl said. "I've got to say, that's a decent resume builder. You're injured, though."

Jason gestured at the bandage. "Just a flesh wound. Ryan shot me in the head on account of me not wanting to murder you."

"He sure had a way with people, didn't he?"

"Yes, sir. I do okay at fighting monsters, and I've got a family to support. I can help."

Earl thought about it for a moment. There was no doubt the man was a Hunter, even if he was from a shoddy outfit. He'd do. "All right. You're hired, but let's call this a probationary period. If we don't die shortly, we'll discuss salary and benefits. Gather what equipment you can and meet me back here in ten minutes. Move out."

Jason seemed honestly relieved. "Thank you, sir. You won't regret this."

Nancy waited for the big man to get out of earshot. "When we were bandaging him up, he was covered in prison tats."

Earl shrugged. It wouldn't be the first time he'd hired a Hunter with a felony record. "I trust him more than Stark already. I'm not hiring him to lead a church choir. I'll pull his records when I get a chance. If he did something particularly vile, like murdering without a good excuse or hurting women or kids, then I could probably get that snowblower going again."

"You're a man of strange sensibilities, Harbinger. But back to what you were saying. I'll feel better when the trash behind this is put away. How do you intend to find him?"

There was a sudden banging on the barricade. Men rushed over to peer through the holes. "Where'd he come from?" someone shouted.

"I didn't see anyone coming!" responded the rifleman guarding the front window. "He came out of nowhere."

There was more commotion around the barricade. Earl confirmed that his Thompson was ready, then waited. Twenty seconds later, a teenage boy ran over to Earl and Nancy. "Mr. Harbinger, there's somebody here to speak with you. Says his name is Nikolai."

"That's how I intend to find him," Earl told Nancy. "If you'll excuse me . . . Oh, and if this asshole tries to kill me, shoot him full of holes."

Two men moved a chunk of the barricade for him. Judging from the shape of it, it was what remained of the trophy case that Heather had broken. Nikolai was waiting outside, arms folded, rifle slung over one shoulder. He'd found some clean winter clothing, probably from the Alpha's closet, and appeared much healthier than earlier.

Earl greeted him. "You're looking sane."

"You, on the other hand, look like shit," Nikolai replied, running one thumb under his eye, indicating the spot where Buckley had tagged him. "You've received a few marks, I see."

Everything on him hurt. "You don't realize just how nice regeneration is, 'til you don't."

"It is rather pleasant. I've fed. Our mystery Alpha has a penchant for Spam." Nikolai patted his stomach. He no longer looked emaciated. "Six cans of lard-soaked protein later, and I feel fine."

"Spam or death . . . Tough call." Earl took out a pack of cigarettes. "I'm a jerky man myself. Smoke?"

"No, thank you." Nikolai studied the blood-soaked walls. The largest identifiable object left in the entryway was a heavily damaged pair of work boots. "I like what you've done to the place. Very industrial."

It was surprisingly *awkward*, trying to be friendly with somebody like Nikolai. "How about we cut the bullshit and get down to business? You with me or against me?"

"You're still alive. I believe even you can extrapolate an answer from that."

"Extrapolate? Where the hell did they teach you English?"

"I'm sorry. The KGB did not have classes in *cracker*."

Earl sighed. "Can you take me to the Alpha or not?"

Nikolai nodded his head toward the hills. "He's out there somewhere. I can feel the amulet. It's been getting stronger all night. I do not know where he is, but I can take us in the right direction."

"Can I trust you?"

"No, but you will," Nikolai answered. "You helped me do something that had to be done. I have regained control. I came here to kill the man that took Lila from me. I will not stop until that is done."

"Fair enough." There was no trust, but there was enough mutual respect to get them through the mission. Earl held out his hand. "Truce?"

Nikolai sneered at the extended hand. "Do not patronize me, Harbinger. We kill this *zalupa* first. Then we can define our terms."

It would have to do. They'd go back to killing each other as soon as the Alpha was out of the way. Earl kept his face emotionless but decided then that when they were done, Nikolai had to be put down. Both of his personalities were too dangerous to live. Nikolai's expression was hard, and Earl knew that the Russian had probably come to a similar conclusion.

"Agreed then . . ." This pained him to say aloud, but Nikolai needed to know. "I think I know who we're after. We go back a ways. I believe the Alpha's a man named Kirk Conover. I don't know if that's his real name, but that's what he went by."

Nikolai thought about it. "The liaison officer at Special Task Force Unicorn?" He seemed dubious. "Unlikely."

"I don't know who he's worked for since the war, but he was some kind of spook. He's the one that told me you'd be here. He roped me into this, and I trusted him like a sucker. I don't know how he hid it, but he smelled human, and he appeared to have aged like normal."

"We met . . . *briefly*, but that was long ago. Why would he have attacked my family?"

"He had a special hatred for you. His wife had nightmares about you until the day she died."

"She would not be the first." Nikolai scowled. "Who was this woman?"

"Your side would probably have known her as Sharon Mangum. Girl had a human father and a siren mother. She was with me on STFU. I found an old photo of Kirk and Sharon at the Alpha's home. It was the only personal effect in the whole place."

"Ah, yes. The Singer. She was right to be afraid. She was considered a very high-value target. Anyone that can so confuse a man's mind is an extremely dangerous asset." The Russian seemed unconvinced. "But there could be other reasons the photograph was there. Could it have been planted to throw you off?"

"Maybe, but it don't feel that way. I don't know. It's the only thing that makes sense. I haven't seen the Alpha yet, but I've spoken to him. He broadcasts his voice somehow, probably using magic. He sounded younger, but he talked like he knew all about me. I didn't get too many details, since you interrupted and drove a snowplow through the wall and blew me up."

"Yes, that was a good one," Nikolai said smugly.

"He didn't sound like Kirk, but he's using magic, so who knows what else he's altered. The Alpha said he'd lured us both here. Kirk lured me here. He despised you, knew enough about your history to manipulate you, and had the resources to find you. You got any other ideas?"

"If Conover is the Alpha, then when did he become a werewolf?"

Earl tossed his partially smoked cigarette into the red snow. "I don't know, but when the Alpha was ripping the curse out of me, he called me *father*."

"Ah, now I see." Nikolai smirked. "So that is why you asked me if you'd spread the curse to anyone during our last battle. It seemed odd that you would not recall having given one of your comrades the curse. . . ." He trailed off, as if lost in thought.

Earl could tell Nikolai was holding something back. "What?"

"You really don't remember? What's wrong with you? I did not know werewolves could become senile."

"Stick it, you vodka-swilling Commie asshole. A demon stole some of my memories a while ago, okay? All I remember is your bomb going off and then waking up on a medevac. I've got memories from before, and memories from after, but not *those*. Quit screwing around. What do you know?"

"Earlier, you asked me if you'd spread the curse to anyone, not if you'd bitten anyone on your side."

Now it was Earl's turn to be confused. "What's the difference?"

"Only humans can be cursed. A divine, or even a half-divine, cannot turn into a werewolf. Only bitten humans can be transformed. Surely you knew that."

"Of course . . . But . . ." The memories just weren't there, but there was only one person on the task force that fit that description. "That's impossible."

"Now you see. In your injured confusion, you did bite someone that day, but it was not Conover. That event would have had dire repercussions, and surely you would have memories of the aftermath, of costing your leader his life. No, you don't recall this, because for you there was no aftermath. Instead it was a minor injury against one to whom the curse meant nothing, who could heal rapidly, and had no fear of being turned. You bit the Singer."

"You're lying."

"Tell me, did you associate with your teammates after the war? Did you keep in touch? Tell me, Harbinger, doesn't Unicorn hold *reunions*?" Nikolai turned away and gave a cold laugh. "And to think that I'd doubted the reports all this time."

"That's enough!" Earl strode over, grabbed Nikolai by the collar and jerked him around, heedless of the fact that the Russian could kill him in the blink of an eye. "What do you know?" Earl snarled. "What happened?"

"You know *nothing*." Nikolai met his gaze evenly. "I know now who we face. After the war, we kept tabs on the surviving members of all four of the American special task forces. I know more about the fates of your former teammates than you do."

That was obviously true. Earl hadn't even ever had a confirmation that there were any other teams active.

"Of the survivors, most, like you, went on to become PUFF-exempt and lived normal lives, a few were still considered too dangerous and were liquidated, and one went on to become a rather legendary MCB asset. Nothing particularly interesting to my superiors, except that two of the survivors disappeared completely within a few years of your return. One special, one human. They married, had children, and held uninteresting government jobs under an alias. Then one day they just vanished into thin air. It was a precise operation. Their existence was totally scrubbed. But before that, we had watched from a distance—"

"Who are you talking about?" Earl asked, exasperated.

"You must not have received the wedding invitation. The Singer had a child *eight* months after our last battle. It was a healthy baby boy."

Understanding came like a kick to the gut. Earl let go of Nikolai and turned away.

Nikolai continued without mercy. "A half-siren? The curse could never take hold in such blood. On a quarter-breed? Perhaps, perhaps not. We do not know. But what of a seed, barely taken hold in its mother's womb, suddenly introduced to the curse through the mother's blood? The mother would be fine, but the child . . . Oh, what an awful fate to inflict on a child."

It was too horrific to comprehend. Normally, small children inflicted with the curse grew sick and died, but if the child was already supernaturally strong, then it was possible they could live through the change. "What have I done?" Earl whispered.

"Can you imagine? A being already blessed with monstrous gifts *and* a werewolf from birth? Such a creature would be a remarkable asset in the right hands. Surely, when such gifts began to manifest, that would be worth whisking a family off into top-secret obscurity, to be protected, to be . . . cultivated."

"You don't know this."

Nikolai shook his head. "There is no confirmation. Only half-whispered legends. You are not naïve enough to believe that your special task force was the last time your government would dabble in such things? Such a being could be very capable if he were to be raised and trained to control his gifts."

A werewolf from birth, but instead of being tempered by a human side, he would have been a conglomeration of two monstrous halves. "Dear God. What have I done?"

"Now, what if this already remarkable being were to go astray, off the reservation as you would say, and found an ancient talisman that magnified his lycanthropic power tenfold?"

"He'd be unstoppable." Earl looked at the carnage around them and felt nauseous for the first time. All of this had been caused by someone he'd created. Biting a pregnant woman . . . He'd cursed an unborn child and created a monster. "This is all my fault."

"Yes," Nikolai answered. "Now that I don't need you, I was debating what to do when we are finished with this Alpha. But now? You should live. Knowing that you are responsible for such madness will wound you more than anything I could do. Your curse is gone, but it lives on through the damage caused by your line. No matter what you do, you are damned. You should have known there is no escape for men such as us."

Nikolai didn't understand. It wasn't about escape. It was about penance. Sometimes the best thing a man could hope for was to set things right. Earl looked to the hills, dense forest stretching for miles, and he knew that somewhere out there, this Alpha, his bastard hybrid creation, was waiting.

⧏ **Chapter 28** ⧐

Harbinger had lied to her. Being a werewolf wasn't nearly as bad as he'd described.

Sure, it had been awful at first; mind-blowing pain, incoherent rage, and thoughts so darkly violent that they'd make a homicidal maniac cringe—that part was exactly like Harbinger had told her it would be. But then she'd found her groove. Thinking was hard, but not impossible. It just took more concentration.

At first, in the dark, encircled in freezing cold steel, she'd been scared. Then she'd gotten angry. There was nothing in the world more important than killing *everyone* for putting her in the box. The black frenzy had blocked out everything else until she'd literally exhausted her anger.

Eventually other thoughts had snuck through the cracks in the madness. Heather had remembered her family. They were all gone now, but they wouldn't want to see her like this. They'd be ashamed to think of her tearing people's limbs off. Since she'd been young, she'd thought of herself as a peacemaker. She had always been the one to break up the fights, to kick a bully's ass, to crack a joke, to try to help someone in need. When she'd gotten older, she'd continued doing the same thing, only more so.

Born with a strong sense of right and wrong, Heather had been an absolutist when it came to doing the right thing. Stubborn, she'd accomplished everything that anyone had ever dared tell her she couldn't. She'd stayed a peacemaker, then added protector to the resume as she'd gotten older. As a female police officer, she'd had to work twice as hard to be considered half as good. So it had been her nature to work herself to death to be considered one of the best.

Back in Minneapolis, she'd risked her life to save a kid from being sold and disappearing into the underworld. She had been undercover, just supposed to be observing a 'massage parlor' for Vice. They'd had no idea what kind of evil really took place there. All alone, the radio failed, no backup, stupidly outnumbered, it hadn't mattered. . . . Nobody else was there to protect that kid, so Heather had. It had put her on the fast track to detective.

But then her mom had gotten sick, and she'd dropped everything and come home. The decision hadn't even taken a second thought; someone needed her help. Unfortunately, the only thing she could do was help make her comfortable. Her mom's death had shaken Heather, and then she'd repeated the process with her grandpa, and then finally with her dad. One after the other. Her grandpa had always been a melancholy and angry man, and when he died it was almost like her dad had inherited that darkness, and then when he was gone he'd passed it on to her, like a family curse. By the time all of the dying was over, she'd been left burned-out and empty. She'd given until there was just nothing left inside, and she'd spent the time since on autopilot.

Then some scumbag had come along and threatened her town. It had awakened that dormant protective nature, and Heather again had a purpose. And she was a force to reckon with when she had a purpose.

The tracks in the snow behind her were paws, but as the distance grew, the tracks changed. By the time they were footprints, she could think clearly again. She continued running through the trees. The ice should have hurt her feet, but there was no pain. The cold should have cut through her naked skin, but she was warm. Faster than was humanly possible, she ran for town, never getting short of breath, never tiring. It felt good to be strong. It would have been so easy to pick a new direction and just keep on running, but Heather focused on the job. People were counting on her, and she couldn't afford to let them down.

Copper Lake donated several snowmobiles with full tanks of gas to the cause. Nancy said their owners weren't around to miss them. She'd sent someone to grab them from a local rental place. They were parked in front of the gym, just outside the pink-slush zone. Earl had sent runners to gather every remaining weapon from his overturned truck and was in the process of strapping the cases onto the back of a newer Polaris while Aino read aloud from Aksel Kerkonen's journal.

"I don't understand this," Aino complained. "It's nonsense words."

"Repeat them to me."

"They're gibberish."

"It's a spell." Earl sighed. He hated magic and had zero talent in that regard, but if you spent enough time hunting, you were bound to gain some familiarity. Earl had intimate knowledge of dark magic's effects; he'd seen the dead rise, seas boil, and fire rain from the skies, but the idea of invoking it himself was abhorrent. But if it meant the difference between beating the Alpha or not, then Earl wasn't above dabbling in the black arts. "Read them to me."

"Aksel wrote that the Baba Yaga walked him through saying these first. I'm no witch of the woods."

"No, you're way too pretty." Earl had never encountered an actual Baba Yaga. They were rare even in the dark frozen corners of Europe they originally hailed from and nonexistent in his usual area of operations, but by all accounts that particular fey was hideously ugly. "Just sound them out, already."

"Well, Aksel couldn't spell for shit, so this should be close." Aino cleared his throat and made an attempt at the words. "*Allut tvar mataw.*"

Agent Stark, having found some supplies and another weapon, joined them at the snowmobiles. "What're you doing?" He was livid. "That sounds like Old Ones' language. You can go to jail just for speaking that stuff."

"Add it to the list of things you're going to prosecute me for," Earl said. "It's all in that journal, Stark. The Soviets had a badass werewolf by the name of Koschei dealing out a lot of hurt during the Winter War. He was so tough they called him the Deathless, and it was all because he was wearing that damn amulet. They couldn't kill Koschei no matter how hard they tried, until some enterprising young officer got tired of retreating and cut a deal with a Baba Yaga for instructions on how to kill him."

"How complicated could it be?"

Aino looked up from the book. "She made some weird magic for them. She killed a bear, and inside its belly was a fox, and inside its belly was a chicken, and inside that chicken was an egg with a silver nugget inside, that she melted into a bunch of needles. Personally I think that part sounds like bullshit she made up so she could charge the army more money. The silver needles, they had to be driven square into Koschei's forehead. Only place that would do, and they'd only work for a minute. Then somebody had to put their hands on the necklace and say the spell before it could be pulled off."

Earl pointed at the antique Mosin-Nagant rifle on the back of his snowmobile. "That's our long-range needle applicator. We find the super-werewolf. Shoot him in the face. Recite a few words. Then go out for coffee and doughnuts. My treat."

Aino grunted. "I better get some damned sprinkles on mine."

Stark was unimpressed. "Sure. Magic chicken egg antique silver bullets . . . How'd that work out last time?"

Earl didn't look up from tying down cases. "Our boy Aksel was the only survivor, but he got the job done."

"Superstitious nonsense. We should play this by the book. Casting spells is against the law."

"I know that, but you want to square off against a super-werewolf that the hardest sons a bitches that ever came out of the frozen north couldn't beat without cheating, be my guest."

"You get an Old One's attention, or even worse, *bring* one here, and we'll be—"

Earl had never realized just how uninformed a senior member of the MCB could be. Myers, in comparison, was remarkably competent. "Okay, okay. Listen . . ." Earl tried to control his frustration, but since he was resisting the urge to strangle Stark, he considered it a win. "Didn't they teach any classes at your fancy MCB school besides witness intimidation? Baba Yaga are fey, not Old Ones."

"What's the difference?" Aino asked.

"Different dimensions. One's a whole lot meaner," Earl explained. "Not that fey are nice, but they tend to keep their unpleasantness to the individual instead of the world-wrecking level. Come on, Stark. Grow a pair."

"Still . . . It sounds like he just made it all up."

"He wasn't an MCB agent bucking for a promotion. Look. I'll grab the amulet and say the words. You just cover me. Worst-case scenario if the Alpha doesn't kill me first, which he probably will, is that I piss off some immortal crone and she hops a flight from Finland and comes over here and puts a hex on me. The bitch can get in *line*."

Stark folded his arms. "You shouldn't joke about that. Curses are serious business."

Earl was the last person that needed to be lectured on curses. "Well, I'm short one, figured I'd collect some more. After this I'm thinking I'll go desecrate a mummy's tomb or something."

"Fine." Stark relented and climbed onto another snowmobile. "We'll see who's laughing when you get turned into a frog. Play with your antique bullets. We need to stop by my car on the way so I can get some *modern* weapons."

Earl just smiled at Stark's ignorance. Sure, he was packing a pair of wheel-guns, a subgun built during the Second World War, and a rifle design that dated back to the tsars, but he also had an 84mm recoilless rifle and enough shells to obliterate half the county. Earl Harbinger was retro-practical. "Aino, would you repeat those words?"

Aino complied. "*Allut tvar mataw. Allut tvar mataw.*"

The words were harsh, grating, unpleasant on the tongue, but at least they didn't seem to bend his sanity like the Old Ones' language did. Earl memorized the words and tried to repeat them. They didn't feel particularly magical. He was probably going to screw this up.

Jason Lococo joined them a moment later, having borrowed some gear from the locals and unceremoniously dumped it on the back of his snowmobile. Earl had left him the biggest vehicle, an 800cc monstrosity. The giant stopped and silently listened to the words of the Baba Yaga. After Aino read the line and Earl repeated it for the fifth time, Jason asked, "If that don't work, what do we do then?"

"Anything you can think of to hurt him, and if that doesn't pan out, run for your life," Earl directed. "If I go down, somebody needs to stay alive to warn everyone else about this guy."

Stark raised his hand. "Maybe I should stay here then. You know . . . to report."

It was an odd feeling, but Earl had never found himself wishing for the professionalism of Agent Myers before. Despite their mutual hatred for each other, at least Myers wasn't a chicken. In fact, if he was going to be stuck with an agent, he would have traded Stark for *any* of the other ones he'd met. Sad to admit, but Franks would be especially useful. Hell, Franks would probably just walk up and punch the Alpha to death.

"Oh, come on, Agent Stark." Jason chuckled. "You were all excited for us to be killing werewolves when you thought you were going to get a cut."

"Shut up, you idiot!" Stark hissed.

"Huh?" Earl's eyes narrowed. "Cut of what?"

Stark held up his hands defensively. "I don't know what this guy's talking about. Cut? What cut?"

"You didn't know?" Jason shook his head. "Yeah, Horst gave Stark something like twenty percent of our PUFF. He told us about the infected deputy in the hospital. That was supposed to be an easy kill."

Stark had called Briarwood? But that meant when Joe Buckley turned early at the hospital and killed all those folks and cursed Heather . . . That all could have been prevented. MCB's own regulations would have required them to stay with anyone they even suspected was infected until it was confirmed if they were or not. Stark had not only known, he'd left someone newly cursed unattended in a crowded place. Earl's gloved hand curled into a fist. Sam Haven had warned him about this guy, and apparently Sam hadn't been exaggerating. He walked toward Stark's snowmobile.

"That's nonsense!" Stark shouted at Jason while trying to look indignant and failing miserably. "He's lying, Harbinger."

"When collecting on the deputy didn't work out, Stark told Horst all about *you*," Jason said. "I wasn't there for that conversation, but Horst thought you were worth so much PUFF that it was worth shooting me in the back and leaving his girlfriend to rot to death to try and kill you."

"You did *what*?"

"Harbinger, I—" Stark's nose was smashed flat as Earl punched him square in the face. He fell over the side of his snowmobile. Earl followed him around and slugged him again as he started to rise. The impact hurt Earl's fist. Stark hit the snow, groaning. Earl took a step back, shaking his aching hand, then changed his mind, came back, and kicked Stark in the ribs.

"I'd suggest that you stay down!" Earl was mad, downright enraged. If he'd still been a werewolf, it would have taken every bit of his self-control not to change right then. Stark had violated a sacred trust. Earl had *earned* his PUFF exemption. Who was this *bureaucrat* to take that from him?

Stark reached into his coat. Earl no longer possessed superhuman speed, but he was by all reckoning still a very quick man. Drawing his Bowie knife, he grabbed Stark by the hood, jerked his head up before he could reach his pistol, and placed the cold steel edge against Stark's jugular. That stopped him cold.

A flick of the wrist and the agent would die. "I did everything they asked me to do. . . . Do you have any idea how many people I killed, how many friends I lost, war after war, so that some government flunky could stamp a piece of paper that said I got to live like a man?"

Blood was running from Stark's nose. "N-no," he whimpered.

"I've seen your kind before, boy. A new generation of assholes comes along, you forget about the sacrifices made by the ones that came before. They mean nothing. To you, we're all the same. You can't tell the difference between a man and a monster. Oh, you've got your *rules*, only they never apply to your kind. And their protections only apply to people like *me* when it's convenient for people like *you*." Earl twisted the bone handle of the razor-sharp knife. Stark yelped as it cut his skin.

A pair of boots stepped into Earl's field of view. "Am I interrupting something?" Nikolai asked politely.

"Not really. I'm just deciding on whether to slit Agent Stark's throat or not."

"I found the scent," Nikolai said. Earl paused and looked up. The Russian gestured toward the hills.

Earl leaned in close and hissed into Stark's ear. "It's your lucky day." He let go of the hood, and Stark flopped facedown into the snow. Earl stood up and sheathed his knife. "Where?"

"He went north along Cliff Road."

"The only thing up there are some farms and . . . That's toward the old Quinn mine," Aino said.

"The one that Aksel worked at?" Earl asked.

"The same. One of the deepest in the world, 'til part collapsed and killed a mess of us."

"That sound like a reasonable place to hide a mystical amulet to you?" he asked Nikolai.

"It was on my list of places to look. A mile underground and filled with water. The amulet would have been extremely difficult to find."

Earl remembered the smell of the creatures that had held him earlier. They'd stunk of the deep earth. "Unless you had some critters that could dig for you. Then it would have just taken time. He's probably using the mine as a base of operations now."

Nikolai stopped and tilted his head. The expression was recognizable to Earl now. Nikolai was listening to the voices in his head. "Yes. Yes, I believe he would. . . . Follow me." Nikolai mounted a waiting snowmobile, fired up the engine, and sped off.

"You trust that crazy?" Aino asked.

"Not at all."

"I better come with you, then," Aino said.

"What're you, seventy?" Earl asked.

"Meh, I'm only twenty. It's the climate. Long winters. Hard on the skin," the old man said. "I can help. I know that place. It's a big facility. And I know the mines, if you have to go down."

Aino Haapasalo was cantankerous and stubbornly brave, but neither of those traits would keep them alive against what they were facing. "It's been a long time," Earl pointed out.

"When a place tries that hard to kill you, you don't forget it very easy. And don't you feel guilty about maybe me dying. I shoulda died years ago. I've just been passing time since then. Besides . . ." He held up Aksel's journal. "I'm the only one that can read this. It might come in handy still."

Regular people never ceased to amaze him. He reached over and slapped Aino on the arm. "All right. Mount up. Follow the crazy Russian."

Stark rolled over with a groan and pressed his sleeve to his broken nose. He flinched when Earl kicked him in the leg. "What're you waiting for? Let's move out."

"But . . . I—"

"Oh, you thought making me mad might get you out of some honest work? I don't think so. See, me and your boss go *way* back. We sure as hell ain't friends, but he's a real letter-of-the-law kind of man, and I know he holds his people to the same standards. You, on the other hand, are taking bribes and breaking PUFF exemptions for money. Help beat this Alpha, and I'll be inclined to forget some of your misdeeds the next time I talk to Myers. Now get your ass up before I change my mind."

Stark glared at Earl as he lumbered to his feet, but he didn't say another word as he reluctantly got back on the snowmobile. He flipped down his goggles over his still-bleeding nose. There may not have been any words, but Earl could see the message clearly etched on Stark's jowly face. *You'll regret this.* The snowmobile engine started with a roar, and Stark took off after Nikolai.

"Now, that's the spirit." Bringing Stark along might turn out to be a mistake, but he didn't particularly like the idea of leaving him here to cause trouble, either. So it was either bring him or murder him. When the MCB did show up, it would be nice if he'd have a chance to explain the night's events before Stark could put his spin on it. *But just in case* . . . Earl turned to Jason. "Do me a favor. If Agent Stark shoots me in the back, blow his fucking head off."

"Yes, sir," Jason answered as he got onto his snowmobile. It looked far too small to carry him. The whole vehicle creaked as he settled in. "You know, I already like this job better than my last one."

≒ **Chapter 29** ≒

The forest was eerily quiet in the predawn stillness. The snow had stopped falling. The wind had died. There were still sporadic gunshots coming from town, but they seemed so distant that it was almost peaceful. The fact that anyone was still alive to be shooting seemed like a good sign, while the fact that there was something still to shoot at was very bad.

Somebody was coming. First she heard the engines. Instinctively taking cover behind a tree, she waited for them to pass. The sounds echoed along the hills a long time before the snowmobiles would be visible. There were several of them, and they were coming from town. That meant they were *probably* on her side, but she wasn't taking any chances.

Next, she smelled them. The engines were hot, the exhaust was acrid. The lead rider was odd; something about his smell distorted her senses, like an air-freshener covering up something pungent. The effect was probably the wolfsbane that Harbinger had warned her about. It was supposed to mess with a werewolf's nose. The others weren't cloaked, though, and she could get a clear fix on them. Some of the riders tasted like fear, others of determination and . . . tobacco?

Heather's nose crinkled. *Harbinger.*

Relieved, she stepped out from the cover of the trees and ran for the approaching headlights. There was no problem navigating down to the road, since her vision had changed. Seeing in the dark was easy now. She raised her arms overhead and waved. Someone shouted, and the headlights turned toward her.

She picked out the other individual scents. Aino Haapasalo smelled like high-blood-pressure medications and the beer he'd had for dinner. The government man that had tried to shoot her earlier was the one giving off the most fear. There was a muscular stranger, bleeding and in pain but trying not to show weakness. Now that he was close enough, she could smell the werewolf under the cloud of wolfsbane. Somehow Nikolai was alive, and his scent screamed danger and made a part of her brain shout *Run!* but she told that part to pipe down. If that lunatic was riding with Harbinger, there had to be a good reason for it.

The snowmobiles stopped in a line. Goggles were lifted. Mildly curious, the big one looked her up and down. "Aren't you cold?"

It took her a moment to realize that she was completely naked. *Shit!* She awkwardly tried to cover herself with her hands and mostly failed. It had felt so natural, even in the freezing cold, that she'd *kind* of forgotten, but now that there were people looking at her, she was suddenly embarrassed.

Earl Harbinger parked the closest. So many ice crystals stuck to his clothing that he nearly shined. He killed the engine, rested one hand on his holstered revolver, and studied her intently, and it wasn't just because of her lack of clothing. "Say something."

She hadn't spoken for a while. Her mouth was painfully dry. "Uh . . . Hi? Now can I borrow some clothes?"

"I'm sure glad to see you." Harbinger breathed a sigh of relief as he jumped off the snowmobile and headed over. He swept off his leather jacket and draped it protectively over her shoulders. The movement struck her as strangely chivalrous. "How're you human already?"

"I don't know. I just . . . changed back when I wanted to." She pulled the jacket tight. It was warm with lingering body heat and smelled like Harbinger.

"You . . . You what? How—never mind. Jason, hand me that blanket."

"It's okay, I'm not cold. Just . . ." The jowly Fed was staring at her. She glared right back. "What? You've never seen a woman before?"

"You're the deputy from the hospital. You're one of *them* now."

"Wow. A brain surgeon. No shit, Sherlock." The big one gave her a blanket, and she wrapped herself in it and leaned against the back of Harbinger's snowmobile. "What gave me away? The naked snow-jogging?"

"Are you okay?" Harbinger asked. "Did you—"

"Hurt anyone? No," she answered quickly. It seemed very important to her that Harbinger knew that. For some odd reason, his opinion mattered. "I got away from town so I wouldn't be tempted."

"You did good. First time's the hardest. If you can keep your head through that, you can do anything. I'm impressed."

That made her blush. "You sure know how to flatter a girl." She caught herself grinning uncharacteristically. Harbinger gave her a hesitant smile in response.

The others dismounted and gathered around. Movement seemed to stand out, with the tiniest flicker easily catching her focus. Every twitch of a finger, every blink of an eyelid. She'd spent the last few hours looking at white snow and black half-covered shapes, so it wasn't until she saw the sheer *dullness* of the brightly colored snowmobiles that she understood just how much her vision had changed. "Everything's so gray . . . How can you stand it?"

"More rods, less cones," Harbinger explained patiently. "That's part of the change. Don't worry—you'll be able to see color again by morning. I'd trade you right now. I'm blind as a bat."

"What's he doing here?" Heather asked as Nikolai approached. The scary Russian stopped and tilted his head to the side, studying her.

"He's on our side. Marginally. I'll explain later."

She'd found the help she needed to get the cure. The words practically spilled out. "I tracked down our bad guy. I didn't see him, but he's in the Quinn facility at building six. There's a bunch of werewolves standing guard around it. I counted at least eight or nine, but there might have been more inside. There's multiple dead bodies there, but I smelled a couple of normal people still alive. Don't know whose side they're on, though. There were portable lights on upstairs, but I couldn't see anyone through the windows."

"You remember that much?" Nikolai asked sharply.

"I do. I was coming back to get help when I heard you coming."

"Impossible." Nikolai addressed Harbinger as if Heather wasn't even present. "No one could have made it through the madness so quickly. Especially a *pup*. She's lying."

"I'm not," she turned to Harbinger. He was studying her, but more with concern than suspicion. "Why would I lie?"

"It's a trick of the Alpha. There is something not right about her," Nikolai said.

"What? No, really. I'm telling the truth."

Nikolai's voice suddenly grew deep. "It's a trap." His entire manner changed. His posture slouched, his knees bent. "Kill her now."

Harbinger tensed and put his hand back on his gun. "Steady, Nikolai," he said with forced calm. "Don't go getting squirrelly on me. That amulet is messing with the natural order of things. That's all. She's okay."

"Hey, I agree with the bipolar guy," the federal agent interjected. "Better safe than sorry. Shoot her."

"Funny. I thought the same thing about you, Stark," Aino said.

"Do it, or I'll do it myself," Nikolai growled with that unnaturally low voice. Heather saw the muscles tense in preparation of movement. Time seemed to slow down as Nikolai's fingers tightened around the stock of his rifle. The barrel rose the slightest bit.

Heather just *reacted*. Without conscious thought, faster than any of the humans could blink, faster even than the other werewolf could register, she shrugged out from under the blanket and struck Nikolai with unexpected strength. The impact of her open palm shattered multiple ribs. Time seemed to stop as she stood there, arm extended, while Nikolai arced through the air. He landed ten feet away, sliding through the snow on his back. Instinctively, she moved in for the kill. By the time Nikolai opened his eyes, she was straddling his chest, pinning his arms with her knees, one hand locked viselike around his throat while the other was lifted overhead, fingers spread wide, ready to tear his face off.

"Heather!"

"Not now, Harbinger," she snapped.

"I gave him my word. We deal with the Alpha first. We're going to need Nikolai alive."

Heather sighed. "*Fine*." Nikolai was staring up at her, shocked. She followed his eyes as they tracked up her bare arm to her outstretched hand. Her nails had already stretched into deadly claws. She studied the claws absently. "Well . . . huh. Where'd those come from?" *Hadn't even felt that.* She turned her attention back to the stunned werewolf.

"What? Didn't expect that from a *pup?* You know what I can't stand? Bullies. I'm sick and tired of bullies. I'm done screwing around. You get me, Nicky?"

The madness in his eyes seemed to subside. There was no way he could breathe, but he managed a spasmodic nod. Giving one last squeeze, as if to say *Got you, fucker,* she reluctantly let go and stood up. Clenching her hand into a fist, she felt the claws shrink automatically. It hurt a little bit, but in a good way.

The four other men were just watching her, mouths agape. She picked Harbinger's jacket out of the snow and actually put it on this time. It was long enough that she was able to retain a tiny amount of dignity. She zipped it up as she walked over to Harbinger. Even he seemed surprised at how quick she'd been.

"What the hell is she?" the Fed shouted.

"She's with us. That's all you need to worry about."

"But werewolves can't do that!"

"Do what?" she asked innocently, making sure to bat her eyes at Stark. The mannerism seemed to unnerve him even more, and she got some enjoyment out of that. *I told Harbinger I'd try not to eat anybody, but maybe he'd make an exception for that one.* Heather banished the thought immediately. She was no murderer, and besides, Stark was probably high in cholesterol.

"He's talking about you partially transforming some body parts at whim . . . and moving damn near master-vamp speed," Harbinger said. "Impressive, even by my . . . or Nikolai's standards. Those are some neat tricks, even with a lot of practice. For somebody on their first night? I would've said impossible." He handed her the blanket. Heather threw it over her shoulders like a robe. It hung to her ankles. "But this night's just *full* of surprises."

The tall stranger and Aino were still gawking at her, obviously scared. Aino had been a friend of the family since before she'd been born. As her curmudgeonly grandfather's only friend, she'd always thought of him kind of like an uncle. To see him staring, wide-eyed and fearful, broke her heart. He was probably waiting for her to just zip over and shred him. He must think she was a complete monster.

Nikolai had stood. There was a terrible crack as he jerked his arm back into the socket. Bones realigned, he could begin to heal. He was watching her carefully, but it looked like the slightly less evil side was back in control. How bad was it that even a werewolf assassin with multiple personalities didn't trust her? If a monster like him couldn't trust her, how could she expect relatively normal humans to? She was really scraping the bottom of the trust barrel here, but she needed all of them if she was going to break the curse.

Heather tried to sound as contrite as possible. "Listen, all of you, please. I'm not like those others. I know this is a little weird, but I'm on your side. All I want is to get that amulet back so I can be cured. Please, I'm begging you. I need your help."

Aino surprised her then as he came over and put an unexpectedly gentle hand on her shoulder. "It's okay, girl. You didn't ask for this. We all know you're doing the best you can. Besides, I didn't shoot you when you got real ugly earlier, not gonna start now. You're the same person as you've always been, and you've always been okay by me."

Heather almost choked up at the unexpected display of affection. "Thanks . . . I . . ."

The old miner had exhausted his supply of empathy. "Eh . . . More? You need a hug or something? Come on, let's go get you cured already. I've been up for like twenty hours. I'm tired."

"My apologies, Deputy Kerkonen." Nikolai's words were polite, his attitude not so much. "It will not happen again." She didn't believe him at all. *It will not happen again* could just as easily be referring to her surprising him and getting the upper hand.

"Thank you," she said. "We cool?"

Nikolai nodded curtly and climbed back on his snowmobile. The others followed suit. Stark was still scared of her. The big one, Jason, seemed ambivalent but kept a real close eye on her. The air filled with the sound of high-pitched engines. One by one, they pulled off to spoil the pristine white swath covering Cliff Road.

Only Harbinger waited. She stepped closer to him. "So, how was that?"

"Unexpected . . . The amulet's magic is doing different things to you than the other recently bitten, and I don't know why. You know, Kerkonen, there's something really special about you."

"Why, Mr. Harbinger, are you *flirting* with me?"

"Huh? No," Harbinger answered before he realized that she was messing with him. He rolled his eyes. "*Special,* as in you're one peculiar werewolf. You're exercising a surprising amount of control for somebody who shouldn't have even turned yet. I just saw you do things that took me forty years to get the hang of. There's got to be an explanation."

Heather found herself grinning again. *Why does he have that effect on me?* She barely knew him, but there was something about Harbinger that just felt *right*. He was a gentleman, but she also liked his no-BS honesty. He was completely fearless but not a brute. This one was a keeper.

Heather had never been the social type. She'd always been the prettiest wallflower, but being a werewolf made her feel kind of *fun*. "Bummer . . . On the flirting that is. I'd gotten my hopes up."

For the first time since she'd met him, which had only been yesterday but seemed like an eternity ago, Harbinger didn't seem to know what to say. "Well . . . I'm . . ."

"Flattered?"

Harbinger actually laughed. "I suppose. You're an impressive lady. Maybe if we don't die, we can . . ." There was an awkward pause. "I don't know, catch a movie or something?"

She'd done the impossible. She'd found somebody who sucked at this kind of thing even more than she did. "You're pretty rusty on the whole dating scene, aren't you?"

"The last picture I took a woman to starred Humphrey Bogart, and it was new. What do you think?"

"Cradle robber." He was over a hundred, after all.

Harbinger shrugged. "That whole werewolf thing is hell on a social life. . . . It's hard when everyone ages but you. Makes anything long term kinda . . . complicated. I hadn't even thought about that part of being human again, but we *will* get you cured, too," he promised, and she could tell that he meant it.

She got closer. "You're sweet." And then she kissed him.

She hadn't planned on it. Harbinger's lips were freezing cold. Hers were abnormally hot. Harbinger was too confused to respond at first, but then he seemed to warm up to the idea.

Out of practice, but he's a pretty good kisser.

A minute later, Harbinger gently disengaged himself. "Well . . ." He cleared his throat. "We'd better get going."

"So, that's a date, then, Harbinger?"

"You can call me Earl. Just don't take that to mean I won't still shoot you if you go all homicidal crazy on me."

Heather put her hands on her hips. "There you go, spoiling a perfectly sweet moment."

Harbinger winked. "Well, I would feel *really* bad about it." He jerked his thumb at the last snowmobile. "Need a lift?"

"Why, I thought you'd never ask."

⊰ **Chapter 30** ⊱

The Alpha's roar shook the building. Dust trickled from the ceiling, dislodged by his bellow, as he stomped down the catwalk.

The wait was agonizing. The amulet was like a burning patch of hate welded to his chest. Even while it fed him, it taunted him with its untapped potential. The power was so very close, nearly at his fingertips, yet the spirit of the forerunner would not give up its secret until this last challenge had been met. He was already a hundred times the man he had been, yet there was still so much more to take.

Dawn was coming too quickly and threatening to ruin everything. Lucinda Hood had warned him that the last vestiges of her spell would fade along with the dark. Soon Copper Lake's story would be told to the world. Time was slipping away, but still the amulet told him to wait. . . .

He had thought about just denying the amulet's order and fleeing as originally planned. Having been raised to always be careful, to always plan for multiple contingencies, to never bite off more than he could chew, this was extremely frustrating. The smart thing to do was to retreat, regroup, and assess his next move. For once training and instinct were in agreement.

Fear kept him in place. The Alpha was worried that if he disobeyed the amulet now, then it would never find him worthy again. He would still be the greatest, but it would be like having one hand tied behind his back for the rest of his nearly immortal life. He would never fulfill his destiny like that. The anxiety tore at his guts. His fist left an indentation in a steel beam.

"I need counsel," he muttered to himself. The pack members that were attending him hung back, terrified at his outbursts. He'd already eaten a few of them, and they didn't even know why. The shadow that remained of his humanity could understand their fear, but the new part was disgusted by their cowardice. "Bring me the prisoner."

The werewolves fled, and the Alpha went back to pacing back and forth on the catwalk overlooking the base of Shaft Six. The catwalk crossed the center of the large space. There were stairs up and down at both ends. He was directly above the massive rusting cable spindles of the deactivated elevator. Being cooped up in this tomb was frustrating.

They returned a few minutes later with a ragged human hanging between them. His head had been covered in a bag, but the blood stains on his torn shirt told the rest of the story. It had been necessary to beat him severely during his capture. That had not been part of the plan, but he had resisted fiercely when the witch's minions had magically appeared in his home. There was no way he would have come willingly, so it had been necessary.

It pained the Alpha's heart to see him in such sorry shape. He should have realized there was no way he would have gone down without a fight. "Put him down." His werewolves did so, and they were wise to do it as gently as possible.

"Get your filthy paws off of me!" the prisoner shouted as the pack withdrew. The prisoner struggled to his knees, and the tilt of his covered head indicated that he was already listening, looking for an angle, for some means to escape. The Alpha walked across the catwalk and pulled the bag from the prisoner's head.

Kirk Conover blinked his blackened eyes as they adjusted from the complete darkness of the bag to the gray dimness of the mine building. Finally, they adjusted enough for him to make out the thin man standing before him in a big black coat and a wide-brimmed hat. "Let me go, Adam. It's not too late to fix this."

The Alpha shook his head and chuckled. "Hey, Dad."

Kirk Conover's hands had been tied behind his back for his own protection. He was still spry for his age and doubtlessly had a few tricks up his sleeve since he had, after all, been trained by the best. He was already looking for something to use to his advantage. This was an endearing trait to the remaining sliver of humanity in the Alpha's heart, but it just made the growing power of the Alpha's inner monster that much angrier. The Alpha whispered for it to be still. He needed wisdom, and his father had always had plenty to spare.

There were cobwebbed chains and pulleys dangling above the catwalk, but nothing that Kirk could utilize with his hands tied. Inventory completed of his situation, *still hopeless*, Kirk turned back to his son. "You need to listen to me. This is crazy. Stricken will lose it when he finds out what you've done."

The government didn't like when its supernatural operatives went rogue, and they were usually dealt with harshly. "I'm not scared of Stricken."

"You should be. I don't know what you think you're going to accomplish here, but it's wrong."

The Alpha leaned against the cold metal railing of the balcony. "This is bigger than me, Dad. This is destiny. You wouldn't listen. Nobody would listen before, but they're not going to have a choice now."

"It's that witch I met earlier. I don't know what she's put in your head. She's a demon's concubine, Son. I recognize her from the briefings. It's that Hood girl. She comes from a long line of necromancers. We'll just explain to Stricken that she brainwashed you."

"Do you really have any room to talk about brainwashing? I'm not the one that made my own child into a weapon. Oh, never mind." Long experience told him where that line of reasoning would take them. There was no need to refight old battles. They'd just have to agree to disagree. "I recruited her, not the other way around. This is my plan. Her god is just along for the ride. I've been working on this operation for three years. . . ." The Alpha paused to let that sink in.

He could see the pain in his father's eyes as he realized what that meant. "Even . . . before your mom died?"

"Since I saw the bones of the forerunner. It showed me *things*. The visions were stronger than the fake thoughts Mom stuck in my head and made me think were my own."

Dad gasped like he'd just been kicked in the stomach. He started to speak, then stopped, nervous and confused. That would have been unexpected. Mother had used her siren gifts to keep him calm and rational during the full moon, but she had also tried to keep him from pursuing his vision, and that had been simply unforgivable. When she'd begun using her powers to try to make him forget about the amulet, that's when it had become necessary to get her out of the way.

He'd always loved his mom. Considering their lifestyle, and the fact he'd been killing people for various black operations since he was a teenager, they'd actually had a pretty normal relationship. His parents had been just, kind, and had done their best to raise him as a normal child, despite his gifts. There had been a lot of love in their home. So that's why, when it came time to remove Mom, he'd made sure the *accident* had been as quick and painless as possible.

Obviously, he couldn't tell that to Dad. There was no need for him to know how far things had gone just yet. Dad would never come around then. "I wish I could show the forerunner's visions to you. Then maybe you'd understand. . . ."

"But, your mother . . . Once she passed away, and you didn't have her to help you, I thought maybe you—"

"Went crazy? No. Nothing like that. Sure, Mom's singing kept me on the straight and narrow, soothing the savage beast and all, just like before, but that didn't mean I couldn't plan for the future. I know you thought you were doing me a favor, helping hold back the wolf, but we both know you were just keeping me under control. I wasn't meant to be a slave."

"You weren't a slave," Kirk sputtered. "If we hadn't agreed to work for them, they would've killed you. But you were the best they've ever had. You were serving your country. You did great things!"

"Sure, but I'm meant for *greater* things," he tried to explain to his father for the hundredth time. "You never listen to me. None of you humans ever listened to me."

"But, son, you're human, too."

"ENOUGH!" The blast of noise made his father cringe. He was sick of this argument, and if his father dared pursue it much further, he'd be staring at a pile of his own steaming entrails. "I don't have to explain myself to you. That's not why I brought any of you here."

"Where's here? And who else are you talking about?"

"We're in Copper Lake, Michigan. Heard of it?" he asked, already knowing the answer. Kirk's face went very pale. "Ah, of course you have. . . . Imagine that. And did you know that I once read a report about an artifact that might have ended up around here somewhere?

Guess what?" The Alpha tapped his chest. "Found it, way down that hole right over there. Damn thing took forever to get to. And I'm the one that brought Nikolai here. Had to gut his wife to do it, too. Turns out he wasn't as bloodthirsty as you made him out to be."

"Maybe he mellowed with age." Kirk's eyes narrowed as he realized just how unstable his son had become. "What's your game, Adam? What're you playing at?"

"I made sure you saw the bulletin about Petrov. Sure, you're retired, but once Unicorn, always Unicorn. I knew you'd call Harbinger. You and Mom used to talk about him like he walked on water, like he was supposed to be some sort of role model for me or something. Of course you'd call your old buddy Mr. Wolf, and all I had to do was sit back and enjoy the show. . . . I actually thought you'd have come yourself, but I guess you're getting a little old for field ops. I wanted you here, too, though, kind of like you're attending my graduation. Sorry about Lucinda's digger roughing you up."

"What happened to Earl?"

"He's dead. Once I knew he was the one, I tore his soul out."

"No, not Earl," Kirk stammered. "Why?"

The Alpha patted the amulet tenderly. "He lives on in me. Ironic. I guess he lived up to that name he picked when he was with you. *Harbinger*. One who prepares the way. I wonder if the forerunner was whispering to him when he picked that name?"

"You ungrateful little bastard," his father snapped. "Earl saved my life and your mother's. If it hadn't been for him—"

"I'd never have been a werewolf." The Alpha smiled.

It was another painful revelation for Kirk Conover. The man was barely able to form the words. "You . . . you know?"

They had tried to keep him in the dark, and, like everything else, they'd failed. "I pieced it together. Most of the files on your original task force had been redacted, but I narrowed it down to two possibilities—Harbinger or Petrov. You never told me who it was, so I invited them both. Harbinger was the superior. He felt right. It was him, wasn't it?"

Kirk just nodded.

"So, he was my real father." The Alpha pumped his fist in the air. "Ha! I knew it."

"I'm your father."

"My *human* father," he sneered. "Cut me in thirds, and that's the most pathetic bit. Part god, part king of the beasts, and what? Human? You want me thank you for my worst parts? You rate a card on Father's Day, but that's about it."

The light in Kirk's eyes died. He bowed his head. "Your mother would be very disappointed in you."

The Alpha grabbed his father by the throat and lifted him into the air. It took all of his reason to stop from ripping the insolent little man in half and throwing him over the rail. Disgusted, he tossed Kirk back on the catwalk. The old man hit the cold metal with a grunt of pain.

This hadn't been what the Alpha was hoping for at all: adversarial, bitter. He'd been hoping for guidance, but now he understood that had only been his remaining humanity being weak and needy. Let it wither and die. It was better this way.

"I didn't abandon man. Man abandoned me. I'm not an attack dog to be kept on your master's leash. I'm the first of a new kind. I'm the next stage of evolution." The Alpha felt the amulet burn hotter. The challenge was *close*. "And I'm only one step away from perfection."

Kirk didn't look up. "My son is dead."

The Alpha was angry that the words actually managed to sting him still. He shouted at his pack. "Put the human back in his cage." He stomped off to face his final challenge. "I'll deal with him later."

"What's the plan?" Stark asked.

Earl studied the Quinn facility through his binoculars. The place was a huge, twisting warren of old buildings and rusting machinery. Heather had said that the tallest structure was Number Six. It was an imposing gray rectangle that dominated the facility. To reach it would require covering a lot of forest, breaching the perimeter, and making their way through a maze of potential ambushes.

At least it was all downhill from here, literally. Earl adjusted his position, trying to find a more comfortable way to lie prone on an icy boulder. Body aching, muscles sore, freezing, bandages pulling . . . He'd forgotten just how much being human could suck. He put down the binoculars and took out a smoke. Then decided against it. Wind was in their favor, but that could change soon enough. He put the pack away with a belabored sigh.

"Plan?" Stark asked again.

Sneaking in would be impossible against that many hyper-sensitive werewolves. The fence was only chain-link, but it was topped in razor wire. Heather and Nikolai could hop it, but the rest were going to have to go through the gate. A full-on frontal assault was their best option.

They were three hundred yards away, on a ridge that provided them with solid cover and a good field of fire. The sun would be coming over the hill any minute, and it would be at their backs. He really couldn't ask for much more. However, it was easy to forget that he'd been up all night, and exhaustion had set in. A tired Hunter was a stupid Hunter, and they couldn't afford any mistakes. He needed another opinion. "Nikolai?"

The werewolf was so quiet and motionless that it was easy to forget he was only a few feet away. "You are thinking what I'm thinking?"

"Square peg. Square hole. Go with our strengths."

"What?" Stark looked back and forth between them. "What's he thinking?"

"Yes," Nikolai answered. "I'm fastest. I will secure the gate. The rest provide covering fire and eliminate the sentries from here."

"What sentries?" Stark asked.

Earl handed Stark the binoculars. "First building in, two stories. Looks like an office. Top window, several of them moving in there."

"At least three more roaming inside. Two more in the trees just outside the main gate," Nikolai said. "Do not bother to look. You will not see them."

"You a good shot, Agent Stark?"

"Qualified expert."

Earl grunted. *Maybe in his prime.* Stark gave him the impression of somebody who spent a lot more time manning a desk than practicing at the range. "Recently?"

"Recent enough," Stark snapped.

Shaking his head, Earl slid back down the boulder. The other two followed him. Stark made more noise than he had, but Nikolai made far less. They made their way through the trees toward where the others were waiting. The snowmobiles were handy, but loud, so they'd parked at the base of the ridge and hiked in. The snow had made for treacherous footing, especially with seventy pounds of recoilless rifle and ammo on his back.

Heather, Jason, and Aino were crouched in a small ravine below.

Aino was using a headlamp with a red lens, still searching Aksel's journal for anything that might help. Jason raised his gun when he heard a branch snap above, then lowered it when he saw his new employer. Earl slipped and slid down the last twenty feet. Exhaustion and grace were mutually exclusive, but he tried to make it look like he'd *meant* to do that. Stark lost it halfway down the incline and tumbled the rest of it, making Earl look like a ballerina in comparison. Nikolai leapt off the top and landed quietly at the bottom. *Show-off.*

"We on?" Heather asked. While he'd been scouting, she had cut a hole in the middle of the gray wool blanket to stick her head through and tied a length of paracord around her waist to secure it. It made for a semi-passable poncho, more for modesty than to protect her against the elements. She was still missing pants and barefoot but had his coat on under there. Earl didn't mind. He figured Travis would have approved of Heather's general attitude.

"We're on. Nice poncho, by the way." Heather took up the edges of the blanket and curtsied. The rest of the group gathered around Earl. "We set up there," he pointed at the ridge above. "Shoot the hell out of anything that moves while Nikolai runs in. On my mark we follow."

"The pup can follow me, if she can keep up. Once inside, stay out of my way," Nikolai said. "When I am excited, it can be . . . *difficult* to tell friend from foe."

Earl grabbed Nikolai roughly by the sleeve. "Don't you dare hurt anybody on our side."

Nikolai struck Earl's hand away. "If you'd followed that advice yourself, we wouldn't be in this predicament now, would we?" Nikolai turned and walked away.

"What was that about?" Stark asked nervously.

"Nothing," Earl muttered. "It's not important. When we leave the ridge, move quick, but stick together. Stay alert. We'll wait until the sun comes over the hill, so we'll have some light."

"Sun'll be up in fifteen minutes," Aino said.

Stark pulled out his cell phone. "Still no signal." The Fed had been checking it every few minutes since they'd set out.

"When there is, you damn well better just call for reinforcements and not an air strike," Earl warned.

"What? They'd actually blow up the town?" Heather asked.

"Of course not," Stark lied as he put his phone away. "That would be overkill. Our primary mission is to protect the population from monster attacks."

"Your primary mission is to contain the truth," Earl said, knowing full well that the MCB was capable of massive overreactions. They'd destroyed population centers before to prevent various supernatural outbreaks. There had been one in Pennsylvania in the eighties, Texas in the forties, and even before there had been an MCB the government had burned a town in Wisconsin. America wasn't the only one with that policy, either. No country would risk a major supernatural outbreak. Areas had been sterilized in Africa, India, Russia, and Europe, blamed on natural disasters or industrial accidents, and those were only the ones MHI knew about. These events were rare and ugly, but they beat the alternative. "We get this guy now and this op is locked down, Stark. There's no need for these people to suffer any more than necessary."

"Blow up my hometown and I will totally beat your ass," Heather said.

"Oh, don't worry about that, missy, but MCB sure isn't done with you," the agent growled. "You know what happens to confirmed werewolves. There's going to be hell to pay—"

Earl cut him off. "*Stark.*"

"What?"

"Another word, and I'll kill you myself and tell Myers the werewolves got you." Earl didn't so much as blink as he let that sink in. Stark began to speak, then thought better of it and closed his mouth. Earl Harbinger had a certain reputation amongst the MCB, and even Stark wasn't pigheaded enough to push him just then.

Earl studied the faces around him. Heather was nervous but seemed predatorily eager. Being a werewolf had that effect on you. If she didn't wig out and go insane on them, everything should be okay. Jason Lococo seemed calm, and despite having come from a crappy company was acting like a professional. Aino was a tough old coot who'd seemingly just tagged along for the ride, but his actions showed he was far more committed to defending his town than his words indicated. Stark was still a belligerent jerk, but he was MCB, and they could usually fight. Nikolai had already wandered off, probably arguing with the voices in his head. They were tired and out of their league. He would have traded them in a heartbeat for his regular team, but they'd have to do.

"All right, everyone. Listen up. We can do this. We're going to beat this asshole."

"You giving a motivational speech?" Aino asked incredulously.

"Damn straight. I always do. . . . We're going to get that stinking amulet, and we're going to cure Heather. If you get scared, keep going. They're werewolves, and they're scary, but they die, just like everything else. Remember, this is your turf. He came here. He started it. He hurt your people. And there's a bunch of folks counting on us back there. We will not let them down. All of you lost someone today—friends, teammates, partners. We're going to get him before he gets away and does this again somewhere else. Now it's *his* turn to lose. It's *his* turn to hurt. It's *his* turn to fucking die."

Earl took the time to look each of them square in the eye. He'd learned a thing or two about leadership over the years, and he could usually tell the measure of a man by looking in his eyes. Whether it was one of his Hunters or a soldier in a trench in France, Earl Harbinger could always see a warrior's heart, and though here it was either too new, too old, too inexperienced, or atrophied by bureaucracy, they were what he had. *They're scared, but they'll do.*

"Good hunting. Move out."

⫷ **Chapter 31** ⫸

"They're here," the Alpha said. "Wake your diggers. Get ready."

Lucinda moved to the window. The sun was just peeking over the mountains. There was nothing moving out there except for one member of the pack, in human form, pacing near the gate. "Who? Where?"

He didn't know who. The smells were confusing. Petrov was one of them, the female was another. There were some humans . . . and something *confusing*. It was Harbinger, but not. The not-Harbinger was what annoyed him. You shouldn't be able to smell a ghost.

"Get away from the window." He took the young witch by the arm and firmly pulled her back. The last thing he wanted was for a sniper to put a bullet in her. Then he'd be stuck walking. "I need you alive."

"Well, thank you. I'm rather fond of you, too." Lucinda's voice dripped with sarcasm.

"You know what I mean." The witch's portal magic was their primary escape route. "Secure my father. I'm not done with him yet. Be careful. He's a tricky one. Get to the bottom and wait for me. I'll meet you at the elevator shaft." His hand unconsciously moved to the amulet. "This shouldn't take long."

Outside, the patrolling werewolf's head opened and tossed out brains. He dropped, cleanly killed. The sound of the rifle shot arrived a moment later.

It had been much more difficult making it back up the ridge with all his weapons, but Earl figured if you were going to bring them, you might as well have some fun with them. He'd made Jason lug the heavy stuff. Being the boss had its benefits.

He watched as the first werewolf fell through his Zeiss scope. *Headshot, asshole.* Though he was right-handed, and the bolt-action was set up for right-hand use, Earl shot left-handed when he was prone and using a bipod. That way he didn't have to break his firing grip or cheek weld against the stock as his right hand quickly lifted the bolt, yanked it back, forward, and back down. It was much faster that way. A spent .300 Winchester Magnum brass case was ejected and a fresh round fed smoothly into the chamber. *Next.*

He picked up the second sentry. The werewolf was beginning to move, having just smelled the spilled blood of his pack-mate. The Zeiss was pre-zeroed for this load, and Earl settled the 300-yard stadia line on the werewolf's chest. The target was moving, so might as well aim for the biggest part. There was no wind to compensate for. Earl exhaled as he tracked his target.

The trigger broke clean. The heavy G.A. Precision bolt-action rifle barely rocked on its bipod. Earl reacquired his target through the scope before the impact. He watched the werewolf shudder as 168 grains of lead and silver pierced his torso. The werewolf stumbled but kept running. *Tough guy, huh?* Earl worked the bolt.

Julie was the team sharpshooter, since the girl just had a remarkable natural talent for putting bullets into very small things, very far away, very quickly, but Earl had been the one who had originally taught her how to shoot, and he was no slouch himself. *Gotcha.* The werewolf was running directly away now. The reticle swayed across the target's back.

He exhaled again as his left finger tightened on the trigger. Earl always shot on the respiratory pause.

CRACK.

This time the bullet hit the werewolf square between the shoulder-blades. He spilled forward in a tumble of snow and blood.

Earl looked up from his scope. The mine facility had seemingly come alive with movement. *Just like kicking an anthill.* He smiled, because there was nothing more rewarding than a target-rich environment. There was a flash of movement from below as Nikolai and Heather sprinted through the trees. "What are you waiting for?" Earl shouted at the others. "Give 'em hell!"

✢ ✢ ✢

This is more like it.

Nikolai could sense the Tvar's pleasure. To the Tvar, it didn't matter who they were hunting, just as long as they were on the hunt. The beast's emotions always seemed to bleed across the lines into his own emotions when it was excited, making it hard to tell who was feeling what. So Nikolai also thrilled to the drama of the hunt. It was intoxicating.

Still in human form, he sped between the trees. The deep snow was nothing to him. Gravity was on his side. Leaping, he moved with incredible speed toward his objective. Faster and faster, he dodged around trees, under branches, and launched himself over logs. Somehow the young female was keeping up. She should have wrapped herself around a tree by now. Even the Tvar was impressed by her performance.

She does not move like a pup.

And she knocked the sense out of us when you threatened her earlier, Nikolai reminded both parts of himself. She was not to be underestimated again. One last jump, branches tearing at his arms, and they were in the open, over the road leading to the front gate. An enemy was caught, surprised and in human form, in the clearing.

But can she do this?

Still airborne, Nikolai aimed his carbine. The Val spat and hissed as the suppressor absorbed the muzzle blast. The burst stitched across the enemy werewolf's abdomen and chest, sending him reeling back. Nikolai landed, sliding through the snow, and struck the inferior creature aside with the butt of his weapon. Two more bullets splattered its head into bits before it could even begin to arise.

His lips pulled back in a grin of semi-elongated canines, and a gush of steam poured out. Nikolai was in his element.

Down.

Tvar sensed danger first. There was another enemy closing. Nikolai dove aside as a bullet passed through the air above. He rolled, and came up ready to fire. The enemy was a black shape coming through the trees. There was a flash of gray and he was gone.

Nikolai blinked. The female had hit the enemy so hard and fast it was as if he had just vaporized. They landed some distance away, a tangle of flailing limbs. Kerkonen got up, grabbed the enemy by the neck, and hurled him into an ancient tree. The wood cracked with a noise audible across the entire clearing. Limbs broken, the werewolf slid down the trunk. Kerkonen approached her fallen antagonist as she freed the shotgun slung over her back. She shouldered the weapon and shot him, once, twice, three times. Satisfied that he was dead, she turned toward Nikolai and gave him a very American thumbs-up signal.

That girl is not normal.

"No. She's certainly not."

Sexy, though. I'd mate that.

For all its flaws, the Tvar was a remarkably straightforward thing. "Mission first." Nikolai ran for the gate.

The ground underfoot rumbled. *Earthquake.* Nikolai lost his balance and fell as the earth suddenly ruptured. Snow flew into the air between the metal posts of the main gate. A square block of rusting metal was thrust into the sky. Three spikes extended from the end. The block crashed down, scrambling for purchase as ungainly limbs stretched behind it. A giant creature was leveraging itself out of the ground.

Burrower!

Despite never having seen one before, Nikolai recognized the creature from his training. They were minions of the Old Ones. According to the KGB analysts, despite their fearsome appearance, they were not supposed to be that tough. He lowered the VAL and fired as he charged. The 9×39 rounds sparked off the monster's armor or tore hunks of stinking green meat from its hide. He would wrench its featureless head from its body. At the edge of the hole, Nikolai leapt for the monster's neck.

One metal claw swatted him across the clearing. The air erupted from Nikolai's lungs as he tumbled through the branches. He hit the trunk of a tree and fell, crashing, face first into the snow.

It appears the briefings were mistaken.

"What the hell is that?"

Earl finished shooting the leg out from another werewolf before he looked up to see what Aino was shouting about. A bubble had formed in the road at the gate. The bulge split, and a monster came crawling out. It was one of the Old Ones' things from the supermarket. Nikolai ran at the monster and got smacked across the road.

"That's the thing that ate Jo," Jason said.

Stark aimed his .308 SCAR at the monster and started popping off rounds. Jason and Aino followed suit. It was a noble effort, but Earl knew how tough these things were. Small-arms fire wasn't going to be enough. "The Gustav! Bring me the big one!" Earl popped up from behind his rifle. "Hurry."

Jason lumbered over with the Carl Gustav recoilless. Earl took the tube from him, flipped the latch, and hinged open the breach. It was far more effective to run these in two-man teams, one gunner, one loader, but there hadn't been time to train anybody. "And the case. Hurry."

He hadn't brought much on the trip. Each round of 84mm ammunition took up a lot of space. Jason hauled the Cordura case over and flipped it open. Earl picked a high-explosive anti-tank, slid it in, and locked the breach behind it. He took a knee and threw the Gustav over his shoulder. "Get back!" he warned. True to its name, the recoil wasn't bad, but the blast was a real bitch. Military regulation limited the number of rounds a soldier could shoot through one of these things daily because they were worried about the damage it could do to your internal organs.

He found the creature in the scope. It was fully out of the hole and striding toward Heather. He just hoped the girl had the sense to get out of the way. Its curious, eyeless head was bobbing back and forth as folds of empty skin spilled and bounced from every unarmored joint. Earl braced himself and fired. The concussion shook the entire ridge.

His aim was true. The round struck the Old Ones' minion in the midsection. It disappeared in a explosive flash. The HEAT round was meant for taking out armored vehicles. Nothing living, short of maybe a dragon, was going to survive that.

Earl watched through the 3× magnification of the Gustav's scope. It was raining meat in the clearing. *Come on, Heather. Where are you?* As the smoke and dust settled, he could see that the monster's torso had been ripped open right through its armor and green liquefied guts had been sprayed everywhere. It was toast, but there was no sign of Heather. . . . *There.* Heather was alive and picking herself up out of the snow.

A bullet whizzed past his head. The werewolves were returning fire from the two-story building at the entrance. It would be difficult for them to aim directly into the sun, but throw enough bullets and they were bound to hit somebody. "I'm done screwing around." Earl tilted the Gustav so he could pop the breach, but there was a tug that stopped him.

"Got you," Stark said as he pulled out the empty shell. The weapon rang like a bell.

So Stark wasn't totally useless. He knew how to act as a loader. "Bunker buster," Earl ordered without looking.

"H-E-D-P," Stark responded as he shoved the shell in and locked the breach behind. He slapped Earl on the shoulder to indicate they were ready, then retreated to keep from getting his eardrums busted. "Go!"

Earl centered the crosshairs on the office building. Though solid looking, it appeared to made of wood and brick. The bunker-buster round had been designed to demolish reinforced concrete, so even though there wasn't any silver involved, this wasn't going to be pretty for the werewolves inside. Earl fired.

The 84mm round hit the front wall, penetrated, and detonated inside a fraction of a second later. Half the building was instantly turned into splinters and brick dust. Ten seconds later the rest of the structure collapsed with an epic groan.

"Best damn thing to ever come out of Sweden not involving bikinis!" Earl shouted.

As Stark ran up and popped the breach, Earl scanned the facility. Heather was picking Nikolai out of a tree. Injured werewolves were moving in the wreckage and in the equipment yard behind it. He only had a few rounds left for the Gustav, but one of those rounds had been specially loaded with six hundred and sixty-six silver ball bearings, because in addition to being a mad genius, Milo also had a sense of humor. "Gimme the Demonsterfier."

Stark yanked the spent shell out. *Pong.*

"De-monster . . . what?"

"The *red* one," Earl growled.

"Are you okay?" Heather asked Nikolai.

"Fine," he said, brushing her hands away. "No need to be concerned."

There was a bone sticking out of his arm, the jagged edge had ripped through his coat. "But—"

Nikolai grabbed it with his good hand and wrenched it back into place. It made a sick crack. "See? Insignificant," he said through clenched teeth.

Heather was still not used to the unnatural toughness aspects of her condition. "The way's clear. Harbinger blew up the—"

Suddenly, Nikolai shoved her onto her back.

He's going to kill me. But then, before she could react, she heard the high-pitched whistle overhead. The shell air-burst in a black cloud over the mine. There was a sound like ten million angry bees and a horrendous rattle of impacts. Then the werewolves began to scream.

"Hunters . . . always with a trick up their sleeves. Come. We're clear." Nikolai got to his feet and plucked his tubular rifle out of the snow. "What are you waiting for?"

"Just catching my breath," Heather said.

"You don't need to catch your breath anymore. That's your human psychology making you inefficient. Come." Nikolai extended a hand to help her up. Heather hesitated. Nikolai seemed relatively sane at the moment, so she took the offered hand. He pulled her upright. "Thinking like you're still human will get you killed."

"I'll be human again."

Nikolai laughed mirthlessly. "I'll believe that when I see it. Why would you want to, anyway?"

"It's a *curse.*" This sanctimonious prick was really ticking her off. "Wouldn't you give it up if you could?"

"Of course . . . *not* . . ." Nikolai stopped, bewildered, then shook his head. "Enough. We're wasting time." He ran toward the screaming.

Since her best bet at salvation meant following the murderous lunatic, Heather followed, the ice crunching between her bare toes.

The facility was clear, seemingly free of targets. The remaining werewolves had taken cover indoors. There was no sign of the Alpha or the other burrowing monster. There was movement as Heather and Nikolai cleared the gates. They had to keep up the pressure.

"Move out!" Earl shouted. There was one HEAT round left for the Gustav. "Jason, sling this." The Briarwood Hunter took the tube and threw it over his shoulder. In Jason's other hand was one of the SCAR rifles they'd scrounged from Stark's Suburban. Visible heat waves were rising from its barrel. Stark had the other SCAR, and Aino was still using his old lever-action .30-30. "Aino, take my bolt gun. You need something that shoots silver bullets." Earl tossed the old miner his last magazine.

"Bulky thing," Aino grunted when he picked up the rifle.

"You want to kill them, or just piss them off?" Earl asked rhetorically as he retrieved his Thompson in one hand and Aksel's Mosin in the other. "Everyone on me." He ordered and he stepped over the edge. The slope was pretty steep, and it would have made a really good sledding hill. It was a fast slide-roll-run to the base. He managed to make it all the way to the bottom mostly upright. He took up a defensive position and waited for the others to catch up.

There was shooting coming from the mine. Heather was in danger. He almost set off immediately, but stopped himself. *Get your head right.* These men needed him. Heather could take care of herself. She was, after all, physically tougher than he was now. His team was going to give him a never-ending ration of shit about this. The first time he takes a vacation day in forever, a town gets slaughtered, some terrible artifact gets unearthed, he gets cured of lycanthropy, and finds a lady friend who unfortunately happens to be a really odd werewolf. . . . It was sad that taking a day off could be more interesting than an average day of monster hunting.

One by one the others slid in behind him. Nobody seemed to have broken anything. Earl set off at the fastest pace he could, which, considering the terrain and everyone's ragged condition, wasn't saying much. Stark was walking with a limp, having twisted his leg earlier. Aino was old. Jason had lost a lot of blood earlier. They weren't going to win any awards for being pretty.

They'd made it halfway when something began to beep.

Stark stopped and began to claw wildly at a pouch on his armor. "My phone!"

Earl signaled a halt. Aino looked like he needed it. He was in good shape for his age, but that age was sufficient to collect Social Security, and his face was red from the exertion. Jason seemed to be hanging in there, though he was walking a little funny, like his side was hurting.

The phone came out. "Headquarters!" Stark said, out of breath. "Yes! This is Stark . . . Wait. I can barely hear you. We've got an emergency. Code Delta-Delta-Five-Niner-Five. You're breaking up."

Earl glanced around the woods. Splitting up was a risk, but they didn't have time to stop, and Copper Lake needed reinforcements.

"Stark! Just men. No carpet bombing. You hear me?" The agent quickly nodded and held up his hand for silence. "Aino, stay with Stark." The old man nodded thankfully, then leaned the G.A. Precision rifle on a tree so he could put his hands on his knees and hang his head to try to catch his breath.

"Jason, you're on me." With the slowest two left behind, Earl picked up the pace. Sweat was rolling down the inside of his armor but freezing solid on his face.

They made it another hundred yards before Jason spoke up. The fence was visible just ahead. "Mr. Harbinger?"

"Just Earl. What?"

He seemed embarrassed. "If I don't make it, I've got a family to support. See . . . I've done some stupid things in my life. It's hard to make an honest living once you've got a record. I used to fight, you know, for money, until this one kid nearly killed me, broke my skull and popped my eye. When Horst offered me this job . . . Well, I don't care about being a hero or nothing like that. I'm doing this for my little girl. What I'm trying to say is, if there's any PUFF . . ."

"You've got no time for doubts. Just know that if anything happens, your family will be covered. Just like I'd do for any of my Hunters."

Jason summoned up his courage. "Give your word."

That stopped him. Earl Harbinger wasn't used to anyone questioning his integrity. "All right. I swear to you that if you don't make it, I'll make sure your family is taken care of forever. You have any idea how many orphans I've sent to college? How many *houses* I've bought? I've lost hundreds of men, but people still keep signing up, so what do you think I'm going to do?"

Jason looked down sheepishly. "Sorry . . . Just that the last bunch I worked for . . ."

Earl had to reach up to clap him on the shoulder. "Was a bunch of shady cut-rate bastards. I'm MHI. So pull your *head* out of your *ass* and get it back in the game. Focus, and you won't have to find out how good the death benefits are."

Chapter 32

The Alpha threw open the doors of Number Six and walked into the sunlight. His senses were overloaded. The air tasted of dust and blood. The pack was being slaughtered. He could feel their pain as the silver seared their wounds. A nearby building was burning. Orange sparks were rising through the black smoke as the beams crackled and broke. And behind all that chaos was the challenge. The amulet was eager. It had been waiting for this moment for thousands of years.

He spread his arms wide. "Here I am! Face me!"

There was a disturbance in the smoke, a whirl of air, imperceptible to any lesser being. The Alpha turned with just a hint of a smile on his face.

Nikolai Petrov leapt through the fire, descending toward the Alpha.

Almost as if the world were in slow motion, he watched the bullets, like fat silver slugs that he could reach out and snatch from the air. He moved aside as they cracked into the steps where he had been standing. The Alpha was so aware that he could watch the action of Nikolai's rifle move back and forth and see every clean bit of brass glinting in the sunlight. Nikolai's eyes widened as he descended, because to him it would have appeared as if the Alpha had just disappeared.

The Alpha casually reached out, caught an ankle, and pulled. The lesser werewolf hit the steps with a meaty thud. The Alpha lifted him effortlessly and hurled him against the wall. Corrugated metal collapsed around Nikolai.

"Well, well, well . . . Comrade Nikolai Petrov, scourge of the steppes, Stalin's favorite werewolf, the ghost of Koh Valley. Killer of man, woman, and child. It's a real pleasure to meet you in person. You've got no idea how much I've heard about you over the years. According to my mom, you were a cross between Freddy Krueger and the Boogeyman. I'll admit I'm a little disappointed. You don't seem to live up to the hype."

Nikolai coughed as he dislodged himself from the wall. He stumbled but caught himself on a piece of scaffolding. "I've come to challenge you."

The Alpha laughed. "I've been waiting."

Nikolai spit a mouthful of blood onto the concrete. "You killed my Lila."

"Was that her name? I forgot. Tough girl. It took her *forever* to die. She was a screamer, though. I never thought she'd shut up. That's why I pulled her tongue out, in case you were wondering."

Nikolai charged. The Alpha let him come. Fists flew. The Alpha just moved around them. It was amusing to watch the effort. It was like a petulant child trying to lash out at its parents. He could smell Nikolai's fury, his desperation, but under that was a hint of fear, and as none of the blows landed, the fear grew. It was delicious. He decided to see if he could taste more of that.

He struck Nikolai down. Bones cracked against the pavement. The Alpha stepped back and casually removed his hat. He carefully hung it on the end of the handrail. The hat had been a Christmas gift from his mother. His overcoat followed, and he was careful not to wrinkle it as he hung the items over the railing. "You want a challenge? Let's do this right. I'll give you time to get ready."

The shotgun blast hit him at the base of his spine. The silver burned briefly before his hyper-regeneration shoved the buckshot pellets out of his flesh. He turned to see the new female werewolf, twenty yards away, pumping her shotgun.

"Nice poncho, Rambo."

She pulled the trigger again, so he moved from the path of the spreading silver cloud. Taking the warm shotgun barrel in one hand, he ripped it away from her. The look on her pretty face told him she hadn't seen that coming. "I'll deal with you in a second." He took the shotgun in both hands and struck her with it like it was a baseball bat.

The wooden stock shattered, and the female went bouncing across the ground.

He tossed the now-bent shotgun aside. "Where were we, Petrov? Oh, yeah. You were challenging my supremacy."

The Russian was transforming, bones twisting, skin stretching. The Alpha calmly removed his ruined shirt, kicked off his shoes, and waited. Nikolai's change only took half a minute, but to the Alpha it seemed to drag on forever. His challenger's body needed to burn its own energy to fuel the transformation. The Alpha knew that the amulet would fuel his instantly.

Nikolai was ready. He rose, snarling, filled with fury. The Alpha had to admit that before he'd found the amulet, he would have thought of Nikolai as an impressive, even fearsome specimen of the lycanthropic species. A century old, hardened by wars, torture, and driven mad by insatiable bloodlust, Nikolai should have been terrifying.

But not anymore. The Alpha didn't even bother to change. He yawned theatrically. "You're not even worth my time."

Nikolai hurled himself at the Alpha.

Stark was pacing back and forth. MCB headquarters was barely audible. He thought it sounded like Agent Archer on the other end, but he had *one* flickering bar, so it was really hard to tell.

"Copper Lake, Michigan. Werewolves, damn it. Hundreds of werewolves!" he shouted.

Buzz-crackle. "—wolves? Status of—" *Hiss-pop.*

"Shit!" Stark kicked a tree. Sadly, that just caused a cascading chain reaction of cold snow to break loose from the upper branches to fall on him. A nasty bunch of ice managed to go down the back of his collar, slide down the inside of his shirt, and lodge in his underwear. "The status is FUBAR!"

The bitter old immigrant had gone off to the side and found a log to sit on. He seemed to be deep in thought.

"—rk." The static was unbearable. Stark had no idea what the agent on the other end had heard so far. "—for extraction?"

"Huh? I can't hear you. Mosher is dead. Most of the town's dead. I need help *now*." He remembered Harbinger's warning, but it had been unnecessary. Stark didn't want the MCB to have the Air Force bombing the place until he was out of here himself. After that? Screw them. But not before he was safely on a flight home. "I need reinforcements. No bombing."

Crackle-buzz. "Request bombing? Please veri—" And then nothing.

Stark screamed in frustration. "No! No bomb!" But the call had dropped. He hit the speed dial for headquarters and then wildly waved the phone overhead like it was a magic talisman that could ward off evil. "I lost my connection!"

"Connection . . ." Aino muttered. "Huh . . . I just thought of something." He pulled the old Finnish journal out of his coat and flipped to the end. It was a good thing no werewolves came up on them at that moment, since Stark was running in circles trying to get a signal while Aino buried his nose in a book.

"Well . . . this sucks." Agent Stark gave up and took a seat on the log next to his only remaining companion. For all he knew, everyone else was dead.

Aino closed the book. "I just figured something out. They're gonna do it wrong. We've got to warn them."

"Probably too late," Stark said. "We need to get out of here before my people blow us all up."

"No," Aino stated with grim determination. "Come on. We can still catch Earl. If I don't, Heather's going to die. I know why she's different than the others."

Stark just shook his head. They were screwed either way. It was a little overwhelming. He hadn't been this tired since BUD/S, and he'd been a lot younger and had actually given a damn back then. He should have been at home, sleeping in his warm bed. He should have caught his daughter's concert, even if it would have been terrible. He never should have tried to game the system to score PUFF money, and now he was going to die for it. . . . Oh well. Being nuked sure did beat having fish monsters lay their eggs in you, so it could always be worse.

"Mr. Stark," Aino pleaded. "I need you to watch my back. We have to reach them. The spell is all wrong. Aksel figured that out afterward. . . . Come on! Get up. I shoulda died a long time ago, buried in that mine right over there. Only Aksel Kerkonen risked his life to drag me out. I owe him, and I never paid him back. So now I owe his grandkid. She's a good girl, and she's about to lose her soul if we don't go get them."

Stark just sighed. He hadn't really been listening to the old hillbilly's blathering. Instead he'd just realized that being nuked was only better if you were close to the impact area. Otherwise it meant a lingering death from radiation poisoning. Bummer.

Aino tried a different tact. "You want to reach your pals?"

"Obviously."

"I know where you'd probably get *great* reception." Aino pointed through the trees at the tallest thing in view. Stark followed his finger to the top of Number Six.

Heather was facedown in the snow. She rolled over and blinked up at the light. Her red hair was spread in a halo around her aching head. Her ears were ringing. She reached up in time to feel the skin crawling closed over a gash in her skull. Her fingers came away covered in blood.

"Why, you . . ." Heather sat up. The dizziness was passing as the bones of her skull fused back together. "Dirty, miserable . . ." She let the anger free, and it washed away the rest of the pain. "Horrible, awful, worthless son of a bitch!"

Her Winchester was there on the ground. The stock was broken and the barrel was bent into an L, but she wouldn't have picked it up even if it was still in working order. She was going to rip this bastard apart with her bare hands.

Nikolai had changed completely. She'd never seen his werewolf, but she had no problem recognizing him. His hair was dark, his form sleek. The power, speed, and ferocity was apparent, but it wasn't doing him a lick of good against the Alpha.

The Alpha was still in human form. He'd stripped to the waist and seemed to be enjoying himself while easily avoiding Nikolai's rending claws and snapping jaws. It was as if he'd appear, then move so quickly that he just reappeared in another place. Heather blinked, but it wasn't her head injury that was causing that effect. He was just that *fast*.

One human hand caught Nikolai's wrist and wrenched it back until it snapped. The Alpha's foot lashed out and caught Nikolai's ankle. Heather cringed as bones shattered. Nikolai fell, held up only by the Alpha's whim. He tried to bite the Alpha, but the man just punched Nikolai in the chest hard enough to leave a dent. Blood sprayed from between Nikolai's jaws as he hit the ground.

Nikolai lay there, gasping, as his chest gradually reinflated. The Alpha turned to her with a confident smile. "Hi. I'm surprised to see you back up and around already. But you're something special. I can see that . . . You're *very* special." Heather's knees turned to water. She felt dizzy and flushed. The Alpha's voice was *so* soothing.

"I can smell it in your blood. You're something different. You've got a birthright, too. Just like me, but you're not the challenge, either. What's your name?"

"Go fu . . . fu . . ." She couldn't finish the insult. She was just too tired. Her eyelids weighed a hundred pounds each. She just wanted to curl up someplace warm and go to sleep.

"What's your name?" he asked again.

Heather wanted nothing more than to make him happy. He was simply beautiful, the most beautiful thing in the world. It was understandable now why his followers were so fanatical. He was beautiful, and he wore the moon around his neck. The Alpha was positively radiant.

And that radiance had murdered half her town. . . .

The anger came boiling back, and the heat of it burned away the haze. Rage was her anchor. He was trying to hypnotize her. *Hell with that.* "My name's Deputy Heather Kerkonen of the Copper County Sheriff's Department. But you"—she spread her arms as she felt the rage turn into strength; she uncurled her fists as her fingers stretched into knives—"you can call me death." She screamed as she rushed him.

"Nice!" the Alpha said. One hand shot out and hit her right in the throat. She slashed his arm, but he didn't seem to notice. His fingers crushed off her air. "Cheesy line, but a good try. Fiery. I like that! I've got a way with the opposite sex. You can say it runs in the family. So it's been a long time since I've had a woman resist me like that. I'm going to enjoy our time together."

Heather thrashed, but he was far too strong. He flipped her around and dragged her in tight. Her back was pressed against his chest. His nose pressed against her hair as he drank in her smell. Blood was leaking from his arms where her nails sliced, but the Alpha didn't seem to care. "Ahh . . . I understand now. So that's why you're so different from my other new children. Your grandfather took something with him when he touched the amulet. A little bit of the forerunner's spirit joined his. He must have passed it on to you."

Heather could sense the truth in the Alpha's words as she thrashed and tried to break free.

"I see now . . . You're his heir. The forerunner's essence is in your veins. That's why you're so in control. You've been prepared for this your whole life—just another thief from a line of thieves. Good thing I came along to take that essence back."

Sensing his distraction, she responded like she'd been trained. She threw an elbow into his ribs, then kicked her heel into his groin. At least that seemed to catch his attention long enough for her roll forward to toss him over her shoulder.

The Alpha hit the ground as Heather backed away. "You're a monster!" The change was on her now. It didn't even hurt this time. She tried to shout something else, but it came out as an inarticulate growl past her sharpening teeth. She nearly tripped over Nikolai, who was coming to and looked ready to get back into the fight. Maybe the two of them together might have a chance.

"I'm a monster?" the Alpha laughed as he stood up. "Look who's talking, babe. You want a monster. I'll show you a real monster."

The humming noise that Harbinger said was the moon multiplied a hundredfold, only it wasn't in orbit. It was ten feet away and closing. She covered her ears and screamed. Nikolai howled. The Alpha seemed to shimmer with heat. The snow around his feet instantly turned to water; then the puddles turned to steam. His skin bubbled and stretched, before it ripped open, revealing tufts of hair.

He was *growing*.

The splits in his skin grew, forked, and grew again. The silver three-clawed amulet shone with a light that threatened to blind. The raw energy of the amulet hammered her soul. Even if she hadn't been changing, the amulet would have forced her to. It was as if the Alpha was sucking energy out of the air and using it to expand. Heather looked up and up . . . and *up*, until the Alpha lifted his tree-trunk-sized arms to the sky and let out an earth-shattering roar of triumph.

His voice crashed into her mind with the sound of thunder. *BEHOLD THE MONSTER!*

There was a noise, so awful, so painfully loud, that for a moment Earl was sure the MCB must have gone ahead and dropped a nuclear weapon to cleanse the area. Except it seemed strangely *organic*.

Earl ran around the underground monster's hole, through the open gates, past a rusting iron sign that read QUINN MINE, and jumped over some flaming boards. The Mosin-Nagant bounced up and down against his back with every step. An injured werewolf came out of the ruins. She had transformed, but her hair had been burned off, leaving her a mottled mass of black burns and red scabs. Earl didn't even slow down as he sprayed her in the face with silver .45 slugs.

Hopefully there aren't any of the new silver-proof ones around. He still had the Mosin's magic ammo, but wanted to save that for the big—Earl totally lost the thought. They rounded the corner and saw the *biggest fucking werewolf ever*.

It was only a hundred yards away, pitch-black as night, at least twelve feet tall, and it was tossing Nikolai around like he was a rag doll. It wasn't just a giant werewolf, it was the living embodiment of the forerunner's bones, cloaked in angry muscle.

There was a flash of red fur as another werewolf jumped onto the Alpha's back. *Heather!* The giant werewolf moved with shocking velocity, snatched Heather out of the air, and hurled her against the wall. Heather shattered a row of heavy-paned windows and disappeared into the bowels of Number Six.

"Whoa," Jason said.

"*Daaaamn.*" Earl was a big proponent of flexible minds on Hunters, but that thing over there was something completely new.

"Is it too late to resign?"

"Probably . . ." Earl looked at the subgun in his hands and then back at the super-werewolf.

"Want your bazooka?"

"That's not a bad idea." Earl traded his Thompson for the Carl Gustav. "Take cover." The Alpha werewolf had his back to them and was busy kicking Nikolai merrily down the road. Earl threw the heavy tube over his shoulder and peered through the scope. The Gustav's optical sight filled with black hair, and Earl fired.

THOOOOM.

The 84mm shell was on the way. Somehow, impossibly, the Alpha turned, lashed out, and *struck* the shell in midair.

BOOOOOOM.

It detonated in a flash of superheated air. The Alpha flew back in a gout of blood and crashed through the wall of Number Six.

Earl dropped the empty Carl Gustav. "Immortal, my ass." There was a groan of metal and a series of crashes as bits and pieces of the interior of Number Six collapsed.

"That shit blows up *tanks*," Jason said happily.

Then the Alpha howled. Only, it wasn't the cry of something mortally wounded. It was the bloodcurdling howl of something injured but still extremely angry. Earl felt the telepathic intrusion as the Alpha invaded his thoughts. *Harbinger? You're alive . . . I don't know how, but it won't be for long.*

"Aw, hell," Earl said as he unslung the Mosin-Nagant. Fighting monsters that could withstand hits from anti-tank weapons was usually a very bad thing. "Back to Plan A. We've got to hit him before he can heal. Come on."

There was a rumble, and the ground lurched beneath their feet. A crack appeared in the ground and snow began to cascade down it. Earl's eyes followed the crack as it travelled across the facility. It widened fifty feet away, and large chunks of pavement broke loose and fell into the growing gap. A giant metal claw appeared over the edge as the second of the Old Ones' minions made its presence known.

The Alpha . . . There was no time to deal with both. He had to get the Alpha before he could regenerate. They were stuck between two awful monsters and out of high explosives.

Jason understood the issue. "I'll keep this one busy," he said. "Go get the big one."

"Alone, you won't have much chance."

"Nobody will if that big one grows his arm back." He tried to hand over Earl's subgun.

Earl was impressed by the kid's bravery. "Hold on to it. You're going to need everything you've got." He pulled out his remaining two magazines and shoved them into Jason's coat pocket. "Stick and move. Don't let it corner you."

"Got it, Coach," Jason said, lifting the Thompson in one hand and the SCAR-H in the other. "Remember our deal."

"Keep your head straight, and I won't need to." Earl ran as fast as he could for the entrance to Number Six. Behind him, Jason opened fire.

⊰ **Chapter 33** ⊱

I am getting really tired of waking up on the ground.

Heather was on a cold slab of concrete. Shards of broken glass surrounded her. Beams of morning light were streaming through the hole in the wall a floor above. One of her hands was in the light. She was human again.

Already? How . . . But she could feel the drain. The Alpha had been hurt. He was using all of the surrounding werewolves' energy to heal himself. For a brief moment, she wondered if she'd been cured. But no . . . she could still hear that damned background sound. She was still cursed. She had to get that amulet.

Standing, Heather cringed when she felt the pull in her leg. Reaching down, she dragged out the bloody hunk of glass that was embedded in her thigh and tossed it away. She'd lost her blanket, but she still had Harbinger's coat. And it didn't even seem damaged. It hadn't so much as broken a seam when she'd changed in it, nor had the glass cut it. In fact, her torso and arms were the only part of her that hadn't been cut by the window glass. No wonder Harbinger seemed so fond of it. The damn thing was like magic.

Where am I? Her gray vision couldn't pick out as much detail as her normal vision, but she could see enough to know that she was on the ground floor of Number Six. Her dad had brought her here once when she was younger, because this was the site of the most tragic thing that had ever happened to their little community. . . . Or it had been, until last night.

Heather limped along, listening to her senses, trying to figure out what to do next. The inside of the above-ground portion was mostly hollow through the center, except for the system that lifted the ore. There were stairs and ladders up each wall leading to various equipment rooms. Below her were the giant cable wheels that led to the elevators down into the mine shaft itself.

She discovered a massive, smoking hole in the wall, and everything around it was *covered* in blood. The Alpha hadn't just been injured: he'd been severely injured. There were fresh boot prints in the blood. She smelled Harbinger, and the scent was warm. He'd only passed a minute ago. The blood trail led down the metal stairs, and that told her exactly where she needed to go.

Earl went down and down the stairs for what seemed like forever. He held a flashlight in his left hand and kept sweeping it back and forth ahead of him. The Finnish rifle was absurdly long, difficult to maneuver inside the close confines of the metal stairwell. The blood was slippery underfoot, but the amount had tapered off. That was either a good sign, as in the Alpha was losing blood pressure, or bad, in that he was healing.

Rounding the last corner, he came onto a catwalk. There was a woman in front of him, filthy, her hair matted with dirt and rust, and seemingly bewildered. She was looking at her hands, confused. Then she saw him, her eyes flashing gold, and asked, "I need to kill you, but why can't I change?"

"Hell if I know," Earl answered as he aimed down the Mosin-Nagant's sights. The sharp report of the $7.62 \times 54R$ was deafening in the enclosed space. The werewolf simply exploded. Everything but her legs disappeared over the edge of the catwalk. Earl lowered the smoking rifle and shined his light over the dripping carnage. "I've got to get me some of these Baba Yaga bullets."

"Earl!" a man shouted below. "Down here."

"Shut him up!" a young woman screamed.

He risked a glance over the edge of the railing. Several portable lanterns had been hung from chains at the base. There were two giant spools of cable suspended on steel girders over a gaping black hole in the gravel floor. A man was on his knees, his hands tied behind his back, and behind him was a young, dark-haired woman in a fur coat.

"Kirk?"

"Down he—" Kirk shouted, but the girl lifted one hand that seemed to be wearing some sort of medieval steel gauntlet and smacked Kirk in the face.

"Get him!" she shrieked. "Kill Harbinger!"

There was movement at the far end of the catwalk. Multiple people, and judging from their golden eyes, werewolves, were headed his way. He chambered another round in the Mosin and fired. Another werewolf flew into bloody pieces. They must not be able to transform for some reason, but these had brought guns. Bullets sparked against the catwalk as they fired wildly at him.

There was no cover. He was dead if he stayed on the catwalk. *Too far to jump.* He saw a chain dangling from an overhead beam off to the side. Earl slung the rifle over one shoulder, vaulted over the edge, caught the chain, and slid roughly down. The rusty steel tore the palms of his gloves. Earl ran out of chain ten feet before the bottom and fell the rest of the way. His boots hit the ground hard and something went *pop* inside one knee.

Metal echoed with footfalls as the werewolves ran above him. One leapt over the side and landed gracefully a few feet away. Earl's revolver was already in hand, and the werewolf's smile of satisfaction barely had time to go away before Earl blew his brains all over the wall.

Before any more could come after him, there was a scream and a crash. The entire catwalk shook, and dust rained down. There was a howl of pain as another werewolf came over the edge. Only this one went sideways and banged off of one of the pulleys with a sick crack. Apparently help had arrived.

Another werewolf was flung over the edge, only this one hit some chains, and was quickly entangled as it spun down until it impaled itself on a hook. The werewolf squealed until Earl shot her in the face. "Harbinger! Clear up here!"

Hearing Heather's voice flooded Earl with relief. He turned back to the only remaining visible threat. The girl was pointing her metal hand at him. Her eyes were blank and her lips were moving rhythmically. The words she was repeating sure as hell were not in English. The already cold air around him grew even colder, like she was sucking the energy out of it. *Magic!* Earl snapped off a quick shot with his Smith and was rewarded with a spark as the bullet ricocheted off the girl's gauntlet. She fell down, and the air temperature returned to just freezing.

Earl reached Kirk a second later. "Nice shot!"

"I was aiming for her head." Earl drew his Bowie knife and slashed the cords binding Kirk's wrists. The girl was sitting up, so Earl pointed his gun at her. "Don't move, missy."

Heather vaulted over the railing, landed softly, and ran over to them. She was covered in healing scratches, and his minotaur-hide coat was dripping blood. She must have recognized the concern on Earl's face. "Don't worry. Most of it's not mine." Heather picked a flattened bullet off of the leather sleeve. "By the way, this is a *really* nice coat."

"Thanks. It's made out of one of my best friends. It's a long story." Earl turned back to Kirk. "What's going on? Where's the Alpha?" And then to the girl: "And who the hell are you?"

"I'm the high-priestess of the new—"

Earl cocked the hammer for dramatic effect. "Short answer."

"I'm Lucinda Hood. Your thugs killed my father."

"Hood? You're Marty's daughter. The Condition is involved?" Earl was stunned. He'd thought for sure they'd been destroyed. "Owen told me about you. What're you doing here? Do all of you evil assholes *network* or something?"

Lucinda began to respond. "You'll pay for—"

"You know what? I ain't got time for this." Earl walked over and slugged her hard in the jaw, knocking the witch cold. "I normally don't hit little girls, but I make an exception for death cultists. Which way did he go, Kirk?"

Conover looked like Earl felt. He'd obviously taken a licking. "Adam? Well, I think it was Adam. . . ." Kirk pointed down the shaft. "But he's changed. That thing's corrupted him."

"Adam? The Alpha . . . He's your son, isn't he?" Earl asked.

Kirk nodded silently.

He, too, was a father, and couldn't even imagine . . . "I don't think he's going to go down quietly," Earl said. "This is—"

"No. He won't stop. Do what you have to do. I didn't know . . . I never expected . . . I thought he had the curse under control. He did fine for years. But then we found that skeleton, and it put images in his mind. He started keeping to himself more. Then, when Sharon died . . . They gave him some leave. Our superiors just thought he needed time to grieve. I should've seen it."

So many questions. Earl shook his head. There just wasn't time. Until that amulet was deactivated by the Baba Yaga's spell, the *vulkodlak* would keep on trying to kill everyone left in town. Earl shone his light down the shaft. It could only pierce so far. He couldn't even see close to the bottom. *How do I get down there?*

"I didn't know, Earl. I promise I didn't bring you here on purpose. I was telling the truth. All I knew about was Nikolai. Adam arranged everything."

The elevator had been left down below. The power was off anyway. It looked like there was usually a safety cage over the shaft, but the Alpha had torn it into jagged pieces. The shaft was a ten-foot-by-ten-foot square. There were several thick cables still dangling in the middle. If he could secure himself to that cable . . . Along with duct tape, Earl always kept a small bundle of paracord in his armor. He pulled it out.

"Why didn't you tell me about him?"

"He's an operative of an agency that doesn't even officially exist. It was classified. I didn't know he'd be here. I just thought Nikolai had come ba—"

"No. I mean how come you didn't tell me that I'd cursed your unborn child?" Earl began fashioning the cord into a basic harness.

"Because . . . Sharon didn't want me to."

Earl tied the paracord around his waist. He despised this acrobatic crap, and wasn't sure how good at it he was going to be as an ex-werewolf. Now he just needed to reach that cable. . . . "Why the hell not? "

"You hurt her while you were trying to save her. Sharon, she . . . she loved you, you know." Kirk's voice grew quiet. "She said that you already had enough guilt on your conscience. She didn't think you could handle much more."

Earl winced. If only he'd known. Maybe he could have made a difference. Maybe he could have stopped this before it had ever begun. Maybe . . . And maybe that was exactly what Sharon had been trying to prevent.

"I don't think you can beat him. Even before he found that damned *thing*. He's powerful, Earl. Like nothing you've ever seen. I'll try to call for help. My old operation has some assets. They might be able to take him alive."

That was a father's desperation talking. There was no help coming in time to save the town. "Too late now," Earl said. "I'm going after him. Wish me luck."

Heather frowned. "Harbinger . . . Wait."

Now was not the time to get mushy and nervous. "I've got to do this."

"No." Heather scrunched up her nose, like she could smell something bad. "He's coming to us."

Stark nervously looked down the hole in the ground at the entrance to the Quinn Mine. That thing had crawled out of there before Harbinger had blasted it with the 84mm. How many more of the Old Ones' creations were hiding under their feet?

There was still gunfire coming from nearby. Stark forced himself to move toward it. The crusty bastard with the accent was right behind him.

Douglas Stark had been brave once. He'd been a member of one of the proudest fraternities of warriors in history, *briefly*. It had been his first operation that had ended up fighting Deep Ones. Stark liked to think that if he would have just stuck with fighting other mortals, he would have been okay and not discovered that he was a coward. But instead he'd been whisked into the top-secret world of monster eradication.

Even then, he'd managed to be brave, a little bit, when necessary. MCB agents were called upon to do all sorts of terrifying things, but Stark had always managed to maneuver himself so that it was somebody else doing those things instead of him. Sure, he'd fought monsters, killed a few, but he wasn't the one to volunteer for it. Following Franks around had been the scariest thing he'd ever done, but Franks had been the one to do all the dangerous stuff, which was justifiable, since it was impossible for Franks to actually die. Stark had always hid his cowardice well. Luckily, since the MCB was a government agency, the keys to success were often more related to time served and working the system than sticking your neck out.

Having spent the last decade in management, though, the part of his brain that controlled bravery hadn't gotten much use. Stark was a good manager, an excellent paper-shuffler, witness-intimidator, and

PR doctor, but always in his heart he knew that he had a tendency to choke under pressure. It was hard to admit, but that was probably the single biggest reason he hated the fact that Dwayne Myers had been promoted instead of him. Myers was just as sly, just as cruelly efficient in the completion of his duties, but Myers actually led from the front. Myers actually was brave, and Myers was also perceptive enough to know that Stark wasn't.

If he could only see me now, Stark thought as he jogged through the burning debris. A bleeding werewolf tumbled out of a smoky corner. Stark bellowed as he shot the werewolf half a dozen times. Another one came out, dragging a leg nearly severed by silver shrapnel. Stark gunned it down, too.

"There! Look over there!" Aino shouted.

Another one of those big underground floppy-skinned monstrosities was chasing the last Briarwood Hunter between some of the parked equipment. Jason saw them, ducked under the bed of a dump truck and sprinted their way. He was holding Harbinger's Thompson, which was a good sign, because maybe that meant the scary bastard had gotten eaten.

Unfortunately, the monster began climbing over the dump truck in pursuit. "Don't run this way! The other way!" Stark shouted, but it wasn't doing any good. The idiot was going to lead that thing right to them. "Damn it."

Jason was soaked in sweat and gasping for air. Blood was running freely from the bandage on his head, and the side of his coat was stained red. Apparently the monster had managed to hit him at least once. "I'm almost out of ammo," he gasped.

"Did you lose my gun? Because that was an issue gun." There was a form for that, and Stark hated paperwork. Except the monster was lumbering toward them, so paperwork could wait. He shouldered his SCAR and started shooting.

Jason fired his last few rounds. The bullets hit, but the monster didn't seem to notice. Its head kept bobbing along. The giant mouth slit was hanging slightly open. Its skin was pocked with dozens of bleeding green bullet wounds. Jason dropped the Thompson and picked up a board. One end of which was on fire. "I'll hold him!" The big man bellowed as he charged the creature.

Now, that was brave. Stark had already gone through twenty rounds and not made a dent in the thing. He dropped the mag and pulled another from his armor while Jason ran right up and smacked the monster in the leg. The flaming board broke into sparks and ashes, but the creature didn't so much as flinch. Jason backed away as the creature raised its two metal hands.

"Big man! Catch!" Aino shouted. Stark was surprised to look over and see the grizzled old man holding a *lit* stick of dynamite. He threw it at Jason, who, remarkably enough, reached out and caught it in one hand.

"Where'd you get that?" Stark asked.

"Been carrying it around all night. 'Bout time I got to use it."

Jason stood his ground, face grim, as the fuse burned down. The creature reached down and grabbed him around the shoulders. Jason's feet left the ground as the horrible gaping mouth opened wide to swallow him whole. He didn't so much as make a sound as he was shoved headfirst down the thing's throat. The skin bag stretched as the Hunter fell inside.

"That is sick and wrong," Stark said.

The monster turned toward them, the pouch on the front bulging and swinging. It took a step forward, then stopped. The head kept bobbing, like it was thinking about something. A green point appeared in the middle of the sack; then it turned into a straight green line as a knife blade sliced cleanly through the skin from the inside. The monster opened its mouth to throw Jason up, but it was already too late.

The incision was three feet long by the time Jason's arm and head fell out. The gasping Hunter and a massive pile of slime spilled into the snow. Jason wasted no time as he sprang to his feet and ran for his life. He'd made it ten feet when the dynamite he'd left behind went off. It wasn't as big of a boom as Stark had hoped for, but it blasted green internal organs six feet in every direction. The blob of a head tilted crazily to the side before the whole monster sank gradually to the ground, flopped over, and lay still.

"That wasn't very big."

"I only had the one stick. Big man! You okay?"

Jason stumbled over to them. He was covered in goo, and so dizzy he could barely walk. He sank to his knees in front of Stark and held out his hand. Under all the slime was a knife. It looked familiar. Just like Stark's SOG knife. Automatically, he reached for the sheath on his armor, but it was empty. "Hey . . . How'd you get that?"

"You lost it sliding down the hill," Jason said. "You can have it back now."

The Hunter had gotten a lot more use out of it than prying open soda machines. Stark looked at the nasty, stinky mess, and said, "Naw. That's okay. You keep it. I've got to try and signal help before they bomb the shit out of us."

"Cool. Gonna rest now. . . ." Jason fell over and hit the ground with a dull thud. "You guys go do what you gotta do."

The man was brave, no doubt about that. That kind of gumption would have gotten him far in the MCB. He looked like he was probably going to die, but he'd managed to kick some ass in the process. He'd already lost one hard-charger today. Stark tried to remember back to his training. . . . Something about an obscure creature like this had been talked about in medical. *That slime* . . . Stark opened the med-kit on his armor and began rummaging around until he found a labeled injector. He gave the Hunter the shot and hoped that he was remembering right.

Stark checked his phone. Still no signal. He looked to the top of Number Six. It was his turn to be the hero. "I've got to go."

Aino handed him Harbinger's sniper rifle. "Just in case you see any more werewolves."

Jason Lococo was mumbling, staring into the distance. "Not so bad . . ."

⧣ **Chapter 34** ⧣

The Alpha was climbing up the elevator shaft. Nikolai could tell that the devil-wolf was fully healed, because that strange draining sensation had tapered off. The Alpha no longer needed the extra energy. When he reappeared, he would be virtually invincible.

Nikolai stopped to watch from the catwalk. He placed his filthy yet all-too-human hands on the metal to balance himself, since the world hadn't stopped spinning since he'd changed back. Harbinger and Kerkonen were below, ready to face their doom with open eyes. Now he needed to decide if he was going to die with them or not.

Flee?

"For what?"

Tvar was silent for a long time. *To survive.*

"Is that all there is to life?"

I do not know.

"Why not?"

Because I am you, and you do not know.

Nikolai was weakened. The Alpha had easily destroyed him just moments ago. To face him again was suicide.

You were willing to commit suicide earlier to stop me from taking control.

It was true. Losing himself had been more frightening than death. Death held no mysteries. Nikolai believed in nothing. The institutions he'd believed in as an adult had been a sham, and he had no faith in the tales of his fathers. There was no happy afterlife for him, no god to judge him, no eternal resting place to lay his weary head.

Bleak but poetic.

"I come from a bleak but poetic people. What would you have us do? Fight and die, or run as cowards."

You are . . . asking me?

"Why not? I'm tired of the struggle. I'm tired of not owning my own head. I'm just . . . tired."

The Tvar seemed to think about it for a long time. The Alpha let loose a howl of rage so intense that it felt as if the entire building would collapse on top of them.

He invaded our territory. He killed our pack. She was mine, too, you know. I did not approve, but he took something from both of us. We fight. Our death will have meaning.

Nikolai was surprised by the answer. "Why?"

Because I am you, and these things . . . I know.

"Incoming!" Heather shouted.

"Get out of here, Kirk," Earl ordered, and, when he hesitated, Earl snapped, "Go call your people. If we die here, he still needs to be stopped." Kirk snapped to and fled.

"Heather, get ready."

He could see the Alpha's eyes far below. They were shining like golden headlights. The mass of the super-werewolf was taking up a large portion of the shaft. He was climbing straight up, throwing himself upward, yards at a time, claws striking deep into rock and steel. It was like standing at the end of a tunnel with a freight train coming right at you.

There was nothing big to drop down the shaft. Heather tossed a wrench, then kicked in a rusty toolbox. The Alpha didn't even blink when they hit.

I'M COMING TO GET YOU, HARBINGER.

Earl had three shots left in the Mosin before he had to reload. Aksel had written that he'd struck Koschei right between the eyes. Earl aimed. Fired. There was a brilliant flash of silver light, and the Alpha roared. The headlights blinked twice, then started back up.

"That didn't work?" Heather shouted. "What now?" She threw over a tarp, looking for something else to toss down the shaft. "What happened to shoot him in the head and say the magic words? Shit. Shit."

KOSCHEI WAS WEAK. HE HAD NOT FED THE AMULET LIKE I HAVE.

Earl chambered another of the Baba Yaga's rounds. He aimed carefully. The old gun seemed to be perfectly zeroed. This time he picked a glowing eye.

YOU'RE NOT EVEN A WEREWOLF! I TOOK YOUR SOUL. YOU ARE NOTH—FUCK!

The Alpha shrieked as the silver bullet obliterated his eyeball. "Felt that one, huh?" Earl shouted as he worked the bolt, chambering the last cartridge in the magazine. There was only one beam of yellow light now. It danced wildly inside the shaft as the Alpha shook his head. He resumed climbing.

OH, IT IS ON NOW.

Heather had found an oil lantern. She hurled it down the shaft. The light fell, then shattered against the Alpha. The oil ignited in hissing flames. The burning werewolf kept ascending.

The fire was dying fast. "Got any more of those?" Earl asked.

"I think the rest are battery-powered."

"Aw, hell." *Last shot.* Earl aimed, trying to time the blinking of the Alpha's massive eyelids. At least the target was getting bigger. . . . Too bad that meant he was closer. "My, what a big eye you have," he muttered. Smoke and the stench of burning hair boiled out of the shaft. He pulled the trigger. The other light went out, plunging the pit into smoky darkness.

AARRRGGGHHH! The roar was in Earl's head and against his ears. *THEY'LL GROW BACK. I DON'T NEED TO SEE TO EAT YOU.*

Earl pulled a stripper clip of five of the magic rounds and began to thumb them into the open action of the Mosin-Nagant. He hadn't used one of these particular rifles since a mission during the Korean War. There was a trick to not getting all the cartridges wedged up against their rims. *There.* He closed the bolt.

And the Alpha came out of the shaft.

Somehow, he seemed even bigger than before. He had to duck his head to get under the cable wheel. *WHERE ARE YOU?* His nostril holes, which were big enough to fit a grapefruit in, flared. The head turned toward Earl, and the jaws opened. Each tooth was the size of a combat knife. *THERE YOU ARE.*

The jaws snapped forward, wide enough to completely consume a man. But they snapped shut on empty air.

Earl hit the ground rolling, entangled with a mass of dark hair. They came to a stop, and for a moment, Earl thought that Heather must have saved him. But it was Nikolai in werewolf form. His teeth were only inches from Earl's eyes, and for the briefest of moments, Earl would have assumed that the fearsome beast, his mortal enemy, smiled. Nikolai turned, snarled, and charged, loping toward the Alpha.

PETROV. Blind, the Alpha swung one mighty arm, ripping thousand-pound girders right out of the concrete. Nikolai spun through the chaos and landed on the Alpha's neck, tearing and biting.

Earl had lost the Mosin. It was a few feet away. He scrambled for it.

Heather, fully changed, joined the fray. She came at the Alpha from behind and attacked his leg, trying to rip through a hamstring. The giant lashed out with one leg, and a paw knocked Heather across the room.

Nikolai never let up to the end. He threw himself at the Alpha, over and over, tearing roast-sized chunks of meat out, spraying blood in great arcs, attacking with unbelievable savagery. One giant claw wrapped around Nikolai's leg and pulled him away. The Alpha held the other werewolf away from his body, letting Nikolai dangle and thrash. The Russian managed to pull himself up, breaking his leg in the process to attack the tendons in the Alpha's wrist. The Alpha roared in agony as Nikolai severed the artery.

ENOUGH OF YOU.

The Alpha reached up with his other hand and took hold of Nikolai's arm. The limb seemed puny between the great claws. The Alpha pulled. Nikolai screamed as one arm was torn off.

Earl's hand landed on the wooden stock of the Mosin-Nagant.

Nikolai was still fighting, still attacking, even as the blood pumped from his torso. The Alpha sunk his claws into Nikolai's chest, and, once locked on, pulled against Nikolai's leg. He screamed again, weaker this time, as his leg was torn cleanly off at the pelvis.

PETER AND THE WOLF. LAST OF YOUR LINE. YOU SHOULDN'T HAVE CHALLENGED ME.

The Alpha wrenched off Nikolai's other arm. Nikolai's head hung, weak and limp. He held Nikolai over the shaft.

LIKE YOUR EMPIRE, TO THE GRAVEYARD OF HISTORY'S FAILURES YOU GO. . . .

Great claws pulled free of Nikolai's body and the Russian tumbled into the dark.

The Alpha turned, satisfied. *NOW, WHERE ARE YOU, HARBINGER?* Still blind, the monster flared his massive nostrils as he sought the scent of his enemy.

And Earl shoved the barrel of the Mosin nearly a foot up the Alpha's nose. He jerked the trigger.

The light was blinding. This time the message that the Alpha broadcast telepathically was an unintelligible signal of so much confusion and pain that it momentarily shorted out Earl's brain.

The Alpha reared back, hit the pulley, did a turn, then fell. Earl dove to the side to keep from being crushed. The impact of the Alpha's body shook the foundations.

NNNNNNUUUUUUUuuuuuuuuuuu.

Earl shook his head. The Alpha was down, flat on his back. The rifle was still sticking out of his nose. There was no time to lose. He had no idea how fast the monster could regenerate from something like this. Nikolai's life had bought him a distraction, and it was his only chance. Earl jumped over one outstretched arm, grabbed handfuls of black, and began pulling his aching body up the Alpha's torso.

The amulet. *There.* It was barely visible through the hair. There was no chain holding it. It was like the silver had turned molten and seared itself to the werewolf's chest. It was an open palm, three claws, just like the forerunner's skeleton, just like the dream from when his curse had been ripped away.

He grabbed the amulet in both hands, sinking his fingers into the Alpha's skin, and shouted the words from Aksel's journal. "Allut tvar mataw!" And he pulled with all his might.

Nothing happened. The amulet didn't even budge.

"Allut tvar mataw. Allut tvar mataw!" Earl roared. Somehow he pulled harder. Veins stood out in his neck. "Allut tvar mataw! Motherfucker!" The amulet hadn't moved a bit. "This is why I hate magic!"

Earl looked to the rifle. The Alpha had to be regenerating. Time for another dose of silver to the old brain-stem.

HARBINGER.

The entire body shuddered beneath Earl's knees. "Aw, hell."
GIVE MY REGARDS TO PETROV.

Earl tried to move, but the arm was so big, there was nowhere to go. It was like trying to dodge a wall. It hit him, and he tumbled overboard. He hit the ground hard, only to be hit again. His body scraped and banged across the gravel as the Alpha shoved him over the edge and into the shaft.

Earl was falling.

Desperate, he reached for something, anything. His hand struck metal, stone, metal, and somehow he grabbed on, for just a split second. The impact wrenched his arm from the socket. The ledge he'd grasped crumbled, and Earl fell again.

Air tore by. Earl hit a center cable. He touched it. Sliding. Then hit it again. Somehow he grabbed it, slowing himself. Friction burned his gloves as he fell.

Can't die. Not like this. Earl got his other hand on the cable. Still falling. *Can't stop.* He hit it with his leg, trying to wrap himself around the cable. It abraded through his armor and into his skin. The pain was horrific, but he squeezed tighter.

He was slowing. *Slowing.* Then there was no more cable. The end zipped past his leg. Past his hands and was gone.

He barely had time to make a noise before the ground hit him.

The Alpha pulled the rifle out of his nose. It hurt like a son of a bitch. The silver needle had literally scrambled his brains. He should have eaten Harbinger, at least for the calories, but kicking him over the edge so he could plunge to his doom had been strangely satisfying, too. He lay there for a moment, using his other senses as his eyes slowly healed. He began to shrink. It took too much energy to sustain the great-form for long. Waves of heat bled from him as he took his human form.

That had to be all. The challenge had to be complete. There was nothing else for him to prove. Listening intently, he waited for the amulet to tell him another secret, but the damned thing was silent. "What more can you want from me?" There was still no response. "Please?"

"Adam!" It was his father. His *human* father. His real father; his *werewolf* father was dead. "Adam, stop." The Alpha turned to face him. Kirk had found a revolver somewhere, probably one of

Harbinger's, and he took it in both hands and aimed it at his son's heart. His father had a surprisingly grim look on his face. "You've got to stop this. It's that thing on your chest. It's changing you. It's messing with your head."

"You can't blame it on the amulet, Dad. It's changing me physically." The Alpha tapped himself on the head. "But I'm the one calling the shots. This is *my* plan. *My* mission. *My* destiny."

"These are silver bullets in here. I don't want to shoot you, but I will."

"I've got no doubt you would. You always were the tough one. You made that decision a long time ago, didn't you? That if your horrible, cursed, monster son ever went wrong, ever went bad, you'd be the one to put him down. Duty, honor, country . . . Family came way after everything else."

The gun was barely moving. "I love you, Son, but I will kill you if I have to."

The Alpha shook his head. "That's what I told myself when I decided Mom needed to go."

"You . . . you . . . what?" Now the gun shook.

"I loved her, but she was in my way." The truth seemed to rob Kirk of his will. The Alpha moved, too quickly for his father to react, and wrapped his hands around the revolver. Kirk fought, but he wasn't nearly strong enough as the Alpha steered the muzzle under his father's chin. "Now you two can be together again." He put pressure on his father's trigger finger and closed his eyes.

When it was done, he felt strangely empty.

The Alpha stepped away from his father's body and touched the amulet. *Still nothing.* He'd just severed the last tie to his mortal life. "What more can you want from me?" He roared in frustration, picked up a wrench, and smashed it to bits against the wall. The sun was up. They couldn't afford to wait any longer. "Let this place be the first test, then. I'll raise *vulkodlak* in other places, larger cities, with bigger populations. I'll satisfy you eventually!" Lucinda Hood was in the corner. Luckily she hadn't been crushed during the melee. He was at her side in the blink of an eye.

The witch was coming to. "Wha—what happened?"

"Harbinger knocked you unconscious. Come on. Wake up. It's time to go."

Lucinda shook her head to clear it. "Give me a moment to prepare." She reached into her coat and began unknotting the rope tied around her waist. The rope was the key element to one of the Shadow Man's perfected teleportation spells.

"Hurry. There's nothing left for us here now." The Alpha checked the air. His vision was shot, but he could still smell—with one nostril, at least. There was only one other living thing on their level. . . . "Wait. That's it!"

Lucinda was still wobbly. "What?"

The female. Her grandfather had somehow stolen a bit of the forerunner's spirit when he'd taken the amulet from Koschei, and he'd passed that on to his heirs. Whatever piece had been stolen was enabling her to exercise remarkable control. That had to be what the amulet needed. It wasn't complete. "Keep working. This won't take long."

He found Heather on the other side of the room, trapped. When he'd struck her, she'd apparently fallen onto a few pieces of broken rebar sticking out of the floor. There was one through her calf and another piercing her thigh, with a foot and a half of metal spike sticking out of each one. Far too high for her to lift herself off of, there was no way out on her own short of gnawing her own leg off.

And from the look of determination in the red werewolf's eyes, he could tell that she was thinking about it.

"Regeneration is a spectacular gift. Except you can't heal around a foreign body. Look at all that *blood*. I'm amazed you're still alive." He reached out one hand and used the gift that his mother's line had bestowed upon him. "Calm . . . calm. Let me take your pain," he whispered. "That's all right. It'll be over soon." The female relaxed. She quit tugging on the bloody holes in her legs. She exhaled as his peace relaxed her, and began to shift back to her human form. He gently stroked her hair. "That's right. It'll be over soon." He waited patiently until she'd returned to her original state.

Once she was fully human, he removed his power and let all the pain come rushing back at once. Heather screamed.

The agony had to be excruciating. "What're you doing?" she hissed through gritted teeth.

"Taking back what's mine. Come on. This won't take long. Stand up." He grabbed her by the old leather coat she was wearing and hoisted her off the rebar. She screamed as the metal tore free. Holding her in his arms like a baby, he carried her back to the shaft. She had lost too much blood to fight anymore. Once the stolen essence had been taken back, he'd toss her down with the others that had dared fight him. It seemed appropriate that way. Someday, in a world full of werewolves, they'd build a shrine on top of this place.

"Heather!" A single, feeble man stood on the catwalk. He was old, pathetically weak, and wouldn't have too many more years on this world, even if the Alpha wasn't about to destroy him for meddling. "It's not too late! I know how to beat him!"

"Somebody kill him already," the Alpha ordered, but then he remembered. The entire pack was dead. One more thing he was going to have to rebuild. He unceremoniously dumped Heather on the floor next to the shaft. "Guess I'll do it myself."

"Heather! It's in your grandpa's journal." The old man lifted a small leather-bound book and waved it over his head. "On the very first page."

Interesting. It would be useful to know exactly how some mere soldiers had been able to defeat the great Koschei. The Alpha picked up a five-foot length of steel girder and tested the balance. He walked toward the human.

"Read the words. Use it!" The old man threw the book at the female. It was actually a very good shot, and the book landed only a few feet from her. She showed surprising fortitude as she dove for it, dragging her torn leg behind.

He looked back at the intruder. He would deal with Heather in a moment. The Alpha hurled the heavy beam through the air. It missed the man but struck the catwalk hard enough to shear all the rusty bolts from the wall.

"Aino!" the female cried.

The entire catwalk assembly broke free and collapsed to the floor with a terrible crash. A cloud of dust rolled across the room. He turned back to the female. She had rolled onto her side and had the book open before her. She was panicked, desperate, as she tried to find a way to stop him.

The Alpha strolled over and snatched the book from her hands. "What've we got here." The handwriting was loose and sloppy. He picked a random spot on the first page.

See, I bear a curse. You learn to deal with it, or it deals with you. Crying about it won't change a thing. Embracing it will destroy you. I have stared into the face of evil, and I've been the face of evil. I've done some bad things in my life. Good thing I've lived a long time, because I'm still trying to even that score. Some folks would call it penance. I call it my job.

I am a Hunter. I am a Monster. I was born Raymond Earl Shackleford Jr., son of the greatest Hunter to ever live, in the year 1900. I've held many names since.

Today they call me Harbinger.

This wasn't the journal of Aksel Kerkonen. The Alpha looked up from the page at the female. Treachery ran deep in her family. She held a different book in her hands and was reading aloud from it.

It was a spell. The air crackled with raw energy. "Bitch." He reached for the true book.

But a claw came over the side of the pit, hooked him by the leg, and pulled him over the edge.

≼ Chapter 35 ≽

Earl had one of those dreams. Where you were falling. And you bolt up in bed, wide awake at the last second.

Only this wasn't a dream, and he'd hit the floor hard enough to break every bone in his body.

He lay there, staring up. There was a single perfect square of light, far above. It seemed so far away. He must've slowed himself quite a bit on that cable, or he'd have been dead on impact.

Earl reached for the wall. One hand wouldn't respond. He gasped in pain when he reached over and touched the bone sticking out of his forearm.

Got to find a way out. Got to move.

He couldn't feel his legs.

Well . . . shit.

They say your life flashes before your eyes when you're close to death. Earl didn't buy that. He'd almost died plenty of times, and he'd never gotten the slideshow. But in those final moments, you did dwell on things . . . Things left unsaid. Things undone. This time was different. Like this, would have plenty of time to think.

Far above, the Alpha was going to kill Heather. She was a sweet girl. She deserved a chance. Then the Alpha was going to get away, and he was going to keep on killing, only he was going to get better at it. All because he was a jerk-off with daddy issues and delusions of grandeur. He'd learn from that amulet, and he'd get stronger. By the time the world knew what they were facing, it would be too late. He couldn't even get word to MHI to pick up where he'd left off. The son of a bitch would flood bastardized zombie *vulkodlak* everywhere.

He'd prayed for a cure. He'd tried to cut a deal with God to be rid of the curse. He'd done everything he could, searched the globe, turned over every rock looking for a way to end it, but never found anything. So he'd accepted his lot in life and made the best of it. He'd used his curse to be a warrior for good. He'd made kicking the shit out of evil into a business, and he'd saved a thousand times more innocent lives than he'd taken, but that entire time, he would have traded it all to be human once again.

Got my wish. Lord, you've got a very ironic sense of humor. He would've laughed if he could have formed the sound. Here he was. Human again . . . only he'd be dead soon. And all the work he'd done, all the battles he'd fought, they'd all be for nothing. *Guess I was wrong to waste all that time wishing for something when I should've just made better use of the gifts you gave me.*

"Harb . . . inger . . ."

The voice was a hoarse whisper. So quiet that the first time he heard it, he thought he was imagining it, or maybe it was an angel come to lead him on. *Now, that will be an interesting judgment day!*

"Harbinger . . ."

Nikolai? He became aware of the presence next to him. The voice was inhuman, struggling to form words with a mouth that was filled with fangs and still partially transformed. "I'm dying . . ."

Obviously. There were limits even to what a werewolf could survive, and three torn-off limbs was well beyond that point. Nikolai being alive was rather surprising. *Stubborn Russki bastard.* "Me, too," Earl managed to croak. *Fitting.* They should've died together a long time ago, the last of their breed.

"No . . . ," Nikolai coughed. "Not yet. Smell . . . no death . . . on you."

Earl lay there, tried to block out the pain, and thought about it. He'd been hurt so many hundreds of times that he could be analytical about his injuries. He knew what broken vertebrae and shattered bones felt like. Nikolai was right. Earl wasn't dying yet. He could survive this.

They'd find him down here. Heather would be dead, and the Alpha would escape, but he could still survive to live as a man.

And as a failure.

There was movement. Nikolai shifted. He was right there, but it was too dark to see, too numb too feel. "The amulet . . . It's surging. Strong. Magic . . . like never before."

What's he getting at? The earlier surges had forced all of the werewolves to change, but Nikolai was too damaged to transform now. Werewolves couldn't regrow limbs. He was melting back into a man as he died. Nikolai was about to punch the clock. And the amulet didn't do anything to a normal man. . . .

It wasn't too late, but it meant giving up everything he'd ever hoped for.

Nobody had ever accused a Shackleford of being a quitter.

Earl lifted his less-broken arm and managed to shove it toward Nikolai. "Bite me."

There was a noise as the dying werewolf shifted. "Finish . . . it . . ."

Crunch. Earl screamed as fangs pierced his hand.

The jaws released, and Earl pulled his mangled hand against his chest. Nikolai was breathing in short, panting gasps. He'd be dead shortly.

"Something . . . to remember me by."

Those were Nikolai's last words.

The ragged breathing stopped, and Earl was alone except for the ringing in his ears and the mind-numbing pain coursing through his broken body.

Would it work? Or would it all be for nothing?

He watched the square of light. It was all he *could* do. The Alpha roared, and the sound echoed down the shaft. Earl's vision darkened as the light darkened from yellow to gray.

No. Not darkening. Changing.

The ringing in his ears was replaced with a hum. *No.* Not a hum. The *Hum.*

The curse was in his blood again. Earl concentrated on the gray light. Normally it took weeks for the change to take place. But with that amulet . . . Heather had changed in hours, Buckley and the other cursed had changed in hours.

He didn't have hours. He'd be dead long before the healing kicked in.

The werewolf-killed had changed into *vulkodlak* within seconds of death. Only, they'd been partial transformations. And what was he supposed to do? Wish real hard for death? And then come back as a mindless undead? No thanks.

Heather had changed in hours because of that false moon. But she'd been a new werewolf. What could it do in the blood of someone already familiar? Somebody who knew exactly what he was looking for, and how to set it off?

Lord, help me. Give me the strength I need to do this. Help me change. I'll do my best. I will be a warrior in your service. Grant me your strength. Please.

Earl cleared his mind and opened his soul to the Hum.

His temperature was rising. Earl still couldn't feel his legs, but he could have sworn that they just twitched.

The Hum was everything. It was calling to him. Earl searched for his other half. It wasn't the enemy. It was an old friend. He thought he heard a noise. *There.* It came again. It was a *crackling* noise.

It was his spine realigning.

Suddenly he could feel his lower body, and it hurt a *lot*. Everything was shattered. *Yes!* Earl welcomed the pain. He welcomed the anger. He welcomed the monster.

Bone fragments ground together, slowly at first, then faster. He lifted his arm, put his hand in front of the square of light. For a moment, he thought he was hallucinating, seeing a vision of the amulet with its three claws. A finger was gone. There was just a bloody hole on the end of his hand.

Nikolai, you son of a bitch, you didn't have to bite my pinky off.

Earl rose, stripped off his tattered armor, and began to climb. The change was fully on him now, but his thoughts were still clear, still coherent, still *his*. He found a handhold and pulled, another, and then he was moving upward. Bones twisted back together, then bent into new angles.

The pain was horrendous. It was just as bad as the very first time, only now, instead of rolling around on the floor and going insane, Earl just kept climbing. He was not the man he had been all those years ago. Twenty feet up, and his nine remaining fingers had turned into claws, all the better to dig into the walls. Forty feet, and his teeth were sharp, ready to rend his enemy's flesh. Seventy, and he was moving with inhuman speed, leaping up the walls, grabbing onto the smallest of ledges. Halfway up and all vestiges of his human form were gone.

He climbed faster and faster, until he was bounding from side to side, kicking off and hurling himself upward.

The square of gray light grew bigger. He heard voices. He felt the false Hum just ahead, like a giant screaming moon. There was Fey magic in the air. The Alpha was vulnerable.

Earl broke into the light. He lashed out, grabbed the Alpha's human leg and pulled. Earl let himself fall. Better to die dashing the evil one against the ground at terminal velocity.

HARBINGER?

The change was nearly instantaneous for the Alpha. One second he was human, the next he was a perfect werewolf. They fell together, striking and tearing at each other. The Alpha was faster, but in free fall, it didn't matter.

WHAT'S HAPPENING TO ME? SHE USED MAGIC!

Earl hit the side. His claws tore divots through the rock as his body lurched to a stop. The Alpha snagged the cable twenty feet below and stopped his fall. He was rapidly increasing in size.

WHY WON'T YOU DIE?

He let go of the wall and fell toward the Alpha.

Because I'm Earl Harbinger.

The two collided. The Alpha held on, and Earl slashed him repeatedly, raking his claws to the bone. The Alpha struck him back with a force that should have killed Earl instantly. Earl hooked his thumb under the Alpha's growing muzzle and tore out his throat. Blood cascaded down the shaft.

King of the werewolves.

They were falling again. The Alpha roared as energy from the amulet flooded the shaft in scalding light. The Alpha had grown so much that he just thrust both arms out to the side and slammed his palms against the wall, stopping himself. Earl fell past but caught the Alpha's leg. Claws raked him, but Earl sunk his teeth into the Alpha's tendons and wrenched his muzzle from side to side. The Alpha screamed.

I only have two rules.

The Alpha's foot claws sliced through Earl's shoulder and knocked him off. Earl dropped like a stone. He looked up as the still-growing Alpha climbed frantically toward the surface. Earl casually reached out and grabbed the madly whipping cable. He stopped himself and began to climb.

Rule number one. Leave humans alone.

As he reached the Alpha, it lashed out at him. Earl launched himself from the cable, hit the wall, and scurried up with an agility that he'd never had before. He reached the Alpha's arm and lit into it with tooth and claw. He tore divots from the bone and bit until he tasted marrow.

Rule one. Violated.

The Alpha was still trying to climb. He was confused how Earl was so fast, so unbelievably strong. He was trying to get into the open, where he could use his superior strength. Earl wasn't planning on letting him. Earl could smell the fear. It was the most beautiful smell in the world. Earl *never* stank of fear. He thrust his claws into the Alpha's neck and bit off his enemy's ear. The Alpha's cry of pain was like beautiful music.

Rule number two. Stay off of my bad side.

They reached the top. The Alpha sunk one massive claw onto the surface and pulled. Earl reached around the Alpha's face and gouged both eyes out.

You done violated the shit out of rule two.

Earl clambered up one giant arm, raised his hand high, and struck three deep lacerations through the back of the Alpha's hand. He hit it again and again. The Alpha wailed as he lost his grip. Both of them tumbled through the darkness, striking walls, careening back and forth. Earl just kept striking until they were falling in a red rain. The cable snapped past Earl's snout; he reached out and took it, but not to slow his fall.

You're no king.

They lurched to a stop in a cloud of broken rock. Earl jerked the cable around the Alpha's neck, then rolled himself over against the Alpha's chest. He sunk his three-clawed hand into the flesh around the amulet.

NO. IT'S MY BIRTHRIGHT.

You have to earn it.

In desperation, the Alpha let go of the wall to try and tear Earl from the amulet. They were falling again. Earl's claws tightened around the burning piece of silver.

They reached the end of the cable's slack. The loop Earl had created snapped tight, and the Alpha's unnatural mass slammed against the noose. Vertebrae and muscle tore. The amulet ripped free of the Alpha's chest as Earl was dislodged and flung aside.

Earl hit the wall, skidding, but managed to sink his talons against a ledge to catch himself. The amulet scorched his hand, but he held on. Above, the Alpha hung, swaying, his limbs dangling, lifeless. The golden light in the giant's eyes began to fade.

He didn't even know if the Alpha could hear his thoughts, only that he could hear the ones the Alpha chose to broadcast, but he had to try. *I'm sorry I cursed you, Adam. I wish I'd known. Maybe I could've made a difference. Maybe I could've helped somehow. Maybe . . .*

The Alpha's body gradually shrank as the amulet's energy left him. The head separated from the body, and both parts plunged past Earl into the darkness.

⚔ Chapter 36 ⚔

The strange words seemed to hang in the air for a time, repeating in her ears, even after the Alpha disappeared down the shaft. Heather's vision blurred, fading in and out of focus in time, as the words turned into a chant. As the world faded, another one replaced it. An older world, long since turned to dust, where one of the four factions had gathered to create their champion.

The mighty beast had been chained. Capturing it had cost many hunters their lives, but it had to be taken alive, for a dead thing had no spirit to take.

Heather stood before a great-demon wolf, more terrifying than the Alpha had been. It was upright, shackled and pinned between two great stone pillars. The ends of a hundred arrows and a hundred spears protruded from its bleeding skin. Its hair had been burned away with fire, leaving it blackened and naked.

It was the last of its kind. The adversary had not created it. He could not create, only corrupt. The sagas said that the adversary had taken the wolf and twisted it to be this, before he had buried himself deep in the world to sleep. There the adversary would lie until time was broken and remade, to fight the great war of the living and the dead, but before his retreat, he had left his great-demon wolves to harry and destroy man.

But man would steal the spirit of the great demon-wolf and make it their own. For when the adversary returned, they would use his own weapons against him.

One of the great demon-wolf's forelegs was lifted with ropes pulled by a hundred of their strongest men. The device was made ready. Designed with plans given by a mad Fallen, built by their wise men using tools stolen from the Old Ones, and given an intelligence of its own, the device had but one purpose: to make the adversary's weapon their own. The wise men surrounded the quaking limb and buried the flaming device into the beast's palm. Its howl had shaken the foundations of the world.

Their greatest hunter had volunteered to be the weapon. He placed his hand against the flames and joined his soul to the beast.

The ceremony had spanned three days and three nights, as the strength had been drawn out, bit by bit, through the device embedded in the beast's palm and fed into the heart of their greatest man. At moonfall, all that could be consumed, had been. The strength of a great demon-wolf had been given to a man. The beast had screamed for all three days of the ceremony, but it was dead now. The transfer was complete.

But something had gone wrong. . . .

The great man could not control the spirit of the beast; instead it had controlled him. At the full moon, he changed into a pale shadow of the great demon-wolf. Madness spread. The vision ended in blood.

Heather wiped her eyes and struggled to her feet. Her head was swimming. The vision slowly faded, and she remembered the broken catwalk. She pulled Aino out of the wreckage and tried to stop the bleeding, but it was too late. Flat on his back, there was blood coming out of his ears and nose. She could sense the weakness, the internal bleeding, and the death that was coming with it.

He'd insisted on holding her hand.

"You can't go back," Aino said. "I'm so sorry."

"Don't talk. Just rest."

"Aksel figured it out too late. The Baba Yaga didn't lie, but she didn't know the whole truth. You've got to give yourself to the amulet first, then it decides who gets it. They fought Koschei twice. First time, Aksel was the only survivor, but part of the wolf spirit went with him. When they fought again, it decided it liked Aksel better."

"Shh . . . Hang on. I'm going to carry you out of here."

"Don't shush me, girl. I'm dying, not stupid. Listen. You've got to know. Aksel fought Koschei twice. Second time . . . said the spell again . . . and he took it. The wolf spirit takes the measure of who's fighting over it . . . decides who's worthy. It used Aksel. That part of the wolf spirit changed him, and when he died it changed your daddy, and then it changed you."

"Why?"

"Something about your people was special. Its job is to pick an heir. It's looking for the last one."

"I don't understand."

"Last heir gets it all. Aksel hid it . . . Because if it picked somebody bad to be the last . . ." He closed his eyes and sighed. "Good or evil . . . it's their call. Your call . . ." He trailed off.

"Aino?" her voice cracked.

"Good old Six," he whispered. "Always thought she'd be the death of me . . ."

"Aino?" She squeezed his callused hand, hardened from a lifetime in the mines, but there was no response. Her eyes burned. "Oh, Aino."

There was a scraping noise echoing from the shaft. Heather turned, expecting to see the Alpha coming out of the hole to finish them once and for all. She scanned the room for help, but there was no one else there. Even the girl Earl had punched out was gone. There was just a weird piece of rope and a burned spot on the floor. She was alone. A sudden *clang* of metal told her he was getting close to the top. *I'm all that's left.* She picked up her grandfather's rifle and, determined to go down fighting, walked to the edge of the pit.

The werewolf was climbing quickly. The Alpha was normal-sized now, but it didn't matter. He was still more than a match for her. She aimed the rifle at the top of the Alpha's skull, but hesitated. Her gray vision could tell that this one was lighter in color. He must have heard her, and golden eyes turned upward. Though she had never seen him transformed, instinctively she recognized *him*. Heather lowered the rifle. "Harbinger?"

Nervously, she backed away. Harbinger wasn't like her. He'd told her about how the moon drove him insane, about how he had to lock himself in a reinforced prison cell whenever the change overtook him. The monster version of Harbinger was an animal, a pure killer, nothing like the honorable man she'd known. It wasn't safe.

The werewolf crawled up the shaft and, with an exhausted grunt, leveraged himself up and over the side. Harbinger stood upright, a foot taller than she was in her human form. His light fur was matted and streaked red. His skin was torn with dozens of deep lacerations. Frothy blood dripped from his jaws and ran down his chest. His head swiveled to study her. He took a step forward.

"Harbinger! Stop. Don't make me shoot you." He took another halting step. She raised the rifle, but there was no growling, no fearsome roar or baring of teeth. He just looked *tired.* "Earl?"

Slowly, he held out one damaged hand. It was covered in blood and hair, and there was a black scab where his pinky-finger had been, but he was offering something to her. She took a step closer. *The amulet!* Harbinger was offering it to her. He took another step and swayed, as if he was going to collapse. Without thinking, Heather moved forward and caught him.

One hairy arm fell over her shoulder. His fangs were dripping the Alpha's blood down the side of her face, but she understood that she wasn't in any danger. She held him upright as the pace of his breathing slowed.

Teeth retracted and flattened. The fur receded. A moment later, he was only a few inches taller than her. She still continued to hold him as the last werewolf features fell away, until she was holding only a very battered man. Heather squeezed him even tighter. She'd only just realized she was crying. He placed one hand on the back of her head and kissed her gently on the forehead. "It's all right," he rasped. "Everything's all right now."

"I know . . ." But she didn't let him go.

He was looking past her and saw the corpses of Aino and Kirk. "Aw, hell. So many . . ."

Harbinger was alive. He had the amulet. "Is he . . . ?"

"Dead." His voice was ragged. "The Alpha's dead, and I got this." He lifted the amulet of Koschei and held it between their faces. "Your town should be safe. Now we need to figure out how to cure you . . . us . . . all of us. Wait . . ." He stopped, horrified, and stared at the rapidly disintegrating amulet. The silver claw was cracking as its outer edges bled into dust. "No. No! NO!" Harbinger shouted. He let go of Heather and tried, futilely, to squeeze the pieces together. Dust streamed between his fingers. Harbinger fell to his knees and tried to collect the ever-shrinking bits. Within seconds, they were gone.

Heather felt the magic leave, and the last fuzzy remnants of the dream went with it.

"I can't believe this. It was a cure. . . ." Harbinger stayed there, on his knees. "No . . . We could have ended the curse."

Heather shook her head, trying to recall her dream. "It was waiting for someone worthy. The curse was on purpose, but the people that took it weren't ready yet. They didn't know what they were asking for. The monster's spirit was stronger than theirs. But the amulet had a mind of its own. It held something back for some reason."

"You saw something, too . . . didn't you?"

"I did, just now. Like it wanted me to know."

"Me, too. Little bits and pieces, when I lost my curse, and when I saw the bones." Harbinger ran his fingers through the dust. "The amulet was a test."

"It wanted to be found. It was waiting for someone. The thing was only making werewolves stronger to attract even stronger challengers." She placed one hand gently on his shoulder. "It found what it was looking for. It picked you."

"No. It didn't." Harbinger stood and took Heather back in his arms. "I wasn't enough. It picked *us*."

"Harbinger?"

"Earl. Really. It's just Earl."

She kissed him, gently. He still tasted like blood. "Let's get out of here."

"You hear that?" Heather asked once they got outside. "It's quiet."

Earl listened, it was good to be able to *really* hear again. "I'd say too quiet, but I suppose that's because we've killed everything in a mile radius."

"No, smartass. There's no gunshots from town."

It was like he'd figured. The *vulkodlak* had only existed because of the amulet. Once it was gone, there was nothing keeping those undead walking. The question was if they'd stopped them in time to make any difference. There was some clothing hanging on the railing at the entrance to Number Six. Which really brightened Earl's morning. He wasn't the self-conscious type, werewolves seldom were, but he was still a Southern gentleman, so walking around buck-naked with a lady seemed rather uncouth. Heather still had his coat, but he passed her the pants. There was a rather nice wool overcoat, so he took that. It smelled like the Alpha. There was a wide-brimmed hat, too. Earl put it on. "Souvenir."

"You look like a flasher," Heather said as she put the pants on. They were too big for her. She unconsciously let one fingernail elongate into a point to poke a new hole in the belt so she could cinch the pants up tighter. "You could just leave it off. You've got a good body for a senior-senior-citizen."

"Damn, woman, you are forward." Earl checked the pockets. Sadly, it appeared that Adam Conover had been a nonsmoker. "In my day—"

"In your day they invented the airplane. Besides, somebody would just call it in and I'd have to arrest you for indecent exposure. Let's see if anybody else survived and find us a ride out of here."

Despite being too tired to think, Earl found himself smiling. The girl had spunk. If she didn't degenerate into an insane killer, he could see this actually maybe working out. It would be nice to have some female company again. "Then some breakfast. I could eat a horse."

"I know where some are near here. The Randall place is just over the hill. I'll split one with you."

Because of the fire, and the smoke, and the dozens of corpses, he couldn't locate any of his companions by smell. So it took longer than he would've liked. They found Jason Lococo near the gates. The Hunter was in bad shape, covered in slime, barely conscious, but breathing. Close by was the exploded remains of one of the Old Ones' diggers.

Earl knelt next to him. "How you feeling, Jason?"

He gestured weakly at an empty syringe on the ground. "Stark . . . Antidote." Jason's good eye rolled back in his head, and he was out. Earl checked the syringe. Atropine. Stark must have known the digger's poison caused nerve damage. Nasty stuff, but it looked like it had been caught in time. His nose was telling him that Jason would live.

"Nice work, kid." Lococo was probably twice his size, but it wouldn't be difficult for Earl to carry him out. "Let's get him to some medical help. Kid's got real potential."

"That just leaves Stark," Heather said as she scanned the compound. "I wonder where he ran off to?"

❖ ❖ ❖

Special Agent Douglas Stark of the Monster Control Bureau of the Department of Homeland Security watched the fire-haired werewolf through the scope of Harbinger's precision rifle. The crosshairs were floating around on the back of her head. He had a solid position. There was zero wind. He'd known they would stop to help the injured Hunter. From the top of Number Six, the range was a piddly hundred and fifty yards. It was an easy kill.

"Agent Stark. Stark! Can you hear me? Are you okay?"

Stark listened to the Bluetooth earpiece. He'd gotten headquarters. He'd gotten help on the way. National Guard out of Marquette were going to cordon off the area while the MCB airlifted in a cleanup team to bag the bodies and intimidate the witnesses. They'd come up with a plausible cover story, like they always did, and the whole Copper Lake mess would just go away.

"I'm here," Stark whispered.

"There are choppers en route to your position. I'm trying to get an ETA. Are you secure?" Agent Archer asked.

There were three dead werewolves that had gotten in his way on the stairs. He was pretty proud of those kills. There were only two werewolves left down there, and he was glassing them with a sniper rifle. "Secure enough."

"Good work, Stark, good work. The outbreak will be contained. Thanks." Archer sounded like he was getting choked up. "Thank you."

Stark moved the crosshairs over to Harbinger's back. A few ounces of pressure on a trigger that would break like a glass rod, and that asshole was toast. Harbinger shouldn't have punched Stark in the face. "What're you talking about, Archer?"

"My hometown is right down the road. If you and Mosher hadn't stopped the outbreak, we might have been forced to . . . Well . . . shit, sir. You know. Just . . . thanks."

"Uh huh," Stark said as he put his finger on the trigger. Obviously, he'd given headquarters his interpretation of the day's events. There was still a lot of explaining to do, but nothing he couldn't handle.

"Well, sir, you're a *hero*. A real hero . . ."

That temporarily floored him. He had never been called that before. A *hero*. Previously, the biggest compliment he'd ever received in the line of duty was *followed orders well*.

Hero. That's what they called you when you risked your life for somebody else, when you saved lives, and they'd probably saved a ton of lives. Anybody that lived through the night in that shitty little one-horse town, and the people in the neighboring towns that weren't getting nuked to glass right now, was because of Harbinger and the people that had followed him.

He couldn't shoot Harbinger or the redhead that had helped him. They really were heroes. They were what Mosher would've been if he'd gotten his way. He was what Sam Haven had been, and Stark was suddenly deeply ashamed of himself.

His finger came off the trigger. "It's your lucky day, hero."

Besides, there was a small chance that he could miss, and then Harbinger would be really mad . . . and that man was *terrifying*.

The responding MCB agents had taken Earl into custody and taken his statement before they'd passed him off to the military. After eating three complete MREs lifted from the Michigan National Guard, Earl had collapsed into a provided bunk and slept like the dead. It had been a long time since he'd been this tired, if ever. He'd slept so deep and dreamless that the pounding on the door had taken a while to even register.

He took the time to light a smoke before getting out of bed. The rubberized food packages hadn't been the only things he'd managed to snag from the National Guard. He made it to the door and cracked it open, squinting at the sudden brightness. "What?"

It was a young lieutenant. "Mr. Harbinger, I need you to come with me, please." He looked a little nervous, unsure why the secretive federal agency in charge of the incident had felt the need to stick this man into a room at the local roach motel and then post a dozen guards to make sure he didn't leave. Their instructions had been to be polite, but *firm*. "Agent Myers wants to see you now."

Earl looked around the hotel room, spotted the shoes and clothing that had been left for him neatly folded on a chair. His old, reliable minotaur coat had been thrown on the floor. "All right. Tell Dwayne to relax. I'll be there in a minute. What time is it anyway?"

"Fifteen hundred, sir. He's using the county office as a command center."

"How's my Hunter? The big fella with the glass eye?"

"We've got him cleaned up, sir. He's very ill. The doctor said it could take him a while, but he should recover."

That was good news. Earl took his time getting dressed. Myers could wait. He was probably busy anyway, what with organizing the cover-up. This one was sure to be one hell of a doozy. Hopefully, Myers wouldn't use it as an excuse to finally have him executed. Satisfied that he was as presentable as he could be in a borrowed set of Army digital camouflage, Earl followed the officer out to a waiting Hummer. The air was crisp and the sky was clear. Copper Lake smelled like dead werewolves, blood, and smoke. It wasn't entirely unpleasant.

Special Agent Dwayne Myers was using what had been the mayor's office. The room was packed with MCB agents and military personnel, poring over maps and arguing loudly. Myers just frowned when Earl entered and snapped, "Everybody out. Out."

Earl waited as the men shuffled past him and out the door. "Hey, Dwayne."

"Earl." There was no offer to shake hands or any other false pleasantries. His old teammate had aged since they'd last spoken. His skin was pale, like he'd been spending too much time indoors, his hair was thinning, and he'd lost weight that he couldn't afford to lose. Even his suit looked more battered than normal. Myers had been run ragged. He gestured at a metal folding chair.

Earl took a seat. He was still smoking but didn't think the rules about not smoking inside government buildings applied after complete anarchy had set in. "So, what's the story going to be this time?"

"Too rural for a plausible terrorist attack. One of my junior men talked to the press too quickly, said that the mine tunnels under the town had caught on fire and that hundreds had been killed in the resulting explosion. Moron forgot it's a copper mine, not coal. Right now I'm leaning toward radon gas. But that's not why I wanted to talk to you."

Myers didn't sit behind the desk, as Earl had expected, and instead wandered over to the window and watched a helicopter landing in the school parking lot. He didn't speak for a very long time.

If the MCB was going to revoke his PUFF exemption, they would've done it already. Something else was wrong. "I'm assuming you wanted to question my account . . ." When Myers still didn't respond, Earl was surprised to find that he was actually concerned. Myers was a prick, but he was a reliable prick. "Are you okay?"

"No, I'm not." Myers shook his head and gave a sad little chuckle, still looking out the window. "It's speeding up . . . isn't it?"

"What do you mean?"

"The events. More incidents every month. They don't seem to be related, but the stats just keep climbing."

Monster attacks were still high. MHI was hopping, there was no doubt about that, but Myers was privy to a lot more intel than he was. He waited for the agent to continue.

"A few years ago, we broke time, nearly opened a portal in Alabama. Scared the shit out of the entire world, but we passed it off as a natural phenomenon. Then the Arbmunep in New Zealand. You have no idea how hard that thing was to bury. Then you probably didn't even hear about what happened in California recently. It was big, but we dropped Franks in and locked it down quick. It's always something different . . . but they're coming faster and faster, like never before. There are so many things I can't even tell you about."

"Keeping secrets from the people is hard work, but you already know my opinion on that bullshit policy."

"It's not just keeping monsters secret anymore. Something's coming, Earl. I can *feel* it. It's not just us, either. The South Africans lost a village six months ago, and we still don't know what did it. Something big happened in a rural area in China just last week, but they won't tell us a thing. Now this."

It was truly odd to have the ultra tight-lipped MCB agent speaking so freely. The government looked at contractors like MHI as a necessary evil, and that was on a good day. "Why tell me this?"

"Because you *get it*. My superiors don't. They're in denial, and they're getting tired of me pushing the issue. They think they can throw enough money and bodies at it and the problem will go away. . . . You know how I feel about MHI."

"Irrational hatred seems to be the words that come to mind."

"You're reckless, careless, and dangerous, *but*, though it pains me to admit it, you're also effective. Enemy of my enemy is my friend and all that. Just think about what I said. I want you to be ready, Earl. I don't know for what, but just be ready."

"Point me at the fight and make sure the checks don't bounce. MHI is *always* ready."

It was back to business as usual. Myers turned away from the window, came over and sank into a cushioned swivel chair. "Now, about your statement. Everything seems in order. According to the locals, you made a big difference here. Even Agent Stark mostly agrees with your account, though he says there was one other surviving werewolf, a sheriff's deputy that was recently turned. So, before you can go, there's just one thing we need to clear up about these other werewolves first. . . ."

Earl had been honest. *Mostly.* "Some died in town. The last of them, including Deputy Kerkonen, were blown up at the Quinn Mine. I want the PUFF on them, the digging things, and all the undead divided up and paid to each of this town's survivors. For the one that started all this, I'm going to demand a one-of-a-kind PUFF finding on him. He was a divine-werewolf hybrid, so he's going to cost you *big.* I'll do the paperwork myself. You'll find that particular werewolf at the bottom of the shaft in two pieces."

Myers put his elbows on the desk and steepled his fingers. "Yes, about him . . ."

"His name was Adam Conover."

"He doesn't exist."

Earl angrily shook his head. "Don't play games. He was government property. A pet monster gone rogue. He was one of yours."

"Not one of *mine*, Earl. Don't bring him up again, don't talk about him, and forget he ever existed."

"So, that's how it has to be?"

"That's how it *is.*" Myers rubbed his face in his hands, as if debating what to say. "Off the record, he worked for an operation you do *not* want to cross. MCB is a shield. They're a sword, or maybe a poisoned dagger would be more appropriate. They answer only to the highest levels. They're small, but they deal with things that I wouldn't want my agency to touch with a ten-foot pole. Nobody talks about them and lives long. Am I clear?"

If there was one thing that werewolves knew, it was how to keep secrets. "Crystal."

⊰ **Chapter 37** ⊱

This will be the last entry in this book. The journals began as a tool to chronicle the holes dug in my mind by a demon, and many of those holes have been filled. There are still things missing, but for the most part, my life is mine again. Up yours, Rocky. I win, you son of a bitch.

The first book was about my history, the second was about my Hunters, and the third was about my curse. But it doesn't feel right calling it a curse anymore. Koschei's amulet changed me. In the four months since Copper Lake, things have been different. The change is easier to control now, and when I do transform, though the madness is still there, it does what I tell it to. Even during the full moon, I'd say I was at least half sane, and that's a pretty decent improvement. I'll still lock myself up, just in case, but I'm more confident than I've ever been. I'm in charge of the beast now, not the other way around.

I've always had family, mentors, friends, and my Hunters are my pack, but in one important way, I've always been a lone wolf. Even my beloved wife, God rest her soul, could never fully understand my other half. Now, for the first time in my life, I've got someone by my side who not only understands what it's like, but who isn't a complete raving nut-job about it, either. I've been teaching Heather, but she's a faster learner than I was.

We're still working the kinks out. Apparently, I can be difficult to live with sometimes. Go figure. But the last few months have been nice. Shit. I'm a master of understatement. It's been great, some of the best times of my life. But if you expected me to write about my *feelings, you sure as hell picked up the wrong journal. Let's just say that life is good.*

Earl Harbinger stopped and looked out the cabin's window. There had been a noise, slightly out of place, just an echo of a sound against the mountain. One hand came to rest on the Smith & Wesson sitting on the edge of the desk. The property was as isolated as possible, just a lone hunting cabin on a barren stretch of nothing a hundred miles from the nearest bit of civilization. He had bought the land a long time ago under a name that had long since ceased to exist. It was the kind of place that a man could disappear for a time; where a young, supposedly dead werewolf could practice and the only things in danger be the local animals. All of which were edible to a werewolf, but only the bears were a challenge.

The logs in the fireplace popped. The cabin creaked against the wind. Scowling, Earl watched the Alaskan night for a while, but the out-of-place sound didn't come again. It must have been nothing. Earl removed his hand from the gun and returned to his work.

I was bitter at first, having chosen to be cursed again by my old nemesis. But Nikolai, evil son of a bitch that he was, had done me a favor at the bottom of that black hole. I'd thought I'd have given anything to be a man again, but I was wrong. I was always meant to be a werewolf . . . Monster and Hunter.

This is who I am.

"Writing again?" Heather was standing in the bedroom doorway.

"Scribbling." Earl put the pen down. He hadn't sensed her come in. She could be downright stealthy when she wanted to be. "Just a few last things to fill in before we trek out tomorrow."

Julie was going to have a plane waiting for them in the nearest town. An identity had been prepared for Heather to use while MHI's attorneys worked on getting a provisional PUFF exemption. They had to tread carefully, but that's why Earl paid them a thousand bucks an hour. MHI had done fine without him there, babysitting, but he hadn't killed a monster since November and was starting to get twitchy. The snows were melting. It was time to return to the world.

"You really think I'm ready?" Heather asked.

"Ready as one of us can ever be."

"You had three years to work on it," she pointed out.

They'd had this discussion several times. "I had to learn all this from scratch. You've got resources, know-how, and one hell of a handsome advisor."

"You're rich, too." Heather folded her arms and watched him with a bit of a smirk. As she had come to accept her new state, Earl found that she'd become increasingly lovely. In his opinion, there was nothing nicer than a pretty girl with the confidence to beat up a polar bear. "Don't underestimate the attractiveness of the being a millionaire part. Mom always wanted me to find a rich guy."

"I invested a few PUFFs way back when. That's the power of compound interest for you."

"You're right. I'm ready." Heather smiled at him. "I'm just going to miss our luxury accommodations is all. Wrap it up, would you? We've got a *long* trip tomorrow. Come to bed."

"I've just got to finish this. When we get to Cazador, I'm going to bury this down in the archives. Maybe it'll come in handy someday for someone else."

"You're pretty serious about recording everything for posterity." Heather came over to where he was sitting, draped her arms around his neck, and whispered in his ear. "But I bet I can distract you."

A grin split Earl's face. "Oh, really?" You got to know someone rather well when you spent an entire winter isolated with them, and Earl knew exactly how distracting Heather could be.

The sound came again in the middle of the night. It was louder this time, and the suddenness of it launched both of them out of bed. Earl was getting dressed as he reached the front door. The noise of the fighter jet lingered on the mountain for a moment. Another aircraft flew past a minute later, skimming terribly low over the lake. It passed the cabin close enough for the noise to rattle snow from the roof.

There were munitions under the wing.

"What was that?" Heather called.

"A flight of F-16s," Earl answered.

Heather was behind him, buttoning her shirt. "Maybe they're just on a training flight?"

The first one was banking back over the mountain. "Doubt it."

"But . . . you're okay, and they think I'm dead!"

The fighters gained a bit of altitude and began a long circle around the cabin. Earl watched the orange glow of their exhaust. That was an awful lot of firepower. There was another noise in the distance. A helicopter. "We've got company coming. Might as well get presentable."

"Should we run?"

"Naw," Earl shook his head. "That's the thing about Hunters. Once they find you, if you run, it just makes them want to chase you that much harder."

The conflict on her face was obvious to read. Instinct was telling her to flee, but she trusted him. "You'd better be right, Earl."

"We'll see what they've got to say. Besides, if they were really out to get us, they'd just have dropped a bomb on the place."

Earl splashed some water on his face, finished getting dressed, and then confirmed that their belongings were ready to go. They'd already been packed to leave in the morning. Heather was too nervous to talk. Earl did his best to comfort her, but he didn't know what was happening, either. You didn't send the air force if you were planning nothing more than a friendly visit. "Stay inside. They might not know about you," Earl warned Heather before giving her a gentle kiss. "I'll be right back."

"You'd better," she warned him. "I don't want to do CPR on you again, okay?"

"You're really good at it, though."

He closed the door behind him. There was an overhang to protect the entrance from the snow, so Earl lit a cigarette and settled down beneath it to wait. Two minutes later, a Chinook helicopter with no markings landed in front of the cabin. Four armored figures disembarked as soon as the ramp hit the ground. They fanned out in a protective circle while a fifth man strolled down the ramp. The stranger walked directly toward the cabin without even taking the time to orient himself. The four soldiers formed a line behind him and followed.

The stranger was tall, and despite his heavy coat, obviously thin. He trudged along through the snow at an energetic clip. Despite their camouflage-painted, ceramic-plate armor that made MHI's heavy suits look svelte in comparison, the soldiers kept up. As they got closer, Earl noted that the leader's head was bared to the elements, and that he was completely shiny-bald. He was also wearing a pair of oddly colored, orange-lensed sunglasses, even though it was pitch dark.

The Chinook's twin rotors were still turning, which made it difficult to understand the stranger's greeting. He had to repeat himself as he got closer. "Good evening, Mr. Harbinger."

Earl just nodded. "Your helicopter's messing up my landscaping."

The soldiers came to a silent halt a polite twenty feet away. Their leader closed the remaining distance and stopped at the overhang. "It won't be there long." The stranger appeared to be in his forties, six-and-a-half feet tall, extremely long-limbed and with skin so pale that if Earl hadn't smelled the warm blood pumping, he would've suspected the man was undead. He was borderline gaunt, but his movements gave off a sense of athleticism. He seemed human, just an odd one. "I'm Mr. Stricken."

Earl made a show of not being able to hear over the chopper. "Sorry? What was that? Strickland?"

"Stricken," he repeated.

"What? No handshake?" Earl asked.

"I've heard your reputation on the subject," Stricken said. "My hobby is classical piano, so I'd prefer you not to break all the bones in my hand. May I come in?"

"No. What do you want?"

"Just a moment of your time. I can be polite or not. Your decision." Stricken took off the orange shades, revealing albino eyes. "And I would like to speak to Ms. Kerkonen as well."

Earl had been afraid of that. "Deputy Kerkonen died at the Quinn Mine."

"We both know that's not true. My time's valuable, Mr. Harbinger. Believe me, this isn't my idea of fun. Cold doesn't agree with me. Bring her out."

Earl looked over at the four soldiers. Their helmets had opaque full-face visors, so it was impossible to read their expressions. He had no doubt he could take them. It was the F-16s he didn't know what to do about. "I don't know what you're talking about."

"Your file said that you could be a pain in the ass. A satellite has been passing over this area every day for weeks. There's a redheaded woman here, approximately five foot eight, one hundred and thirty pounds. Nice rack. Spends her free time turning into a werewolf and terrorizing the squirrels. Wave, dumb-shit. You're on camera," Stricken said. Earl tilted his head to peer suspiciously around the overhang. "Don't bother looking, you idiot, you can't see it. It's in fucking outer space."

"She can control it. Just like me."

Stricken's laugh was mean. "You think I give a shit? You think I'm MCB? They're losers. You think they'd get permission to go rerouting satellites for one measly lycanthrope? If popping her was my mission, I'd have vaporized this whole valley with one phone call." The laughter died, and Stricken's pink eyes bored into Earl. "Call her *out*."

This man wasn't to be trifled with. Earl opened the door a crack. "Heather?"

"I heard," she muttered as she came through the door and stood proudly at Earl's side. "What do you want from us?"

"Werewolves have to earn the right to exist. PUFF immunity is a rare and precious thing. Luckily, werewolves are an *amazing* creature, and I happen to need one."

Not again. Earl tossed his cigarette butt in the snow. "How long this time?"

"Two years, beginning immediately. Upon satisfactory completion, there will be a certificate granting full PUFF immunity to the bearer."

"Until the government changes its mind again."

"Of course. This offer is valid for the next five minutes. Yes or no. If yes, then we board that helicopter and for the next two years you have zero communication with anyone outside of my organization. No friends, no family. For all intents and purposes, you'll be government property for the next seven hundred thirty days. Seven hundred thirty-one if there's a leap year. I haven't checked the calendar."

"And the job?"

"You will complete assignments as specified. These assignments will be dangerous but should be well within your capabilities. Everything you need will be provided. At the end of this term, you're free to go. However, you will be required to keep all information pertaining to my organization classified for the rest of your life, or your immunity will be revoked and you'll be terminated."

"And if the answer is no?"

Stricken smiled that same unnerving smile. "Harsh words may be exchanged . . ." An F-16 roared past. "And cluster bombs."

Earl glanced at the eerily silent soldiers. They hadn't so much as twitched. There wasn't even a hint of fear smell, nor excitement or any other recognizable chemicals. Their smell was an indeterminate mixture of gun-oil, synthetic fibers, meat, bone, and blood. They were either inhumanly well trained, or just plain inhuman. Their armored faceplates gave no clue.

He turned to Heather. She was still holding his arm. Now *she* was frightened. The soldiers were terrifying, not as physical threats, but as what they represented. Heather was barely learning to control herself. He was her anchor, he was her teacher, he was her lover, but now these strange men were here to take him away. Stricken wouldn't just be hurting Earl, he'd be hurting her.

But if he didn't go, they were both as good as dead. Even if he killed these men and they escaped, the hunt would just be beginning. He was a Hunter, and as such, he understood just how awful it was be to be the hunted. It would never stop.

Earl gently raised his hand and touched Heather on the cheek. She turned to him, and he could see the understanding in her eyes. She knew what he had to do. Heather was strong, even stronger than he had been at the beginning. She'd be fine. There was just the slightest hint of a nod. No matter what, she trusted him.

Stricken was waiting for an answer. The man, if he was a man at all, was still smiling, only his eyes weren't. The strange eyes were utterly cold. It was just like before. Different decade, and it would be a different war, but the game was always the same. To them, a werewolf wasn't a person with a curse, they were an asset, a weapon. They'd give him a new name, and then they'd point him at a target. He'd do his job, just like before.

Only this time, there would be a woman that loved him waiting at the end. So at least he'd have something to look forward to. Earl cleared his throat. "I'll do it."

"Not you." Stricken shook his head and pointed one long finger at Heather. "I want her."

The words took a second to register as Heather's fingers tightened around Earl's bicep. "You bastard!" he snarled as he took a step forward. The faceless soldiers' guns came up with a clatter.

"Wait!" Heather shouted as she pulled on Earl's arm.

Stricken raised his hand. The soldiers immediately stopped, their carbines shouldered, muzzles trained on Earl. Four laser dots danced on Earl's shirt, but Stricken would die before Earl felt the sting of the first bullet.

"Up yours, Pinky. You can't have her. You want a werewolf, you take me."

"You know how it works, Mr. Harbinger. Monsters have to earn a place in our world, and you've done it. No one doubts you. You're a *patriot*. You are living proof that the system works. Unfortunately, times have changed, and I'm afraid recruiting a man with your known personality quirks would be a bad human-resources decision. Ms. Kerkonen, on the other hand remains an unknown quantity. She needs to prove herself, and, as you know, my organization is now short one werewolf."

"So, Adam was yours?"

"Yes," Stricken said unapologetically. "And he was the best I've ever seen. I had a great deal of respect for his parents as well. They worked for me, too, before they retired so Sharon could dote on her grandkids. Operative Alpha was just like you once, a superb killer. He also earned a place in a human world, only he decided that wasn't good enough."

"Your boy went nuts and killed my hometown," Heather spat.

"I let my guard down, began to think of him as an equal. I'll never make that mistake again." Stricken looked at Heather pointedly. "Clock is ticking. You know how much it costs per minute to run a fighter jet? That's all getting billed to my operating budget."

Earl was calculating the time it would take to incapacitate the soldiers. Then he'd grab Stricken as a hostage and force the chopper to fly them out. . . . Heather squeezed his arm again. She knew exactly what he was thinking.

"I'll do it," Heather said. "I can prove myself. Just let him go."

Earl closed his eyes and died inside.

"Wise choice, Ms. Kerkonen," Stricken said. "Get your bags and let's go."

Heather turned to him. "Earl . . . I'm sorry. I've . . . I've—"

He took Heather in his arms and held her close. "Don't do this."

"I'll be back." Heather was trying not to cry. "I'll stay strong."

"It's not you I'm worried about. Don't trust anyone," Earl whispered. "I can—"

"Excuse me," Stricken interrupted. "I said grab your shit and let's *go*. Time is money, Ms. Kerkonen."

Hesitantly, Heather broke away and entered the cabin. Earl watched her go, and there wasn't anything he could do. The government was the most merciless monster he'd ever dealt with, and it was the only one that he could never truly beat.

"Don't try to contact her. That will only make things worse," Stricken said.

Earl's hands curled into fists. "Heather serves her time. Then she goes free. You stick to the deal or you deal with me."

Stricken nodded appreciatively. "And I'd expect no less. I would hate to sully our blossoming friendship. I'm not the bad guy here, Harbinger. I'm just doing my job, just like you had to. I don't get off on dragging monsters into slavery. We're doing important work, and it absolutely has to be done."

If hate could kill, Stricken would have burst into flames. "Fuck you and your important work," Earl whispered.

The door opened in a rectangle of firelight as Heather came out of the cabin, backpack in hand. Earl held her again, stroked her hair, lied and told her everything would be okay. "I love you, Earl. Wait for me." He couldn't form a response, other than to nod desperately. They kissed good-bye, lips salty with Heather's tears, and then Heather was walking away, a soldier flanking her on either side, and there was nothing Earl could do but watch.

"You'll get her back," Stricken said. "You have my word."

"Your word means nothing. I don't even know who you people are."

Stricken paused, weighing his answers. "We're nobody. You think monsters are secret? They're *famous* compared to us. I'd tell you to remember that, but you're better off forgetting this ever happened."

The soldiers escorted Heather up the ramp. She turned, waved, and bravely blew him a kiss. A solider took her by the arm, and then she was out of view. Earl exhaled, and did his best to retain both his composure and his humanity.

"Listen to me carefully, Stricken. She's a good girl. She's got a human's heart. She's not like Adam, and she's sure as hell not like me. You go back on the deal, and I swear you'll be worried about a lot more than me talking. I swear to God, if anything happens to her, nothing in the world will save you."

"I'm not worried about you talking or your threats. Kill me, and somebody else will take my place. I'm humble enough to know I'm a little cog in a big machine. Talk? Well, no one would believe you, anyway." Stricken put his odd glasses back on as he turned and walked to the waiting Chinook. He called over his shoulder, "Because remember, Mr. Harbinger, everybody knows there's no such things as *unicorns*."